something like thunder

Jay Bell Books
www.jaybellbooks.com

Did you buy this book? If so, thank you for putting food on our table! Making money as an independent artist isn't easy, so your support is greatly appreciated. Come give me a hug!

Did you pirate this book? If so, there are a couple of ways you can still help out. If you like the story, please take the time to leave a nice review somewhere, such as an online retail store (my preference), or on any blog or forum. Word of mouth is important for every book, so if you can recommend this book to friends with more cash to spare, that would be awesome too!

ISBN-13: 978-1511774932

Cover art by Andreas Bell: www.andreasbell.com

Something Like Thunder

by Jay Bell

Acknowledgements

Special thanks go to the wonderful Jo Sowerby for presenting me with an intriguing idea that finally found its place in the following story. I'm also grateful to my friends and family for putting up with me, and my editors for being so diligent in their work. And hey, this is my tenth novel, so thank you! That's right! You there with your nose pressed up against this book. Without such a faithful and kind reader, I probably would have given up on this dream years ago, so thank you for all the love. The feeling is mutual!

This book is dedicated to the good people of Germany for showing me endless hospitality and for giving me a nice quiet environment in which to write. I'll miss your pragmatism and offbeat humor. Oh, and the beer and chocolate. Thank you for letting me take one of your kinsmen with me when I go.

Prologue

When the past catches up with the present, returning from the realm of broken dreams and dented hopes, the best course of action is to roll over, expose the belly, and pray that it will be merciful. Or at least quick.

As the elevator doors slid closed behind Nathaniel Courtney, instinct told him he was trapped. And not in a good place, because the normally bright office in front of him was now dim, the overhead lights lowered, scented candles placed strategically around the room to turn the gloom into warmth. A bottle of wine attended the two crystal glasses next to it, and as Nathaniel searched the room for evidence of another living soul, he heard soft music playing just loud enough to banish awkward silences while still allowing for murmured conversation.

Oh yes, this was hell. One of his own making.

After determining he was alone, Nathaniel sighed, turned around, and pressed the elevator button. The doors didn't open. He jabbed the button a few more times, despite knowing the gesture was hopeless. The software that ran the elevator could be remotely controlled. He had little doubt as to whom was chuckling from some distant location.

"It won't work," Nathaniel said, addressing a security camera in one corner. "If you have any love for me, you'll let me go right now, because this is going to kill me."

He swallowed and felt tightness in his throat. The camera lens remained impassive, the elevator unresponsive, so Nathaniel moved toward the two lounge couches that faced each other. How many business deals had he successfully negotiated here? Perhaps that's what convinced his boss, Marcello Maltese, that this was the right environment to negotiate this deal, albeit for a prize far more valuable than money. The sentiment was misplaced because the battle had been lost years ago.

Instead of sitting, Nathaniel picked up the wine bottle and read the label. Another dart pierced his chest when he saw the vintage. He turned to the camera briefly, hoping the pain showed on his face. Then he set down the bottle and considered the two wrapped gifts. The first was flat and hard. He lifted the small card in one corner and read:

What was once thought lost can still be recovered. The past can be a gateway to the future. I do this for love, with love. -Marcello

Nathaniel clenched his jaw and sat. He wasn't gentle as he tore away the wrapping paper. One swipe revealed glass, a black and white photo behind it. He stared, willing his pounding heart to stop racing—to go still as possible in the hope of tricking these feelings into thinking he was dead. Maybe then they would finally go away.

But no. With more care now, he pulled away the shreds of paper. The photo's backdrop was a high school running track. Nathaniel was in the forefront, arms pumping as he ran. Next to him, leaning forward and so horizontal that he almost appeared to be flying, was someone he still thought of every day. A slender build with ropey muscles. Dark skin and shrewd eyes—at least that's how Nathaniel chose to remember them. In the photo those eyes were joyful, surprisingly so, considering their owner was about to trip over a dog. The mutt's face was just as gleeful as the runner's, tongue hanging out one corner of his mouth as he cut across their path.

Nathaniel swallowed, his attention darting down to the mat board where in light pencil, the words *Before the Fall* were written. Somehow he didn't think "fall" referred to the season, or even the inevitable collision with the ground. Next to this was a dash followed by a single letter. *-K*

Nathaniel felt like moaning in misery. Instead he grimaced and considered the other wrapped box, opening the gift tag only long enough to see who it was addressed to.

Kelly.

Nathaniel set the framed photo on the table and tossed the paper on top of it. Then he stood and walked around the room, extinguishing the candles. Kelly wouldn't be happy to see them lit. He'd feel insulted that mood lighting and smooth jazz could be expected to undo what had been done. Forgiveness—if not already impossible—would take so much more than that.

Nathaniel killed the music. Then he went to the desk and called a technician who could open the elevator doors, no matter how rapidly Marcello's fat fingers poked at the screen of his phone. Then Nathaniel waited. He sat, trying not to bite his nails. As time wore on, he began to pace. What was taking so long? He was eying the bottle of wine, wondering if he should get drunk, when he heard the elevator motor whirring. When the doors opened and a familiar figure stepped out, he stared for a moment before his need to escape returned. He leapt over the couch, an arm stretched out, reaching for freedom.

"Don't let them close!" he shouted.

Brown eyes widened, taking him in. Nathaniel saw so much reflected in them. Apprehension, hurt, and perhaps worst of all, love. After all this time. Even though it was merely a flickering spark. Even though—like the light past the closing elevator doors—it was soon hidden again, Nathaniel had no doubt it was still there.

Fuck. That complicated everything, because now he had hope.

Nathaniel slammed into the elevator doors and felt like pounding his head against them. Too late. He had missed his chance, in more ways than one. Nathaniel jabbed at the button anyway, a growl escaping his lips. He couldn't deal with this— couldn't let himself believe even for a second that Marcello was right, that the past could be resurrected.

"Nice to see you too," Kelly said. "What's next? Are you going to try jumping out a window just to avoid me?"

Nathaniel sucked in air, using the precious substance to tell a lie. "I'm not avoiding you. I just don't like being trapped. I called a technician over an hour ago."

Kelly's eyes travelled over him briefly. They were soft, not hard and criticizing. "Marcello has someone waiting at the door. He probably sent the technician away already. So where is he? Hiding behind his desk, or can he control all of this from home?"

"From his phone." Nathaniel turned, pressing his back against the elevator doors to feel more steady. "I don't want to know what he's playing at."

"He probably thought this was the only way he could get us to talk." Kelly crossed his arms over his chest. Now those eyes turned hard, a sight so familiar Nathaniel nearly smiled. "I saw you at the gallery. Why did you run off?"

"I had an awkward conversation."

Kelly blinked. "That's it? That's why you didn't even say hello?"

"You wouldn't understand."

"What else is new?"

Fair enough. Nathaniel had kept plenty from Kelly—from just

about everyone. He had good cause, wanting to protect Kelly, to keep him safe, not just from his own clumsy attempt at love, but from life's cruelties as well. Nathaniel had a feeling that, before the night was over, they would be forced to face some of those ugly truths.

Nathaniel headed for one of the couches and sat, resting elbows on his knees, his face in the dark warmth of his palms. What now? He listened to Kelly's footsteps, the dress shoes clicking across the marble floor and pausing, no doubt taking in the strange scene as Nathaniel had upon first arriving. The silence grew thick. Then Kelly spoke. "I know about the prosthetics. You've been paying for them all this time."

Nathaniel let his hands fall away and looked up, and for one moment, allowed himself to feel happy that Kelly seemed to be doing so well. "Marcello told you?"

"I figured it out. I'd offer to pay you back, but I don't have any money. Maybe someday I can—"

"No," Nathaniel said. "I want to do this. For you. Please let me."

Kelly appeared confused. "Why? I know you promised I would never have to worry about it, but I don't hold you to that anymore. It made sense when you loved me, but not now."

A question. Despite being presented as a statement, Nathaniel recognized it for what it was. "That's not fair. Don't make me say it."

"Why not?" Kelly said. "Is that the cure? Does staying silent keep the feelings at bay?"

"No."

"And did it ever stop hurting? All these years we've been apart, can you honestly say you avoided what you fear most? Because my heart has been aching since that night. No matter how far I go and how many other people I welcome into my life, there's always still a part of me that yearns for you. I've learned to live without you, Nathaniel, and I can keep on doing so. But I don't want to, and the pain is never going to go away. I'm guessing the same is true for you."

"Yeah," Nathaniel said, hating that this suffering was mutual. He'd never wanted that. Ever. "I love you, Kelly. I'm a piece of shit and I ruined everything, but I love you so much that I think it might be worth the pain."

"It doesn't have to hurt," Kelly said, taking a step closer. "Not all the time. I swear."

Kelly had been right about so much. Maybe he was right about this too. That heart of his was resilient, had been dragged across more than one battlefield. Maybe it was strong enough to forgive, to shrug off the damage that had been done. To give one more chance. If so…

Nathaniel stood, eager to bridge the distance between them.

Kelly gave an almost imperceptible shake of his head. "We need to talk."

Of course it wasn't that simple. So much time had passed between them, and Kelly was just as beautiful and sharp and everything wonderful that he'd been when they'd parted. Maybe even more so. Nathaniel sat back down. "There's someone else?"

Kelly laughed. "There's only you. You made it so I could run again, and believe me, I've been running long and hard. Whenever I look back, I see you're not there and I feel like I got away. But the truth is, you're inside me so deep that there's no escape. All this time I've been running, all I've been doing is carrying you with me. So no, there is no one else. I don't think there ever will be. But I'm finally ready to get to know the man I love. All of him."

"So what do I do?" Nathaniel asked.

"Talk to me." Kelly sat, gingerly at first, as if not to scare him away. Then he settled in and made himself comfortable. "Tell me everything."

"My past?" Nathaniel said, eyes darting briefly to the mess of wrapping paper on the table. He could see the partially obscured card, opened just enough to reveal the edge of Marcello's handwriting, one truncated phrase catching his eye. *–for love, with love.* "It's a long story."

Kelly's smile was subtle. "In case you've forgotten, we're both stuck here. It might help pass the time." His face grew more somber. "Please."

Nathaniel nodded. Then he began.

**Part One
Houston, 2004**

Chapter One

I'm on trial. The person I love most is demanding an explanation from me, but so often the truth can lead to heartbreak. Lying is immoral, but so is deliberately causing someone pain. Silence would be the best course of action, but some truths aren't so easily covered up. Although in retrospect, a little powder and base might have avoided all of this.

"Is that a bruise? My God! How in the world did you get that?"

Nathaniel fixed his mom with a stare before letting loose a playful smile. "Paid cash for it. They had a sale on bruises at Walmart. I went there looking for a paper cut, but they were out of those. Stubbed toes were in stock, but you'd be surprised how expensive they are."

Star shook her head, grasped his chin, and turned his face toward the kitchen light. "Who would do this to my baby?" She winced as she considered the injury on his left cheek. "It's darkest in the middle. Did you get hit by a rock?"

Not a rock, a ring worn on a meaty fist, but Nathaniel didn't want her figuring that out. "It was a stupid misunderstanding. During lunch we were talking about snowball fights and how rare they are down here. I took an ice cube from my drink and tossed it at a guy, making sure it was easy to dodge, but when he threw it back he wasn't so careful. Hurt like hell."

"An ice cube did this to you?" His mother pursed her lips. "Is that the truth?"

"If I was lying, I'd come up with something better than that." Given more time, maybe.

Star scrutinized him a little longer. "You're too old *and* too smart to start a food fight."

But she believed him. That's all that mattered. Already she was turning back to the steaming pots on the stove. "Maybe you could start packing my lunch," he said. "Equip me with more appropriate ammunition. Olives, cream pies, maybe a few bananas I can use as boomerangs."

"I'd rather you eat your food instead of throwing it. Speaking of which, could you set the table?"

The grin slid off of Nathaniel's face. "Sure."

He went to the cabinet and took out three plates. He could

feel his mother watching him. When she spoke, he already knew what she would say.

"Four plates, honey. I want us to eat dinner together."

"I have to get to the learning center."

Star pulled the wooden spoon from the mashed potatoes, tapped it on the edge of the pot, and set it aside. Then she turned to him. "It's my cooking, isn't it?"

Nathaniel relaxed a little. "Your cooking is fine. Most of the time."

His mother swatted at him playfully, Nathaniel leaping backward. She grabbed the wooden spoon, wielding it like a rapier, and stepped forward to jab at him. He swiped at the makeshift weapon, both of them laughing as he wrested it from her. Then he handed it back.

"Save me some. I'll be starving when I get home."

Star put a hand on her hip and frowned. "Seriously? You can't go an hour later? I moved back three of my yoga classes just so we could have family dinners again. I even lost a few students."

"I have students of my own," Nathaniel said. "For some of these kids, having a tutor there every day can make the difference between passing and failing." Then, in more dramatic tones he added, "Won't someone think of the children?"

"It's my own child I'm thinking of." Star exhaled and looked toward the stove, as if no longer interested in preparing a meal. "Are you avoiding your father?"

As usual, her motherly instincts were right. Just slightly off target. Nathaniel's afterschool tutoring job was indeed his way of avoiding someone, but not his father. And certainly not his mother, who continued to express her concern.

"He mentioned that he hasn't seen you for weeks."

Nathaniel shrugged. "I'll make sure he sees me this weekend. I really gotta run."

"Okay. I love you."

He stepped forward for a hug. His mother was slight in his arms, her head barely reaching his chest. "I love you too."

Once Nathaniel was buckled in his car, the tension left his shoulders. As he drove, he slowly transitioned from being on constant alert to feeling like a normal human being. He put on the debut album by *Keane*, and as they sang about a place no one else knew about, Nathaniel hit the gas pedal and breezed by every other car on the road. By the time he reached a strip mall and parked, he felt wrapped in a protective cocoon. He shut off the car and the music along with it.

He practically bounded into the learning center, the interior just as uninspiring as the exterior. Worn desks lined the walls. On them sat equally exhausted computers. If not for the people, Nathaniel would dread coming here every day. He loved working with the kids, especially the younger ones. Some of his fellow tutors weren't bad either. One had even become his friend.

He scanned the room, searching for Rebecca, which wasn't difficult considering how tall she was. Six foot one—just an inch shorter than he was. Her build was lanky, but she carried herself upright. His first impression had been of a pole vaulter, not that she was athletic, as it turned out. She was smart though. Pretty too. She didn't wear much makeup, and her medium-length ginger hair was worn loose, never styled. Rebecca was too practical to fuss with such things. Nathaniel had once overheard two students call her "horse face" behind her back, perhaps because of her long features. He liked her face. He could stare at it all day, especially when lit up, as it was now.

"The new software came in," she said, walking over to join him.

"For the tests?"

Rebecca nodded enthusiastically. "We've got graphs! And it pinpoints areas that need to be strengthened. I have no idea how accurate it is, but this might save some guesswork. Come see!"

Nathaniel shook his head ruefully as she led him toward one of the computers. He might like it here, but Rebecca loved it. He wasn't as fond of computers as she was, preferring to rely on direct interaction with each student. After enough enthusiastic nodding to convince Rebecca he was equally excited, he was free to start working. He sat down with a third-grader who despised math. She understood all the concepts correctly but abhorred doing the work, so Nathaniel focused on teaching her as many shortcuts as possible.

While he was doing so, he felt someone watching him. He glanced over at the next desk. A high school student, although Nathaniel couldn't remember if they went to the same school or not. The guy had bronze skin, dark hair pulled back into a pony tail, and thick framed glasses that appeared black at first glance but were actually dark red. Nathaniel gave a friendly upward nod in greeting before turning his attention back to tutoring.

Except he continued to feel that gaze. Every time Nathaniel checked again, the guy would quickly avert his eyes. He didn't seem to be doing anything but ignoring the computer in front of him. Rebecca must have noticed because she went to investigate.

"So I add the first column before the last one?"

Nathaniel shook his head to clear it and explained the trick once more. Halfway through, Rebecca offered to take over. "He wants to work with you," she said.

"Oh, okay." That wasn't so unusual. When students did well, they often sought out the same tutor during their next visit. Sure enough, when Nathaniel pulled up a chair, the guy revealed a paper they had worked on together. He held it clutched to his chest, like it was precious.

"Ninety-eight percent," he said, voice almost too faint to hear.

"Just ninety-eight?" Nathaniel teased. "Let me see that."

The guy licked his lips and held out the paper, the pages still warm from being pressed against his body. Nathaniel casually checked the name in one corner. Caesar Hubbard. Of course! How could he forget a name like that? Then he flipped through the pages until he spotted a circle of red ink around one word.

"We misspelled 'intellectual,'" Nathaniel said. He glanced up in time to see Caesar smile. "That's embarrassing. Remember when we ran the spell check?"

Caesar nodded. "You thought the computer was wrong."

"I figured it was recommending the British spelling or something. I guess you're here because you want a refund?"

Caesar's grin widened before he bashfully forced it away. "My parents said I'm supposed to work with you from now on."

"They must think I'm an intellectual," Nathaniel said with a wink.

Caesar's cheeks turned red. Then he broke eye contact, staring downward instead. Okay, so maybe it wasn't a great joke. Nathaniel considered him for a moment, the light sweat and the even lighter hairs barely visible on his upper lip. How old was he? Fifteen? Sixteen? He definitely wasn't a senior yet or Nathaniel would have noticed him before. "So what are we working on today?"

Caesar opened his backpack and pulled out a sophomore

biology book. In a voice so quiet Nathaniel was forced to lean forward to hear, he rambled nervously about an upcoming test. For the next hour, Nathaniel helped him study for it, teaching him techniques to simplify memorization. Caesar hung on his every word but seemed to have few of his own, only speaking when Nathaniel asked direct questions. At the end of an hour, once Caesar had demonstrated a thorough understanding of the scientific method, Nathaniel got him started on a computer test and moved to the next student. By the time he looked over again, Caesar was gone. A big red "completed" flashed on the computer screen. Nathaniel went to check the results.

Perfect score. Not bad! Nathaniel saved the information to Caesar's profile. Then he turned his attention to the next student. By the time he was finished working and had stepped outside, the sun had gone down. He had mixed feelings about this. Not for the first time, he wished the learning center had longer hours. He stood facing the parking lot, trying to ignore any thoughts that caused his stomach to churn. When he felt a hand on his back, he flinched.

"Easy cowboy," Rebecca said. Her fingers continued down his back, angling across to his hand. Once she had taken it, she loped toward her car, dragging him along. "Smoke a cigarette with me?"

"No thanks. You managed to get more?"

"Kind of." Rebecca opened the passenger-side door and dug around. When she stood again, she was holding a blister pack.

"Is that nicotine gum?"

Rebecca sighed. "Desperate times. You know the freshman I used to buy cigarettes from who stole them from his mother? She quit smoking."

"Good for her."

"Bad for me. My parents have been on to me for years, so I finally 'fessed up."

"So they would buy you the next best thing." Nathaniel shook his head. "If only you would use your powers for good and not evil."

Rebecca smiled shamelessly before popping the gum in her mouth. Then she relaxed visibly, even though the effects couldn't have kicked in yet. "That's better. I thought I'd never make it through the day."

"If it's gum, why did you wait until you're outside?"

"The ritual is important! That's why you're here. Smoking is a social activity."

"You're ridiculous."

Rebecca shrugged. "Everyone should have a vice. You could do with one. It would make you more interesting."

"You think so?"

"Definitely. Any ideas?"

Nathaniel leaned next to her against the car. "Boys."

Rebecca breathed out, as if exhaling smoke. "Okay. What's your type?"

This gave him pause. "I don't really have one."

"You must. What sort of guy do you find yourself lusting after?"

Nathaniel shrugged.

"Seriously?" Rebecca narrowed her eyes. "Are you sure you're gay?"

"Last time I checked, yeah."

"But have you ever *done* anything with a guy?"

"Have you?" When she looked hurt, he hastened to add, "I'm just a lowly virgin. We both are."

"Yeah, but I figured you managed more than I have. A kiss or a little dry humping maybe."

Nathaniel laughed. "There *was* this one guy."

Rebecca smacked her gum more enthusiastically. "What happened?"

"This is back when I lived in California. My friend's parents both worked full-time. They had this porn video. Not like the stuff you see online. This was totally retro, like seventies. All the guys had mustaches, and trust me when I say you've never seen so much bush in your life. It's like they had afros downstairs instead of up."

"Ew!"

"Yeah, but the video got my friend all riled up. One day he suggested that we—" Nathaniel made a pumping motion with his fist.

Rebecca stopped chewing so her jaw could drop. "Together?"

"Yup."

"And did you?"

"Of course! The first time I didn't even let myself look at him, because I was worried it would give me away. The next time, I saw him checking me out. He even complimented me on… Uh, anyway. This went on for a while."

"Wow."

"Yeah," Nathaniel said, smiling at the memory. "That's not all."

"I'm going to need another piece of gum," Rebecca said. "Keep talking."

"Okay. Right before we moved, like the day before, I figured I didn't have anything to lose. I reached over and knocked his hand away. Then I grabbed his you-know-what, and started pumping like my life depended on it. When he did the same for me, I realized we could have been doing that all along."

Rebecca's cheeks were red, but she smiled. "Lucky!"

Nathaniel considered the pavement around his feet. "I guess. The next day wasn't so great. I'm used to moving every few years, but that one hurt."

"Oh. You liked him."

"A little." Nathaniel bit his bottom lip, then forced a smile. "Just a crush. No big deal. He never answered my emails, so I don't think it was mutual."

When he looked up again, he found Rebecca studying his face.

"That bruise still looks nasty," she said.

"It'll fade."

"You need to tell someone."

"Rebecca…"

"I know, but I'm sure your mom will—"

"Becky!"

That shut her up. If there was one thing they both hated, it was cutesy abbreviated names. Especially since their parents were so fond of them. He and Rebecca only used them when the other person was seriously misbehaving.

"Staying silent is your choice, *Nate*, but you can't stop me from worrying."

"Fine."

"I want to kill the bastard."

"I know." He fixed her with a pleading expression, begging her to change the subject.

After a moment her features relaxed, but she continued to study his face. "How often do you shave?"

"Every other day."

"So if you stopped, you would end up with a full beard. Right?"

He allowed himself to look offended. "I'm not aging myself prematurely just to buy you cigarettes."

"Come on! Just think how rugged you'll look!"

"No way."

"Fine." Rebecca slumped. Then she perked up again. "Shoplifting is a vice. Ever give that a try?"

He playfully pushed her away. When she came back and wrapped an arm around his waist, Nathaniel put one around her shoulders. Then he hugged her and tried not to think of how, eventually, he would have to return home again.

Meatloaf, green beans, and mashed potatoes. Nathaniel worked methodically on consuming massive portions, his mother sitting across from him with watchful eyes. She needn't have bothered. Cleaning his plate had never been an issue for him, but he knew she couldn't rest until certain he wouldn't starve.

"Want me to get your father?" she asked.

"I think I can manage on my own," Nathaniel said.

"We're having a family meal this week, even if it means tying each one of you to a chair."

Nathaniel managed a smile. "What's dad doing?"

"Watching one of his boring documentaries."

He kept his attention on the plate, his tone neutral when he asked, "Where's Dwight?"

Star exhaled. "You know your brother, always chasing after some girl."

"He's on a date?"

"If you can call it that. Did you know he broke up with Angela? I was shocked too. She was the sweetest girl. Pretty as can be. I thought for sure—"

Nathaniel tuned out the rest of her comments, his jaw feeling less stressed. Finally able to relax, he tackled his food with renewed gusto, finishing in record time.

"Want to watch TV with us?" Star asked, standing to take his plate.

Nathaniel hopped up and grabbed it before she could, taking it to the sink. "Watch TV? In your bedroom?"

"You're not too old to cuddle up with your parents," Star said, opening the dishwasher.

"When exactly will I be too old? Forty?"

"Nope. You'll still be my baby."

Nathaniel made a face. "I think I'll pass. I need to burn off some of these carbs."

After suffering a kiss on the cheek, he went to the back of the house. To the gym, as Dwight called it. Nathaniel wasn't sure if a weightlifting bench, some yoga mats, and a treadmill qualified as a full-blown gym, but he wasn't stupid enough to argue the point. He stripped down to his boxers, stopping in front of the mirror. He had a darker shade of his mother's blonde hair, the bangs just long enough to frame hazel eyes like those of his father.

The height he inherited from his mother's side, his grandfather in particular, since Nathaniel was a few inches taller than both his father and brother. He only wished he shared their build. Six months of lifting weights had not yielded the desired results. He had enough muscle to make his pecs bounce, his shoulders had grown meaty, and flexing his arms revealed nice curves that hadn't been there a year ago. But it wasn't enough. Dwight had played baseball his freshman year, had been a wide receiver on the football team sophomore year and a quarterback the next. The trophies in the room attested to how athletic he was, and on any other guy, his body would have been drool-worthy. That all those muscles belonged to Dwight gave Nathaniel nightmares. Literally.

No need to despair. A good body and the strength that came with it were within anyone's grasp. So claimed his favorite advertisement. He went to the side table and picked up a workout magazine. It flopped open in his hands, its bent spine leading to the page he so often stared at. The model wore nothing but simple red shorts, the bulge beneath a source of many fevered fantasies. Nathaniel rarely lingered on this detail since the body was sculpted perfection. The veiny arms were nice, as was the six-pack, which Nathaniel envied because he had yet to find his own. The chest intrigued him the most. It was wide and densely covered with muscle, reminding him of an ancient Roman breastplate. Surely that mighty chest could protect Nathaniel. Or be a pillow for him to rest his head against after he'd been rescued. He let his attention dart up to the face, the eyes watery and sensitive, as if understanding his pain. The guy looked like a hero. *His* hero.

Nathaniel let himself bask in the fantasy, his hormones

kicking in. Deciding to channel them in the right direction, he bent back the spine of the magazine and propped it up on the table for extra motivation. Then Nathaniel headed to the weight bench and got to work. Every repetition brought him closer to his dream, the sting of sweat in his eyes and the salty taste on his tongue spurring him onward. He was on his back, hands clenching the barbell as he did a series of bench presses, when an upside-down face appeared above him.

And a handsome face it was. A strong jaw, a crooked smile, and deep blue eyes that gleamed beneath jet black hair. The expression was kind, but as usual, the intention was cruel.

"Working out, baby brother?" Dwight said. "Need someone to spot you?"

"No," Nathaniel said, trying to stay calm. Glancing over to see that Dwight had closed the door did little to soothe his nerves. "Just finishing up."

"You're looking a little shaky. Here." Dwight took hold of the barbell and suddenly the weight felt light as air, his brother not showing any sign of strain. "Slow and steady is the key. A lot of guys thrust, like they want the weights to hit the ceiling. That's not how it's done. First you go down..."

Dwight relinquished control, the barbell growing heavy again, but his hands remained, keeping it steady.

"...and back up again. And down. That's it. Nice and smooth. You train as much muscle on the way back down, but only if you work to maintain control. You feel that burn?"

Nathaniel nodded, eyes locked on Dwight's, searching for any warning sign.

"Elbows at a ninety degree angle. Good. Back up... and down. Up. And down. Up and... *down!*"

Dwight's arms flexed as he pressed. Hard! Had Nathaniel not been braced for something like his, the barbell would have smashed into his chest, crushing his lungs. Instead, Nathaniel pushed back, arms shaking, tissue tearing.

"Mom asked me about that bruise on your face," Dwight said, his smile a grimace now. "Why would she do that?"

"I don't know," Nathaniel grunted. "I didn't say anything, I swear."

"You'd have to be pretty fucking stupid to, which is exactly why I'm worried." Dwight pushed down harder, the metal bar pressing against Nathaniel's neck, making it hard to breathe. "You sure you didn't say anything? How stupid are you, Nate? Huh? Tell me how stupid you are!"

"Not… stupid," Nathaniel managed to grunt. Gritting his teeth, he summoned his last reserves and shoved. The barbell moved. Just a few inches, but it took the pressure off his windpipe. Dwight's expression registered surprise. Then his face twisted up in rage, and Nathaniel felt like whimpering. He tried to remain strong—tried not to lose this small advantage—but Dwight leaned over, adding the weight of his body to the strength in his arms. The barbell came back down, cutting off Nathaniel's oxygen supply.

Almost. He was still able to wheeze air in, but already he was getting lightheaded. He didn't know how much longer he'd be able to hold out. As soon as his arms buckled, the full force of the weight would crush him. Nathaniel saw stars and realized this might be the day he died.

Then the barbell rose and was ripped from his hands. As his vision cleared, he saw Dwight placing it back on the rack before he looked down at him again, those blue eyes calm and collected, as if nothing had happened. "If that leaves a mark, ask yourself again how stupid you are. Understand?"

He tried to respond, but the sound that came out was pathetic and unrecognizable. Dwight smiled, then turned and left the room.

Nathaniel sat up, panting to catch his breath, blood pounding in his ears. He stared at the image in the propped-up magazine, at the look of pure sympathy. Or maybe the expression was apologetic, because his hero had failed him. Nathaniel stood, picked up the magazine and tossed it aside. After forcing himself to calm down, he returned to the weight bench and lay his back flat against it. The guy in the magazine advertisement was no hero, nor would he ever come to his rescue. That left only one option.

Steeling himself, Nathaniel picked up the barbell and continued working out.

"Rise and shine, honey."

Nathaniel blinked against the light and smacked his mouth a few times, tasting stale drool. His mother sat on the edge of the bed, a hand on his back. He scowled at her encouraging smile. "It's not a school day."

"No, but breakfast is almost ready. I want you in the dining room."

Breakfast? Since when did his customary bowl of cereal require waking him up? Then again, he did detect the faint aroma of bacon in the air. Or wafting from the apron his mother wore. This almost made him laugh. Normally she always dressed so stylishly, more than once being mistaken for his older sister. Recently she had watched some old black and white television show and fallen in love with how wholesome families appeared back then. Now she struggled to recreate what she had seen, if only for one meal.

"I tried having a family dinner and failed," she said, confirming his suspicions. "If I can't get everyone at the table during the evening, it'll have to be in the morning."

"Do I have time for a shower?"

"Nope. I need you at the table. Now."

He grunted his agreement, remaining stationary a few minutes after she had left. Then he sighed and dragged himself from bed. He pulled on the jeans he'd worn the day before and reached for the T-shirt before remembering that he'd used it to wipe up a sticky mess just before falling asleep.

"Nate!"

He rolled his eyes at his mother's voice and stumbled out of the room. He felt more annoyed when he reached the table, because no one else was there. Dwight showed up a few minutes later looking bleary-eyed, dark hair sticking up. Their father came next, having long since awakened and dressed. His work was demanding enough that he was usually out of the house before Nathaniel rose. When he was home...

His father set a laptop on the corner of the table before he sat down. He gave both his sons a crinkle-eyed smile before he opened it and started clicking. Nathaniel considered him a moment longer, his attention briefly darting over to Dwight to compare them, since his father and brother looked like younger and older versions of each other. He could understand how his mother had found Heath so attractive when they met. The muscular build was slowly losing its firmness, but he was still handsome. Heath's hair was brown rather than black, his eyes the same striking shade of blue, although they never appeared cruel.

He didn't possess the same demons that Dwight did. His only flaw was being a hopeless workaholic. Ironic, since providing treatment for addiction was his line of business. Maybe Heath needed to check into one of his own clinics.

Nathaniel smirked at the idea, but his smile faded when he saw Dwight staring at him with open irritation. Feeling rebellious, Nathaniel glared and looked away. He felt a lot happier when his mother set a plate in front of him. Scrambled eggs, hash browns, and bacon. He reached for the bottle of ketchup and doused the food until his plate was mostly red. He glanced up to see his mother looking around the table with a bright smile, her dream coming true. Of course people on those old shows would never sit at the table while looking rumpled from bed, but she seemed happy enough.

"Dig in," Star said. Then she raised her eyebrows. "Heath!"

His father blinked, then clicked a few more times before closing the laptop. "Looks delicious," he said. He made a big show of inhaling through his nostrils directly over the plate. "Smells delicious!"

"Judging from the human vacuum over there," Star nodded toward Nathaniel, who already had his mouth stuffed, "it tastes good too."

He shrugged unapologetically, looking to the stove to see if there was more. The sound of utensils clinking against plates filled the room. After a few bites, Star set down her fork, still appearing pleased. "What's everyone doing today? I thought maybe we could all go shopping or—"

"I need to pop into the office," his father said.

"Work," Nathaniel said when his mother looked at him.

"I'm staying home to watch the game," Dwight said.

Star ignored him, still staring at Nathaniel. "What happened to your neck?"

He stopped chewing, a wave of cold panic crashing over him. Over the last few days he'd been careful to wear tight-necked T-shirts that didn't reveal the mark the barbell had left. Only light bruising remained, which had already faded to yellow. The worst was the broken blood vessels, all in a neat red line across his upper chest and in full view at the moment, since Nathaniel hadn't put on a shirt. He glanced over at Dwight, seeing the same angry expression from before.

"I keep telling him he needs a spotter," his brother said.

"You did this while working out?" Star asked.

Nathaniel cleared his throat in an effort to make it feel less dry. "I pushed myself too hard."

Her mouth dropped open, one hand thunking the table. "You could have been seriously injured! Why didn't you say something?"

"Because I knew you would be upset!" Nathaniel shot back.

"Of course I'm upset," she replied. "You need to be careful!"

"I'm always willing to spot for you, baby brother." Dwight smiled at him. "You know that, right?"

Nathaniel gritted his teeth. "Thanks, but I'm fine. The weight slipped and I caught it, but not before it bumped me. It won't happen again."

"Heath," Star said, looking to her husband.

He glanced up. "Let your brother help you."

"I don't need—"

Heath raised an eyebrow. "It's that, or you don't work out at all."

Nathaniel clamped down on his anger. "Fine," he said. "I'll ask him for help next time. Or maybe you can help me, Mom. I've seen your yoga muscles."

Star appeared somewhat placated by this, but only just. "We should buy one of those resistance machines instead. You know, the kind that use elastic bands instead of weights? They must be safer."

Dwight snorted.

Nathaniel nearly joined him. "What we've got is fine."

His mother looked him over. "How much bigger do you plan on getting? If you were trying out for the football team or something I would understand. Wait, is there some guy you're trying to impress?"

"No," Nathaniel said with a nervous chuckle. "I don't have time for stuff like that." Then he realized that he should have said yes. His parents didn't care that he was gay. His father had gay coworkers, and back in California, his mother had more than one gay friend. Even Dwight hadn't cared when Nathaniel first came out, never needing a specific reason to hate him. So pretending he was steadily building muscles in the hope of winning some imaginary guy would have been the most sensible excuse. Now his efforts to beef up had surely raised suspicion, and it wasn't his mother who concerned him.

He focused on his food, refusing to look up from the plate. When he finally did, his fears were confirmed. Dwight was considering him with fresh malice. *You want to challenge me?* his expression seemed to say. *You think you can be the bigger man?*

Nathaniel hid any reaction, making polite conversation with his parents and declining the offer of more food, even though he would have gladly eaten more. Maybe going without would be enough to quell Dwight's suspicions. Probably not.

Nathaniel was first to leave the table, heading down the hall to take a shower and listening for the easily-picked lock to pop, for the knob of the bathroom door to turn. Dwight had never attacked him there before, but he wasn't exactly predictable. Once Nathaniel was dressed, he drove to the learning center. It wasn't open yet, so he sat in his car and allowed himself to feel all the emotions that Dwight was so good at stirring up. Then he flipped an inner switch to silence the fear and anxiety. By the time he saw the manager unlocking the door, he felt normal again. At least as normal as he ever did. He watched the clock on the dashboard, waiting until he was due to begin work before he went inside.

Working on Saturdays was always the least fun. Nathaniel might be glad to get away from home, but most of the learning center students hated having to do school work on the weekend. Saturdays tended to draw a different crowd, many coming in only on this day. This made effective tutoring more difficult, but Nathaniel was up for the challenge. He soon saw one familiar face. Caesar was quietly sitting at a computer, waiting to be noticed, still bashful even though they had worked together all week.

Nathaniel went to join him, asking for a status update. "Geometry test," he said.

"Ninety-seven percent," Caesar mumbled.

Nathaniel nodded as he pulled up a chair and sat next to him. "Spanish quiz?"

"I got an eighty-nine."

"Not bad considering I've never been good at foreign languages. My friend Rebecca, she's practically fluent. You should work with her next time you have a language test coming up."

Caesar didn't say anything. He seemed… uncomfortable? Then he turned, his chair creaking as he looked toward the front door. An older man who shared Caesar's bronze skin tone stood there talking with the manager. His hair was graying at the temples, his mustache the color of cigarette ash, the polo shirt and slacks not quite casual enough for a Saturday morning. Nathaniel was instantly reminded of his own father. Both men had a middle-management sort of vibe. At the moment, the older man appeared none too pleased as he listened to what the manager had to say. Then both adults turned in their direction. Nathaniel quickly focused on the computer, catching Caesar's eye along the way.

"What's that all about?"

Caesar sighed. "I didn't do so well on the biology test."

"You had that material down!" Nathaniel said, not hiding his surprise. "You aced the practice test!"

"I got distracted."

Nathaniel glanced over at him. "How?"

A shrug was the only response.

Nathaniel made sure his tone was neutral. "I'm on your side here. I'm just trying to figure out what went wrong."

Caesar took a deep breath. "I had something on my mind. Something I couldn't stop thinking about. I knew I was supposed to be focusing on the test, so I tried clearing my mind, but that made it worse somehow."

"Because you started thinking about not thinking about that thing you weren't supposed to be thinking about."

Caesar's eyebrows rose in surprise. Then he flashed a bashful smile. "Exactly."

Nathaniel nodded his understanding. "Look, next time that happens, just stop what you're doing and allow yourself to think about whatever is distracting you. That will help get it out of your system."

"Does that work?"

Nathaniel thought about all the times he'd sat in his car before work or school, thinking about Dwight, entertaining each fear so it became easier to push away. "Just remember that the worst rarely comes to pass. Whatever is most likely to happen, it's got to be better than that. Right?"

Caesar considered him, the eyes behind the red-framed glasses a curious golden hue. Then he turned to look toward the front door again. Nathaniel did the same. The older man was gone, but the manager was flustered. Nathaniel would probably hear about it later. Many parents blamed the tutors when their students' grades weren't high enough. Nathaniel didn't let it get to him. All he could do was try his best. With that in mind, he helped Caesar get a head start on the coming week, then set him up with one of the computerized programs. Nathaniel moved on to his next pupil. And the next and the next, the hours melting away until it was time for his half-hour lunch break.

He left the building, intending to walk down to the sandwich joint. He only made it a few yards before a car pulled up next to the sidewalk and parked. The black SUV reflected a distorted version of himself in the freshly polished surface. Then the passenger door opened and Caesar slid out wearing a miserable expression. From around the front of the car appeared the stern businessman who had exchanged tense words with the learning center's manager. Except now he was smiling and extending a hand.

"Todd Hubbard. Nice to meet you. I'm Caesar's father."

"Nathaniel Courtney," he replied, taking the hand and feeling uncertain as his arm was pumped up and down. "Mr. Hubbard, if this is about the biology test—"

"It's about *all* of Caesar's grades, and please, call me Todd."

"Okay," Nathaniel said, wondering if he was supposed to repeat the name. The eyes fixed on him were still shining, which was confusing. "What can I do for you?"

"More of what you've been doing. Caesar's grades started slipping over the previous year, but in the last two weeks, they're on the uptick again." Mr. Hubbard winked. "He says you're to blame for this."

Nathaniel glanced at Caesar, who had his hands in his pockets, his shoulders slumped as he stared at the sidewalk. This had to be embarrassing. They were practically the same age and here was his father, talking to Nathaniel like he was a school teacher or something. "He's been doing all the work. I'm just a study buddy. Human flash cards."

"There's more to it than that." Todd glanced toward the learning center and lowered his voice. "I was disappointed to learn that extra hours aren't an option. I could understand if it was a scheduling issue, but apparently it's company policy."

Ah. Now it made sense. Occasionally parents requested one-on-one tutoring, but for legal reasons, any learning had to be done in the center itself. "Not up to me," Nathaniel said. "I'll try to spend more time working with Caesar when he's here."

Todd nodded. "From what I saw, there are more pupils than tutors. I imagine your time will always be divided. That must be frustrating."

"Dad," Caesar said pleadingly.

His father ignored him. "If you don't mind me asking, how much do you earn an hour?"

"Dad!" Caesar stared at him in disbelief. Then he groaned and rolled his eyes when Mr. Hubbard took a business card out of his pocket and handed it to Nathaniel.

"I'm offering you a job. The same hours but more pay. Think about it and give me a call."

Nathaniel stared at the card before realizing he was expected to respond. He raised his head and nodded, figuring that was vague enough for now. Caesar shot him an apologetic expression, then nudged his father back toward the car. After the SUV had pulled away, Nathaniel looked down at the business card again and laughed. Wait until Rebecca heard about this!

"You've been head-hunted!"

Nathaniel held back a smile. "Not exactly."

"By a talent scout!" Rebecca continued unabashed.

"Not exactly." Nathaniel plopped down on the bed next to her. He had paced excitedly while telling his story, chuckling on more than one occasion. Now he felt embarrassed by the whole thing. "It's simply another parent who thinks he can pay for perfect grades."

"Just tell them no refunds," Rebecca said, pulling up her legs and resting her head on her knees. "Money is money."

"You think I should do it?"

"Normally I'd be selfish and say no, but of course Caesar changes everything."

Nathaniel furrowed his brow. "He does?"

Rebecca mirrored his confusion. "You don't think he's cute?"

"I don't know. I guess I haven't thought about it."

She scrutinized him before coming up with an explanation. "Maybe you need him to do a nerd girl twirl."

Nathaniel laughed. "A what?"

"Nerd girl twirl. That's what I call it anyway. You know how on TV shows or movies, they'll have a nerdy girl nobody likes? Eventually she takes off her glasses and shakes out her hair, usually while twirling around dramatically. Then everyone sees she's pretty, suddenly making her worthy of attention. It's totally sexist." Rebecca bit her lip. "Except if it was a guy instead of a girl, I'd be okay with it. Call me a hypocrite, I don't care. Could you imagine Caesar with his hair down? Or ripping off his glasses, followed by his shirt?"

She giggled shamelessly. Nathaniel smiled in response, but felt distracted by the visual image. He hadn't considered Caesar in that way before and couldn't imagine what sort of body he would have. Nor could he imagine someone so shy and reserved being comfortable with nudity.

"So you think I should take the job?"

Rebecca tilted her head back and forth as she considered the question. "I like that we work together, but it's not like we have much time to interact while there. So… maybe?"

"Maybe it is," Nathaniel said. "I'm sick of thinking about it. Movie time?"

"Definitely."

Rebecca got up to put a DVD in the player, Nathaniel rising to help her pick one. Then they settled back on the bed, their arms and legs pressed against each other. Not long into the film, Rebecca took his hand, which he was fine with. They might both be perpetually single, but at least they had each other. The physical closeness gave him comfort, as did the environment. Rebecca's room was smaller than his own, the walls covered in posters of her favorite eighties bands and movies. The bedspread was pink and Strawberry Shortcake-themed. One of their thrift store finds. He often teased her for being nostalgic about a decade she may have been born in, but definitely didn't remember. He liked her passion anyway, and how she decorated the room. He felt safe here. Able to relax. No creepy older brother. Just Rebecca's parents and little sister, none of whom ever disturbed them.

"You're going to love this one," Rebecca said. "Wait till you see how many baby-faced celebrities are in it. Talk about humble beginnings."

He turned his attention to the screen and soon felt less relaxed. The film quality appeared more seventies than eighties, a low-budget high school movie. Young actors gave stiff performances, many of them big names who now probably hoped this film would remain forgotten. He pretended to laugh along with Rebecca at certain points, but the subject matter made him uncomfortable. A geeky guy got bullied until the day he enlisted the help of a gentle giant. His own personal hero. The fantasy was nice, but the lofty tone of the movie only made his own life seem that much darker.

His palms were sweaty by the time the credits rolled. Rebecca released his hand so she could wipe her own on the bedspread. "Movie get you all hot and bothered? Who do you like better, Clifford or Linderman?"

"Huh?"

"Who do you think is cuter?"

He shrugged.

"Neither of them? Just think how manly Adam Baldwin grows up to be!" She shook her head, as if he were hopeless. "At least tell me you found Matt Dillon attractive. I know he's a jerk in this, but come on!"

"I love him in *Drugstore Cowboy*," Nathaniel replied.

"But in this movie, no one caught your eye?"

"You and Joan Cusack sort of look alike. I've never noticed that before."

"That's not what I mean." Rebecca got up to eject the DVD and put it back in the case. She kept her head down, seeming to stare at the cover. When she looked back up, her expression was vulnerable. "You don't notice guys very much, so maybe..." She exhaled and turned off the television. After more hesitation, she returned to the bed and sat cross-legged, facing him but keeping her attention on the comforter, where a little girl harvested strawberries with her pink kitten. The image seemed too innocent to belong to the modern era, making him long for a time he wasn't sure ever really existed. "I was reading online about how most guys mess around with other guys, especially when they're younger. Hormones or something, but I guess it can be confusing to them. Like they might think they're gay—"

"Rebecca," he interrupted. "Trust me, I know what I want."

She looked up, her eyes searching. "Maybe you don't. Maybe you just need to try something different. Then you could decide for sure."

He finally understood what she was attempting to say, but

tried his hardest to pretend he didn't. Acknowledging the truth would only ruin their friendship, make the closeness they enjoyed feel awkward instead of endearing. She had feelings for him. That wasn't a complete secret, but he never dwelled on it because for him it was impossible. It would never happen. He thought she understood that.

"Maybe something's wrong with me," he said, standing to put distance between them. "You're right. I don't notice guys. At least not very much." His former magazine hero was the exception, but most of that had been about wanting to be saved. "Maybe it's all this stuff with my brother. If I'm not busy with work or school, I'm waiting for the next bad thing to happen."

"Hypervigilance," Rebecca said with a sigh.

"What?"

"It's a condition the body goes into when threatened. A sort of non-stop fight-or-flight reaction. Your body is in a constant state of hyperarousal. And no, that's not as sexy as it sounds. This has an effect on your mind too. You're unable to focus on more normal things, like who you find attractive, because your system is constantly on alert for the next time Dwight jumps you."

He looked back at her. "I don't notice guys often, but I never notice girls. If I did, you'd be my type. You're pretty, but it's your brain that really makes you sexy. If I could find a guy as smart as you, I'd be all over him."

Rebecca didn't swoon. Instead she seemed frustrated, which he supposed he could understand. "It would be nice if you weren't the only guy in the world who felt that way."

"There's someone out there for you," he said. "Wait and see."

She didn't look convinced. Maybe that's why she changed the subject. "You can't keep going on this way. Diminished sex drive, strain to your heart… You'll probably start losing your hair next. Bald at seventeen. How would you like that?"

"Are you serious?"

"Not about the hair loss. But I'm totally serious about Dwight. Tell your parents or lure him out into the street at night so I can run him over. And then back over him. Then I'll run over him again."

Nathaniel smiled at the idea, but his expression became more reserved. She was right. Something had to change. And soon.

* * * * *

Nathaniel stood in front of a large two-story house in a neighborhood that could best be described as affluent. He considered his own parents to be well-off; the homes they had owned over the years often had an extra room or two that wasn't needed as a bedroom. He thought that seemed grand enough, so as he peeked through the etched glass window on one side of the door, he tried to imagine why any single family would need so much space.

Mr. Hubbard must be upper-management, not middle. The business card hadn't provided any clues as to his position. It just listed a company name, a stylish logo, a phone number, and the name "Todd Hubbard" emblazoned in gold letters. Nathaniel had called to say he was interested in the offer. Mr. Hubbard had then jokingly suggested that Nathaniel come in for a job interview. At least he thought it was a joke. Mr. Hubbard had chuckled, but maybe he wasn't fooling around. Unsure of what to expect, he steeled himself and rang the bell. The door swung open, and an older woman with a shrewd face looked him over before smiling. "You must be Nathaniel," she said, stepping aside so he could enter. She offered her hand, but not her name. "I'm Caesar's mother."

"Nice to meet you," he said. "And there's the man of the hour," he added, when Caesar tromped down the stairs.

"Hey." Caesar still looked embarrassed by all of this.

Nathaniel offered a sympathetic expression. "Should we get started?"

"Actually," Mrs. Hubbard said, "I believe my husband wanted to speak with you first. He's in his office. This way, please."

Caesar shrugged helplessly, but didn't follow. Nathaniel felt stiff-legged as Mrs. Hubbard led him down a hall. This *had* to be a job interview. He should have brought his résumé! Not that he had one, but now he wished he did. Instead he was woefully unprepared.

Mrs. Hubbard knocked on a closed door. "Can I get you something to drink?"

"No," he answered. "Thank you."

"You're welcome. Well, I'll leave you to it. Good luck!"

She pushed the door open, then turned and headed back down the hall. Nathaniel took a deep breath and stepped into the room, only getting a brief impression of his surroundings: bookcases and office furniture made of dark wood, mounted antlers behind a large desk, framed degrees, and a fishing trophy. He tore his eyes away from all of this and focused on Mr. Hubbard, who had stood and walked around his desk to greet him.

"So good of you to come!" he said as they shook hands. "Please, have a seat."

Nathaniel nodded numbly and sat. Then he flipped that inner switch, the one he always used when emotions became a hindrance, when he needed to forget about Dwight for a while. Now was not the time to be nervous. In fact, he could imagine Mr. Hubbard responding well to a little reckless confidence.

"It's nice to see you again," Nathaniel said. "You have a very nice home, but I was under the impression that Caesar needed study help. Not you."

Mr. Hubbard raised his eyebrows. Then he laughed, that same amused chuckle that had followed his mention of a job interview. "I was hoping we could get to know each other better. Then I'll set you loose on the boy."

"Sure," Nathaniel said easily. "What would you like to know?"

"Are you from around here? I thought I heard a Midwestern accent."

"Is there such a thing?"

"Well, I haven't heard a single 'y'all' out of you. Of course I don't say it now, but that was a habit I broke for the sake of my business. I try to make sure my family doesn't say it either." Mr. Hubbard sniffed and leaned back. "I'm pretty sure I heard a 'ta' instead of a 'to' when we talked on the phone. I'm going *ta* the store…"

"…*fur* some eggs and bacon." Nathaniel grinned. "Blame my parents. My mom is from Missouri, my dad from Kansas. I haven't lived either place, but listening to them while growing up must have corrupted me. Worried I'll pass that along to Caesar?"

"Not at all," Mr. Hubbard said, smiling at his humor. "So you're a Texan?"

Nathaniel shook his head. "Born in Kansas City, but I spent most of my life on the West Coast. California feels the most like home, although we tend to move every few years."

"How do you like it here?"

"It's nice," he said. "I miss the beaches. And the ocean."

"The Gulf of Mexico doesn't count?"

Nathaniel grinned. "It's not quite the same. That's all right. I was never any good at surfing."

"Do you play any sports?"

"Nope."

Mr. Hubbard's attention darted down to his body, but not with much interest. "You must stay active."

"I try."

"You like fishing?"

Nathaniel's eyes went to the large fish mounted on the wall. "I'm going to say yes, but only because I want this job."

Mr. Hubbard chuckled again. "The job is yours. I'm impressed with your work ethic. The manager at the learning center had nothing but praise for you. Are you saving up for anything in particular? A college fund, perhaps?"

"I'm lucky enough to already have one, thanks to my parents, but I'm hoping to get into a good law school, so—"

Mr. Hubbard appeared impressed. "Any school in particular?"

Nathaniel shook his head. "I haven't decided yet."

"I was hoping you'd say Yale."

"They've got my application."

"Do they?" Mr. Hubbard beamed at him. "I graduated from there in—well, no sense in giving away my age. Sorry, I interrupted you."

"I started tutoring because I thought it would look good on my application."

"So would a glowing reference. I have contacts at quite a few law schools. Including Yale. I'm sure I could help you."

Nathaniel opened and closed his mouth, but it took a few tries before a sound came out. "Seriously?"

"It's certainly possible." Mr. Hubbard leaned forward. "Listen, the reason I'm giving you the third degree is because I'm looking for more than just a tutor for my son. My business demands a lot from me, especially time. Occasionally I have to travel, and when I'm in Houston, I put in long hours. I'm providing for my family, but I'm concerned that Caesar doesn't always get the guidance he needs. Even when I'm home, I worry he might not turn to me if he needed advice about girls or such things. I expect him to provide that guidance for the other kids living here, to be a big brother, but he doesn't take much interest in that role. Then it occurred to me that maybe he needs his own role model."

Nathaniel took a deep breath. "I'm not sure I'm qualified."

Mr. Hubbard waved a hand dismissively. "You're humble, and that's admirable. I understand it's a lot to take on. I probably should have let things develop naturally, but I've always believed in being upfront. Just go about your tutoring duties as you normally would, but also don't hesitate to reach out to him on a more personal level."

"Okay," Nathaniel said.

"I'll stop yammering and let you get to work." Mr. Hubbard stood. Nathaniel did the same. "One more thing. Is that a bruise on your cheek?"

Nathaniel felt like groaning. The bruise had faded to an ugly yellow and wasn't nearly as visible now. He had hoped it would go unnoticed. "Yeah."

"Get into a fight?"

"Not really," he said.

"An accident?"

Nathaniel meant to nod, which would have dismissed the subject, but instead he found himself shaking his head. Maybe because Mr. Hubbard didn't know his parents and wasn't associated with the school. He didn't have the power to make him see a counselor or anything like that. He was, in effect, a stranger. Somehow that made it easier to be honest. Besides, he seemed genuinely concerned.

"Do you feel comfortable telling me what happened?"

Nathaniel considered his answer carefully before he said it aloud. "I have a brother who gets a little rough sometimes."

"Rough?"

"Yeah," Nathaniel said, trying to sound casual. "We horse around. It's no big deal. That's just how he is."

Mr. Hubbard didn't appear reassured, the concern in his features deepening. "I like to think we have an open house. If you ever need to come by, even if Caesar isn't here—even if *I'm* not here, please don't hesitate. Or if there's someone you want me to talk to on your behalf—"

"Thank you," Nathaniel said, cutting him off before the offer

3 3 4 1 212

22111

could turn into a question. "I'll keep that in mind. I think Caesar has some vocabulary he needs help with."

"Of course." Mr. Hubbard offered his hand again. "He should be in the dining room. If you don't find him there, just keep looking until you do. As I said—open house."

Nathaniel nodded his appreciation and left the room. Once he was in the hallway, he glanced back, a strange feeling overcoming him, one so alien he needed a moment to recognize it for what it was.

Hope.

Chapter Two

Nathaniel lingered in front of the bathroom mirror and sighed. Sometimes he wished for a normal weekend—sleeping in and staying in bed, even after waking up. A quick excursion to the kitchen for a bowl of cereal before heading back to his room for a movie marathon. Some of Terry Gilliam's films, starting with *The Adventures of Baron Munchausen*, since it made him believe fantasy could become reality.

Nathaniel exhaled and checked his watch. Time to tutor Little Lord Hubbard again. Over the past week, Caesar's grades had remained steady, but as a good role model or whatever, Nathaniel was failing abysmally. Try as he might, he struggled to make any sort of personal connection with Caesar. The environment didn't help. They always sat at the dining room table, Mrs. Hubbard appearing frequently to check on their progress. Nathaniel felt pressured, like they needed to remain on track or risk being reprimanded, so he didn't even attempt small talk.

He also tried to view Caesar as more than just a pupil, still bothered by Rebecca's claim that he didn't react to other guys the way he should. Yesterday, while Caesar was distracted with reading a paragraph out loud, Nathaniel had looked him over, noticing the jumble of homemade friendship bracelets he wore on one wrist. Who had given them to him? Had Caesar returned the favor, making and distributing his own? Or, like Nathaniel had done before Dwight gave him hell about it, maybe he had made the bracelets for himself, just because he thought they looked cool. Nathaniel had been on the verge of asking about them when Mrs. Hubbard made another of her appearances.

Today wasn't likely to be any different, but he had a job to do. If he didn't get a move on, he'd be late. Nathaniel had grabbed his things and was heading for the front door when he heard shouting. At first he thought it was his parents. His father was a patient man until he wasn't. His mother felt deeply or nothing at all. When they butted heads, they did so loudly. Nathaniel always remained on the sidelines, but watching them go round and round about issues that didn't seem important to him was tedious. He was just about to step outside when he realized one of the voices was wrong. He recognized his mother, but shouting back at her…

Nathaniel spun around and raced toward the commotion. He found himself in the kitchen, where he saw his mother backed up against the counter, Dwight's finger thrusting at her repeatedly as the shouting continued. Nathaniel didn't think. He lurched forward, grabbed Dwight's shoulder, and pulled so hard his brother spun like a top before he caught himself. His handsome face was twisted with rage, an arm cocking instinctively before the flames flickered in his eyes. Dwight remembered that a witness was present. His arm lowered, but his fists remained balled.

"Everyone just calm down," Star pleaded.

"What's going on?" Nathaniel asked, chest heaving from adrenaline.

"Mom's pissed at me *because I got a job*," Dwight spat.

Star exhaled. "No, I'm angry because I found an account statement showing that your college fund is nearly depleted!"

"Which is why I got a job!"

"That money is supposed to be for your education!" She shook her head. "I told your father we shouldn't let you take a year off. I knew this would happen!"

"Oh really? Then why act so damn surprised?" Dwight turned and stepped into her personal space again. "I'm not a kid anymore. You can't tell me what to do!" He kept shouting, ranting that he didn't need a college degree to sell cars, and that he would be the best salesman the dealership had ever seen. Nathaniel barely heard the words. Instead he focused on his mother's bewildered expression, like she had been cornered by a wild animal in her own home, and for a moment—just the tiniest fraction of time—her features betrayed fear. That's what set him off.

He grabbed Dwight's shoulder again, clamping down so hard it was sure to be painful, shouting his own furious words. "Leave her alone, you piece of shit!"

Dwight turned, knocking away his hand and gritting his teeth. The look he shot Nathaniel promised there would be hell to pay. But not now. Dwight grabbed his keys and stomped from the room. They listened as the front door opened and slammed shut. Then Star sighed, rubbing her temples as she took a seat at the table.

Nathaniel sat next to her. "Are you okay?"

"Of course." Another exasperated sigh. "This is my fault. I didn't raise him well or… I don't know how I got it so right with you but not him." She shook her head. "I was too young to be a mother."

"I'm glad you didn't wait," Nathaniel said, trying to interject some humor. "Otherwise I wouldn't be sitting here. It's not like Dwight and I were lined up inside you, just waiting our turn. It's all down to chance. Right?"

"In that case I don't have any regrets. I just wish I knew what he needed."

"Have you tried slapping him around?" Then, more carefully, he added, "Maybe this will be good. All he's done the past year is laze around the house. Now he's got a job. Maybe he'll get his own place too."

"That's not what I want for him," his mother said. "His independence, yes, but he needs more to fall back on than his good looks. Those won't last forever. I'm living proof."

"You're beautiful."

His mother put a hand over his and managed a smile. "You make me proud. You know that?"

"I'm glad," Nathaniel said, gently pulling away his hand. "I have to get going. If Dwight comes back, let Dad deal with him. Okay?"

His mother nodded distractedly. He watched her for a moment longer, wondering if he needed to fear for her, but he knew he didn't. As usual he would be the one to take the brunt of Dwight's anger. In this circumstance, he would do so willingly.

Nathaniel didn't feel quite so noble when he stepped outside. His car was tilted at an odd angle. Sure enough, when he walked around the vehicle, he spotted a flat tire. The timing was no coincidence. Revenge. Just a down payment. The rest would come later. Nathaniel flipped his internal switch, preferring to feel numb rather than sorry for himself. Then he went to the trunk and dug around for the jack. The spare tire was low on air when he got it out, but it would be enough to get him to the nearest auto repair shop. Once there, he called Mr. Hubbard, leaving a voicemail explaining he would be late. It took almost an hour for the tire to be fixed, Nathaniel remaining detached inside. Once the tire was repaired, he drove to Caesar's house.

Mrs. Hubbard opened the door. "We thought you decided not to show," she said.

"I had car trouble," Nathaniel replied. "I left a message with your husband."

"Todd is out of town." She pursed her lips before stepping aside so he could enter. "Caesar is upstairs with a friend. I'll go get him for you."

"No," Nathaniel said quickly. "I don't want to trouble you. I'll run up myself."

"Oh. Very well."

Nathaniel hurried up the stairs before she could change her mind, wanting to avoid another awkward session at the dining room table. He found himself in an unfamiliar hallway with more options than he liked. He counted under his breath. Six doors! Of course he knew now that the Hubbards had quite a few kids, at least some of which were adopted. He stopped halfway down the hall, unsure how to proceed. A boy with a pug nose and freckles appeared, halting in his tracks when spotting him.

"Carrie or Caesar?" he asked.

"Caesar," Nathaniel said. "I'm his tutor."

The boy snorted, jerked a thumb over his shoulder at a door, then walked on. A moment later, Nathaniel heard a toilet seat clanking against the tank. Weird kid, but helpful. Nathaniel went to the door at the end of the hall. He was raising his hand to knock when he heard voices inside. Loud ones. A girl giggled before responding to a question. The other voice sounded cocky. He barely recognized it as belonging to Caesar, who was normally so soft-spoken. Nathaniel glanced back to make sure he was still alone and pressed his ear to the door.

"—cutting yours next," Caesar was saying. "I'm thinking a flat top. Or a mohawk! Or maybe we'll buzz it all off completely."

"That wasn't the deal," the female voice responded. "Now hold still or I'll cut you."

"By accident?"

"Nope!"

A flushing toilet from farther down the hall prompted Nathaniel to stand upright again. He cleared his throat to avoid appearing stealthy. Then he knocked. The voices grew quieter, whispering to each other. He heard footsteps before the door swung open. A girl with a head full of black corkscrews stood there. Her eyes were equally dark, but they shone with amusement as they looked him over.

"Are you the tutor?" she asked.

"Yeah," Nathaniel said. "I'm running a little late."

"Fine by me," she said, gesturing him inside.

He entered a bedroom larger than the one belonging to his parents. A bed was to one side, beyond it a loveseat and cluttered coffee table. Except for a few windows in the vaulted ceiling, the only light came from the attached bathroom where—

Nathaniel stared. Caesar was standing in the doorway, framed by light. He was shirtless, his bronze skin in full view. His body was lean, his shoulders broad, the muscles wiry. His waist narrowed as it disappeared into his jeans, the band of his underwear visible. His hair was currently down. On his left side it rested on his shoulder. On the other it had already been cut, but not drastically so. The length stopped just above his jaw line and appeared even shorter when Caesar brushed it behind one ear. He looked good. It wasn't a full nerd girl twirl, since he still had on his glasses, but Nathaniel liked those anyway. He hadn't minded the ponytail either, but he wasn't sad to see it go. So much for Rebecca's fight-or-flight theory, because Nathaniel had to force his eyes away.

"Should I go?" the girl asked. "I can finish cutting it some other day."

"No way!" Caesar said with a laugh. Then he looked a little more shy. "Nathaniel, this is my girlfriend, Steph. Steph, this is my Nathaniel. I mean my tutor. Nathaniel. Uh."

"You're such a dork," Steph said, rolling her eyes at Caesar. Then she cocked her head at Nathaniel, her long curls fluttering like a curtain. "I don't suppose you know how to cut hair."

Nathaniel smirked. "I'm not that kind of tutor."

Caesar looked panicked. "You said you knew how to do this!"

"I figured it couldn't be that hard," she shot back. "I was wrong."

Caesar's face fell. "Oh crap. I'm ruined!"

"Looks like she's on the right track," Nathaniel said, following Steph so they could consider him up close. "Turn around."

He stood off to one side, examining the jutting shoulder blades and the small of Caesar's back. Then he remembered the bathroom mirror, which probably revealed him doing all of this, and quickly focused on the hair instead. It really did look fine. "Just keep doing what you're doing."

"Think I should trim around the ears?" Steph asked.

"No. Leave it long. See how it looks when you've done the rest. Then we can decide."

He stepped back so she could get to work, happy for an excuse to stare at Caesar. He wished he could let his eyes wander wherever they wanted, but more than once, he saw Caesar's reflection staring back at him. Nathaniel went to sit on the edge of the bed and glanced around the room. His impression of Caesar had always been of someone bookish and shy, but he saw no thick tomes or dusty stacks of fantasy novels. The room was little different than his own. Just as disorganized, although instead of movie posters on the wall, those here involved a video game, a bikini-clad model, and one of Eminem looking squinty and pouty. The television opposite the loveseat was nice. Widescreen, instead of the old 4:3 aspect ratio he had back home. Nathaniel had been saving up for a new TV. Maybe he should pull a Dwight and raid his college fund.

"You were right about the ears." Steph plopped down on the bed next to him.

Nathaniel looked to where Caesar had last been, but the door was mostly shut now, the sound of a shower running beyond.

"I've been trying to axe that ponytail for months," she continued. "I even had a dream about sneaking in here and cutting it off."

Nathaniel refrained from sharing his own opinion of Caesar's appearance. "How long have you guys been together?"

"A little over a year."

"Geez."

Steph eyed him. "Most people don't wince when I tell them that."

"I'm just surprised, that's all. None of my friends have made it more than a few months." He glanced over at her, trying to determine her age. "Are you a senior?"

"Oh, I like you!" Steph beamed at him. "I'm just a sophomore. What about you?"

"I'm a senior."

"Uh huh. And how long have you made it before?"

"In a relationship?" Nathaniel thought about junior high, when a girl he hadn't known had asked him out. They shared the same English class, but they never talked. He had said yes, because it had seemed the right thing to do. Then she started calling his house, which was awkward, because he never knew what to say. That had only lasted— "Two weeks."

"That's it?" Steph looked surprised, then narrowed her eyes suspiciously. "Oh I see. Now that I think about it, it's obvious."

Nathaniel resisted a gulp. "Yeah?"

"Yeah. You're a player, aren't you?"

Nathaniel recovered enough to smile. "Busted."

"Just don't teach Caesar any of your moves."

Nathaniel laughed nervously as the bedroom door opened. Mrs. Hubbard. Naturally. She looked at them both, then toward the bathroom.

"He's taking a quick shower," Steph explained. "We trimmed his hair."

Mrs. Hubbard didn't appear impressed. "He's supposed to be studying."

"I guess that's my cue." Steph shot him a 'same shit, different day' expression. "Have fun hitting the books." She stood, grabbed her purse, and swept past Mrs. Hubbard, who ignored her.

"Would you rather wait downstairs?" she asked.

"Actually," Nathaniel said, grasping for an excuse. "I thought we'd try studying in here. A familiar environment can be conducive to stronger focus. You know, fewer distractions, like siblings walking through the room." Or overbearing mothers. This logic seemed to appease Mrs. Hubbard, who left him alone.

Nathaniel turned forward, listening as the water stopped, the last drops no doubt running down to Caesar's pointed chin. Or down his neck, over that smooth chest, across his stomach and ending up at his— The shower curtain pulled back, the rings clattering along the pole, but the door wasn't open enough to confirm his fantasies.

"It definitely feels better!" Caesar said. "I hated how it stuck to my back when wet."

Nathaniel didn't reply, feeling the words weren't directed at him.

"Are you sure it isn't too short?"

Again he stayed silent until Caesar's head popped out from the door. "She went home," he explained.

"Oh."

His glasses were off, completing his nerd girl twirl, but the new look was no major revelation. Nathaniel had noticed his eyes before, and found him just as attractive with the glasses on. Definitely a cute guy. Steph was a lucky girl.

"Uh," Caesar said. "I'll be right out."

The door slammed shut. Had Nathaniel been staring too long? He exhaled and tried to get himself into a professional mindset. Studying. Learning. Not toweling off a sopping-wet boy in his bedroom. When the bathroom door swung open, Caesar was dressed, this time with a shirt. The eyes behind the glasses darted in his direction and away again as he stood there awkwardly.

"What do you think?"

Nathaniel stood, like he just spotted his prom date coming down the stairs. What did he think? Impure thoughts, that's what! He tried to focus on Caesar's hair. Even wet, he could see the natural curl. Not like Steph's hair. Not even close, but now that his hair wasn't pulled back, Caesar's locks were free to proceed in gentle waves across each temple and ear. He liked it but wasn't dumb enough to say so. "It'll grow back."

Caesar looked crestfallen.

Nathaniel rolled his eyes. "I'm sure Steph will love it. Try parting it on one side, not the middle. Yeah, exactly. Now if beauty hour is finished, maybe we could get to work."

"Ugh." Caesar checked the mirror once more, making a face. "I was hoping we wouldn't have to. It's the weekend, you know."

Nathaniel exhaled. "Yeah, but the next time your mom walks in here…"

Caesar walked to the bedroom door and pushed the lock in the knob. "Oops!"

Nathaniel liked that. A lot. And why not? Maybe this was the sort of bonding Mr. Hubbard had been hoping for. He only wondered how they would fill the time. He glanced around for inspiration, noticing a framed photo of a sports team hanging on the wall. He moved closer to examine it. About twenty guys were lined up in three rows, all of them wearing sky-blue singlets. He scanned each row until he found Caesar, who was sandwiched somewhere in the middle, his bulge hidden behind some guy's elbow. Too bad. Nathaniel turned around and asked the obvious.

"You're on the wrestling team?"

"Yup."

"You any good?"

Caesar raised his chin. "My mom keeps the trophies downstairs in the living room. She's even more proud of them than I am."

Nathaniel nodded appreciatively, glancing at the photo once more. The school name confirmed they didn't go to the same one. Some of the guys on the team looked pretty tough. One even had facial hair. He tried to imagine Caesar on the mat, fighting to pin any of these opponents, and couldn't. Then again, the wiry muscles Nathaniel had seen earlier, and the confident way he had joked with Steph, implied he didn't know the true Caesar yet.

He moved to a narrow shelf full of DVDs, searching for more clues.

"Nice movie collection," he said. Once he started reading the spines, he wished he hadn't spoken so quickly. Most of them were action films. He didn't have anything against big budget explosions, but Caesar's collection was devoid of any that had defined the genre. No *Kill Bill*. No *The Bourne Identity*. Not even *Die Hard*. Most of the movies here were just a flash in the pan, pushed heavily by the studios but soon forgotten afterwards. He noticed *Independence Day* and tried not to wince. The collection wasn't completely hopeless though. He unshelved *North by Northwest* and held it up.

"You like old movies?"

Caesar shrugged. "Christmas present from Dad. It's his favorite. I've never actually seen it."

"Your dad has good taste. All of Hitchcock's stuff is excellent. Well, except for *Mr. & Mrs. Smith*. Or some of his wartime propaganda films, although *Lifeboat* starts out good."

Caesar stared at him blankly.

"Or not," Nathaniel said, turning to place the movie on the shelf. Then he hesitated. He couldn't think of anything else to do. Maybe a movie would help break the ice. Besides, the DVD was still shrink-wrapped, which seemed tragic. "We could watch it together. If you want."

Caesar nodded. "Okay."

Nathaniel dug a thumbnail along the case to break the seal, watching as Caesar bent over to turn on the DVD player. Once the disc was in the tray, they settled down on the couch, but Nathaniel didn't feel comfortable. How could something as simple as sitting together feel so awkward? It didn't help that he was so aware of Caesar's every movement, like the way his leg bounced impatiently as the FBI warning flashed on the screen, or how one of his hands rested on the cushion between them, looking lonely all by itself. Maybe Caesar wished Steph was sitting there so she could hold it for him.

The movie finally started. Nathaniel immersed himself in a world before his time, paying attention occasionally to Hitchcock's directing style, but mostly getting caught up in the plot. Caesar seemed to enjoy himself too, tensing up at the right moments. At first, anyway. The movie wasn't exactly short, and as it neared the two-hour mark, Nathaniel could sense him getting restless. He realized then how boring he must seem. Maybe Caesar wasn't actually shy. Perhaps he simply didn't have anything to say to Nathaniel any more than he would to one of his teachers at school. All they did together was study. When Caesar asked to do something else, Nathaniel had suggested they watch his father's favorite movie. Caesar probably saw him as another boring adult. So Nathaniel did something he usually abhorred and started talking during the film, sharing some of the more interesting trivia about the production, or some of the scandals that surrounded the stars. Some of this Caesar responded to. Other times he just nodded to show he was listening.

"When I lived in California, I made a list of filming locations and went to as many of them as possible."

Caesar perked up. "What city did you live in?"

"San Diego at the time, but we move every few years."

Caesar sighed wistfully. "Must be nice. I've been here my whole life."

"At least you know who everyone is. I'm tired of feeling like a stranger."

Caesar thought about it. "I would definitely miss my friends." He looked over and made eye contact. "It must suck having to say goodbye each time."

"I try to minimize that by being antisocial." He laughed at himself. "I always have at least one friend or I'd go crazy, but there's no point in getting too attached."

"How long have you been here?" Caesar asked. "I mean, will you be moving again soon?"

"Why? Will you miss me?"

"Yeah." Caesar returned his attention to the screen. "I would."

The response sounded genuine. And a little too sentimental, because they didn't really know each other. Still, he couldn't help but find it endearing. "I don't know what's going to happen after I graduate. I guess that depends on whatever college accepts me. Maybe I'll stay local."

Now he was being sentimental. The plan had always been to move as far away as possible. College was his best chance to escape Dwight forever.

"I'm going to Yale," Caesar said.

Nathaniel raised an eyebrow. "Hard school to get into."

"That's why you're here," Caesar said.

True enough. This wasn't a social call. Mr. Hubbard was paying him good money to make sure his son got into the right college. Nathaniel returned his attention to the television and watched Cary Grant scramble over Mount Rushmore. When the film reached its epic conclusion and the credits started to roll, he grabbed the remote and shut it off. "That was a waste of time. On Monday we hit the books again."

Caesar looked chastised, but that was fine. Nathaniel had a role to play. Drooling over a sophomore and trying to imagine what was beneath his wrestling uniform was the opposite of what he should be doing.

"I gotta run," Nathaniel said. "If you have any homework this weekend, make sure you get it done."

Starchy, but necessary. If Caesar wanted to have fun, he could spend time with his girlfriend. Nathaniel got up and left the room, wishing he had someone like that in his life. Someone he could always be himself around instead of having to pretend he was responsible or anything but fucked up. Then again, he kind of did.

"So he's straight," Rebecca said, making sure she understood his story correctly. She was flipping through her CD collection, tossing those she no longer wanted on her bed so she could feed them to eBay.

"Yeah, he's straight," Nathaniel said. "His girlfriend was my first clue. That he's actually happy and outgoing around her confirms it."

Rebecca shrugged, her attention still on her task. "One less thing for you to worry about."

"Easy for you to say." Nathaniel said with a huff. "I was

starting to like him. You have no idea how it feels to meet someone you like, only to find out you're not compatible on the most basic level."

Rebecca stopped sorting and looked at him pointedly. "Yeah, that must be rough."

"Oh. Sorry. It's just so frustrating."

Rebecca sighed, her shoulders relaxing. "I know. I'm sorry too. You finally noticed a guy, but he'll never notice you. Not in the same way. Why does love have to suck so bad?"

"I don't know, but you're right. I have bigger things to worry about. My mom and Dwight got into an argument today." He told her everything that had happened. Rebecca pushed aside the pile of CDs so she could sit on the bed and listen. He didn't have to explain the implications—she already knew what he had waiting for him at home.

"Sleepover time?" she asked when he was finished.

He nodded gratefully. On occasion, when the situation was dire enough, she would sneak him up to her bedroom late at night and out again in the morning. This only delayed the inevitable, but occasionally Dwight cooled down by the next day and returned to being just a jerk instead of a vicious monster.

"Spring break is coming up," Rebecca said.

Nathaniel groaned. "Don't remind me. At least I don't have to worry about him when I'm at school."

"But you said he got a job. Find out his hours. We'll make plans for whenever he's off work." She hopped up and grabbed a notebook and pen, turning to a blank page. "Let's come up with an idea for every single day. We can hit a bunch of museums in Houston or—"

"Road trip to Galveston?"

She nodded and scribbled it down. "What else?" When he remained silent, she looked up, seeing the relief on his face. "It sucks that you have to hide from your own brother, but we're going to have fun."

"You're my best friend," Nathaniel said. "Of all time."

Rebecca smiled, her cheeks a little flushed. "Then let's make this a spring break to remember!"

Time was Nathaniel's greatest weakness. No matter how often he promised himself to remain on guard or how much he prepared for the worst by working out each day, eventually his memory blurred at the edges, his instincts growing lukewarm. That's when it would happen. His mind would be somewhere else—such as the old Savage Steve Holland movie he was watching at the moment. When his brother plopped down on the couch next to him, Nathaniel knew he should have gotten up before Dwight's butt hit the cushion. But he didn't, his intuition having failed him.

Dwight reached for the remote, flipping over to a football game. Nathaniel was pushing himself up to stand when his brother grabbed his wrist, squeezed, and yanked him back down. He tried pulling away, but Dwight's grip was strong, ensuring he couldn't escape.

"Watch the game with me," he said, blue eyes flicking over to meet his. Then he smiled.

Nathaniel felt sorry for any girl taken in by the perfect white teeth, the strong nose, and the eyes that danced with joyful glee. How many girls had been lured in by that handsome face, and how many had walked away damaged by the experience? Nathaniel tried jerking away, but Dwight's jaw clenched and his expression grew dark.

Nathaniel stopped struggling. He attempted to relax, to pretend that none of this really bothered him. He even tried flipping the switch to kill his emotions. Dwight still gripped his wrist, making Nathaniel want to recoil in fear, but he distanced himself from the situation as much as possible while staring at the television. The increasing pressure on his wrist made this impossible. Like a python squeezing its prey to death, Dwight's grip grew tighter and tighter. For half an hour they sat together, but Dwight never stopped. His own hand must have been aching from effort. Nathaniel—brow sweating now—looked out of the corner of his eye to see Dwight's forearm flexing, his knuckles white. Nathaniel's hand had lost sensation, the circulation cut off. Not his wrist though. That seared with maddening pain, the bones seeming to be on the verge of cracking and splintering. Then the garage door rumbled, signaling their parents' return. Dwight didn't let go until the door connecting to the kitchen swung open. Then he released Nathaniel, casually wiping the sweat of his palm on the couch. When their mother called for help unloading the groceries, he reached for the remote, turning up the sound a few notches.

Nathaniel stared at him, heart pounding. Then he rose to help his mother. His hand tingled painfully as sensation returned, his wrist burning, but he ignored this pain as best he could and carried in plastic bags filled with food. Once this chore was done, he went to his room, shut and locked the door, then curled up on his bed. Rebecca's plan wouldn't work. Any second that Nathaniel was at home meant being at risk. He needed more than an after-school job or a day at the museum. Karate lessons? A knife? A gun?

Help. That's what he needed most. Perhaps that's why the next day, when his wrist had turned dark red and purple, he left it in plain view. His mother didn't notice at the breakfast table because she was running late for an appointment. His father had already left for work. Dwight was still in bed. If anyone noticed at school, they didn't say anything. Just Rebecca, who only needed confirmation of her suspicions. She shook her head in frustration, knowing he wouldn't listen to her advice. One other person noticed, but after school. Science books were spread out over the dining room table and Nathaniel was trying his best to explain chromosomal inheritance when Caesar interrupted him.

"What happened to your wrist?"

Nathaniel looked up from the books in time to see Mrs. Hubbard in the doorway. She had heard Caesar and was moving toward the table to investigate. For some reason Nathaniel didn't want her to see it, so he quickly slid his arm under the table.

"Tennis injury," he mumbled, which was a ridiculous claim, but he hadn't prepared a good excuse.

Caesar was confused. "You play tennis?"

"Let's focus on studying," Nathaniel said. "You have a test tomorrow."

Caesar appeared slighted, his eyes returning to one of the open books. Mrs. Hubbard's curiosity must have been appeased because she turned and left the room. Close call. Tomorrow he would start wearing long-sleeve shirts until the bruises faded. He thought that was the end of the subject, but when he and Caesar were wrapping up, Mr. Hubbard strolled into the room.

"Nathaniel!" he said with an easy smile. "How nice to see you. Join me in my office, won't you?"

Nathaniel nodded, gathered up his things, and followed Mr. Hubbard down the hall.

"Take a seat," he said once they were in his office. Mr.

Hubbard remained by the door long enough to close it. Then instead of walking around his desk, he leaned against the edge, looking down at Nathaniel. Or more accurately, at his wrist. "More horsing around?"

Mrs. Hubbard must have reported what she'd seen, which also implied that her husband had asked her to be on the lookout for such things. Mr. Hubbard knew. He had to, so Nathaniel nodded in confirmation.

Mr. Hubbard exhaled. "I have two brothers. I was the youngest, the lowest in the pecking order. My oldest brother treated me like a slave. My mother was always working, struggling to raise us on her own, which meant she wasn't around much. So my older brother would make me fetch drinks for him or make sandwiches. Sometimes he would do worse. We had a cat, and one time he dumped out the litter box on the carpet right in front of me, and said that if I didn't clean it up, Mom would put Ginger to sleep. He wasn't the nicest guy. Occasionally I would get fed up with him, and a few times we got into physical altercations. Scratches, bumps, and bruises were part of that." Mr. Hubbard nodded at Nathaniel's wrist. "But not like this. You know what that looks like to me?"

"What?" Nathaniel asked, his throat raw.

"Abuse."

All of Nathaniel's excuses rose to the surface—that brothers play rough with each other, or that his own clumsiness was to blame, or even that he bruised easily. But he was tired of hiding the truth. He needed to tell someone, just one adult, to see if they had a magic solution, a useful course of action he hadn't thought of himself. "I don't know why he hates me. Most of the time I'm just minding my own business when it happens."

Mr. Hubbard frowned. "Do your parents know?"

Nathaniel shook his head. "I don't think so."

"It's hard to miss a bruised cheek."

"I'm a pretty good liar."

Mr. Hubbard studied him a moment. "My mom had an awful lot on her plate. That's why I never told her what was going on. My situation wasn't as severe as yours appears to be. Most siblings torment each other to some extent, but what you're going through is far outside the norm. It needs to stop."

"It wasn't always this bad," Nathaniel said. "When we were

younger, I would tell on him. Back then it was just friction burns or noogies. I would tell and he would be punished. I have good parents. I really do. But then Dwight started retaliating. One of my favorite toys might go missing, or once when I had a bunch of tacks in my backpack for a school presentation, he must have opened the box and dumped them out, because the next time I reached in—" Nathaniel's fingers twitched at the memory. "There was never any proof, but these things always happened after I got him in trouble with our parents. So I stopped telling them."

Mr. Hubbard's expression was sympathetic. "Sounds to me that matters have escalated beyond a missing toy or a mean-spirited prank."

"I guess so."

"I would be happy to talk to your parents with you. Or even on your behalf."

Nathaniel shook his head. "What are they going to do? Ground him? Kick him out of the house? Neither of those things will stop him from getting back at me. He'll find a way, believe me, and when he does it'll be far worse than what I go through now."

"Then perhaps we should contact the police."

Nathaniel's head whipped up. "No! Think about my mother! One of her sons putting the other in jail? That would kill her. How long would they hold him anyway? Eventually he'll be free to get back at me. I just need to stay out of his way. Soon it'll all be okay. Dwight was supposed to go to college last year. I thought I'd be free of him then. Doesn't matter because when I graduate, I'm *definitely* going to college. Somewhere far away. Dwight hates me, but not enough to travel across state lines just to punch me around."

Mr. Hubbard's brow was furrowed. "I don't feel comfortable with this. I really think we should talk to someone."

"I'll deny everything," Nathaniel threatened. "I'm sorry, but I will."

Mr. Hubbard considered this. Then he rubbed his mouth and mustache, stood to walk around his desk, and took a seat. Once there, he seemed lost in thought.

Nathaniel watched him, heart pounding, hoping that he hadn't made a major mistake. "I just need to avoid him. This job you gave me already helps. The less time I'm home, the better.

Dwight got a job recently too. Everything will be fine. Honestly."

Mr. Hubbard nodded reluctantly. "I'll respect your wishes. I hope you know that you can always turn to me if you need help."

"I know that now," Nathaniel said. "Thank you."

Mr. Hubbard nodded again, still not looking pleased. Eventually he sighed and leaned back in his chair. "Spring break is coming up. We're taking a family trip. Camping, if this good weather continues. If not, there's always the cabin. Why don't you come with us? Give yourself a break by getting away. Besides, I enjoy your company. I know Caesar does too."

Nathaniel wasn't sure about that last bit, but the offer had his chest feeling tight, his eyes a little teary. He blinked, hoping Mr. Hubbard hadn't noticed. Then, not trusting his own voice, he simply nodded. Nathaniel had always wanted help. He just never expected to get it.

Chapter Three

Pine needles, most of them dark green bristles, some more vibrant where they had freshly burst forth in this new spring. The rest were brown, carpeting the ground, absorbing sound underfoot and preserving the silence. No roar of a distant highway, no airplanes buzzing overhead. The Hubbards had driven him four hours away from Houston and now, so detached from civilization, Nathaniel felt safer than he had in years. These woods were his sanctuary.

Behind him... that's where things became complicated. He glanced back, making sure Caesar was keeping up. Every time Nathaniel looked over his shoulder, Caesar flashed him a reassuring smile before quickly averting his eyes, usually down to the path. Awkward as hell, but still enough to whip Nathaniel's hormones into a frenzy because he found the guy adorable. If only he wasn't so difficult to penetrate.

Nathaniel allowed himself a covert smile at the double meaning as they continued their hike. This was Mr. Hubbard's idea. During the drive, his eyes kept shining at them in the rearview mirror, as if they were already off to a great start. Nathaniel tried not to disappoint, bringing up topic after topic. Conversation remained one-sided. Caesar occasionally offered a few quiet words or nodded to show he was listening, but no lighthearted banter resulted. Nathaniel had been his private tutor for a few weeks with little progress. When added to their time at the learning center together, he felt even more like a failure.

While helping to set up the tent, Mr. Hubbard had been encouraging when Nathaniel broached the subject.

"He's really quiet around me. I feel like I'm doing something wrong."

"Caesar? Quiet?" Mr. Hubbard had winked. "I noticed that too, and it is unusual for him. I think he just admires you."

"Really?"

"Sure! Why don't you two spend some time together, man to man." Mr. Hubbard then suggested the hike they were currently on, mentioning an old ghost town a few hours away from camp, and offered one more piece of advice. "Take him into your confidence. Pull the curtain aside and show him that you're human too. That'll help get you down from the pedestal he's put you on."

Nathaniel wasn't sure what to make of that. Was he supposed to open up about Dwight? Right now, that was the last thing he wanted to think or talk about. Escaping felt too good. Why sully this paradise by invoking his brother's spirit? Still, they had to talk about something. Nathaniel slowed, stepping off the path to walk beside Caesar.

"Miss your girlfriend yet?"

Caesar nodded.

"Spring break without you watching out for her. I hope she doesn't get into trouble."

Caesar managed a nervous chuckle.

"Seems like a good girl. I can tell she's crazy about you."

A smile that didn't reveal teeth.

Ugh, so boring! Nathaniel decided to stop being cautious. "So, have you guys fucked yet?"

Caesar's cheeks grew red and he smiled. More of a leering grin, really. A hint of swagger came into his step too. Promising.

"Well, well!" Nathaniel said. "Make with the details!"

"Like what?" Caesar said, not completely averse to the suggestion.

Like how big is your dick and what can you do with it? Nathaniel struggled to find a question that didn't center on Caesar. "Is she wild? Tame? Somewhere in between?"

Caesar thought about it, still grinning. "Sweet," he said eventually. "When we're just hanging out, she's got a wicked sense of humor, and she loves to tease me. Not in a sexual way. Uh… She's fun to be around. But in bed it's like she's vulnerable. Delicate."

"Huh," Nathaniel said. He would have preferred raunchy details, because now he was picturing Caesar being gentle and tender, calling on his emotions rather than his hormones.

"It's kind of a shame," Caesar said quickly. "Don't tell her I ever said this, because it would break her heart, but I wish she was the same Steph in bed. I'm always worried I'm going to hurt her. I don't mind being gentle. Occasionally though I just want to get nasty."

"Nasty?"

"Freaky," Caesar said.

Nathaniel wished he could casually adjust himself. His jeans were starting to feel tight. He wanted to ask what Caesar meant, but if his dick got any harder, there would be mounting evidence—literally—of how turned on he was getting.

"What about you?" Caesar asked.

"I'm down with freaky," Nathaniel said, pretending to misunderstand the question. "Nasty too."

Caesar chuckled. "No, I mean what's it like with your girlfriend?"

"I don't have one."

"Really? Oh. What type of girl do you like?"

Nathaniel sighed inwardly, his erection subsiding. Coming out sucked. He had no regrets about having done so originally, the feeling liberating. What no one had told him was how he would have to keep coming out over and over again. People couldn't tell just by looking at him, which meant he often found himself in situations like these where he needed to explain. There was always something to lose. Friendships were put at stake, casual acquaintances could end before becoming more. Telling his boss at the learning center had been an intense experience that would be repeated at each new workplace. Maybe someday being gay would cost him his job. Maybe this one, because Mr. Hubbard didn't know. Nathaniel wouldn't let that stop him. He refused to let fear dictate who he was. That was the deal. No gray areas. No compromises.

"My type?" Nathaniel repeated. "Tall is good, as is a deep husky voice. That always drives me wild. A six-pack is cool too, since no matter how many sit-ups I do, mine never surfaces. I'm not big into facial hair, although a little scruff is okay."

Caesar continued to walk alongside him, appearing puzzled.

"I'm gay," Nathaniel said helpfully.

He held Caesar's gaze, refusing to show shame as he waited for judgment.

"You're gay?" Caesar repeated. "Seriously?"

"Yup."

"Wow. That's…" Caesar stared off into space before his eyes focused again. "That's really cool!"

Pine needles rustled underfoot as Nathaniel considered his words. "You think it's cool that I'm gay?"

"Yeah! I never would have guessed. Do you have a boyfriend?"

"No."

"Why not?" Caesar said. "I mean, just look at you!"

Without any convenient mirrors hanging on nearby trees, Nathaniel had only his memory to rely on. He had a strong brow, which Dwight insisted made him look like a Neanderthal. Aside from that, he didn't consider any of his features noteworthy. More than a few girls had shown interest in him, but he never took much comfort in that. What he really wondered is what guys thought of him.

"You think I'm hot or something?" Nathaniel asked, grinning to show the question was a joke.

To his delight, Caesar chose to answer him seriously. "You could have anyone you wanted. I'm sure of it."

Nathaniel wasn't convinced. "Maybe. Finding the right sort of guy isn't easy."

"Have you tried online?"

"Yeah."

"And?"

Nathaniel smirked. "Are you asking for details?"

Caesar grinned back at him. "Sure."

"Mind your own business." In truth, he didn't have an exciting story to share because half the guys didn't look anything like their profile pictures, and those who did were more interested in getting into his pants than talking to him. Occasionally Nathaniel was tempted, but ideally he wanted his first time to be with someone he actually liked.

Caesar looked disappointed, but he didn't retreat back into himself. "Do my parents know?"

"That I'm gay? Nope."

"Is it a secret?"

"Not really. My policy is when it comes up naturally, I'll talk about it. I don't see the need to broadcast it."

"That makes sense," Caesar said. "They'll be okay with it though. They're good people."

Nathaniel arched an eyebrow. "You'd be surprised how much hate can come from people convinced they are doing good. All those Bible thumpers telling me I'll burn in Hell? They think they're doing me a favor by trying to save my immortal soul. Are your parents religious?"

"Yeah," Caesar said. "We go to church every Sunday. They really are good people. All my siblings are adopted. You know that, right?"

The oldest girl was Asian, so Nathaniel had suspected as much. "What about you?"

"I'm their only biological child. For medical reasons. My parents didn't let that stop them. They take in a lot of foster kids. I can't count how many have come and gone."

"I'm sure they're good people," Nathaniel conceded. "They wouldn't have let me tag along if they weren't. With the gay issue though, it's hard to guess how anyone will react."

Caesar nodded. "I know."

Nathaniel was pretty sure he didn't, but he let it slide. "It gets lonely. Sometimes I wish more gay people were around. Maybe there are, but I can never tell who. I don't want to hang out in some anonymous chat room just to meet someone, you know?"

Caesar shrugged. "Whatever it takes. It's not like a grocery store or whatever is much more exciting."

Nathaniel snorted. "You're right. Maybe I just like being lonely." He wasn't sure what he meant by that, and he didn't really want to dwell on it because at the moment, his stomach was more demanding than his heart. "I'm hungry," he said, coming to a stop. "Let's eat here."

"The ghost town isn't far away," Caesar said.

"Then let's pick up the pace. You lead."

Once Caesar was ahead of him on the path, backpack bouncing on his shoulders, Nathaniel allowed himself a smile. It was nice to be accepted, although he'd have to watch himself now. If Caesar noticed any lingering gazes, he would know they weren't completely innocent. Maybe he would take it as a compliment, but Nathaniel was meant to be playing big brother, not would-be lover.

His stomach was grumbling by the time the trees thinned out, the shadows replaced by daylight that warmed their skin. At first he thought they had entered a natural clearing, but the land continued stretching outward, unhampered by anything but the skinniest of trees.

"Which way is the ghost town?" Nathaniel asked.

"We're already there." Caesar stopped, beaming at everything around them. "My dad and I discovered this place a few years back."

"Did you eat some magic mushrooms along the way? Because I don't see anything."

"Wait." Caesar walked forward, kicking occasionally in the dried yellow grass. "In the summer it's impossible to find much. I tried once and came back with an army of ticks. One even got on my— Here!"

Nathaniel joined him. Buried in the earth was a long rectangular stone. A brick. Its shortest edge touched another, and after brushing more dirt away, they found a third attached to it. "The foundation of a building," he said, glancing upward at the seemingly empty field. "Are there more like this?"

"I counted around twenty last time," Caesar said. "A few still have walls. Mostly ruined, but you can get a better idea. I'll show you."

His hunger forgotten, Nathaniel followed him around the edge of the field. Rounding a curve they found even more empty space.

"Dad thinks most of the land had been cleared for farming. That's why there's not much out there in the middle. Most of the houses are toward the woods. Hey, there they are!"

In the underbrush, just before the first row of trees, were crumbling walls barely higher than their shins. Only the front steps stood taller, three of them, leading to a doorway that no longer existed.

"It's kind of sad." Caesar stepped onto one of the stones, its edges rounded with age, the flat surface stained green with moss. "At one time, this house must have been new. Like brand new. Somebody probably stood right here, feeling proud of his new home, and thought it would last forever. Maybe he pictured his grandkids inheriting it. Their kids too. I bet he never imagined this ruin when he carried his bride across the threshold. Or maybe his husband."

Nathaniel scoffed. "If you want to get progressive, maybe a woman built this house and carried *her man* over the threshold."

Caesar didn't seem to hear him, his eyes moving over the former interior of the house, which was now sunken earth filled with wet leaves. "Even the town didn't survive," he added eventually.

"Are you sure one was ever here?" Nathaniel asked. "It could have just been a farm."

Caesar nodded toward the field. "There was a church. And a graveyard. I'll show you."

Nathaniel followed him into the cleared land. They walked past enough half-buried foundations and toppled bricks to convince him this was more than just a farm. They reached the graveyard first, where the stones had been worn down by so much weather that only the occasional number or letter was visible. They hovered on the edges, unwilling to walk over any graves.

"Dad found one from the eighteen hundreds. He said he was going to check the county records and find out more about what had been here. Never did. I guess he's too busy."

"You should do it yourself," Nathaniel said.

"Maybe." Caesar turned away from the grave. "The church was right over here. See? If you follow what's left of the foundation, it makes a long rectangle. With it being so close to the graves, we figured that's what it must have been."

"You sure it wasn't a crematorium?" Nathaniel asked. He laughed at Caesar's worried expression, since they were standing in the middle of the space now. "Don't worry. I'm sure this is hallowed ground. Perfect place to eat lunch."

Caesar just stood there.

"And unless you open your backpack soon," Nathaniel added, "we'll have to call it dinner."

"Oh!" Caesar hurried to free his arms from the pack.

They were both curious about the contents, since Mrs. Hubbard had packed lunch for them. Inside was a blanket, which Caesar spread out on the ground, making a place to sit. Then he pulled out a few sandwiches, two slightly browned bananas, two cans of Coke, and some of her homemade brownies wrapped in aluminum foil.

They gobbled down the food, Nathaniel finishing first. Caesar was still chewing the second half of his sandwich and wearing a thoughtful expression. He swallowed a bite and took a swig from his can. "What did you mean earlier, about my parents being good people for letting you come along?"

Nathaniel paused. Caesar was a quick learner, but he was no Sherlock Holmes. The information he was after had nothing to do with such a vague statement. "How much do you know?"

"About what?" Caesar said innocently.

"How much?" Nathaniel repeated.

Caesar shrugged and looked away. "I was surprised you

were coming with us. Peter wasn't allowed to bring a friend, and I never was allowed before. Normally these trips are about 'the family spirit,' as my mom likes to say. So I was surprised, that's all."

Nathaniel continued to scrutinize him. "Did you ask your father?"

"Yeah. He just said it would be good for both of us, whatever that means."

"He's hoping I'll be a good role model to you," Nathaniel said. "Nothing more."

"Then why did you get so defensive about the question if you've got nothing to hide?"

Fuck. Okay, maybe he wasn't Sherlock, but he did have a touch of Columbo. "Don't worry about it."

Caesar wasn't discouraged. "Did it have something to do with your wrist being all bruised?"

Nathaniel snapped. "Just shut up, okay?"

The loudness of his voice carried through the clearing, birds pausing before continuing their chatter. Caesar looked away and resumed nibbling on his sandwich. He didn't make eye contact again. Nor did he try to make conversation.

Nathaniel sighed. "My brother and I don't get along."

Caesar's eyes met his and widened. "He did that to you?"

"We got into a fight." That kept things simple. Two brothers arguing until they started swinging wasn't hard to imagine. How he had sat still and let his brother slowly hurt him, not offering any real resistance—that would be difficult to explain. "We get on each other's nerves a lot, so your dad thought me getting away would help cool things down."

"Oh," Caesar said. "Sorry."

"It's fine. I just don't want to talk about it. The point of being here is to leave it behind." Nathaniel flopped onto his back, considering the clouds until the sun came out from behind them and brightness forced him to close his eyes. "I like it here. Your dad was right. This is what I needed."

Caesar was silent, probably wondering how a person's wrist could be bruised so badly during an ordinary fight. Or perhaps he just wanted to respect Nathaniel's wishes. "Usually I hate these trips," he said eventually. "Especially the last few times. I'd rather be with my friends."

"Or Steph, I imagine."

"Yeah." The blanket rustled, the fabric beneath his back tugging a few times. When Caesar spoke again, his voice was lower, like he too had opted for a sun bath. "I'm glad you came along. Forget the family bond. I'd rather have fun."

"I'm glad you're glad," Nathaniel murmured.

Caesar laughed. "I'm glad you're glad that I'm glad."

Nathaniel's thoughts felt sluggish, his stomach full. "I'm having fun too."

The only response was a light breeze that rustled the grass around them. Then Nathaniel didn't hear much of anything, his thoughts abstract until he was no longer aware of them at all.

Something cold and wet splattered on his forehead, jerking him awake. The sky was gray now, just a hint of optimistic blue visible on the distant horizon. Caesar was sitting up, staring at him. Nathaniel expected him to look away, as he so often did. Not this time. Caesar watched him until a drop of rain struck his own cheek, causing him to flinch.

"I guess we should get going," Caesar said, wiping it away.

"How long was I asleep?" Nathaniel asked, head feeling light as he rose.

"An hour. Maybe more."

"Why didn't you wake me?"

They didn't have time to discuss it further because raindrops were coming faster now. Together they shook out the blanket, everything on it tumbling off. They stuffed the blanket messily into Caesar's backpack, leaving little room for anything else.

"Let's just go," Nathaniel said, glaring up at the clouds.

"It's a church!" Caesar insisted, crouching to pick up the litter.

The gods had a funny way of thanking him, because as soon as he was finished, the skies really opened up. Rain pummeled Nathaniel as he broke into a sprint, Caesar soon catching up and running alongside him. They were heading for the nearest line of trees, which wasn't near at all. Nathaniel wished at least one building in this old town had survived, because they were getting seriously soaked. By the time they reached the trees, their clothes clung to their bodies. Caesar laughed, wet hair framing his face. Nathaniel grimaced, pulling at his T-shirt until it let go of his skin. At least the trees provided some shelter. Water still broke through, but it was better than nothing. Hopefully the storm would blow away so they could dry out on the way back to the campsite.

First they needed to find the path. Caesar seemed to know where to go. As they slowly picked their way over brambles and small bushes, Caesar stopped to get his bearings. He took off his glasses and wiped at them with his wet shirt, which didn't do much except move the water around. When he put them back on, they began to fog up.

"Damn it," he muttered, removing them again. "I hate these things! I'm getting contacts."

"I like your glasses," Nathaniel said.

"I like being able to see. I'll get contacts and pop the lenses out of these so I can still wear them. Happy?"

"Thrilled."

"Good." Caesar folded up the glasses and shoved them in his back pocket. "You'd better lead the way. The path should be right over there."

He was right. Soon they were on the path again, which made travelling easier but exposed them to more rain—just a drizzle now, but enough to ensure they wouldn't dry out. After the better part of an hour, the clouds finally parted. The sun was too low in the sky to provide heat, but exertion helped. Half an hour later, Nathaniel was feeling warm. Odd then that Caesar was shivering visibly. All the weight and muscle Nathaniel had put on over the last year might be useless against Dwight, but apparently it protected him against the cold.

"You okay?" Nathaniel asked, bringing them to a halt.

Caesar nodded, putting on his glasses again. This time they didn't fog up. "I'm okay."

"Try saying that without your teeth chattering."

Caesar ignored him, glancing around. "Does this look familiar to you?"

"A bunch of pine trees, a few squirrels, and the occasional armadillo? Yup."

"Seriously," Caesar said. "What about the big rock where I stopped to tie my shoes? Remember? We should have passed that by now. Do you remember seeing it?"

"No." Nathaniel looked farther down the path, just in case it was there waiting for them.

"I would have seen that, even with my glasses off." Caesar stopped shivering long enough to scan their surroundings. "Maybe this is the wrong path."

"There's more than one?"

"Yeah."

"How many?"

"I'm not sure," Caesar said, giving up and turning to him. "I wish we hadn't left our phones behind."

"There's no reception out here," Nathaniel reminded him. "I don't know about you, but I don't feel like backtracking for more than an hour. This path has to end up somewhere, right?"

"I guess so."

Nathaniel led by example, setting off down the path again. After what felt like another half hour, he stopped. The sky above was growing dark, the path they were walking becoming thinner, as if less traversed. He was starting to wonder if this path didn't lead *to* somewhere, but *away* from somewhere instead.

He turned to find Caesar hugging himself, his normally olive skin a paler shade than normal. "You're still wet!"

"A little. This shirt is made from sponge or something crazy. Maybe I should take it off."

"Do it." Nathaniel unshouldered the backpack, shoving the trash to one side so he could pull out the blanket. "Here." He stepped forward, wrapping Caesar's bare torso in the light material. That would probably be enough, but he gave into temptation, pulling Caesar close and putting arms around him. "Just warming you up," he said.

"Thanks," Caesar responded.

Nathaniel breathed in, as if concerned by their situation. He was, but he also yearned to inhale the scent of Caesar's skin. At the moment it smelled like rain water with a hint of sweat, a combination he didn't mind at all.

"What are we going to do?" Caesar murmured. "I don't think this is the right way."

"I don't know," Nathaniel replied, forcing himself to focus on the matter at hand. What choice was there besides turning around? No other paths had crossed this one. They could only backtrack to the open field, find the original path, and go from there. Reaching the ghost town originally had taken hours. That, added to how long they traveled in the wrong direction, meant they would be walking in the dark long before they got back to camp, increasing their chances of becoming lost again. Surely if they kept walking, they would reach a river or— "Hold still," he said. "Listen."

Caesar forced himself to stop shivering. Nathaniel held his breath. There! Off in the distance! Maybe it was just wishful thinking, but it sounded like tires cruising along a gravel road.

"Did you hear that?" Nathaniel asked.

"Maybe," Caesar said.

Nathaniel released him and stepped back. "Either you heard it or you didn't."

"I don't know. Over there, maybe?" Caesar nodded in the direction Nathaniel thought he had heard a vehicle.

That was all the confirmation he needed. They would have to leave the path, but it was worth the risk. "Keep the blanket around you and pay attention to where we're going in case we need to backtrack."

"Maybe we should do that now," Caesar said.

"Ten minutes. If we don't find anything, we'll turn back."

Caesar didn't seem convinced, but he nodded. Nathaniel led the way, moving as fast he could now that he was on a time limit. He kept checking his watch, not saying anything when they reached the ten minute mark. He pushed it another five, about to admit defeat when he noticed a crushed beer can on the ground. He glanced upward, the dwindling light slightly brighter just ahead. After pushing past a few more trees, they stumbled out onto a road.

This road wasn't built for high traffic, so he wasn't worried about them getting run over. No pavement or painted lines. Just flattened beige dirt and a bunch of small stones. They celebrated regardless, Nathaniel whooping and jumping around while Caesar grinned at him.

"Okay," Nathaniel said once he calmed down. "Which way to the campsite?"

"Forget that," Caesar said. "Take me to the nearest hotel. I want a hot shower!"

Nathaniel filed away that fantasy for later. He considered the setting sun, determined that direction was west, and admitted to himself that knowing the cardinal direction didn't help one bit. Then again, they were walking toward the sun earlier in the day, so heading away from the sunset might make sense. Without mentioning his flimsy reasoning, Nathaniel led them down the road, hoping with each curve that they would see some encouraging sign. They didn't. Just more trees and dirt. Hope was beginning to ebb when the road behind them lit up. A car!

Or an old pickup truck, as it turned out. Nathaniel stepped in front of Caesar, waving it down. The vehicle wasn't travelling fast, so the driver didn't have to slow much to stop. Nathaniel went around to the window, seeing a face tanned by a lifetime spent in the sun. Old gray eyes looked over both of them. Then the man spat off to the side with practiced skill.

"You boys look like you've survived a shipwreck, which is odd, because we're a long way from the sea."

"We were just—" Caesar began.

"Looking for the campsite when you got lost?" The old man seemed amused. "You ain't the first, you won't be the last. Hop in."

"I can't believe he knew the name of the ghost town and everything!" Caesar raved. If the tent was taller, he'd probably be pacing back and forth. As it was, he stood on his knees, his gestures animated. "Warton. What a name!"

"Like the town had been a wart on Texas," Nathaniel said with a smile.

"Until it was burned off."

Caesar wasn't just being poetic. From the old man who had given them a ride, they had learned that Warton's population had dwindled to almost nothing before a fire spread across the town, reducing the remainder to ash. The old man had also told them his grandfather had lived and farmed there, so while the town might not have survived, its descendants still formed its legacy.

Once the old man dropped them off at the campsite, and Caesar was showered and dressed in dry clothing, he told their story to his family, making it sound like some grand adventure. In truth they had only stumbled around in the woods for a few hours, soaking wet, but his enthusiasm was contagious. Best of all, the ice was broken between them. Whether the experience itself or Nathaniel's openness had done the job, he wasn't sure. Regardless, he was in Caesar's inner circle now. No more clamming up. No more averted gazes.

"What now?" Caesar asked, glancing around the tent. They had their own, and aside from a couple of sleeping bags, an electric lamp, and privacy, they didn't have much to work with.

"What now?" Nathaniel repeated with an incredulous twist. "You're ready for the next adventure already?"

Caesar grinned at him. "Sure!"

"I'm ready to sleep," Nathaniel said. "It's late."

Caesar groaned, as if disappointed. Then he stripped off his shirt, tossing it casually aside before reaching for his jeans. "What about tomorrow?"

Nathaniel forced himself to focus on unzipping his sleeping bag. "Up to you. Maybe we'll go back to Warton. But at night, this time. We'll hang out in the graveyard, light some candles, spill some blood. Then we'll see if any ghosts want to share their secrets with us."

"Dude," Caesar said. "You're freaking me out. Seriously."

Nathaniel smirked. "Don't like ghost stories?"

"Nope."

He looked over to find Caesar already in his sleeping bag, his jeans a crumpled pile next to him. He didn't see any underwear, but that still seemed awfully undressed for a chilly spring night. Nathaniel left his clothes on and reached to turn off the lamp. A few minutes later, he started sweating. Whatever material these bags were made of, they were hardcore. He squirmed out of his to shed some clothes.

"What are you doing?" Caesar whispered.

"Getting naked."

"These sleeping bags are hot, huh?"

"Yeah."

The silence was thick with sexual tension, even if it was one-sided. Stripping down to his underwear this close to Caesar felt erotic. Nathaniel started to hurry, becoming aroused and wishing he had taken care of business in the communal shower room earlier. Maybe he could wait until Caesar fell asleep or—

"Hey."

Nathaniel made sure he was back in his sleeping bag before he answered. "What?"

"You're not alone."

Nathaniel scrunched up his face in confusion, despite his expression being invisible in the dark. "Huh?"

"What you said earlier, about being gay. You're not alone."

Pep talk. That was sweet, but he didn't need it. "Okay," Nathaniel replied, rolling over and getting comfortable. His eyes shot open soon after. Was Caesar simply trying to cheer him up? Or was there more to it? "I know there are other gay people," he whispered. "I told you, I've been on dates and stuff."

A long pause. Had Caesar fallen asleep? No. "There was this guy I met once. Well, I didn't *meet* him. I called an ambulance because my grandma was having a stroke and he picked me up— Not like that! I don't mean he flirted with me. Ugh, I'm telling it all wrong."

Nathaniel tried not to laugh. "You met a paramedic once, and he turned out to be gay. Unless you've got his email address for me, I don't see your point."

"That's not what I was trying to say."

Caesar sounded hurt, so Nathaniel made sure his voice was softer when he spoke. "Try again."

"He was beautiful," Caesar said hurriedly. "Even though he was only in my life a few minutes, I never stopped thinking about him."

A guy calling another guy beautiful… That didn't happen often. Any guy could tell if another was hot and might mention that in conversation. *Johnny Depp sure is a good-looking motherfucker. Guy probably gets all the girls!* Banter like that didn't raise red flags. But a gentle word like 'beautiful,' was something different. Still, Nathaniel didn't leap to any conclusions, despite being tempted.

"There's a difference between admiring a guy and finding him attractive."

"Sometimes it's both."

"But you and Steph…"

"I love her," Caesar said. "I'm into girls. Especially her. But I've always noticed guys too. I used to think I lacked a filter or just hadn't made up my mind about who I am. But I don't wonder anymore. Like I said… Sometimes it's both."

Bisexual? Nathaniel felt like sighing and groaning at the same time. Over the past few weeks, he had wished more than once that they were compatible, that Caesar was gay. He should have been more specific because he got his wish. He and Caesar *could* be together. Except Caesar already had someone he loved. The revelation was bittersweet. Mostly bitter though.

"Nathaniel?" Caesar said.

"Hm?" he managed.

"I'm really glad we met."

Nathaniel kept his expression neutral. When he remembered he couldn't be seen, he allowed the pain to show. "Yeah. Me too."

Chapter Four

Nathaniel stood outside Rebecca's house, buzzing with energy. The last day of spring break was usually depressing, since it meant returning to school. The next hiatus wouldn't be until summer, and with college looming, the future seemed a very stressful place. Nathaniel now felt ready to take it on. His trip with the Hubbards—with Caesar—had refueled him. The family outings had been nice enough. Horseback riding, grilling huge meals in the afternoons, or taking a boat out on the lake—all of that had been great. But what Nathaniel loved most were the countless hours spent talking to Caesar.

His shy guy was long gone. They didn't have enough time or oxygen for all the words they wanted to share. No longer were they strangers. Nathaniel knew a lot about Caesar, even dumb stuff like his severe allergy, which made it impossible to have pets. Or his passion for wrestling—not just the sport but its history, everything except for the costumed variety on television. Or little embarrassing truths, like how prone he was to nightmares, Caesar shaking him awake more than once in the middle of the night. Nathaniel never minded. Back at home he woke up at least once an hour, checking the door to make sure it was still shut and doing a quick sweep of the room to ensure he was safe. He was used to a living nightmare, so mere dreams were easy. Nathaniel would make conversation to distract Caesar, waiting for him to calm down enough to sleep. What Nathaniel really wanted was to comfort him physically. Surely his arms could do a better job than his clumsy words.

Unfortunately, the one topic that came up most often was Steph. Caesar really cared for her. This knowledge didn't dampen Nathaniel's spirit. He had finally met a guy he liked, one he couldn't stop staring at. Nathaniel couldn't wait to share the news with Rebecca. She'd be thrilled for him!

When she opened the front door, her smile wasn't quite as broad as his. She accepted his hug, but instead of leading him upstairs to her bedroom as usual, she pulled the door behind her closed and walked to the cast iron furniture off to one side. She sat in a chair, placing her hands in her lap.

"Have a good time?" she asked.

"Yeah!" Nathaniel said, too excited to sit. "You wouldn't

believe all the stuff we did, but honestly, the best part was Caesar. We really hit it off, and get this: He's bisexual!" Rebecca frowned. He pressed on anyway. "You wouldn't believe how nice he is. Sensitive too. I guess that's not so surprising, since it took him forever to stop being shy. Now he's really..."

Nathaniel trailed off. Rebecca had looked away and no longer seemed to be listening. Her mouth was set in a way normally reserved for when kids at school made fun of her.

"You okay?" he asked. "Did something happen?"

"Nothing happened!" Rebecca snapped. "That's what sucks! We had all those plans together, and you totally ditched me so you could run off with some guy you're crushing on. Now you show up here, and all you're doing is bragging about hooking up with him!"

"That's not what happened," Nathaniel said. "He's got a girlfriend. We're not together."

"Gee, too bad," Rebecca said sarcastically. "You could still show a little tact and not brag about how awesome your spring break was when mine totally sucked."

Nathaniel grimaced. "You're right." He angled one of the chairs to face her before sitting. "I'm being a dick. I'm sorry. But you know why I bailed on you. Even with all our plans, there was still a chance that Dwight—"

"I know," Rebecca said. Then she exhaled. "Part of me was happy knowing you were safe. The rest was bored out of my mind."

"That bad?"

"Worse. My mom got on this kick about how I'm going off to college soon, and decided we needed to spend quality time together. That meant visiting an arts and crafts fair at the public library. Or taking stupid square dancing lessons."

Nathaniel tried not to laugh. "Seriously?"

Rebecca's features tensed. "Yes!"

Nathaniel tried a more sympathetic tone. "I'm sorry. I'll make it up to you somehow, I swear."

"You're taking me on a date," Rebecca announced. "You don't have to put out, but I want dinner. And a movie. You're also taking me to the prom."

Nathaniel grinned. "It's a deal."

Rebecca eyed him a moment, then became more friendly.

"The break wasn't a total bust. The acceptance letters were exciting. Who did you hear back from?"

"I don't know," he said. "I haven't been home yet."

"Really? You came to see me first?" Rebecca smiled. "Of course you only wanted to brag, but I'll still take it as a compliment."

"Your turn. Tell me everything you learned about square dancing. No, forget that. Just show me your new moves."

She shook her head, then invited him to her bedroom. There they lay on her bed and went through her acceptance letters one by one. They had made sure to apply to the same schools, hoping to enter college together. She didn't have a response from every school, but she did save the best letter for last.

"Oh, and here's one more," she said with a twinkle in her eye. "Some no-name school on the East Coast. What were they called? Ah, I remember! Yale."

Nathaniel's jaw dropped. Then he snatched the letter from her. After absorbing its contents he handed it back with more reverence. "Makes your decision easy."

"Not necessarily," Rebecca said with a casual shrug. "We'll see."

"What's there to see?" he asked incredulously.

Her freckled cheeks grew a little red. "If they accepted you too."

"No way," he said, shaking his head. He wasn't going to let her feelings for him ruin an opportunity like this. "You're going. There's no way in hell you're not."

"And what if I don't, *Dad*? What are you going to do? Ground me?"

"You're going," he said, ignoring her sarcasm. "I won't be the one to mess this up for you."

"Then you'd better get accepted too."

They talked over her news a little longer, Nathaniel's anticipation about his own results increasing until he couldn't wait anymore. After a kiss on the cheek, he headed home to see if he had any mail. The usual anxiety he felt when nearing his house was absent today, replaced by dreams of the future and a longing to see his mother. He found her in the living room, flipping through channels on the big screen TV. When she heard him, her head turned, surprise registering before joy. One hand pushed a button to silence the television as she stood. She only managed a few steps because Nathaniel got there first, hugging her and lifting her off her feet.

His mother laughed, then winced as he squeezed, so he set her down gently.

"Sorry," he said. "I forget my own strength."

"Maybe take it easy on those weights," Star said, placing a hand on one of his cheeks. "Look how much sun you got! And when's the last time you shaved? You look like Paul Bunyan."

"Rugged, isn't it?" Nathaniel rubbed the scruff. He hadn't grown a real beard, but he still felt proud.

"Sit down and tell me all about your trip," his mother said. "Oh, are you hungry? There's a cucumber salad in the fridge or—"

"Yuck."

"—or I can nuke you a chicken pot pie."

"That sounds better."

Half an hour later, Nathaniel was sitting at the kitchen table, a scraped clean cardboard pie tray in front of him. He had managed to eat and tell his mother the highlights of the trip at the same time, which is probably why she kept making faces. For once she didn't chastise his table manners, clearly happy to have him back.

"What's been going on here?" he asked.

His mother sighed, looking weary. "Your brother lost his job."

Cold dread hit his stomach. "Already? What happened?"

"Dwight got into an argument with a client. You know his temper. He actually—" His mother pressed her lips together and shook her head. "He forced the customer from the car he was trying to sell and told him to leave if he didn't agree with the price."

She wasn't doing the story justice. Nathaniel could visualize how it probably really happened. The customer was behind the wheel of a car—maybe on the showroom floor or out on the lot. In the process of trying to haggle down the price, he must have injured Dwight's ego, so his brother grabbed the man by the arm and yanked him out of the car and to the ground, no doubt swearing at the top of his lungs as he did so.

"It's still not clear if the customer is going to press charges," Star continued. "I almost hope he does. I feel terrible for saying that, but maybe going to court is the wakeup call your brother needs."

"Do you think he'll go to jail?" Nathaniel said.

"For something so small?" Her forehead crinkled with worry. "I hope not! Anyway, I'm glad you're home. It's been a nightmare around here lately. I need you by my side." She reached across the table to take his hand.

Nathaniel's eyes met hers. "I'm here."

"Good. Your father had to take an emergency trip to the Oklahoma City clinic. One of the managers there went AWOL, but not before disappearing with most of the schedule two narcotics. He's looking forward to seeing you. He'll be home later tonight."

"Where's Dwight?"

Star frowned. "Probably drunk somewhere. He brought around a new girl who smelled like a distillery. I found a bunch of empty bottles in his room too, so it looks like he's got a new hobby. I told him if he's so interested in binge drinking, that he should have gone to college." The tension in her face disappeared. "Hey, speaking of which, you've got mail!"

Four envelopes. As soon as his mother set them on the table, Nathaniel grabbed them and stood, heading for the kitchen door.

"Where are you going?" she asked.

"My room."

"But I want to know what they say!" she called after him.

"I'll show you later." He hurried to the hallway before she could complain further. He couldn't open them in front of her, mostly because she could read him like a book. The slightest hint of disappointment would have her trying to comfort him, which tended to make him feel worse. He needed to do this alone.

Once shut safely in his bedroom, he placed all four envelopes facedown on the bed. Then he picked up the first, opening it even after he saw it wasn't from the college he was hoping for. Funny, because when he sent out the applications, he didn't have a strong preference. He wanted to be out of state. Simple as that. Now everything had changed, and why?

Yale, or more accurately, the people who would be going there. Rebecca of course, but she would probably follow him to any college he chose. If not—as much as he really did like her—Nathaniel was accustomed to saying goodbye to friends. Only one person tipped the balance. Maybe he was still high from the carefree days of the camping trip, but he very much liked the idea of Caesar showing up at the same college a couple of years after him, a nervous freshman on a big scary campus. Never fear, because Nathaniel would be there to take him under his wing.

The fantasy filled his chest with yearning. Nathaniel flipped over the second letter. No luck. He opened it anyway, reading it carefully, like a birthday card, when all he really wanted to do was rip open the next present. Or in this case the next letter, which he soon did, his disappointment tripling. He had been accepted. That was great. Just not to the right school.

He eyed the final letter, all of his hopes now resting on it. His pulse was racing as he used one finger to flip it over. Once his eyes focused on the return address, he sighed. Not Yale. Feeling dejected, he opened it, finding his fourth acceptance. Four out of four. Most people would be jumping with joy. Nathaniel just sat on his bed, reading through the letter. Then he made himself go through them all again, trying to imagine himself at each place. He even booted up his laptop, looking at the official websites. After half an hour, he went to Yale's website instead, unsuccessfully trying to discover if all admission invitations had been sent out.

He shut his laptop and gathered up the letters. His mother would want to hear the news. He wandered down the hall, passing the master bedroom, and heard the water running in the bathroom beyond. The door to the hallway was still open. He could see his mother standing in front of the mirror. She still had on her bra, thank goodness, and the jeans from earlier. College talk could wait. He was turning to go back to his room when something caught his eye. His mother was twisting at the waist, jutting one shoulder forward so she could see the back of her arm in the reflection.

He noticed the spots first, dark ovals the shape of flattened olives. Or fingerprints. As if someone had pressed the tips of each finger in a pad of ink, then touched her arm—or grabbed it, the way Dwight had grabbed his wrist, the muscles of his forearm flexing. Exactly like that. Nathaniel thought he could see lighter lines, showing where the fingers had squeezed, so he stepped forward for a closer look.

His mother noticed him and swiped a robe off a nearby hook to slip it on, which was odd, because Nathaniel had seen her in her bra plenty of times. He never thought much of it, and neither did she. Not normally. Now she was tying the robe closed and looking displeased.

"How about some privacy?" she said. "I'm trying to take a bath here."

"The door was open," Nathaniel said, his eyes still on the spot where he'd seen the bruises, even though it was covered now. "Your arm..."

Star's expression became neutral. Remarkably neutral, in the way most people appeared only when sleeping. "What?"

"Your arm," Nathaniel repeated. "What happened?"

Star studied him in silence, then sat on the edge of the tub, shutting off the tap and moving her hand through the water to stir it. Her answer came, but only after a lengthy pause. "Oh, you mean the bruises? Take a beginner at yoga, make her eight months pregnant, and then get an instructor dumb enough to show her the tree pose. The only thing I did right was keeping my balance when she grabbed me on the way down." Still his mother studied the water, weaving her hand along the currents she had created.

"Can I see?" he asked.

She finally looked up at him. "Stop being weird. So what's the news?"

"News?"

"Your colleges. Which ones accepted you?"

"All of them."

"All of them?" Star sat up straight, pulling her hand from the water. "My gosh! There's so much to discuss! Have you chosen one yet? Forget my bath. We've got your future to plan!"

"No," Nathaniel said, not matching her smile. "It's all right. Enjoy your bath. We can talk about it afterwards."

"Are you sure?"

"Yeah."

Nathaniel couldn't be sure, but just before he turned and left the room, he thought he detected a hint of relief. Or maybe that's how he felt, because he needed time to think this through, to let his emotions come unhindered without having to hide them. Or emotion, singular, because at the moment his only dancing partner was fear. This tango had been going on for a long time, most recently while camping with the Hubbards. A little voice in the back of his mind always wondered who would be his replacement. Who would fulfill the role of punching bag while he was away? Dwight's girlfriend of the week? What about those times when he was single? When Nathaniel was away at college, who would bear the brunt of so much rage?

His mother. Nathaniel had never wanted to believe it. Parents were authority figures, not to be messed with. Like striking a police officer, only the deranged would attempt such a thing. But those bruises on her arm, the silence before her answer, the way she had winced when Nathaniel had hugged her…

Blood became a drum in his ears, a steady beat that refused to cease. Anger. Dull disbelieving anger. Somehow he still functioned, some distant part of him conversing with his mother when she came to his room. Which campus was the most beautiful, which town would be the most fun to live in, where was he most likely to meet the right sort of guy? Playful discussions, the kind that made his mother feel like his best friend. He was beginning to fear they had a little too much in common. Eventually she went to start dinner. Nathaniel began to wait. At first in the living room, his ears tuned to the driveway, listening for the sound of a car's engine. When it came, the drums picked up the beat, but the person who entered was his father. Nathaniel greeted him, even managing a smile, then watched as his parents embraced, kissing affectionately. At least with his father home, she was safe. That's what he tried to tell himself, but he knew it didn't work that way. How often had Dwight found ways of hurting him, regardless of their parents being just one room over?

Waiting. During dinner. While watching a movie afterwards. In a silent living room once his parents had gone to sleep. He even went inside Dwight's room, a place forbidden to him. Nathaniel hadn't stepped foot in there for years. Doing so was to invoke wrath, but now Nathaniel welcomed conflict. He sat surrounded by clutter, his brother's room representative of his ugly insides. Unlike his handsome face, the wrinkled dirty laundry on the floor, the drywall with a hole punched through it, the dusty blinds hanging askew over the window to obscure the daylight—all these things reflected who Dwight truly was. A fucked-up mess.

Nathaniel remained there, waiting, even stretching out on the bed and closing his eyes, tempting fate. But he didn't sleep.

When he finally returned to his own room, he didn't find any respite from his violent fantasies or the ceaseless drumming in his ears. Is this how Dwight felt all the time? Is that what drove him to lash out so often? Had he somehow passed on this disease to Nathaniel?

When dawn came, he rose and showered, checking his brother's room once more. Empty. He ate breakfast and waited until the very last moment before leaving the house. His brother had to come home eventually. Then he would pay. School dragged on, Nathaniel barely aware of his surroundings, completely missing his teachers' lectures. Instead his mind entertained various nightmares. Maybe the camping trip with the Hubbards hadn't been the trigger that turned his mother into a victim. Maybe Dwight had been hurting her all this time, both her and Nathaniel keeping the same secret from each other.

When the school day ended, he didn't even consider driving to Caesar's house. A single desire pumped through his heart, compensating for his lack of sleep, his entire being fueled by hate. He returned home to find his brother's car in the driveway. The sound of the television led him to the living room. With their parents both at work, he knew it could only be one person. In his mind, he saw a flash of his mother arguing with Dwight, pleading with him to get his life together before his brother had grabbed her by the arms and shaken her, spittle flying from Dwight's mouth, tears from his mother's eyes.

Nathaniel strode into the living room, standing directly in front of the coffee table, blocking the view of the television. Dwight's eyes were bloodshot, like he'd been up all night drinking. Indeed, when he spoke, Nathaniel could smell stale alcohol.

"You've got five seconds to get the fuck out of this room."

Nathaniel didn't budge, barely even heard him, because a whole drum circle was pounding in his head now. "I know about the bruises," he growled. "On Mom's arm. I saw them."

He stared straight into his brother's eyes and saw a flicker of recognition. Understanding. Something else was there too. What the hell was that? "You saw?"

"Stand up," Nathaniel said.

"Why?"

"Stand up!" Nathaniel noticed a glass of water on the table

and picked it up. He needed all his willpower not to pitch it like a baseball. How satisfying it would be to see the glass shatter against Dwight's head! Instead he tossed the contents at his brother, the water splaying into his chin and soaking his T-shirt. That's all it took. The uneasy expression left Dwight's eyes, replaced by fire. The bull was ready to charge.

"You little shit!"

As Dwight stood, Nathaniel grabbed the edge of the coffee table and yanked, jerking it out of the way. His brother was reaching for him, hands still open. Didn't he know this was a fight? Nathaniel didn't hold back. He balled up a fist and swung, a lunge that struck the side of Dwight's neck. Those bloodshot eyes looked ready to spurt. Now it was a fight! Dwight snarled and attacked, fist curving toward his head. Nathaniel had no choice but to take the blow. He was good at handling pain, thanks to his brother. All that mattered was keeping his balance so he could retaliate. Dwight struck him in the cheek, rattling his skull, but Nathaniel barely blinked. He kept his eyes focused on his brother's position, put all the force he could muster into his arm, and swung. When his fist connected with his brother's head, it sounded like a thunder clap. To Dwight it must have been even louder, because Nathaniel got him right in the ear. He'd been hoping to strike his jaw but Dwight had pulled back and—

He was swaying! Dwight was still drunk or that punch really had been something. Nathaniel wasn't taking any chances. He swung with his left, then his right, striking two more blows. When Dwight stumbled backward, tripping over one corner of the coffee table, Nathaniel popped him right in the mouth. His brother hit the floor, landing on his ass, his head bouncing off one of the sofa cushions and resting there, like he'd decided to watch TV sitting on the carpet.

He was down, but the drums were still beating in Nathaniel's head. Every instance of terror he had felt: the endless wondering of when the next attack would come, what form the abuse would take, if Dwight would push things far enough to kill him. His mother wincing when Nathaniel hugged her, or twisting to see the bruises on her arm. All these sickly visions, all those boiling emotions, were ready to erupt outward at last.

Nathaniel was on his knees. He didn't remember how he got there, but his brother's body was below him, that stupid handsome face sneering at him. But not for long. Nathaniel swung. Again and again and again. Nathaniel's vision became a blur, but he could still hear the smacking noises, feel something wet and hot on his knuckles, even registered the strangled animal noises his brother was making. A plea for mercy? A defiant roar? He didn't care. All that mattered were the memories flashing through his mind and the nightmares that haunted his future.

"Stooooop!"

The sound was like a wounded animal. A bleating lamb. Nathaniel blinked, his arms losing strength. Dwight's eyes were wide with fear. Nathaniel had never seen him afraid. His right eyebrow was cut open, blood trickling down his face. Another crimson river was pouring from his left nostril. His bottom lip was split. The rest of his skin looked pink, one of his eyes already puffing shut.

Nathaniel scurried backward, wanting to get away from this abomination. Then he stood, still staring at the sniffing, gasping mess that was his brother. He kept standing there, mostly because he wondered if Dwight was going to survive. As his breaths became less ragged, Nathaniel's anger clawed away at his brief concern.

"If you ever touch her again…" he began.

"I didn't touch her!" Dwight spat, saliva and blood dribbling down his chin and staining his shirt. "She's our mother!"

"I'm your brother, but that never stopped you."

Dwight shook his head wearily. "I never touched her."

"Then how'd she get those bruises?"

Dwight looked away, but not before Nathaniel saw the strange reaction again. His stomach sank. The question wasn't how. The question was who. Dwight knew about their mother getting hurt, but if it wasn't him—

"Dad." Nathaniel whispered the word, feeling punched in the stomach.

Dwight laughed humorlessly. "They always sheltered you. God forbid their precious baby see the truth! I'm the one who had to deal with all their shit. I was what—six years old the first time I saw it?"

"Saw what?" Nathaniel said.

"Him slapping her around like a whore." Dwight wiped at his mouth, wincing with pain and grimacing when he looked at his hand and saw blood. Then he glared up at Nathaniel, some of that fire returning. "Want a demonstration?"

Dwight slowly got to his feet. Then he staggered back and flopped down on the couch. "I'm going to kill you," he said, on the verge of tears. "You might have got the drop on me, but I'm going to fucking kill you!"

Nathaniel watched him a moment longer, not doubting the truth of those words. Some mad part of him even considered getting there first. But he didn't have it in him. That compassion would probably cost him his life. Dwight would heal, then find some way of killing Nathaniel. Who could he turn to for help? His father, who had some incomprehensible dark side? His mother, who was too weak to protect either of them? This house wasn't safe. He couldn't stay here.

Nathaniel turned and left the living room, patting his jeans pocket to make sure his car keys were there. As he reached the front door, his brother shouted after him, repeating the words that ensured Nathaniel would never return.

"I'm going to fucking kill you!"

Nathaniel stood in front of an elegant front door, the dark wood polished, gold metal framing the delicate windows. He touched the brass knocker with a finger crusted with maroon smears and felt bewildered by the contrast between two worlds. He had just come from Hell, and here was a place tranquil and perfect. The stillness of the neighborhood, the manicured lawns all around him, were almost upsetting in their serenity. He wanted to disappear into this world, but felt forever marked by what he'd been through. Damned.

He missed the anger. Without it he was left shaken. Could it be true? Had his father been abusing his mother all these years? On the drive over, he tried to convince himself his brother was lying, that all of this was calculated to hurt him. Dwight had never relied on mind games before. His abuse was always physical. This wasn't his style, nor was how he had looked away, like he too was eager to deny. To flip the switch.

Nathaniel tried to do the same and couldn't. Not yet. The pain was too fresh. He needed a safe place where he could calm down. He needed protection. Who could he turn to? Rebecca, of course. Or even Caesar, but neither could give him the sort of help he needed. Nathaniel grasped the knocker and used it. Three short raps. The door swung open half a minute later, Caesar grinning at him.

"Why didn't you use the doorbell?"

Nathaniel swallowed against the lump in his throat. "I need to talk to your father."

"What? Why?"

Caesar looked him over and noticed his hands, gawking a moment before taking a few steps back. The door was still open, so Nathaniel made this an invitation. When he shut the door behind him and turned around, Caesar's eyes were wide.

"Are you okay?"

"Your dad," Nathaniel said. "Go get him. Please."

After more hesitation, Caesar spun around and went down the hall. When he returned, he was behind his father. Mr. Hubbard walked right up to him, his voice gentle.

"Let me see."

Nathaniel held up his hands. He'd noticed when gripping the steering wheel that some of his knuckles were cut open. All of them had begun to swell. Mr. Hubbard examined them, then turned to his son.

"Why don't you go to the kitchen and make us some coffee?"

"How?" Caesar said. Then to Nathaniel, "Do you even drink coffee? Are you okay?"

"Now," Mr. Hubbard said. Caesar loitered a moment longer. Then he slinked away. "Care to join me in my office?"

Nathaniel nodded, then followed Mr. Hubbard to the place where they always talked. Once the door was shut and they were seated, Mr. Hubbard offered him a sympathetic expression. "Looks like your brother pushed you too far this time."

Nathaniel tried to respond, but his voice only squeaked. After composing himself, the story came pouring out. All of it, even the ugliest, most shameful details that he hadn't dealt with yet.

"I don't know what do to," Nathaniel finished. "I ruined everything."

Mr. Hubbard cleared his throat. "No reasonable person could blame you for what happened." They were interrupted by a knock on the door. Mr. Hubbard went to answer it. A hushed conversation followed, and when Mr. Hubbard returned, he was carrying two steaming mugs. "Do you drink coffee?"

Nathaniel shook his head.

Mr. Hubbard set one of the mugs in front of him, then leaned against the desk. "Now's a good time to start. Coffee is one of life's little miracles. It gives you energy when you're tired, warms you when you're cold, and gives you something to hide behind when life keeps throwing shit your way."

Nathaniel glanced up and managed something close to a smile. He'd never heard Mr. Hubbard curse before. Picking up the mug, he took a small sip, wincing at the bitter taste. "Got any milk?" he asked. "Or sugar?"

Mr. Hubbard shook his head. "Always drink it black. Anything else shows a lack of commitment. You'll grow accustomed to the taste. You'll even learn to savor it. Sort of like marriage, but let's not get ahead of ourselves. Begin with coffee. You can figure out the mysteries of matrimony some other day."

Nathaniel took in the sparkling eyes, the friendly expression. "I wish you were my father. I never talk to my own. Not like this. Maybe if I did, I would have seen the truth. I thought he was a good person. I should have paid attention. For my mother. I should have known better."

Mr. Hubbard sighed. "You couldn't have. Parents have an unfair advantage. Our children can't hide anything from us, but we're exceptionally adept at keeping the truth from them. Usually with the intent to protect. There are exceptions though. Your parents didn't know about Dwight abusing you. That's about to change."

Nathaniel shook his head. "Dwight will tell them he got in a bar fight or something."

"No," Mr. Hubbard said. "They're going to hear the truth from me." He held up a hand when Nathaniel tried to protest. "They'll need a reason why you're staying here from now on."

Nathaniel stared. "What do you mean?"

"You said you feel like your home is no longer safe. I agree. Not until matters with your brother are resolved. Until then, I'd like you to stay here. It's up to you, of course, but we have a spare bedroom no one is using and—"

"Are you serious?"

"Absolutely. But I would need to talk to your parents first. About everything."

This kept his optimism in check. He wasn't escaping his

problems, but at least he wouldn't have to face them alone. "Okay."

"Good." Mr. Hubbard lifted his mug of coffee, holding it up until Nathaniel did the same. "Here's to happier times."

Caesar was on his feet the second Nathaniel entered the dining room, like a new father waiting outside the maternity ward. Nathaniel almost expected him to ask if it was a boy or a girl.

"Is everything okay?" Caesar said. "Are you all right?"

"Everything's fine," he replied, not knowing if it was true. Elsewhere in the house, Mr. Hubbard was trying to call Nathaniel's parents. He had been given the option of staying in the office but had mumbled some excuse about an important test they needed to study for. In reality, he couldn't handle speaking to his parents yet.

Caesar's attention was on his hands. "Does it hurt?"

Nathaniel held them up, flexing his fingers, tearing the skin a little around the most damaged knuckles. "I've had worse."

"Come upstairs. I have stuff I can put on them."

"It's fine."

"Seriously. Come on."

Nathaniel followed Caesar up the stairs, wondering how to deal with his inevitable questions. He didn't want Caesar to know about his home life. Not that he didn't trust him or feel like he couldn't be open. Caesar looked up to him, which made Nathaniel feel good about himself. Proud, although he probably didn't deserve it. He didn't want to ruin that by revealing he'd been a beaten dog for most of his life, only standing up to his brother when trying to protect his mother. Even that he had gotten wrong.

"In here," Caesar said, leading him through his bedroom to the private bathroom. From under the counter he pulled out a large red case with a white cross on the front. This was no average first-aid kit with the bare necessities, rather it was a suitcase loaded with multiple kinds of gauzes and bandages, ointments and sprays. Nathaniel had trouble recognizing most of it, but Caesar seemed delighted, sifting through different items and examining some before setting them aside or putting them back in their designated places.

Nathaniel eyed the metal implements. "You aren't planning on giving me stitches, are you?"

"Do you think you need them?" Caesar asked. "I can't sew you up, but I've got some butterfly bandages. Um… Mind if I take a look?"

Nathaniel leaned against the bathroom counter and held out his hands. Caesar bent over to see, but he didn't touch them. Then he gave his diagnosis. "The dried blood probably makes it look worse. Let's get them cleaned up. I have a spray—"

"No," Nathaniel said, anticipating the sting. "Soap and water is fine."

He washed his hands in the sink before Caesar could protest. This stung too, but he made sure not to show it. Shutting off the tap, he flung the water off his hands and held them up. "All better. See?"

Caesar shook his head. "Antibiotic cream will help everything heal faster."

Nathaniel eyed him. "You're really into this, aren't you?"

"Yup." Caesar's smile was subtle as he opened a tube. "I told you about my paramedic, didn't I?"

"You started to."

Caesar reached out, placing a hand beneath one of Nathaniel's to support it. The physical contact made him feel hungry. His world had always included pain, but now he was reminded of a different sort of touch.

"I was a kid," Caesar said, gently applying ointment. "My grandma was taking care of me when she had a stroke. It was just me and her at the time, so of course I freaked out, but at least I remembered to call 911. When the ambulance came, there was this paramedic…" Caesar shook his head. "I was worried about my grandma. Don't get me wrong. I wasn't lusting after some dude while she was potentially taking her final breath. The attraction wasn't sexual at all. Not at that point. Instead this guy was like a mythical hero, you know? Like he strolled out of some mysterious fog at the darkest moment of my life to save me. Or my grandma. But me too, since if she had died then… Like I said, I was just a kid, and we were all alone. That would have messed me up pretty bad, so in that way, he became my hero."

Nathaniel felt a pang of jealousy. Partly because his own hero had always failed to show. And also because being someone else's hero must feel good "So you wanted to be like him?"

Caesar shrugged. "Sounds dumb, I know. When I hit a certain age, I started wishing I could be *with* him instead. I never saw the guy again, but in a way, he also helped me figure out my sexuality. Funny how that works. He probably doesn't even remember me. To him it was just another work day. For me, it was life-changing."

Caesar continued smoothing in the cream, using a circular motion. If the skin beneath his touch wasn't so damaged, the experience would have been pleasurable. Even so, Nathaniel's body was beginning to react. "I think that's enough."

"Okay. A few of your knuckles will need bandages. You don't want them getting infected."

"Fine." He watched as Caesar dug through his kit again. "I'm guessing you're not going to Yale to become a paramedic. A doctor?"

Caesar didn't answer. Instead he peeled the paper off an adhesive bandage and asked a question of his own. "What happened?"

Nathaniel wanted to snap at him—tell him to mind his own business. Considering he was carefully tending to his wounds, Nathaniel decided instead to give back. Just a little. "I got in a fight with my brother."

Caesar looked up, searching his face for any damage. Or maybe for faded signs of the bruise he'd had when they'd first met. "Does that happen a lot?"

"We've never really gotten along."

Caesar was quiet while finishing his work. When he was done, he asked, "My dad is going to help you, right?"

"He's trying."

Caesar nodded. "Good."

Nathaniel shifted, uncomfortable with the topic. "What should we do now?"

"You mean for fun?" Caesar chewed his bottom lip. "Wanna watch a movie?"

"Yes. Please." Movies were the perfect medicine. No matter how bad the day, once at home and in the safety of his room, Nathaniel could lose himself in another character's life. An hour and a half of being a spy or a treasure hunter or even a starship pilot. Each had their problems, but none were as grounded in reality as his own. Trying to figure out how Godzilla could be defeated was infinitely more appealing than trying to find new ways of avoiding Dwight. Nathaniel loved losing himself in stories, and he found movies the most immersive form.

"What should we watch?" Caesar asked, leading the way back to his room.

Nathaniel flopped down on the couch. "You pick one."

"Oh." Caesar considered his DVD collection, touching one occasionally before turning around to look at him. Then he would second-guess himself and continue his search.

"There's no wrong answer," Nathaniel grumped after minutes of this. "This isn't one of our study sessions."

"Yeah, I know. Hold on. Uh… Have you seen *Midnight in the Garden of Good and Evil?*"

"Clint Eastwood, right?"

"The cowboy?" Caesar asked, looking puzzled.

"The director, and no, I haven't seen it. Let's give it a spin."

Nathaniel wasn't into the movie at first. His knuckles were starting to ache, and his back and neck were still tense from the fight. He found himself more interested in the person sitting next to him. Nathaniel kept his head forward but stole glances at Caesar from the corner of his eye. One of the hands that had so recently been touching his was resting on Caesar's leg. Nathaniel thought about placing his own hand over it, consequences be damned, but he found himself paralyzed.

Then the movie picked up pace, and Nathaniel was swept up into the strange world of Savannah, Georgia, where every resident seemed to hide a dark secret behind a façade of manners and etiquette. By the time the credits rolled, Nathaniel was spellbound.

"That was fucking excellent!" he said.

Caesar relaxed, as if relieved by his verdict. "I caught the second half on cable one night. It totally resonated with me."

In what way? Did he relate to the bumbling journalist, who found himself in a world of unspoken rules? Or the drag queen, who despite all her bravado, seemed strangely vulnerable? Or maybe the male escort, who was fought over by men and women alike? Nathaniel could ask, but felt he should already know. He wanted a connection with Caesar that transcended words.

"Of course the parts about voodoo freak me out," Caesar continued, "so I never watch it alone."

Nathaniel made a face. "It's not exactly a horror movie."

"Yeah, but it is kind of a ghost story."

Nathaniel shoved him playfully. "You're a wimp, you know that?"

Caesar grinned. "Hey, we can't all be bruisers."

"Bruisers?"

"You know. A fighter."

"You think that's what I am?"

Caesar nodded toward his hands. "I'd say you're pretty tough, yeah."

Nathaniel didn't feel that way. Not normally. Then again, he had just recently beaten the crap out of the biggest monster in his life. If only he hadn't been replaced by another. "You're the wrestler," Nathaniel said. "You could probably take me in a fight."

Caesar perked up. "You really think so?"

Nathaniel snorted. "No."

"Sounds like a challenge to me!"

Nathaniel jerked a thumb at the floor. "Let's go!"

Before they could get tangled up, there was a knock at the door. Caesar opened it to find Mr. Hubbard standing there. "Nathaniel. A moment, please."

"Saved by the bell," Nathaniel said playfully, even though his stomach was twisting up. He followed Mr. Hubbard down the hall, entering a bedroom on the left. The walls were blank, the bed and mattress bare.

Mr. Hubbard shut the door. "I spoke with your mother just now."

Nathaniel swallowed. "What'd she say?"

"She would like to meet with you after school tomorrow. To talk things over."

"Just her?"

Mr. Hubbard nodded. "I made sure of that. If you want me to go with you..."

"No." Without his father or Dwight there, Nathaniel had nothing to fear. "Thanks."

"In the meantime, you're welcome to stay the night. We can get this room ready for you and—"

"No need," Nathaniel said quickly. "I don't want to make more trouble for you than I already have. I can crash in Caesar's room tonight. If you think he won't mind."

Mr. Hubbard smiled. "I'm sure he'll be thrilled by the idea. But I wanted to show you this room, because you're welcome to it. I want you to know you have options. You have a safe place to stay for as long as you need."

Nathaniel appreciated that, but he had bigger concerns. "What about my mother? I know it's asking a lot, but when we talk tomorrow, I'd like to offer her a safe place too."

Mr. Hubbard became very still. "You would need to discuss that with her first."

"But can I make her the same offer?" Nathaniel knew he was asking a lot, but he needed to know.

Mr. Hubbard exhaled. "You really need to speak with her. She was very defensive about your father."

That was impossible, or at the very least, a misunderstanding. His mother was probably uncomfortable discussing such things with a stranger.

"Regardless," Mr. Hubbard said, "we'll do what we can to help you both."

Nathaniel felt so emotional that he had to steel himself to keep from crying. "Thank you," he managed.

Mr. Hubbard clapped him on the shoulder. "Now, go have fun. Just don't forget that this is a school night."

Nathaniel nodded, headed back down the hall, and swept into Caesar's room. "The good news is that our camping trip has been extended by one night. The bad news is that you have to sleep on the couch. Your bed is mine."

Caesar looked him up and down. Then he smiled. "Wanna wrestle for it?"

Nathaniel stood by the entrance of the high school, feeling like a little kid waiting to be picked up by his parents. When his mother's car arrived, he peered at it until certain she was alone. Then he hurried to meet her. She stepped out of the car, trying to look him over, but he didn't give her a chance as he squeezed her close in a hug.

"I'm so sorry," she was whispering.

Nathaniel felt like apologizing also, if only to put this whole ordeal behind them. But he couldn't. Not until he got answers.

"Have you eaten?" his mother asked once they finished embracing. "Hop in. We'll grab a bite to eat."

"I have my own car," he reminded her.

"I don't care." Her smile was gentle. "I'm not letting you out of my sight."

She drove them to his favorite bar and grill. Not that he ever drank when there, but they made the best burgers. When he held open the door for her, his mother noticed his hands and gasped.

The bandages were fresh. Caesar had insisted on changing them this morning, applying fresh antibiotic cream and still behaving as if the injuries were life-threatening. He had even backed out of the promised wrestling match, too concerned about Nathaniel hurting his hands further. Nathaniel's only concern was his own self-control, but the night had been good anyway, not ending until nearly three in the morning. When they became too tired to talk or watch TV, Nathaniel had taken the couch, despite Caesar's insistence that the bed was big enough for two. He was right. It's just that Nathaniel knew he wouldn't find sleep there.

"You're quiet," his mother said as they waited to be seated.

"There's a lot on my mind," he said, feeling guilty for not considering more important matters. "We need to talk."

"First we eat." They followed the hostess to a booth, Nathaniel frustrated by the typical restaurant rituals but happy when their food finally came and the waiter left them alone. His mother seemed more concerned with making sure he ate than with discussing anything, but for once he understood. She appeared gaunt. Star was normally so pretty and vibrant, but now… Maybe knowing the truth made the difference. Nathaniel felt like reaching across to tug up her shirt sleeve, wanting to see if the bruises were still there or if any new ones had been added.

They ate mostly in silence, their worry for each other deepening. Then Star pushed away her unfinished food and sighed. "Your brother needed stitches."

"Awesome."

Her eyes searched his features. "You're a good boy. Or man, I should say. You've always been a good person, so I know in my heart that you have a reason for what you did. Talk to me. I need to hear your side of the story."

"What did Dwight say?"

"It doesn't matter. Tell me what happened."

"The same that's always happened. What would have

kept happening, if I didn't do something to stop it." Nathaniel struggled to sum up years worth of fear and pain. "This has been going on a long time."

"How long?"

"Since I was a kid."

Star's expression was pure anguish. "When you got that bruise on your cheek, I *knew* something was wrong. I thought maybe—"

"That Dad was hitting me? Like he does you?"

His mother's cheeks were pale. "Your father never hit me. Not like that. He might lose his temper on occasion…" She shook her head. "I thought maybe kids at school were giving you a hard time. Because of who you are. But—"

"It's Dwight," Nathaniel said. "It's always been Dwight, and as far as I can tell, he doesn't need a reason for hating me. Or for hitting me."

"He's your brother!"

The way she said this sounded like a desperate plea for the world to make sense again. Nathaniel could sympathize. Over the years, he'd observed other pairs of siblings, and while not always on the friendliest of terms, their relationships weren't nearly as screwed up. Or as violent. So he tried to explain how it had all begun, how bullying had escalated into constant abuse. By the time he was finished, her hands were trembling as she wiped away tears.

"Why didn't you say anything?" she asked. "Why didn't you tell us?"

"What would you have done? Grounded him? It never made a difference. He always found some new way of making me suffer."

"Had we known, we wouldn't have let it go on like this."

Nathaniel crossed his arms over his chest. "You know now. What are you going to do about it?"

His mother turned away to blow her nose. When finished, she still looked shaken. "He has to go. He's old enough that he should be out of the house. He'll get his own place and—"

"—show up at the house one day when you're not there or wait until a family get-together before pulling me aside to choke me or some other nightmare he's cooked up. You can't do anything. No one can. The only solution is for me to leave. That's the only option. For both of us."

"Nate." His mother looked at him like he was being silly.

"What? Are you seriously going to feel sorry for me when the same thing is happening to you? They're monsters! Both of them."

"Dwight has always had emotional problems, but your father... You know how hard he works for the family, and on occasion, *very rare* occasions, he crosses a line. Each time he does, I make sure to let him know how displeased I am. How unacceptable that is."

"Which stops him from doing it again?" Nathaniel leaned forward, his voice cracking. "We can escape. Together. The Hubbards are willing to take in both of us. I talked to them about it. We don't have to live like this anymore. No more fear. No more pain."

His mother smiled at him, as if he was being sweet, like he had just recited a poem he'd written as a Mother's Day present. "I love you, honey. But I'm not living in fear. Or pain. Your father and I love and respect each other. We failed you. I see that now. We should have realized sooner that something was wrong, but we will fix this."

"*He hits you,*" Nathaniel stressed, the words making his heart ache.

"He doesn't hit me," Star said in hushed tones, glancing around the restaurant. "He might grab me too hard or—"

"Slap you around? That's what Dwight said he saw. When he was a kid." Nathaniel clenched his jaw a few times. "I always wondered what made him so messed up. Maybe that's the reason."

"I don't know what he thought he saw," Star said, "but he was mistaken."

"Bruises don't lie. Whatever Dad does to you, it's wrong."

His mother stared at the table, lost in thought.

"Please," Nathaniel pleaded. "Please come with me! We'll get away from them both."

She remained silent a little longer. When she looked up again, she seemed determined. "Every family goes through rough patches. This is ours, and I *will* get us through it. But until we can get things sorted out, if you feel safer staying with the Hubbards, then that's what you should do. For now."

"I don't care about me. I care about you!"

"Then you need to trust me. I'm fine. Your father isn't a

monster. He's human and he loves you very much. He's worried sick about you right now."

Nathaniel grunted and looked away. He didn't want to hear it.

"I don't know what's wrong with your brother, but it isn't your fault. Maybe you're right. Maybe I'm to blame."

"That's not what I said."

Star placed a hand on his arm so he would look at her. "Just don't blame yourself. Please. And think about coming home. I still want to see you every day. Okay?"

"Yeah," Nathaniel said, unsure how that would work. "But I don't want to see them again. Ever."

Star took a deep breath. "We're going to get through this."

All he cared about was escaping from his father and his brother. With her. "The offer still stands," he said. "If things get too bad, I know some good people who are willing to help you. Don't forget that. Promise me you'll ask for help."

His mother managed a small smile and nodded. "I promise."

Chapter Five

Fear's presence is impossible to ignore, a cold serpent slithering through the veins, reaching the heart and injecting it with venom. Oppression is more subtle—a heavy cloak that wraps around the body, weighing it down and restricting movement. Nathaniel knew brief respites from fear when he was at school or on the camping trip with the Hubbards, but in the back of his mind he dreaded the inevitable return home. Now he had escaped suffocating oppression and for the first time, the future was no longer a burden.

Only the essentials had been moved to the Hubbards' home, creating a sanctuary Dwight couldn't find. His mother alone had the address. Nathaniel still worried about her, but they saw each other often, usually for a dinner out. He even insisted on paying, when she would let him. Each time they met, he scrutinized her for any signs of abuse. He didn't find any. Except for deepening worry lines, she looked good. Maybe she had been telling the truth and his father rarely lost control, but that wasn't enough for Nathaniel to forgive him.

He tried his best to enjoy his good fortune. The letter from Yale had finally arrived, welcoming him to their campus. He and Rebecca had accepted without hesitation, giving them reason to celebrate today.

"You're so lucky," Rebecca said, strolling around his new room and examining everything. "You get to live with your boyfriend."

"He's not my boyfriend," Nathaniel said, "and having to flee from my psychotic brother hardly sounds like luck."

"Sorry," she said, picking up and looking at the few DVDs he had brought with him. Most of his things were still in his old room. "At least you've gone from somewhere terrible to a place you like. And where you really like someone."

"He's just my friend."

"Of course. Still…" She turned in his direction but continued looking around the room. "You know, now that everything is out in the open, I could ask my parents if you could come live with me. We don't have a spare bedroom, but we could put two twin beds in mine. Sort of like married couples did on old TV shows."

He remained silent, waiting for her to look at him. When she did, he shook his head.

"Can't blame you," she said. "I'd choose this place over mine any day. They've got a nice house." She nodded to the dumbbells sitting in one corner. "Although I'm surprised they don't have a dedicated gym somewhere on the fifth floor."

He laughed in response.

"You still feel like you need those?" she asked.

This made him more somber. "Nobody is going to hurt me again. Not if I can help it."

She considered him, then smiled. "So, where are you taking me for our big night out? Somewhere with tablecloths and wine glasses, I hope."

"I was thinking the mall."

"Oh."

"And uh… Do you mind if Caesar and Steph tag along?"

"Seriously?" When Rebecca saw he wasn't kidding, she scowled. "Is Yale accepting high school sophomores now, because I thought we were celebrating *our* major achievement."

"We are," Nathaniel said. "This way we'll have an audience we can brag to."

"Is this some weird plan to get into Caesar's pants? Because I know all about lost causes, and this sounds like—"

"He's my friend," Nathaniel repeated. "So are you. I want you guys to get to know each other. That's all."

"That's it? You swear?"

"Yes! I live with the guy. If I wanted to seduce him, I'd just wait until he's in the shower, get naked, and hop in with a washcloth and a hopeful expression."

He let her digest this mental image. A knock at the door soon followed, and as it turned out, Rebecca wasn't the only person anticipating romance.

"Oh!" Steph said when noticing Rebecca. "Is this a double date?"

"Sure is," Rebecca said, not missing a beat. She walked over and took Nathaniel's arm. "Ready to go, hon?"

He decided not to contradict her. At least she seemed happy again. They piled into Nathaniel's car, Rebecca sitting up front with him. That left the lovebirds in the backseat, but they didn't seem too cozy at the moment. Caesar was bobbing his head along with the music on the radio, Steph staring out the window at the traffic whizzing by. Strange that she would think they were on a double date. That suggested she didn't know he was gay. Did that mean Caesar didn't talk about him much? He wasn't surprised. When alone together, they probably had more interesting diversions keeping them occupied. So lucky!

Once at the mall, Rebecca continued the pretense of them being a couple, hanging off his arm or holding his hand. While dining at the food court, she even fed him some fries.

"How long have you two been together?" Steph asked, amused by this display.

"Just a few weeks," Rebecca said. "Honeymoon stage."

"That's the best." Steph sighed. "Maybe that's why Caesar and I keep breaking up, so we can experience it again."

"We only broke up once," Caesar replied.

Steph raised an eyebrow. "Twice."

Caesar looked exasperated. "We broke up during lunch and got back together before the school day was over. That doesn't count!"

"Yes, it does," Steph said, but she was smiling. Then she addressed them again. "No relationship is perfect. Just remember that when the honeymoon is over."

Nathaniel pretended to consider her words of wisdom when really he was distracted by the revelation that they had problems. Caesar had never mentioned that. Apparently they had weathered many issues, because Steph kept dishing out advice: Walk away and cool down when arguments get too heated. Don't try to hurt the other person just because you feel hurt. Always be honest and open. Nathaniel listened with fascination, especially when she gave examples of previous tiffs.

"Let's catch a movie," Caesar said, eager for a change of topic.

"Sounds to me like you're living one," Nathaniel said.

The girls laughed. Caesar just blushed.

They went to the mall cinema, but the movie they wanted to see didn't start for another half-hour, so they spent that time shopping. Or at least Rebecca and Steph did. Nathaniel and Caesar sat on a bench in the mall corridor, watching through a store window as their dates perused pop culture T-shirts and gothic jewelry.

"Your girlfriend is really pretty," Caesar said, getting his revenge.

"Shut up. She's had a crush on me since the first day we met. I love her, but it's annoying at times."

"You should be flattered."

Nathaniel glanced over to see he was serious. "You really think she's pretty?"

"Yeah! Totally."

"You have good taste. Most guys ignore her. I don't get why."

Caesar shrugged. "They're probably scared to admit what they like."

"Maybe. You sure are open-minded."

Caesar grinned. "I pride myself on it!"

Nathaniel looked around, spotting an Asian woman in her twenties. "What about her?"

"What?"

"You think she's pretty?"

"Yeah," Caesar said. "She's all right."

"And what about him?" Nathaniel nodded to a portly old grandpa. "Feel like sitting on his lap and telling him what you want for Christmas?"

"Blech!" Caesar stuck out his tongue. "He's *way* too young for me. I like them more mature than that. I wanna marry a mummy."

Nathaniel laughed, the warm feeling spreading through his chest. "And what about me? Am I the marrying type?"

Caesar's cheeks grew red, making Nathaniel confident of the answer. Until he was proven wrong.

"I don't know."

"You don't know?" Nathaniel looked away. "Whatever. It was dumb question."

"There's a big difference between finding someone attractive and wanting to spend the rest of your life with them."

"I wasn't proposing to you," Nathaniel snapped. "It was a joke. Chill."

"I wish I knew you better."

That got his attention. "How?"

Caesar seemed a little wary, probably worried about offending him again. "Let's try an experiment, okay?"

"Sure."

"What's my favorite color?"

"Blue."

Caesar smiled. "And my favorite musician?"

Nathaniel grimaced. "Eminem."

"Don't hate," Caesar chided. "What's my middle name?"

He needed a full minute to answer that one but felt pleased when finding the answer. "Anthony. See? We know each other just fine."

Caesar shook his head. "I can't answer any of those questions. Whenever I ask you about yourself, you always change the subject."

Nathaniel shrugged. "Okay. Gray, Danny Elfman, Edward. Now you know the answers. Happy?"

"Those were just examples. It's more... I wish you trusted me. That's all."

Nathaniel studied him. "Because I don't want to talk about my fucked-up family? Think about one of the worst days of your life, one that was really shitty and embarrassing. The kind you just want to forget. Ask yourself how much you like telling other people about it."

"I get that," Caesar conceded, "but—"

"I don't talk much about myself because most of my life has consisted of shitty days."

Caesar was quiet. "That bad?"

Nathaniel exhaled. "No. Not always. It just feels good pretending none of it ever happened. That's where I'm at right now."

"Okay," Caesar said. "Sorry I mentioned it."

"I'm not mad at you."

"I know. It's not a big deal."

But it was, because Caesar was basically saying he didn't know who Nathaniel was. Nathaniel wasn't okay with that, but he didn't know how to fix it without unleashing a horde of ugly demons.

"Here they come," Caesar said.

Rebecca and Steph were walking toward them. Maybe they'd had their own uncomfortable conversation because they appeared tense. No one spoke much on the way into the theater or while waiting for the movie to start. Nathaniel was glad when the lights dimmed. Rebecca, seated on his left, seemed a little jittery. As far away from her as possible, Steph was seated on the opposite side of Caesar. Their friendship was already over, it seemed. He didn't let this concern him. Instead, as the movie started, all he could think of was how close he felt to Caesar and how one-sided that connection had turned out to be. He didn't know the solution, because even if he opened up about every terrible thing Dwight had done to him, that still wasn't Nathaniel's identity. He hated the idea of letting the abuse define his personality. There had to be more to him than that.

For now all he could do was casually shift his leg so it bumped against Caesar's. He left it there, neither of them reacting. Maybe Caesar didn't notice it over the car chases and explosions, but Nathaniel felt a little better knowing they were connected in this most superficial of ways.

Once the movie was over and they were in the parking lot heading toward the car, Steph pulled Caesar aside. They walked far enough away that they couldn't be heard, but they were obviously arguing. Nathaniel turned to Rebecca for an explanation.

She looked sheepish. "I sort of let it slip that you're gay."

"What? Why?"

"I didn't mean to! I saw a gay pride bracelet, and without thinking about it, I said I should buy it for you. That it might help you find a boyfriend."

Nathaniel glanced back toward the ongoing argument. "I don't see why Steph would care."

"Me neither. All I know is, we hit zero degrees Celsius in about two seconds flat."

When the happy couple returned, neither had much to say. It wasn't until Nathaniel had dropped off Rebecca and Steph that he got his answer.

"She felt like we were making fun of her," Caesar explained. "Like she was the butt of a joke. She was giving you guys all that relationship advice and—"

"Oh," Nathaniel said.

"Yeah. So that made her feel embarrassed."

Nathaniel slowed at a stoplight. "Seemed more angry to me."

"That too." Caesar picked at the fabric of the armrest. "I guess our legs were touching during the movie or something."

"Were they?" Nathaniel asked, his voice sounding a little high.

"No idea. She knows I like guys too, so I guess she felt threatened by it or whatever. I don't know. It's silly."

Nathaniel wouldn't agree with that. He'd preferred to think it was serious or had the potential to become so. But first, he'd have to find a way of showing Caesar who he really was.

The solution came to him a week later while he was helping Caesar with a social studies assignment. The book was open to a map of the United States, and when Nathaniel mentioned again that he'd lived in California, Caesar asked a question.

"Where else have you lived?"

Nathaniel went backward through his own life history, struggling to relate the locations to who he was. "Colorado was okay. Tons of roadkill, especially in the fall. Lots of deer and elk, which can be messy. Er..." Rather than explore that charming topic further, he moved on to the next state. And the next. "I've lived here too," he said, putting his finger in the middle of the map. "In Missouri."

Caesar squinted at where he was pointing. "Warrensburg?"

"Yeah. But only when I was really little."

"So you don't remember it much?"

"Not really, but I still go back there to see my grandparents."

Caesar perked up at this. "Really? Do you..."

"Get along with them?" Nathaniel laughed. "Yeah! I love them!"

For once his family wasn't a taboo subject. That's when the idea came to him: Why not visit his grandparents together? The timing was perfect too, since they were facing a three-day weekend. He asked Mr. Hubbard first, because he didn't want Caesar to get excited about the idea if he wouldn't be allowed.

"He's a little young to be taking a road trip," Mr. Hubbard said sternly, but a twinkle in his eye gave him away. "Then again, it *would* broaden his horizons. Besides, I know you'll keep him safe. We trust you."

These three simple words gnawed at Nathaniel during the drive to Missouri. They left shortly after breakfast, Caesar hyper and talkative over the next three hours. Only after they blew through Dallas and entered Oklahoma did his passenger settle down, leaning the seat back and closing his eyes. Nathaniel occasionally glanced over, catching little glimpses. Like the olive-toned skin of his bare forearm. Or the muscles of his neck and the slightly agape mouth, his breathing heavy in sleep. Even the twist of denim between his legs, just in case morning wood revealed tantalizing details. Or road trip wood, Nathaniel supposed, but his wry smile soon faded.

We trust you.

Not just Mr. Hubbard. The "we" implied Mrs. Hubbard did too. She certainly checked up on them less. When he had begun tutoring Caesar, she often stuck her head into the room to see how they were doing. Even after he'd moved in, she tended to find excuses to look in on them. But not anymore. Nathaniel was an honorary member of the family. And what was he doing with that trust? Hell, what was he doing at all? He wanted to open himself to Caesar, to prove that they knew each other well, but not so their friendship could thrive. Nathaniel wanted much more than that. He harbored no delusions of Mr. Hubbard's reaction if he learned the truth.

He tried to put these thoughts out of his mind as they drove. The only other option was to stop the car and turn around. After a pee break in Oklahoma City and a meal courtesy of the gas station microwave ovens, they pressed on, Caesar becoming less excited and more restless.

"Maybe we should have flown instead," he complained as they crossed another state line.

"Warrensburg isn't exactly near a major airport," Nathaniel pointed out.

"So what does it have?"

He thought about the question, feeling confident of the answer. "Nothing."

Caesar groaned dramatically. Then he perked up again. "Can I drive?"

"Do you know how?"

"No."

Nathaniel glanced over at him quizzically.

"Relax," Caesar said. "I'm in Driver's Ed."

"Gosh, that *is* comforting. Do you have your learner's permit?"

"Nope. So can I drive?"

Nathaniel thought about it and shrugged. "Yeah, okay."

He heard a distant echo of *we trust you* as he pulled the car over, but the road ahead of them was clear and straight, empty of any challenging curves. Besides, the way Caesar was grinning as they passed each other in front of the hood already made the risk worth any consequences. That didn't mean Nathaniel would let down his guard. Once buckled up in each other's seats, he coached Caesar through every maneuver, the role of tutor and student familiar to them both as they pulled out onto the highway. Caesar was doing well. Until he got daring.

"Slow down," Nathaniel said, eyes on the speed gauge.

"I just want to hit eighty-eight miles per hour. Like in that one movie."

"Back to the Future," Nathaniel said automatically, "and I want you to slow down."

Caesar bit his lip, looking more amused as he pressed down on the pedal. The little arm reached eighty and kept going. Nathaniel didn't normally find speed intimidating, but the way Caesar constantly adjusted the wheel was making the car wobble back and forth. They were coming up on another vehicle too.

"Either brake," Nathaniel said, pressing himself against the seat, "or switch lanes. Now!"

The car weaved a few more times, the rear of a minivan filling much of the windshield. At the last possible moment, their car careened into the other lane and then back again, cutting off the minivan. An angry honk sounded at the same time that Nathaniel swore, censoring the f-bomb. He was sure Caesar heard it anyway, not that he seemed to care. Instead he was laughing, tears in his eyes.

"You almost killed us," Nathaniel said. "Scratch that. You *are* dead! Just as soon as you pull over."

"Then I better keep driving." Caesar glanced over, acting confused by the anger that greeted him. "What? I remembered to signal!"

Nathaniel scowled. Once Caesar's attention was back on the road, he allowed himself a covert smile. "Take the next exit."

"Are we there already?"

"No, but I have to take a piss. And check to see if I shit myself."

Caesar went into another fit of laughter. Nathaniel reached over to stabilize the wheel until he calmed down. He remained on edge as they left the highway, Caesar bringing them to a gas station full of more obstacles. Somehow he managed to park without taking out one of the gas pumps and blowing them up.

"How'd I do?" Caesar asked.

Nathaniel answered him with a glare and a swat to the back of the head.

Thankfully, the rest of the journey wasn't so eventful. They reached their destination a few hours past dinnertime, their stomachs grumbling, but Nathaniel knew his grandparents would have food waiting for them. They owned a home on the edge of town, meaning Caesar would have to wait to see glorious downtown Warrensburg. For now they were both eager to escape from the car. His grandparents lived at the end of a cul-de-sac, their house nestled up against undeveloped land—woods that Nathaniel had memories of playing in as a child. The home was ranch style, the windows lit by a warmth that welcomed them inside.

The door was open before he could knock. His grandmother, of course. She resembled her daughter—his mother—although her hair was gray instead of golden and always worn in a bob. She squeezed him tightly while squealing with joy. Then she moved to do the same to Caesar, despite never having met him before.

"Come in, come in!" she said, ushering them inside. "I thought you'd never get here! I was about to send out a search party. What time did you leave?"

"After breakfast," Nathaniel answered.

"On the phone you said you were leaving early!"

"That is early!" Nathaniel retorted.

"Teenagers," his grandmother said playfully. "Introduce me to your friend."

Before he could, his grandfather appeared in the entryway. Nathaniel had inherited a lot from him physically. They shared the same large build and tall height. The strong brow too. Star insisted their blond hair came from him as well, although he had been white-haired and balding for as long as Nathaniel could remember. Hopefully he hadn't inherited that genetic tendency.

"Good of you to come," his grandfather said, clapping a hand on his shoulder. "I didn't think we'd see you again until Christmas."

"I didn't want to wait," Nathaniel said. "You guys are ancient. Who knows if you'll still be around in December?" His grandmother giggled, sounding like his mother and making him feel homesick. "Granny, Gramps, this is my friend Caesar. Caesar, this is Joe and Laura."

"Or Granny and Gramps, if you prefer," Laura said. "Now come to the kitchen. You must be starving!"

"Let them eat in the living room," Joe said. "They'll be more comfortable there."

Laura rolled her eyes. "There's a game on."

"I don't mind," Nathaniel said. "You've already eaten, right?"

"That's right," Joe said before his wife could answer.

After declining offers of help, she went into the kitchen while his grandfather led them into a large living room. The house had been designed at a time when stylish walls were plastered with flat misshapen stones. Exposed dark brown beams graced the ceiling. Nathaniel didn't know when the house was built or what people had been smoking back then, but he found it sort of appealing. The sunken floor and chocolate-colored carpet in the living room gave the room a cozy feel, partly due to the soft glow of the lamps. He plopped down happily on the couch, Caesar doing the same next to him.

His grandfather settled into his favorite chair, one eye on the widescreen television where a poker game was in progress. "So why are you here?" he asked. "Money? On the run from the law?"

"Chasing down my past," Nathaniel said.

"Oh? Why's that?"

To impress the guy next to me. But that would be too awkward a confession. "Homework assignment. Caesar has to write a biography of someone he knows, and since I'm his tutor, we figured that would be easiest."

"What's this I hear?" his grandmother asked as she entered the room.

"Nate's going to be famous," Joe said. "Caesar is writing a book about him. They've already got a six-figure deal with a major publisher."

"Exactly," Nathaniel said. "No, it's just a school paper about where I come from. Figured it was a good excuse to see you guys."

"Well, be sure to thank your teacher for me." Laura grabbed two of the TV trays from the corner and set them up. That was another childhood memory, since there was always something on television they wanted to see. Perhaps that's where his passion for cinematography came from. Regardless, most meals he remembered eating here were served on wooden trays in front of the TV. After refusing another offer of help, she returned first with drinks, then made another trip for two plates of potato salad and fried chicken that had cooled to room temperature.

"So what do you boys have planned?" she asked when finally able to sit.

"I figured we'd wander around town tomorrow," Nathaniel said. "See what memories I can dig up."

"I'll be surprised if you remember anything," Laura said. "You were so little when your family moved the first time. It nearly broke my heart."

"We always came back to visit though. This is the closest thing I have to a hometown."

"It *is* your hometown," Joe said. "You were practically born here."

"Does Warrensburg have its own hospital?" Caesar asked.

"Yeah," Nathaniel said with a chuckle. "It's not *that* small."

"Warrensburg has its own university too," his grandmother said. "Have you decided yet? Is that why you're really here, to visit the campus?"

His grandfather chuckled. "Careful! She'll put sugar in your gas tank just to keep you from leaving again."

"I was accepted into Yale," Nathaniel said.

"Oh, I see. Well…" She sounded so disappointed that they all laughed.

"Most people would break out the champagne," Nathaniel teased. "Not look sad."

Joe twisted around in his chair and smiled. "You boys want a beer?"

"Yeah!" Caesar said.

"No," Nathaniel said firmly.

More small talk followed, Laura grilling Caesar about who his parents were and what they did for a living. Little details that mattered to adults, for some reason. Bowls of ice cream followed the chicken and potato salad, and as the night wore down, they were shown to their room. Singular. And this time there wasn't a couch for Nathaniel to crash on unless he returned to the living room, which he wasn't willing to do. He didn't even offer to take the floor. If Caesar had any complaints, he'd have to voice them. Nathaniel was setting himself up for a restless night, but he could always nip off to the bathroom for a quick—

"They're really nice," Caesar said, sitting on one corner of the bed.

"Yeah."

"I'm surprised you don't live with them since… You know."

"I love my mom," Nathaniel said quickly. "I never wanted to get away from her. Just my brother." And his dad, but that was recent.

Caesar waited, maybe thinking they drove all this way just so Nathaniel could tell him everything. But that wasn't the deal. Nathaniel unpacked his stuff, ignoring the silence. Eventually, Caesar chose to fill it.

"Do they know about you?"

"That I'm gay? Yeah."

"How'd they take it?"

"Granny had lots of questions. Gramps gets uncomfortable when the subject comes up, but he doesn't treat me any different. Aside from no longer asking if I have a girlfriend. Why? You thinking of telling your parents?"

"No," Caesar said. "I just wondered if they think I'm your boyfriend."

His expression was innocent when Nathaniel turned around. With a hint of mischief. "Keep dreaming," Nathaniel said, tossing a pair of socks at him.

Caesar caught them and threatened to throw them back. Before he could, there was a knock at the door. His grandmother opened it, but only a crack. "Can I come in?"

Geez, maybe she really did think he and Caesar were a couple. "Get on in here," Nathaniel said.

Laura entered the room carrying two large photo albums. "I thought these would assist with your paper," she said to Caesar. "Always helps to have a visual aid. Anything you want to take back with you, we can get copies made of. Nathaniel isn't in all the photos but—"

"This is great!" Caesar said, standing to relieve her of the albums. "I can't wait to go through them!"

And he didn't. As soon as Laura shut the door behind her, Caesar flopped stomach-first on the bed and opened an album.

"Hold up," Nathaniel said, plopping down beside him. "I need to check for embarrassing photos first."

"No way!" Caesar said, yanking away the album. He returned it front and center when he saw Nathaniel wasn't serious. "Who's this?"

The black-and-white photo was of two thin people in formal clothing. "I don't know. My great-grandparents maybe."

"Oh."

Caesar kept turning pages, giving each photo a few seconds of attention before continuing. Nathaniel stopped him at a photo of his mother when she was just a kid, sitting between her parents on the couch—his grandparents, who looked younger than he had ever seen them.

"Only child?" Caesar asked.

"Yeah. Lucky her."

As Caesar turned the pages, she slowly aged before their eyes, finally becoming a teenager, the innocent smile replaced by a self-assured grin.

"Is that your dad?" Caesar asked, tapping a photo.

Nathaniel craned his neck to see. The guy next to Star had dark hair, the sides buzzed short, giving him a sort of mohawk. He wore an old army jacket along with a cool expression, his hands shoved into his jeans. "Does that look like my dad?" he asked incredulously.

"I don't know," Caesar said defensively. "I've never met him before."

"Oh. Right."

"He sort of looks like you."

Nathaniel scoffed. "No, he doesn't!"

"You've got a similar nose." Caesar brought his face closer to the page. "Same lips too. He's kind of cute!"

Nathaniel looked again, not agreeing. "He looks weird. But no, that's definitely not my dad."

As Caesar turned the pages, Nathaniel tried to name what relatives he could and to come up with interesting stories for those he remembered. Only on the last page of the album did Nathaniel finally appear, still a toddler, his mother stooping over him and holding onto his hands so he could remain standing.

"She looks so young," Caesar said.

Nathaniel smiled. "She always has."

"She's a hottie too!"

Nathaniel gave him a look. "You've got issues."

"Hey, it's not my mom. She's a total MI—"

"Don't even say it!"

Nathaniel grabbed the book to shut it. He pushed it aside and reached for the other, this one covering more familiar territory. A family photo, his young father looking so much like Dwight that Nathaniel felt uneasy. As for his brother, in the photo Dwight was still chubby-cheeked and anything but intimidating. His family must have moved away by this point, because most photos had Christmas decorations in the background, the season when they returned to Warrensburg for visits. That made for good conversation, since his holidays were full of happy memories. They found a few summer photos too, one of Nathaniel skinny and sunburned, sitting with his legs dangling in the pool. That sunburn—and how Dwight had delighted in it—brought back bad memories, making him eager for Caesar to turn the page. He did so and stared at a shirtless photo of Dwight, his brother's smile just as bright as the sun beaming down on him.

"That's him?" Caesar asked.

"Yeah."

At least he had the decency not to mention how hot he was. Caesar wordlessly flipped through the remaining pages, probably wondering how Nathaniel could turn his back on all those smiling faces. He felt guilty by the time they shut the photo album, but soon forgot those feelings when Caesar grinned at him.

"That was cool!" he said.

Nathaniel searched his eyes. Were they good now? Is that all Caesar needed to feel close? "I'm surprised it didn't bore you to death."

"Nope!" Caesar yawned. "Maybe we should crash though. It's late."

"Yeah, you don't want to be tired for our big day tomorrow."

Caesar looked interested. "Really?"

Nathaniel laughed. "No. Not really. Lower your expectations. Trust me."

Caesar went to the bathroom to brush his teeth. Nathaniel did the same once he was back. When he returned from the bathroom, Caesar was already in bed, his glasses on the nightstand, his eyes closed. Nathaniel stood in the doorway and watched him for a while. Then he flipped off the light, stripped off his T-shirt, and let his jeans drop before stepping out of them. He slipped between the sheets, remaining on his side of the bed. Eventually though, he slid one hand across, leaving it splayed in the center of the mattress like an open invitation.

Chapter Six

A tediously cheerful breakfast greeted them the next day. Nathaniel's grandparents were in high spirits and certainly more animated than the night before. What was it about early mornings that seemed to super-charge the elderly and why did people his own age find them so damn hard to get through? A couple of hot showers brought them back from the dead. Gramps was in front of the television, watching ESPN, and Granny wanted to go grocery shopping, her sights already set on dinner. Neither activity sounded appealing, so they hitched a ride downtown with her and set out on their own.

Warrensburg was small enough that getting around by foot was ideal. If they tackled the town by car, they'd probably be done within an hour and be left with little else to do. They walked through the oldest part of town, which looked nothing like Houston or other cities where Nathaniel had lived. Most of the brick buildings were featureless boxes, the architecture uninspiring, which is perhaps why so many businesses had cloth awnings above their doors. Even the old church they passed could have been designed by a child—a rectangle with a pointy steeple on top.

"This is wild," Caesar said. "It's like something out of a Western movie!"

Nathaniel smirked. Take away the occasional spindly tree and replace the paved road with dusty dirt, and it did have that feel. "Too bad there's not a saloon. Plenty of bars for the college students though. And the unemployed."

"I can't imagine growing up here," Caesar said in hushed tones.

"Hey, it's not exactly a third-world country." He frowned at their surroundings. "But yeah, I'm glad we moved."

They wandered aimlessly, weaving in and out of neighborhoods with small houses, eventually ending up on the university campus. They walked the pathways between buildings as if enrolled there, and joined a slew of other people for lunch in the student union. Caesar grinned throughout the meal, enjoying the experience. Nathaniel felt a little intimidated by all the unknown faces, and by getting turned around so easily while exploring. This university was small compared to Yale. How would he ever survive there? Of course he wouldn't be alone. He'd follow Rebecca around like a duckling if need be. And eventually, he'd have a duckling of his own.

Nathaniel nudged Caesar playfully. "What do you think? Should we talk to admissions?"

"It's better than high school, that's for sure!"

They explored the campus a little longer, ending up at the stadium where Caesar insisted on stretching out on one of the bleachers to soak up sun. Nathaniel sat a few rows up while he did so, his attention on the horizon, the blue sky above, the sports field below, and when he dared, the six feet of cat-napping temptation just ahead of him. Caesar's T-shirt had pulled away from the waist of his jeans, revealing a strip of skin that Nathaniel imagined running his tongue along.

When a fat white cloud thoughtlessly came between them and the sun, Caesar stirred and got up so they could continue their journey. This time they backtracked through the downtown area toward Route 50. Across the highway was a more modern commercial zone full of the generic restaurants and supercenters found everywhere in the United States, which somehow made the crummy downtown area more appealing. Nathaniel didn't take them into this area, leading Caesar instead to Bernie's Stop and Shop where they bought Cokes. Not far from this were two vehicle dealerships, one specializing mostly in pickups, the other in tractors.

"Here's the family fortune," Nathaniel said without ceremony.

Caesar looked back and forth between the two parking lots. "Your family owns these?"

"They used to. Gramps sold them years ago. His plumbing business too. He used to always say 'Trucks, tractors, and toilets—I've got your ass covered!'"

Caesar scrunched up his face. "Huh?"

"Because you sit on all three things. It was funnier when I was a kid, but not by much." Nathaniel stared at the dealerships and tried to drum up an interesting memory, something cute, like him being allowed to drive a tractor around at an adorably young age. Nothing like that had happened though. "I guess that's it," he said. "Show's over. Sorry."

"What are you sorry for?"

Nathaniel sighed and headed for one of the side streets. "I wanted you to learn more about me. I guess there's not much to tell."

Caesar laughed. "I don't really have a paper to write."

"I know." Nathaniel walked in silence, eying the homes around them. Inside each was a family of some kind. Young couples just starting out, single parents with kids, or maybe even an older person who had already lost their other half. But all of them had achieved a relationship, which seemed miraculous, because he couldn't figure out how to get there. How did two people go from being strangers to meaning everything to each other? How did anyone bridge that gap?

Nathaniel sighed. "You said you don't really know me. I thought coming here might change that."

"I never said that!"

"You did. At the mall a few weeks back."

"Oh."

Nathaniel glanced over at him.

Caesar met his gaze, looking a little sheepish. "All that stuff about your favorite color or whatever?"

"Exactly."

"Little details like that don't matter. They're nice, but I was hoping you'd be more open." Caesar hesitated. "About other things."

Nathaniel stopped walking. "About my brother?"

"Yeah. I guess so."

Nathaniel glared. "This isn't a game! That information isn't a prize to be won, or something I hand out to people who get close to me. If you're hanging around me waiting for some juicy gossip, you can fuck off!"

Caesar's jaw dropped. "That's not what I meant! I figured it's an important part of you, and if you keep it from me—"

"That's not who I am!" Nathaniel snarled. "It might have shaped me, but I'm sure as hell not going to let it define me!"

"Fine!" Caesar held up his hands in surrender. "I just want you to feel like you can confide in me."

"I do. But that doesn't mean I need to."

"Okay." Caesar looked dejected. "Sorry my stupid comments made you feel like you needed to bring me here."

Caesar resumed walking, which was silly, because he didn't know which direction to go. Nathaniel stared after him, then hurried to catch up.

"I'm the one who is sorry," he said. "I just find this whole experience frustrating. I mean, I like being on this trip with you. I just... Never mind."

Caesar shot him a glance. "What?"

Nathaniel held back a growl, hating himself in advance for being dumb enough to say it. "I want you to like me."

Caesar's attention immediately returned to the sidewalk as he paced along. He didn't say anything. Nathaniel grimaced and seriously considered bonking him over the head in the hope of inducing amnesia. Or turning around and running in the opposite direction, consequences be damned.

"I do like you," Caesar said at last. "A lot. You're amazingly smart. When I first saw you at the tutoring center, how you just moved from person to person, helping them all. It's like you know everything and—"

"That's not how it works," Nathaniel interrupted, but Caesar didn't seem to hear him because he kept rambling.

"I was always checking you out. You've got those big shoulders, and I felt like I could hang off them and you wouldn't even notice. Ha ha! I don't even know what that means, but I kept thinking of you and wanting to make you proud, because you're so perfect. When I saw that bruise on your face, I got obsessed. I wished there was something I could do. I wanted to help, to give back to you. Then you kept getting hurt, and it was my dad who figured out how to fix it all. I'm glad, but I sort of wish it could have been me, because he doesn't— Not like me. He doesn't feel the way I do. Now you're saying you want me to like you, which is crazy because..." Caesar stopped and turned to face him, his chest heaving, attention still focused on the ground. "I'm in love with you."

Nathaniel stared at him—at downturned eyes the color of honey that seduced him with every glance, despite being hidden behind goofy red frames. At the strong jaw, the waves of dark hair, the flaring nostrils that accompanied each quick breath. *Love.* He hadn't even considered the word, didn't even know if he was capable of loving after everything he had been through. Then his gaze darted down to those lips, and he knew what he wanted.

Two things stopped him. One was a bright-eyed girl with corkscrew hair who was probably missing her boyfriend right now, counting the hours until he returned. The other was a phrase—the three words that had haunted him this entire trip. *We trust you.* He couldn't imagine a more efficient way of breaking that trust than giving in to his urges now.

And yet, he had been through so much, bearing as much suffering as he could in silence. Perhaps he had earned this. One moment of bliss to help balance out the pain. Just once and never again. He reached forward, placing a finger beneath Caesar's chin, tilting his head upward and locking eyes with him. Nathaniel stared deep into Caesar's soul, creating an entire relationship in his mind that started right now, went through college and careers, vacations and retirement, ending with them falling asleep in each other's arms and never waking again. He tried to compress all of that down to one instance, one kiss. Then he leaned forward and touched Caesar's lips with his own.

The details were lost to him. Who embraced whom, or how long they stood there or the exact motions of their mouths. All he took from the experience was the sensation of being whole, and the certainty that Caesar had chosen the correct term. Love. That's what this was.

When reality resumed, Caesar was smiling bashfully, but Nathaniel couldn't. Those three little words had returned, altered slightly now. *We trusted you!* An image of a crying girl accompanied the accusation, high school sweethearts ruined by this indiscretion. Her tears were much more bearable than the angry glares of Mr. and Mrs. Hubbard.

"We can't do that again," Nathaniel said.

Caesar looked crestfallen. "Why not?"

"You know why." He watched realization arrive.

"Oh."

Nathaniel couldn't be sure if Caesar grasped all the reasons, but he clearly understood enough. Nathaniel put an arm around his shoulder, guiding him down the sidewalk, breaking contact when he was certain Caesar would keep walking on his own. "But for the record, I don't regret it. As long as we don't let it ruin anything, I'm glad that it happened. In fact, there's no way in hell I'll ever forget that kiss."

"Me neither," Caesar said, managing to sound upbeat.

Nathaniel glanced over and smiled, even though inside he was already wishing he could turn back time.

They returned to the house in a thick silence. Caesar was no doubt worrying about Steph, perhaps struggling with his guilt. Nathaniel's thoughts focused more on salvaging his connection with Caesar and steering them back toward friendship without either of them getting hurt. That already seemed impossible.

"You want something to drink?" Nathaniel asked as they entered the kitchen.

"Thanks."

These were the only words they had exchanged in the last half-hour. The drive home tomorrow was going to be hell. Nathaniel was rustling around in the refrigerator when his grandmother entered the kitchen. She seemed troubled when she saw them, as if she could sense the tension, but her expression was soon whisked away by a smile.

"Are you boys hungry?" she asked.

"Just thirsty," Nathaniel replied, handing Caesar a can of Coke.

"I'll start dinner soon. Did you have fun?"

"It was great!" Caesar said. "I really like Warrensburg. Especially the university. We had lunch there."

"How nice." Laura's smile seemed frozen in place. Then she took a breath, sharp and quick. "Caesar, why don't you go relax in the other room? I need Nathaniel's help with a few things."

"Oh. Okay!"

Nathaniel took a sip of his Coke while watching Caesar leave the room, raising an eyebrow quizzically at his grandmother once he was gone. "What's up?"

His grandmother pulled out a chair, indicating he should sit. Once he had, she joined him at the table. "I spoke with your mother this morning."

"Oh."

"I only called to let her know you had arrived safely. She was surprised. She didn't know you were coming for a visit."

"I'm a big boy now," he said, trying to inject humor into the situation. "I can do what I want."

Laura remained serious. "She said you had moved out, that you're living with Caesar's family."

Nathaniel grew more somber. "Did she tell you why?"

"She wouldn't say much, other than you not getting along with Dwight. But really, what sort of reason is that? Siblings always have their problems. I know how strong-headed your brother can be, but you can also—"

"He's not my brother," Nathaniel spat. "And the other man living there? That piece of shit? He's not my father!"

Laura pursed her lips, which was all it took for him to feel bad. He never acted up around his grandparents. When he was younger maybe, but he tried to be on his best behavior. Especially around his grandmother, whom he loved dearly.

"Sorry," he mumbled.

Laura placed a worn and wrinkled hand over his, patting it a few times. "I understand now."

"You do?"

"Yes. I didn't realize they had told you. I know it's a big adjustment, but honey, there's more to family than blood. Heath raised you. He works hard to provide you all with a good home. That makes him your father. That's what counts. And I don't know what you and Dwight are struggling with, but believe me, even biological siblings drive each other crazy. Coming from the same womb doesn't mean you'll get along."

Nathaniel remained very still, which was difficult because he felt very much like jumping to his feet or spluttering a number of questions, all of which boiled down to wanting to know what the hell she was talking about. In the end, he managed to utter one hoarse word. "What?"

His grandmother searched his eyes, realizing her mistake. "I thought they told you! Why else would you say— Why would you be living with another family, especially so close to graduation when you'll be moving out anyway?"

Nathaniel pulled his hand away. "He's not my father?"

"Of course he is!" Laura said. "That's what I was trying to tell you. Let's calm down, shall we?" The suggestion could have been directed at herself, since her hand was now placed over her heart.

"He's not my biological father," Nathaniel said, refusing to let the truth be swept away so easily. "If he's not, then who is?"

Laura opened her mouth a few times, then looked toward the living room, calling her husband's name. "Joe!"

"Who's my real father?" Nathaniel demanded.

"How could I be so foolish?" His grandmother leaned back in her chair. "I'm sorry for dropping it on you like that. I thought you knew!"

"Just tell me," Nathaniel pleaded. "Who?"

"I think it's best if we get your mother on the phone." Laura stood and went to the kitchen counter. "We'll do this the right way."

Nathaniel watched her pick up the phone and punch in the number. Once the receiver was pressed against her ear, she looked back at him as if he might bolt. She needn't have worried. Nothing would get him to leave this room. Not when he was so close to the truth.

"Voicemail." His grandmother made it sound like a cuss word. She set down the phone reluctantly before turning to him. "This needs to be done the right way."

"You keep saying that, but I don't know what it means."

"That the rest of the story needs to come from your mother."

Nathaniel eyed her disbelievingly. "You won't tell me who he is?"

"It doesn't matter," his grandma said pleadingly. "The man who raised you *is* your father."

But it *did* matter, because Nathaniel felt like the world had kept spinning without him, leaving him scrabbling to catch hold of anything solid. He needed something to anchor him again—a name, a location, a physical description. Or a photo. He stood, the chair skidding across the floor before it tilted and fell. Then he rushed from the room. The bedroom door was cracked when he reached it, so he used his shoulder to shove it open, surprised to find the room occupied.

Caesar spun around, arms hanging limp, a cell phone in one hand. Then he smiled. "I broke up with her."

"What?"

"With Steph. I broke up with her."

"Why?" He didn't wait for an answer. Nathaniel pushed past him to get to the far side of the bed where they had left the photo albums on the floor. He knelt to grab one of them, tossing it aside when he saw it was the wrong one. Once he had the other open, he flipped through each page impatiently until he found a photo of a punky-looking guy standing next to Star, his expression cool, like all this drama didn't faze him. Nathaniel tore back the protective layer of transparent plastic and snatched the photo free. Then he stood, finding Caesar in his way once again.

"What's going on?"

"Nothing," Nathaniel snapped. Then he sighed. "Everything. I don't know. Just stay here, okay?"

Caesar seemed unhappy, but he nodded.

Nathaniel squeezed past him, noticing his expression. "Sorry about your girlfriend," he said, before his mind returned to the dizzying truth. He glanced down at the photo as he left the room and walked down the hall. Were they a couple? The guy wasn't holding his mother's hand. He didn't have an arm around her possessively. Their shoulders weren't even touching.

When he returned to the kitchen, Gramps was there, listening intently to his wife's hushed words. When he turned around, his features showed pure concern. Then he opened his arms, as if expecting a hug. Nathaniel ignored him, tossing the photo on the table but not watching where it landed. Instead he examined their faces closely, his grandmother's in particular as she turned it over. Her eyes widened enough to know he was right—that Caesar had been correct. This man was his father.

"What's his name?" Nathaniel demanded.

His grandfather, arms at his side now, gave him the answer. "Victor Hemingway."

"And where is he now?"

"Joe," his grandma said, her tones concerned. But why?

"Does he live in Warrensburg?" Nathaniel asked.

Gramps shook his head. "No."

"Where is he then?"

"You'll have to ask your mother about that." His grandfather gestured at a chair, but Nathaniel was too on edge to sit. "We're not trying to be difficult. We're respecting Star's wishes. I hope you understand. She was awfully young when she had you, and this other fellow wasn't ready to be a father. Your mother wasn't ready to raise a child either. Not on her own. We helped until she met Heath."

Nathaniel strained, trying to find any memory, no matter how foggy, to support this story. He couldn't remember a time when his father—or at least Heath—hadn't been around. Then again, Nathaniel did have fond memories of being at his grandparents' house. More than normal perhaps, and in most of those memories, he had been their sole focus. King for a day. For many days. He hadn't shared the spotlight with his brother. Not back then. That had come later. Speaking of which…

"Dwight," he said.

"Heath's boy," Gramps said. "I don't know much about his mother."

"But he has a different mom," Nathaniel said, mind racing. "And a different dad. That means he's not my brother!" The realization summoned a manic smile, but also a sinking sensation. It took him a moment to recognize why.

While his grandfather gave him a pep talk on what constituted a family bond, Nathaniel searched his heart until he understood. All he had suffered through, all the abuse he had taken, had been at the hands of a stranger. Not his brother, but some other kid Nathaniel was forced to live with. Why? The reason was simple. His mother had chosen the wrong person to fall in love with. If she had walked away the first time Heath hurt her, she would have spared them both so much pain. Or at the very least, had she been honest with him about his true father, Nathaniel would have had somewhere else to go. Another home, one where he was safe.

"I want to see him." The words cut off his grandfather's lecture, but he didn't care. Nathaniel's need was too strong. "Right now."

"We don't know where to find him," Gramps said. "That's the honest truth."

"Why didn't she stay with him? With Victor?" Nathaniel's voice cracked. "Why'd she have to choose Heath? Victor couldn't have been worse. Believe me."

His grandparents looked concerned, but he stopped caring what they thought when they gave him the same old answer.

"You'll have to talk to your mother about—"

"Fine!" Nathaniel said, turning away. "Then I'll go ask her."

He swept from the room, pausing briefly in the hallway to wipe at his eyes. He clenched his jaw a few times, summoning up anger again so he wouldn't be weak. When he barged into the bedroom, Caesar was sitting on the bed, his legs pulled up to his chin.

"Pack your things," Nathaniel said. "We're going home."

Caesar's eyes went wide. "Is this because I… Did I mess up?"

"This has nothing to do with you," Nathaniel insisted,

grabbing his backpack and shoving yesterday's outfit into it. "Hurry up!"

Caesar had just hopped out of bed when there was a knock. Gramps was standing in the doorway. He gestured for Nathaniel to join him in the hallway. Nathaniel knew what was coming, but he followed on the off chance that he was wrong.

"Heading home?" Joe asked.

Nathaniel nodded, "Yeah."

"It's a twelve-hour drive. Don't you think it's too late to start?"

"Not that long," Nathaniel replied. "I drive fast."

"Even if you don't take breaks and you manage not to get pulled over, you'll be lucky to reach Houston by three in the morning."

He shrugged. "I've stayed up later than that. I'll be fine."

"I know you will, but your grandmother doesn't. She'll be worried. You might be used to staying up late, but she's not and won't get a wink of sleep until you're home. God forbid anything happens to you! She'll only blame herself. She's already sick with guilt, so I'm not asking you to stay for your own benefit, or even for mine. But if you respect that woman, you'll stay and show her you're okay. And that you don't blame her."

"I don't," Nathaniel mumbled.

"I know, but she needs more than just words to reassure her. One night won't make a difference. I'll even wake you tomorrow so you can get an early start. Deal?"

Nathaniel took a deep breath. Then he exhaled and nodded.

"That's my boy."

Gramps opened his arms for a hug again, and this time there was no getting around it. Nathaniel stepped forward, holding back tears as his grandfather squeezed him affectionately, which was weird because this was good news, right? He despised Dwight and had all but disowned the man he had once considered his father. Now he had discovered that he wasn't related to either. And yet, a strange sense of loss hung over him.

Gramps patted him on the back a few times before ending the embrace. "Now go be a good host to your friend. He looked scared out of his wits."

Nathaniel composed himself. When he returned to the room, Caesar was indeed a little wide-eyed, like he didn't know what mood to expect next. After staring at him dumbly, Caesar resumed rushing around the room, gathering his things.

"Forget it," Nathaniel said. "We're staying another night."

"Oh." Caesar opened his mouth, no doubt about to ask what was wrong, before he thought better and snapped his jaw shut.

Nathaniel felt a twinge of guilt. "Later," he said. "I need to get things straight in my head. Then we can talk."

Caesar nodded, occupying himself with unpacking. Nathaniel watched him work, wondering how he would explain a situation he barely understood. And couldn't. Not completely. Not until he had the missing puzzle pieces.

They tried to pass the evening as if nothing had happened. With Caesar there, neither Nathaniel nor his grandparents felt comfortable discussing the topic openly. Probably for the best, since all Nathaniel had were questions, and all they had were secrets. Perhaps in an effort to cheer him up, they ordered a cheesy comedy from pay-per-view, but the movie failed to provoke an ounce of amusement in him.

Afterwards, his grandmother changed tactics, putting on old home videos instead. These were indisputable proof that Nathaniel had been a happy, giggling child, smashing his hands gleefully through his first birthday cake or looking pensive as he rode a pony, his father walking beside him to make sure he remained securely in the saddle. His father. Not Victor. And when the ride came to an end and little Nathaniel was lifted off the pony, his arms wrapped instinctively around that man's neck. As a child, he'd had no doubt. Only one man was his father, and back then Heath had still been perfect. Or had seemed so to him.

As the home videos continued, he began to view them with suspicion. What else in this picture-perfect world was false? What other secrets did the colorful birthday banners or sunny days at the beach conspire to hide? Then he started searching the background of each scene, almost expecting to see a guy with a mohawk casually leaning against a tree, watching his son from a distance. But Victor wasn't anywhere to be found.

When the evening ended, Nathaniel hugged his grandmother good night, pretending not to hear her ask if he was feeling better. Then he made a detour to the kitchen, finding the photo on the table. He took it and went to meet Caesar in the bedroom.

Nathaniel quietly closed the door behind him. Caesar was sitting on the edge of the bed, pajama bottoms already on as he worked at getting his head through a change of shirt. Nathaniel stared at the bare skin until it was covered by cotton. Then he moved to sit next to him.

"You were right," he said, handing over the photo.

Caesar looked at the image before raising his head to search his eyes. He was a smart guy, enough that Nathaniel knew he wouldn't need to explain. The emotional outburst earlier, the evening's entertainment, all slotted into place nicely with this piece of information. The only thing Caesar didn't know was a question Nathaniel also struggled to answer.

"I feel like I should say I'm sorry, but... Is this good news or bad?"

"I don't know," Nathaniel said. "I guess that depends on what he's like. Maybe he won't want to see me, or maybe he's a creep. It's pretty damn ironic either way. I brought you here to show you who I am, only to find out that I don't actually know."

"That's not true," Caesar said, handing back the photo. "You know who Carrie is?"

The Asian girl, the oldest kid in the Hubbard household.

"She's my sister," Caesar continued. His expression welcomed challenge. When it didn't come, he explained. "We're not blood. She doesn't know who her biological parents are, but she has a mom and a dad, and she definitely has a brother. Anyone who says otherwise is asking for this."

Nathaniel tried not to laugh when Caesar held up a fist. He failed. "But what if her real parents—sorry, her biological parents—showed up one day?"

"So what?" Caesar said. "It wouldn't change who she's been this whole time. She hasn't been living a lie or pretending to have a family. That's not how it works. Your parents should have been honest with you, but they're still your family."

"I'm not sure I want them to be," Nathaniel said. "That's the difference between Carrie and me."

"I guess so." Caesar nodded at the photo. "Are you going to see him?"

"Yeah. I don't know where he is, and nobody wants to tell me, but I'll track him down."

"I'll help you," Caesar said. "If you still want me to."

"Of course!" Nathaniel said. "Why wouldn't I?"

"Because earlier... I don't know."

Earlier. The kiss now seemed a million miles away. Nathaniel had been so preoccupied with what he had learned that he'd nearly forgotten. Now it all came rushing back, not that it mattered because the Hubbards still expected better of him and Steph— Oh shit!

"You broke up with her."

Caesar flopped back on the bed with a sigh. "Yeah."

"Why?"

"We've been arguing a lot lately, and both of us have said we'd be better off as friends. She still cried, which makes me feel like crap, but I wanted to do the right thing."

Nathaniel scowled. "Because of the kiss? It was a one-time thing. I wouldn't have told her."

Caesar was quiet. When he spoke again, his voice sounded vulnerable. "What's the bigger betrayal in your mind, kissing someone else or having feelings for them?"

"I wouldn't have told her about that either."

"Her not knowing doesn't make it okay!"

"So what are you going to do, never date again just because you have feelings for me?" Nathaniel exhaled. "We can't be together. It's not just Steph. If your parents found out—"

"I won't tell them."

"Not knowing doesn't make it okay." Nathaniel glanced back to find Caesar grinning, like he'd already solved the problem. "I'm serious."

Caesar studied him. "So am I."

Nathaniel had lost so much tonight: a brother, a father, maybe even a part of his own identity. That he might gain something new, something he had long desired... the temptation was too great. Still, he had to try to do the right thing. Just once more.

"I'm tired. It's time for bed."

He rose to switch off the light, but turned around before doing so. Caesar was settling beneath the covers, his back to the room. Nathaniel didn't blame him. The poor guy had dumped his girlfriend, only to be rejected after a very misleading kiss. As Nathaniel got undressed in the dark and slipped between the sheets, he realized he couldn't have made a bigger mess of things. Anything he could have done wrong, he had. Except that wasn't quite true. Not yet. His final mistake would be falling asleep and waking up again to find their potential swallowed up by the morning chill.

He reached out, the tips of his fingers touching warm cotton. Caesar breathed in sharply and went still. Nathaniel froze too, but not for long. Touching him felt good. His fingertips traced an abstract shape across Caesar's back, summoning a sigh. Nathaniel pressed his palm against him, slowly moving it up and down, delighting in the friction that was pulling the fabric upward. He reached down for the hem, Caesar quickly helping to remove the shirt before lying back down. Nathaniel touched his back again, this time feeling warm skin. He caressed the boney shoulder blades, then let his fingers crest the side of his torso to the ribs. Caesar captured his hand, tugging on his arm so that Nathaniel was forced to scoot closer.

Their bodies made contact piece by piece. Nathaniel's knee bumped the back of Caesar's thigh before nestling into the nook of his leg. Toes touched ankle before sliding beneath Caesar's foot. His arm flexed as Caesar's back made contact with his chest, drawing them even closer together. This only left one area, which he was purposefully holding back. Caesar had other ideas, pressing his rump against Nathaniel's crotch and squirming a little, just to make a point.

That was pretty damn exciting, but Nathaniel's attention was on Caesar's ear, which he delicately nibbled. Caesar's face turned to meet his, eyes shining. He looked so happy! Nathaniel stared, astonished that he could make anyone feel that way. Then he realized he could make them both feel a lot happier by leaning forward. Their lips met, Caesar smiling briefly in the middle of their kiss. He scooted away, but only to roll over so they were facing each other.

"This isn't a one-time thing," he said. "Promise me."

"It might not be a thing at all," Nathaniel said. "Not if you keep talking."

"I like talking," Caesar said mischievously.

"Really? Then give me something to work with." Nathaniel managed to sound cocky, when in reality, he was the inexperienced one. He knew from previous conversations that neither of them had really been with a guy, but Caesar had been with a few girls, one of them a regular partner. Nathaniel had no idea how he was expected to compete with that.

"Roll over onto your back," Caesar said.

Nathaniel did as he was told, sucking in air when Caesar's hand slid over his pecs before moving south. The tips of Caesar's fingers snuck beneath the band of his boxers and found his cock, gripping it tightly. Nathaniel supposed that was one arena where Steph couldn't measure up.

"Nice," Caesar hissed in appreciation, pumping his hand up and down. "You like how that feels?"

Nathaniel answered by grabbing Caesar beneath the pits and yanking him over so he was lying on top. Then he reached for the waist of his pajama bottoms and shoved them down enough for something hard to thwack against his thigh. As Nathaniel gripped this and stroked it, a memory flashed of that final day with his former friend. At least this was familiar territory.

"That's it," Caesar said, voice husky like he was auditioning for a porn movie. "Tug on my dick."

Nathaniel stopped what he was doing. "You talk too much, you know that?"

"Steph liked it."

"Probably because she didn't have a convenient way of shutting you up."

"Such as?"

Nathaniel put a hand on top of Caesar's head and pushed downward, but he didn't really need to. They both wanted the same thing. Caesar gleefully scurried beneath the covers and farther down the mattress. Nathaniel braced himself, wondering if the reality could possibly feel as good as his fantasies.

It was better. Even the way Caesar kept nicking him with his teeth summoned pleasure. Part of Nathaniel was eager to return the favor. The rest of him was caught up in selfish bliss. He remained on his back, trying to moan quietly, the spell broken when Caesar stopped suddenly and threw back the covers.

"Hey. Are you uncut?"

Nathaniel glanced down. "Yeah. So?"

"Can we turn on the light? I want to see."

Nathaniel rolled his eyes, reaching down to pull Caesar up to his level. He kissed him before another conversation could start. Then he flipped Caesar onto his back, making the same journey south. He noticed first the musky smell, which made his cock flex in anticipation. He felt wiry pubic hair on his cheek as he grabbed Caesar's searing hot cock. Then he took it in his mouth to help cool it down.

He gagged a few times before he got the hang of it, listening intently to Caesar's breathing, taking it as a good sign when he started to moan. Then Caesar started talking again, making requests, asking Nathaniel to return so they could swap. His pleas were ignored, Nathaniel focusing on the task at hand. He had fantasized about this for so long and felt like he could never do it enough to make up for all those years of wanting. Eventually Caesar stopped talking and started whimpering. Nathaniel bobbed his head up and down faster and was rewarded with hot spurts of liquid in his mouth. He wasn't sure if he'd like it, and admittedly it was a little weird, but being drunk on hormones made it easy to swallow.

Caesar pushed him away when he tried to keep going, so Nathaniel crawled back up to his level, rubbing himself against Caesar's hip to express his need.

"Don't worry," Caesar said. "I'll take care of you. I promise. But first…" He swung out of bed. A moment later, the lights flicked on.

Nathaniel growled in protest, blinking. "What are you doing?"

"I told you. I want to see."

Caesar returned to bed, pulled back the covers, and hopped in. He leaned across Nathaniel's waist, propping himself up with one elbow. This gave him perfect access to Nathaniel's cock, which he took hold of gingerly. Nathaniel glanced down to see him rolling the foreskin up over the head before tugging gently on the loose skin.

"Wow! This is so cool!"

"It's not a toy," Nathaniel complained.

"I beg to differ. Does this feel good?" Caesar ran his tongue around the ring of skin, causing him to moan. "What else do you like?"

"I don't care," Nathaniel said, his head flopping back on the pillow. "Do whatever you want. Just don't stop."

Caesar kept playing, trying out different techniques, all of which felt good. When Nathaniel whispered a warning that he was getting close, Caesar replied with "Yeah. Do it!"

Nathaniel did, his hips bucking. Caesar didn't swallow, choosing instead to watch the show. From the impressed noises he made followed by a happy laugh, he wasn't disappointed.

"We're going to need a towel," he said. "Maybe two."

"Just get up here," Nathaniel replied.

"Seriously. This is really—"

"Now."

Caesar obeyed, Nathaniel grabbing him tight.

"Ew! We're going to get glued together."

"I don't care," Nathaniel said. "You know why?"

Caesar stopped resisting and relaxed into his arms. "Why?"

"Because you're right. This isn't a one-time thing."

"Promise?"

"Yeah," Nathaniel said with a squeeze. "I promise."

Chapter Seven

The drive back to Texas was more relaxed than Nathaniel had imagined it would be. Sure, he was still racing toward home in the hope of learning the truth, but now he had a boyfriend at his side. One who went down on him somewhere in Oklahoma. Caesar had seemed so shy and repressed when Nathaniel had first met him. Then he had discovered a more confident side, a guy who liked to make his girlfriend laugh. And now… Nathaniel didn't have anyone to compare him to, but he sure seemed wild. Not that it mattered. He didn't focus on the sex much because best of all was how Caesar kept reaching over to take his hand during the drive, eyes shiny as he grinned.

As they passed through Dallas, Nathaniel decided they needed to talk. "We could tell your parents," he said, testing the waters. "We aren't doing anything illegal."

Caesar mulled this over. "I don't think they would let you keep living there, and right now I'm *really* liking the idea of you being around."

"Yeah, me too. We'll have to be careful. No messing around at the house."

Caesar snorted. "So anytime we want to do it, we'll have to find a bush somewhere? That doesn't sound safe."

"We just have to be smart. That's all I mean."

He wasn't so cautious when they reached Houston. He dropped off Caesar at the Hubbards' house before driving over to his former residence. He didn't worry about Dwight being home or running into his father. Heath. Nathaniel didn't concern himself about any of that. He simply hoped luck would be on his side. And it was. His mother met him in the entryway. As much anger that had pounded through his veins over the past twenty-four hours, he never felt he had lost her, which made accepting her hug easy.

"I'm sorry," she said. "I didn't want you to find out like this."

"I need answers." Nathaniel took a step back. "I want to know everything."

Star nodded. "Come to the kitchen with me. Are you hungry?"

"No," he lied. "I just want to talk."

His mother had been expecting him. Or maybe she needed to

revisit the past because a handful of Polaroids were spread out on the table, next to them a thick stack of photos. Star sat in front of these, Nathaniel looking over her shoulder until she scooted aside and patted one of the wooden chairs. Nathaniel took a seat, eyes not leaving the images. Most of them were of Victor and her.

"This was from our European trip," she said, tapping a photo of Victor sitting on the banks of a river, an open bottle of wine next to him. "Paris. He liked it there, but not nearly as much as he liked Dublin."

"Where was I?" Nathaniel asked. "Had I already been born?"

His mother nodded. "Your grandparents did a lot of babysitting back then. Mostly because I was still naïve enough to think—"

"Wait," Nathaniel said with a huff. "You were gallivanting around Europe with this guy and just left Granny and Gramps to raise me?" He snatched one of the photos. In it his mother stood with one hand on her hip, the other pointing a long baguette at the camera like it was a sword. She looked so young. "How old were you?"

"Fifteen."

He scrunched up his face. "And they let you go to Paris?"

"No. I was fifteen when I got pregnant. With you."

Nathaniel's anger ebbed. He felt… weird. Like he'd been a burden his entire life, an unhappy occurrence. An unwanted baby. He just never knew it before.

"I love you," his mother said, searching his face. "I wanted you! I never once thought about giving you up. I never considered… There was no alternative in my mind. The second I found out I was pregnant, I knew I would keep you. It wasn't easy at times, but I have no regrets."

"Then how come I'm not with you?" Nathaniel said, gesturing to the photos. He reached for the stack and started flipping through. Most were of Victor, his hair grown out and messy before a trim and gel returned definition to the mohawk. He only smiled in a handful of the pictures, his nose lightly sunburned. Others were of them together, Victor with an arm around his mother's neck as he threw a peace sign. But they remained a lonely duet. Nathaniel looked up and swallowed. "You wanted me. He didn't."

Star shook her head. "That's not true."

"Then why hasn't he been around? How come he never calls or sends a stupid Christmas present to make up for being such a shitty father?"

"Nate," his mother said, pleading with him.

"Tell me!"

"He didn't know."

Nathaniel stared. "What?"

"I was fifteen. He was thirteen." Star licked her lips nervously, then hurried to explain. "You have to understand, Victor wasn't like other people. He wasn't like anyone I had ever met before. Or since. He was an old soul, or seemed mature back then, because I thought he was my age when we first met. Victor was running with his cousin at the time. That's who introduced us. We used to be friends, I guess. We were so wild. Victor too, but he was thoughtful. Always thinking, always talking. Pretty soon he was all I cared about."

"Why didn't you tell him?" Nathaniel said, his throat tight.

"He was thirteen." Star exhaled. "Victor got into trouble for stealing a gun. Not a real one. Just an air pistol, but it was enough to scare his mother into taking action. She sent him to a military academy, and I found out shortly thereafter that you were on the way."

"He wasn't allowed to get mail?" Nathaniel said. "You couldn't write him a letter?"

"Victor had a lot of complicated philosophies."

"Meaning?"

Star hesitated. "He wasn't fond of the idea of relationships. Or commitment."

Nathaniel crossed his arms over his chest. "He sounds ridiculous."

"He wasn't." Star sighed wearily. "Or maybe he was. I thought I could change him, that I could slowly win him over and make him mine." She shook her head. "I was so stupid. So young and stupid."

Nathaniel studied her, clamping down on the sympathy that her sad expression summoned in him. Instead he focused on reading between the lines. "You didn't tell him about me because you thought it would scare him off."

"It would have terrified him," Star said. "I know, because I was freaking out myself. As much as I wanted you, I worried

I wouldn't be a good mother, that I wasn't ready, and that I wouldn't be able to take care of you. What help would a thirteen-year-old boy be? So I turned to my parents, and we made a plan. I went to stay with my aunt in Kansas City and— Jesus, I know how old-fashioned this sounds, but it wasn't like that. I needed my privacy, needed to get away from the prying eyes in that awful small town. So I had you, and when I returned to Warrensburg, I didn't feel the need to tell anyone where I had been. Or why."

"They must have seen."

"It's not like I took you to school with me." Star chewed her bottom lip. "I'm not proud of this, but when in public, we pretended you were my little brother."

Nathaniel's stomach turned. "Is that what you told him?"

"Yes. He was surprised, but your grandma was a lot younger then. It wasn't impossible, but we made sure to call you Nate."

"How come?"

Star's smile was sad. "Victor Nathaniel Hemingway."

Nathaniel felt raw inside. "You named me after him?"

"Yes."

"And he never noticed?"

"I don't think he ever knew your full name. At the time he was… distracted. Whatever happened to him in the military academy nearly broke him. It took a while before he found himself again, and when he did, he was even more aloof than before."

"Poor guy," Nathaniel said without sympathy. Then he reminded himself that he wasn't angry at Victor. How could he have been a good father when he was never given a chance? "Did he ever meet me?"

"Of course!" His mother reached for the photos he had been sifting through, finding one and handing it to him. Nathaniel was very small, just finding his feet, which is probably why his smiling mother held one of his hands. Victor held the other. In the photo, Nathaniel was looking up at him and wearing a slightly puzzled expression, as if he wasn't sure who this person was. Or why he seemed so familiar. As for Victor, his head was turned away from both of them, looking at something off camera.

"Is this the only one?" Nathaniel asked, swallowing against the lump in his throat.

"The only photo of you together?" Star asked. Then she nodded. "I think so."

"I want it."

"Okay."

"I also want his phone number and his address. You chose not to tell him about me back then, but now it's my decision. He needs to know that he's my father."

Star appeared strained. "Heath is your father."

"He's nothing to me!" Nathaniel snapped. "Him or his stupid son! I can almost forgive the decisions you made, but I can't forgive them." He thumped one of the photos of Victor. "I don't care what his issues are. I'd rather you stayed with him!"

"I was trying to give you a family. I wanted you to grow up with a father, but with Victor that wasn't possible. Heath wanted a family."

"Dwight knows all of this, doesn't he? That's why he hates me."

"He doesn't hate you. And no, aside from a few confusing memories, he has no idea. His mother was an addict. That's how she and Heath met. They were together a few years, but she always struggled with drugs. Eventually, she chose them over her own child. Heath wanted his son to have a mother just as much as I wanted a father for you. I know it must sound cruel or manipulative, but you were both young enough that we felt it wasn't too late. We were trying to do the right thing."

"Well you failed. I'd rather have been raised by Granny and Gramps than live the life you gave me." His mother appeared hurt and more than a little ashamed, which made him feel bad. His tone was gentler when he continued. "You should have left him the first time he hit you."

Star looked away. "I thought about it. I really did. But I didn't want to abandon Dwight. He was just a little boy. Besides, if I have one weakness, it's thinking I can change the men I love."

Nathaniel put a hand on her shoulder. "It's not too late. You don't have to stay with him. We'll get a place of our own. I'll get a full-time job. College can wait, or I'll do night classes. All that matters is us being together. And you being safe."

His mother took a deep, shuddering breath and dabbed at the corners of her eyes. "You're the only thing I ever did right. You know that?" Then she composed herself. "I made my choices.

Now I have to live with them. I won't screw up your life more than I already have."

"Fuck college," Nathaniel said. "Fuck everything else. You're all that matters to me."

"That's not true," his mother said. "I don't want it to be. I'll leave when I'm ready to leave. I'm stronger than you think."

Nathaniel considered it all from a distance, how scary it must feel to get pregnant at fifteen; how even at his age, he wouldn't be ready or capable of dealing with something like that. "I know you're strong," he said. "That's what makes it so hard to understand."

"Love rarely makes sense," his mother said. "You'll discover that for yourself."

He frowned and considered the photos, moving them around as if trying to solve a puzzle. "I want to see him," he said. "Maybe I won't tell him who I am. But I at least want to meet him face to face."

"I'm sorry," his mother said. "I really am."

He didn't understand what this meant until he saw the tears spill down her cheeks. Getting out the next two words made his throat ache. "What happened?"

"He's gone," Star said, shaking her head as if even she didn't want to believe it. "Victor died a long time ago."

"Suicide." The word felt acidic on his tongue, as if it would burn through his mouth, leaving him unable to speak again.

Caesar was wide-eyed, his expression uncertain as he stood up from his bed. Nathaniel could hardly blame him, since he too found all of this difficult to comprehend. He hadn't told Caesar everything. Just that Victor had taken his own life. The story was easier that way. Cleaner. The reason his real father wasn't around was because he was dead. He didn't need to know all the details about Heath. Nathaniel didn't want to focus on those. All he could think about was a man he had never met and never would. He didn't feel justified in mourning his passing. And yet he did.

"Why?" Caesar managed.

"Nobody knows. She thinks he had some sort of mental illness." He said this unwillingly, as if the words increased the possibility that he might suffer from the same problem. Then again, even the darkest moments of his life didn't stir such thoughts.

"Come here," Caesar said, offering his hand.

Nathaniel hesitated. A hug, or even a kiss, wouldn't make this better. He stepped forward anyway, certain this was a bad idea when Caesar reached for the hem of his shirt. "Now's not the time."

"I know," Caesar said. "I just want to feel close to you." He lifted Nathaniel's shirt tentatively, pulling it off completely when he didn't meet resistance. Then he did the same with his own, reaching next for the button of his shorts. Nathaniel didn't look, wasn't aroused as Caesar stripped down to his underwear. Instead he locked eyes with him, astounded that Caesar's were watery with sympathy. Nathaniel felt the need to cry but was unwilling. He removed his jeans. Caesar extended his hand again, and this time Nathaniel took it and was led around the bed. Caesar climbed in first, remaining on his knees so he could pull Nathaniel in after him.

Caesar kicked the covers down enough to slip under them, still pulling on Nathaniel, reluctant to release him. "Lay down," he whispered. "Turn around."

Nathaniel felt puzzled as he did so, stretching out on his side while facing the far side of the room. A moment later, Caesar slipped an arm around his chest, pulling him close. The body pressed against his was warm. Comforting. He leaned into Caesar and allowed himself to bask in the sensation. He felt the reassuring beat of another heart against his back, listened to the calming sound of breathing as Caesar's lungs filled and emptied.

"I'm sorry," he said.

Nathaniel wasn't. Not right now because all the pain he had been through, all the hard truths he had just learned, convinced him of one thing: He wouldn't make the same mistakes. Regardless of what it took, his time with Caesar wouldn't end badly. They wouldn't be separated, wouldn't lie to each other, no matter how good their intentions. Nathaniel would do everything in his power to see them through to their happy ending. He pulled on Caesar's arm to draw him even closer.

"I love you," Nathaniel said, not taking another breath until the answer came.

Caesar placed a kiss between his shoulder blades. "I love you too."

* * * * *

"I wish there was something I could do," Rebecca said.

"It's fine." Nathaniel met her gaze in the bathroom mirror. This was an awkward setting to have this conversation, but they had work to do in here.

"It's not fine," she said, calling his bluff. "I can see from your face that you're hurt. I wish I had a magic spell to bring him back to life for you. Or at least make it possible for you to speak to him."

"I think I'd rather forget the truth."

"*Obliviate*," Rebecca said, waving the hair clippers like they were a magic wand.

"Sorry," Nathaniel said. "Even J.K. Rowling can't fix this mess."

"He must have family. Have you tried tracking them down?"

"Sort of." Nathaniel turned around to face her and leaned against the counter. "I keep calling my mom with questions, and each time I do, I regret it. Victor's dad ran off when he was young and she doesn't know his name. Something ending in Hemingway, presumably."

"That was Victor's last name?"

He nodded.

"Nathaniel Hemingway. Sounds poetic."

"Sounds like somebody else, not me. Anyway, Victor was close to his mother. I found her on the Internet."

"You did?"

"Yeah. In an obituary from a few years back."

"Oh."

Nathaniel took a deep breath. "The only other family my mom knows of was his cousin. Last she heard, he went to prison for sexual assault. I haven't tried finding him. I'm not sure I want to talk to someone like that."

Rebecca grimaced. "I don't blame you."

"Yeah. That one stuck with me. Makes me wonder where exactly I come from. To be totally honest, I don't feel like I know who I am anymore."

Rebecca cocked her head. "You're the same person you were before you found out the truth."

"Am I? I have family I've never met. My real dad probably had a mental illness, and at least one member of his family is a criminal of the worst variety. What does that make me?"

"Remember my Aunt Teresa? The one with the huge collection of clowns? Clown paintings, clown plates, clown figurines, and that terrifying mannequin head that she bought a wig and makeup for to make it—come on, say it with me now."

"A clown," Nathaniel droned with a wry smile. "What's your point?"

"That I don't like clowns. She's family, but we have jack squat in common. Hell, neither of my parents like to read, which drives me bonkers. I don't know where I get that from, and I don't worry about it because they aren't my identity. I appreciate that they donated their genes to me, but I'm my own person."

Nathaniel frowned. Then he nodded. "Maybe you're right. I still wish I had some way of connecting with him, just to see what kind of man he really was."

"Which is why we're here." She held up the hair clippers. "You sure about this?"

"Yeah."

"A mohawk? Really?"

"Yes!"

Rebecca shrugged. "Take off your shirt."

"I bet you've been dying to say that."

She held up the clippers like they were a weapon, prompting him to hastily apologize, even though taking off his shirt really did seem to improve her mood. Then he sat on the toilet seat so she would have an easier time buzzing the sides of his head. He often kept his hair short, so he wasn't too worried about the procedure. The top was long enough that, once she trimmed it with scissors, he would have a decent strip of hair sticking up in the middle.

He was eager for her to finish, feeling like this really was some sort of spell, like Victor's ghostly image would appear in the mirror the second they were done.

"There you go," Rebecca said, setting aside the scissors and brushing the shorn hair off his shoulders.

He stood to consult the mirror. He looked doofy. Nothing about him was punky enough to compliment this style. His hair wasn't even the right color. His eyes darted to the photo resting on the counter—Victor holding his son's hand distractedly. Then he returned his attention to the mirror.

"You're definitely right. This isn't who I am. Shave it all off."

Rebecca nodded approvingly. She grabbed the clippers and waved them as if some magic had indeed been worked. Then she turned them on and gestured at the toilet.

"Your throne awaits!"

"What happened to your hair?" Caesar was sitting on the loveseat in his room. After staring a moment, he tossed aside the video game controller and stood. "It looked better before."

"You'll learn to like it." Nathaniel grunted. He grabbed Caesar's hand and rubbed the palm against the short bristles of his scalp. The goose bumps travelling down Caesar's arm were in plain sight. "You already like it."

"Okay, maybe I do." Caesar yanked away his hand and hurried to the bedroom door, which could only mean one thing.

"Don't," Nathaniel said. "Locking the door is too obvious. It isn't safe."

"It's a lot safer than my parents walking in on us," Caesar said. "Take off your clothes."

"Keep your voice down," Nathaniel hissed. "I'm serious. We need to be careful!"

Caesar appeared dejected. "Then how are we going to... You know."

"I've been thinking about that lately."

"Yeah, so have I!"

"Not like that." Nathaniel reconsidered. "Okay, like that too. But I've also been trying to figure out how we can do it without getting caught."

"I'm all ears," Caesar said.

Nathaniel nodded to the bulge in his pants. "You're all something. Remember what we did on the drive back down here?"

"Yeah. Fondly."

Nathaniel smirked. "Well..."

Caesar managed to focus. "That's not risky?"

"Not if we find a country road."

"This is Houston, not Warrensburg."

"Fine," Nathaniel said. "Maybe we should take up hiking. The Wilderness Park has lots of secluded trails. Right?"

"That it does," Caesar said. "So we can only do it outside from now on? You're making me feel trashy."

"Sorry."

"No, I like it!"

Nathaniel shook his head. "You're a bad influence on me. I used to worry the opposite was true, but of the two of us, I'm pretty sure you're the most depraved."

Caesar grinned shamelessly. "You have no idea."

As much fun as they had turning the great outdoors into their own sexual paradise, they both became more frustrated as the weeks rolled on. Caesar snuck into the shower with Nathaniel once, an especially dangerous move considering how bathroom time in the morning was strictly scheduled. Nathaniel had lectured him over that, but only after giving in. He broke his own rules a few nights later by creeping down the hall to Caesar's room. Neither of these events gave them much satisfaction, since they still rushed through the process, trying to remain silent all the while.

They both wanted more. Without freedom and security, they didn't feel comfortable exploring new possibilities, despite discussing them often. They craved more than just a hurried blow job in the woods. A hotel would be ideal, but neither of them was old enough to reserve a room. Nathaniel was having dinner with his mother one night, toying with the idea of asking her to get one for them, when she inadvertently provided a solution.

"Your father has a business trip in Quebec this weekend," Star said. "I'm going with him. Maybe I can escape this heat for a few days." When she saw his longing expression, she misinterpreted it. "Would you like to come with us? You haven't seen your father since—"

"No," Nathaniel said. "I was wishing I could have the house to myself. Well, not *completely* to myself."

Realization made his mother's eyes light up. "You mean Caesar? Hoping for a romantic getaway of your own?"

"Yeah."

"Well, why not?"

"You know why."

His mother leaned forward. "I told you that Dwight hasn't been home for weeks. He's really serious about this new girl. He's living with her now."

Nathaniel perked up. "Really?"

"Yes! Come home for the weekend." Her eyes pleaded with him. "Come home for good."

"Dwight's relationships never last."

"Then I'll tell him he needs to find his own place. He's too old to be mooching off us. Please. Just consider it. I miss you."

Nathaniel couldn't make any promises, but he looked forward to a trial run. His plan was simple. He asked permission to take Caesar camping, which Mr. Hubbard readily agreed to. On Friday night, Nathaniel went to the house to make preparations and to make sure it truly was safe. His mother hadn't deceived him. He saw no sign of Dwight.

The next morning, after sleeping in, they loaded up his car with a tent, sleeping bags, and even a cooler of food, just for appearances.

"It's sort of ironic," Caesar said. "We really could just go camping. That would give us plenty of privacy."

"But not a nice comfy bed," Nathaniel said. "Besides, as much as you like to talk, we'd probably attract every park ranger in the county."

"Communication is crucial to every relationship," Caesar said solemnly.

As if to prove his point, Caesar talked during the entire way to the house. He only quieted down once they pulled in the driveway. This probably felt like another revelation to him, finally getting to see Nathaniel's former home.

Nathaniel led the way to the front door, unlocking it and letting it swing open. He didn't enter yet. Not right away. Instead he swept Caesar off his feet—literally—and carried him over the threshold.

"Welcome home, Mrs. Courtney," he said. "We just got married. The reception was great, but we're both eager to escape the guests and start our honeymoon."

Caesar laughed. "What are you talking about?"

Nathaniel set him down. "This is your house now. Our house. For the weekend, anyway."

"We're playing house?"

"Yup."

Caesar grinned. "I like it."

"I hope so. Now go cook me dinner."

"You're living in the past," Caesar said, shaking his head.

"I might be the wife, but I'm also the breadwinner. I work long hours too, so you best be ready to rub my feet."

"Fine, I'll be the househusband. I already cleaned the place for you."

That wasn't entirely true, since his mother kept the place tidy. He *had* changed the sheets in his parents' bedroom and whipped up a pasta sauce that was a little salty, but he hoped a heaping helping of cheese would disguise that.

He followed Caesar as he explored the house, watching him soak up every detail. Family photos interested him the most, at least until they reached the master bedroom.

Caesar bounced onto the bed with a naughty smile. "Ready for round one?"

"I thought we'd spend the day together first. Let the anticipation build."

"And I thought we'd do it twelve times. At least."

"Have fun," Nathaniel said, walking out of the room.

Caesar followed, looking pouty, but he cheered up when they entered Nathaniel's old bedroom. Then he got hyper, examining everything, asking a million questions, and even opening drawers and the closet door without permission. Nathaniel considered telling him to stop, but was flattered to have someone so interested in his life. They spent a long time exploring the house, skipping only Dwight's room. Caesar insisted on peeking in the door, but that was it. Eventually they ended up in the backyard, where Caesar jumped on the normally ignored trampoline, even dragging Nathaniel onto it with him. A movie next, then an early dinner, since they had skipped lunch. Caesar started making bedroom eyes afterwards, but Nathaniel insisted they go for a walk, wanting to feel less stuffed.

"You're driving me crazy," Caesar said as they strolled. "Either take me to bed, or I'm locking myself in the bathroom. Just don't expect to have any lotion left when I come back out."

"Fine, you horndog. Just so you know, I had more romantic stuff planned."

"Ugh."

Nathaniel glanced over at him and saw the playful expression. They intended to make the most of their privacy, a prospect that made him nervous. This would be his first time. Caesar's too, in a way, but at least he had experience being the giver rather than the receiver. Nathaniel was completely out of his element. He felt like he should be the one guiding Caesar as he did in other matters. Browsing porn hadn't helped, since most movies followed a formula of rimming before shoving it in. A few forum posts had been a little more informative, if Nathaniel could trust them.

The walk was cut short when it started to rain, sending them running for the house.

"Again?" Nathaniel complained. "What did you do to piss off the gods of weather?"

"Just be glad we're not actually camping."

Once they were back inside the house, Caesar grabbed his hand. He was panting slightly, winded from their run, and this made him resemble an eager puppy, one that dragged him toward the bedroom.

Nathaniel felt like tugging in the opposite direction. "Should I light—"

"Nope!" Caesar said.

"Maybe we could—"

"Nuh-uh."

"Do you need—"

"I'm ready," Caesar said. "I'll probably only last two seconds because you've been making me wait, but it's going to be an awesome two seconds."

Nathaniel gave in. He wanted this too. He just needed it to be perfect for Caesar, who didn't seem to share these concerns, so Nathaniel left his worries at the bedroom door. He grabbed Caesar's shoulder and spun him around. A kiss, an embrace, then he lifted Caesar off his feet and hobbled forward to throw him on the bed.

"That's more like it!" Caesar said.

They began in their usual manner, using their mouths and hands to bring each other pleasure. After a frenzied beginning they slowed, intending to enjoy this rare seclusion. They brought each other to the brink multiple times, taking breaks in between to cool down. Then they would start again.

"I'm more than ready," Caesar said.

Nathaniel reached for the lube, squeezing a line out along his finger like mustard on a hotdog. Caesar made the same connection and laughed as he rolled onto his stomach. "All you're missing are some buns."

"I think you can help me with that." Nathaniel reached for Caesar's butt, letting his finger slide up and down the crack. Then he carefully slid a finger inside, looking to Caesar for feedback.

"It's fine," he breathed. "I've been practicing. By myself," he added when Nathaniel appeared concerned. "Try another. Two at the same time."

Nathaniel did, his cock twitching when Caesar started to moan. After lubing himself, he flopped forward on his hands. Caesar flipped over, hips rising to meet him, legs wrapping around his waist. One of his hands reached down to position Nathaniel's cock, the head rubbing against his hole. Then he nodded. Nathaniel pushed forward.

Caesar grimaced. "Okay," he wheezed. "Uh. Ow!"

"Should I—"

"Don't move! Actually..." Caesar shoved him away.

Nathaniel rolled over. "Not good?"

Caesar's face remained contorted with pain. "You're a little bigger than two fingers."

"Sorry."

"It's fine," Caesar said, but he was only half hard now. "Can we just lay here a minute?"

"Yeah. Of course."

What a disaster! Nathaniel flopped onto his back and silently chastised himself. If only he'd known better! There had to be some trick, or so many people wouldn't be doing it. But somehow he had managed to mess it up.

"Okay," Caesar said a while later. "Let's try it again."

Nathaniel shook his head. "We don't have to."

"I'm not a quitter," Caesar said.

"I don't think it's a good idea."

"I'll be the judge of that." Caesar sat up and swung a leg over Nathaniel's hip. Then he settled down. Nathaniel had gone limp, but Caesar kept grinding his rump against him and thwapping his stomach with his rock-hard cock. "Come on now. Giddy up cowboy!"

Nathaniel laughed, which helped him relax. All but one part of him, which stood at attention again. He let Caesar remain in control. After applying more lube, they both held their breath as Caesar lowered himself. The movement seemed to take an eternity, but this time when Nathaniel eased inside, Caesar didn't wince. He proceeded cautiously, moving a fraction of an inch each time before retreating again. Eventually the speed and depth of this motion increased, and their concentration turned to pleasure.

For once Caesar didn't have much to say. As Nathaniel reached forward to touch him, all he could do was gasp. "Same time," were the only words he managed.

"Just tell me when you're ready."

Caesar nodded. A few minutes later he took hold of himself and nodded emphatically. Nathaniel closed his eyes, his hands sliding over Caesar's hips, which he gripped. Overwhelmed by euphoria, he forgot to be careful, thrusting hard and fast. Caesar seemed okay with this though, since his every breath was a moan. When Nathaniel felt hot liquid shoot across his stomach, he knew he didn't have to hold back any longer. He groaned and grunted, pulling Caesar close as he snarled with release. He held on even as the piston slowed and slipped out. Caesar stayed trapped in his arms, his whole body shaking.

"You okay?"

"Yeah," Caesar said. "That was intense." After a few haggard breaths he added. "I want to do that to you."

Nathaniel raised his head. "What?"

"Next time," Caesar asked. "Why not? There aren't any rules."

"I guess," Nathaniel said. "I don't know if I can handle it."

"A big strong guy like you?"

"Maybe you're stronger," Nathaniel conceded. "In fact, I'm pretty sure you are."

"I don't think so." Caesar rolled off him, pushing himself up on his side. "Wanna hit the shower?"

"Not really. I feel clean enough."

"Probably because you don't have lube covering your ass. I feel like a glazed donut. Now come support me in the shower. I'm still shaky. Or do I need to file for divorce?"

"You're the boss," Nathaniel said. Funny thing was, he wasn't sure if he meant it jokingly or not.

A thud woke Nathaniel. This happened a lot in the movies, the actor lying flat on their back so they could sit upright in shock. He wished he could do the same. Instead he was on his side, face sticky with drool. He opened his eyes blearily, noticing that Caesar's half of the bed was empty. That would explain the noise. Caesar probably got up to use the bathroom and bumped into something. He started drifting off again when he heard the crash of shattered glass. Then voices. Plural.

He jolted awake. Nathaniel shoved out of bed with one syllable on his tongue. Dwight. Who else could it be? Caesar had probably heard him and gone to investigate. Nathaniel stooped to pull on his underwear, then rushed from the room, following the light to the kitchen. He noticed Dwight first, standing next to the counter, a bottle of vodka in one hand. On the ground was a shattered drinking glass and ice cubes. Closest to the door was Caesar, who faced Dwight and was in the middle of an explanation.

"—your brother's boyfriend. He knows I'm here. We can wake him up."

Dwight's scowl only increased when Nathaniel came into the room, placing himself between them. Already his chest heaved with adrenaline. Dwight's bloodshot eyes searched his, breath full of fumes when he spoke. "What are you doing here?"

"Mom said I could have the place for the weekend. And that nobody would be here."

"I'm here," Dwight said helpfully.

"I thought you were living with some girl."

"I dumped her, you little fuck." Dwight's tone was bitter. "Mind your own business."

Nathaniel eyed him. He hadn't seen his brother since learning they weren't related. Before he had felt handcuffed to a person who terrified him, unable to escape the bonds of family. Now that illusion had been lifted, and Nathaniel found himself apathetic. Almost. That wasn't quite accurate because he still wanted to get away from Dwight, but now that felt like a viable option. "Fine," he said. "We'll keep to ourselves. Just make sure to sweep up the glass."

Dwight didn't budge. "I told you what would happen if you returned."

Nathaniel sighed. "What's the point? You hate me. Fine. Before too long, I'll move away to college and you'll never see me again. You made my life hell while we were growing up, and last time we saw each other, I got back at you. What's the point in starting all of this again?"

Dwight strode forward, broken glass crunching beneath his

shoes. Then he cocked back his arm and popped Nathaniel in the face. He was drunk enough that his aim was clumsy. His fist hit Nathaniel's cheek before sliding off. The blow still hurt, but lacked the force to make his head whip back. Nathaniel winced. Then he repeated his words. "What's the point?"

Dwight lunged again. Nathaniel wasn't looking for a fight, but he wasn't going to take a beating. He dodged to one side, Dwight stumbling past him like an inebriated bull. Then he turned around, because of course Dwight was coming back for more, swinging at the air, his teeth bared. Nathaniel walked backward at an angle, avoiding where the glass was, until he felt himself bump up against the kitchen counter. No choice remained. He'd either have to fight or—

Caesar leapt onto Dwight's back, wrapping one arm around his neck and both legs around his torso. Dwight was built, but he wasn't particularly tall. Or sober. The added weight had him teetering, arms jerking in a hopeless attempt to elbow Caesar off. Then he lost his balance completely and fell on his back, Caesar taking the impact. Nathaniel winced in sympathy, but his boyfriend rallied quickly. In fact, he seemed more in his element than ever, rolling them both onto their sides and using his free arm to add pressure to the chokehold around Dwight's neck. Caesar kept squeezing with his legs, effectively trapping his prey. This was wrestling! The real deal! Or more like one pro and one amateur, because at the moment Dwight was nothing more than a spitting, frothing victim. Then he stopped moving completely, his body going limp.

Caesar released him, catching his breath before smiling.

"Thanks," Nathaniel said. "Uh… Is he dead?"

"He's fine," Caesar said, rolling Dwight onto his back. Then he tapped him a few times, as if to rouse him. Dwight didn't move. Caesar froze, a hand pressed against Dwight's chest. Then he relaxed. "He's breathing. I guess he's not waking up because he's drunk."

Nathaniel stared in fascination, not used to seeing Dwight so vulnerable. They could do anything they wanted to him, make sure he was never again a threat, but those thoughts were too dark to entertain seriously. Nathaniel shook his head to clear it. "If he's going to be all right, we should go."

Caesar stood. "What about tomorrow?"

Nathaniel nodded to the ground. "What about him?"

"He can find somewhere else to stay," Caesar said, approaching with a seductive expression. "I'm looking forward to—"

Whatever else he planned to say was lost in a gasp. Caesar's eyes went wide, as did his mouth. Then he started hopping. The broken glass!

"Shit!" Nathaniel moved to help him. Then he forced himself to be cautious. Most of the mess was off to one side, but he knew how a dropped glass could scatter shards everywhere. He chose his steps carefully. When he reached Caesar, he offered support, moving them toward the kitchen door, away from the glass. And Dwight.

"Help me onto the floor," Caesar said. Once he was sitting, he grabbed his ankle and pulled his foot close so he could examine it.

Nathaniel did the same, leaning over so he could see. Blood oozed from around something hard and transparent. "That looks bad."

"Yeah," Caesar agreed. "Got a first-aid kit?"

Nathaniel hurried to the master bathroom, opening the cabinet beneath the sink and shoving aside cleaning chemicals and rolls of toilet paper to find a small white box. It was nowhere near as fancy as Caesar's, but he hoped it would be enough. He returned to the kitchen, eying Dwight to make sure he hadn't moved before handing the kit to Caesar. "Do your stuff."

He remained on edge, watching Caesar use a pair of plastic tweezers to remove a fat glass shard from his foot, wincing with him in sympathy. Caesar examined the wound, murmuring words that sounded unhappy. Then he wrapped his foot with gauze, the cotton turning red.

"I'm pretty sure I need stitches."

A trip to the hospital. He knew where that would lead. "You can't just hold it shut while I put a Band-Aid on it?"

Caesar's expression was incredulous. "No!"

"Okay," Nathaniel said. "Do we have time to put on clothes?"

Caesar laughed. "Yeah. I'm not showing up at the emergency room in my underwear."

The emergency room. Fuck. Nathaniel got dressed, then brought clothes to Caesar and helped him do the same. All the while he grappled with a decision. On the drive to the hospital, he navigated wet roads distractedly and reached the only reasonable conclusion: This wasn't a secret to be shoved to the far corner of his mind and forgotten. Flipping the switch wouldn't help. As soon as Caesar was seated and puzzling over clipboard paperwork, Nathaniel pulled out his phone.

"What are you doing?" Caesar asked.

"Calling your dad."

"Wait! Why?"

"It'll show up on the insurance. Besides, he has a right to—"

The phone clicked. Then Nathaniel took a deep breath and told Mr. Hubbard where they were and what had happened. Sort of. He explained that Caesar had stepped on glass, but not the circumstances leading up to it. Mr. Hubbard didn't stay on the phone to ask for details. Instead he said he was on his way and hung up, eager to join them.

"Cover story?" Caesar asked when the phone call had ended.

"People can step on glass just about anywhere," Nathaniel said.

"I left my tent to take a piss in the middle of the night. That's why I was barefoot. While looking for somewhere private… The rest is obvious, right? Give a hoot—don't pollute."

Nathaniel nodded. "Yeah. Okay."

He felt guilty about lying to the Hubbards. Doubly so for failing to keep Caesar safe. Both Mr. and Mrs. Hubbard arrived just as Caesar was being called to an examination room. The nurse had put him in a wheelchair so he wouldn't have to walk. This only made the scene more dramatic. Mrs. Hubbard was distraught as she accompanied her son. Mr. Hubbard stayed behind. As did Nathaniel.

"I'm sorry," he said.

"It was out of your control," Mr. Hubbard said, settling into one of the plastic seats. Nathaniel sat at his left, but soon wished he had chosen the other side, because Mr. Hubbard was looking at him. Carefully. "You weren't camping when this happened."

Nathaniel raised a hand to his face, feeling tender skin where Dwight's fist had grazed him. He could tell by touch alone that there was swelling.

"I understand," Mr. Hubbard said.

"You do?" Nathaniel responded.

"Yes. Once it started raining, camping lost its appeal. That tent leaks. I meant to replace it after our last trip. I'm surprised you decided to stay at your parents' house though."

"They're out of town," Nathaniel admitted.

Mr. Hubbard exhaled. "And returning to our place would have felt like marching home after a humiliating defeat. I can't blame you for wanting to prolong the adventure."

Nathaniel swallowed, the taste unpleasant. Mr. Hubbard put far too much faith in him, none of it deserved. "I'm sorry."

"I feel sorry for you. One night back in your own home and this happens? Your brother, I presume?"

"Yeah."

"Care to share the details with me?"

"Do I have to?"

Mr. Hubbard frowned. "I've tried to respect your privacy, but now it involves my son. I won't turn a blind eye this time."

Nathaniel told him the truth, leaving out that they had been sleeping in the same bed. The rest was innocent enough, for such a damning situation.

"I'd like to talk with your parents," Mr. Hubbard said, his face flushed and features tense. "Not just your mother this time. Your father too."

"He's not my father," Nathaniel murmured.

"I agree with you," Mr. Hubbard said. "And not just because of what you told me. That you're not his biological child doesn't matter. He failed to provide you with a safe environment, he set a bad example, and he is oblivious or willfully ignorant to what happens in his household. That's no way to raise a child!"

"I wish you were my father." The words came quickly, Nathaniel feeling their meaning so strongly that he had to rein back on his emotions.

"That's not impossible," Mr. Hubbard said, his voice calmer now. "You're practically a grown man, but everyone should have a safe haven, a family who will love and protect them. Right now we're both agitated, but if things don't improve for you... Well, we can talk about it."

Nathaniel didn't know how to respond. Mr. Hubbard didn't seem to need words. He patted Nathaniel on the back. Then they waited together in silence. Conversation would have been preferable, because when left to think, Nathaniel soon lost that warm feeling. Adoption wasn't a viable solution. Nathaniel still loved his mother, and as much as he wished Mr. Hubbard was his father, that wouldn't work for one very good reason: Caesar. He couldn't be his brother, and any love the Hubbards felt for him would dissipate if they were caught. Wouldn't it? He looked at the man seated next to him, who had been amazingly generous so far, and wondered if his kindness could survive learning the truth.

The lawnmower rumbled, the vibrations coursing along Nathaniel's arms. He freed one to wipe the sweat from his brow, glancing up at a perfectly blue sky and wishing for one small cloud to block the sun so he could cool off. After crossing the yard back and forth a few more times he stopped, let the engine sputter into silence, and stripped off his shirt.

"Now we're talking!"

Nathaniel spun around to see Caesar approaching from the house. He reached out a finger, like someone wanting to swipe frosting from a beater to taste it. Or sweat from a bare chest. Nathaniel knocked his hand away, shooting a glance toward the house.

Caesar rolled his eyes. "Nobody's home. They're still out shopping. Let's go."

"Go where?" Nathaniel asked.

"Anywhere you want!" Caesar said with a lewd grin. "Pick a room."

"We talked about this," Nathaniel said with a shake of his head. "No more risks."

"Awww, come on! It's been weeks!"

Nathaniel raised an eyebrow. "More like four days. I woke up in the middle of the night to find you sucking my—"

"That doesn't count."

"Sure felt like it counted to me! And it went against the rules."

"Oh, the rules!" Caesar said, waving his hands sarcastically. "Scary! I meant it's been weeks since… You know."

Since their pseudo-honeymoon. Nathaniel looked at the house again, feeling a longing before he steeled his resolve. He tossed his sweaty shirt at Caesar, then yanked the ripcord to start the mower again, steadfastly ignoring his boyfriend. Even when he stood in the way, Nathaniel plowed on, forcing Caesar to leap aside. When the grass was thoroughly tamed and the air free from the engine's growl, Caesar wasted no time in continuing his plea.

"Just think how good it'll feel. How good it felt the first time."

Nathaniel worked on removing the canvas bag full of clippings. "Why don't you go think about it in the bathroom. By yourself."

Caesar sighed. "I've done plenty of that lately, believe me. Besides, I wanted to return the favor."

Nathaniel glanced up sharply. "Uh. No."

"Uh. Yes. It's only fair."

"That's not how this works. There are roles."

Caesar shook his head. "No there aren't."

Nathaniel furrowed his brow in confusion. "I thought you liked it."

"I did, but that's like visiting London, loving it there, and never going anywhere else. I want to try new things. Visit new places. Paris. Moscow. Vienna." Caesar grinned. "Bangkok."

Nathaniel considered him carefully. "You need more from me. Something fresh."

Caesar shrugged. "Yeah. Exactly."

"Fine." Nathaniel thrust his hand into the bag of grass, grabbed a fist full, and pulled it out again.

"Not that kind of fresh!" Caesar said, taking a step back.

Before he could escape, Nathaniel flung the clippings at him, picturing the grass swirling around his head like confetti. Instead the clump hit him square in the face with a wet smack, spreading across his nose before falling to the ground. "Sorry!" Nathaniel said hurriedly. "I thought—"

"You're sorry?" Caesar said incredulously. "Like that was an accident?"

He came closer, so Nathaniel grabbed another fistful of grass in self-defense. Caesar, with nothing to lose, lunged for the canvas bag to arm himself. Nathaniel pelted him with another clump, this time hitting his shoulder, but Caesar wouldn't be dissuaded. He thrust both hands into the grass clippings, pulling out two huge bundles.

"Oh, come on!" Nathaniel pleaded. "That's too much!"

"An eye for an eye," Caesar said.

"But I'm all sweaty and—"

Nathaniel didn't need to continue. Grass splattered against his chest and stuck there. He tried wiping it off, but that only spread it around. He looked up, ready to complain, when the next batch hit him in the face. For a moment, all he could see was green. Once he wiped his eyes clean, all he could see was red. He grabbed the entire bag of grass, hoisting it into the air. Then he moved forward.

"No!" Caesar said, hands raised to ward him off. "We're done!"

"We're not done," Nathaniel snarled. "Not by far. After I dump this over your head, I'm going next door and mowing the neighbor's lawn for more."

Caesar took off running, Nathaniel giving chase. They zigzagged across the yard, much of the grass spilling out on the way, but Nathaniel still had enough to get revenge. Caesar stumbled and fell, rolling onto his back, eyes wide with terror when he found Nathaniel standing over him. "I'll do anything!"

Nathaniel's grin was vicious. "Anything?"

"I swear!"

"So the next time we're alone. *Really* alone. Who's going to be on top?"

"You," Caesar said instantly.

Nathaniel tilted the bag slightly, a few blades spilling out. "I have your word?"

"Yes!"

Satisfied, he tossed aside the bag and offered his hand. Caesar allowed himself to be pulled to his feet.

"You'll be on top," Caesar said. Then with a wicked gleam he added, "Bouncing up and down on my cock."

Nathaniel shook his head. "You're hopeless."

"I know." Caesar came close, reducing the space between them.

"I'm disgusting," Nathaniel said, pulling back.

"I don't care. I love you."

Nathaniel kept his eyes locked with Caesar's as they wrapped their arms around each other. "Say it again."

"I love you." Caesar said this with his head held high, proud of the fact.

Nathaniel swallowed. "If you ever want to get me in the mood, that's all you've got to do. Just keep saying those words."

"I love you, I love you, I love you."

"I don't mean now!" Nathaniel said with a laugh.

Caesar's eyes were pleading. "Then when? Give me something to look forward to."

Nathaniel leaned forward and kissed him. "Soon. I promise."

Caesar squeezed him tight. Then he hopped up and wrapped his legs around Nathaniel's waist. Nathaniel stumbled forward, but regained his balance. He spun around a few times, then lurched around the yard like a drunk. After one more kiss he fell to his knees and bent forward, lowering Caesar to the ground.

"Let's go get clean."

Caesar nodded. "Okay."

"Let me finish up here. I'll meet you inside."

Nathaniel took the bag and patrolled the yard, scooping up some of the bigger piles of grass. Then he put away the mower in the garage. A car was parked there. Nathaniel flinched from it, as if confronted by a bear, but it was only Mrs. Hubbard's minivan. How long had she been home? His stomach felt queasy as he put on his shirt, closed the garage door, then went to investigate.

The garage led directly to the kitchen. The groceries had been brought in, the counters covered in loaded bags. The kids had already disappeared upstairs, leaving Mrs. Hubbard unpacking food in the kitchen. Caesar was helping. Had they been seen?

Caesar, as if hearing this unspoken question, made sure he wasn't being watched before shooting Nathaniel an uncertain expression. Mrs. Hubbard continued to place cans and jars in the pantry. Was she a little too focused? Nathaniel rinsed his hands in the sink, and despite feeling too grubby to do so, pitched in.

"That's great," Mrs. Hubbard said, noticing him. "Caesar, why don't you go upstairs and get freshened up?"

Caesar hovered a moment before doing what he was told. Once they were alone, Nathaniel braced himself for confrontation. Or at least a probing question.

"No, don't put the bread in the refrigerator," Mrs. Hubbard said. "Does your mother do that?"

"Yeah. She says it makes it last longer."

"How interesting. I've always preferred a bread box."

Okay. Not exactly the conversation he would expect from someone who had just seen her son kissing another man. Nathaniel relaxed a little. They made small talk, all of it

Jay Bell

innocuous. Another close call. Another lesson learned. Once the groceries were put away, Nathaniel expressed his intent to go take a shower.

"Do you know how to peel potatoes?" Mrs. Hubbard asked.

"No," he admitted.

"I'll show you. Wash your hands. With soap this time."

Some of the tension returned to his shoulders and neck. Was she trying to keep him and Caesar apart? After Mrs. Hubbard demonstrated how the job was done, Nathaniel stood at the sink and peeled potatoes. When Caesar came back with damp hair and clean clothes, Mrs. Hubbard took the paring knife from Nathaniel. "Thank you. Why don't you hop in the shower now? Caesar can take over."

"Okay."

He trudged upstairs, trying to make sense of the situation. Maybe she was simply being practical, knowing that simultaneous showers would cause the water temperature to fluctuate uncomfortably. If so, that was very considerate of her. Or maybe she really was trying to keep them separate.

After his shower, Nathaniel dressed in his room, then had an idea. He grabbed his cell phone and sent a quick text to Caesar. *what do you think?*

A minute later the response came. *I don't know. All clear?*

He thought about it and nodded to himself. Surely she would have said something to one of them by now. Mr. Hubbard was out of town, so she wasn't waiting for him to get home.

all clear, he texted back. *we'll be fine.*

He pocketed his phone and headed downstairs. He didn't join Caesar, who was watching music videos with Carrie. Deciding to play it safe, Nathaniel sat at the dining room table and worked on homework. When Mrs. Hubbard came in to set the table, he moved aside his books and helped her. At dinner, the mood at the table wasn't tense. Mrs. Hubbard wasn't talkative, but she often wasn't. Nathaniel tried to get everyone conversing, which didn't take much effort. Especially with Peter, who loved talking about himself.

After dinner, Nathaniel remained in plain sight, proving he had nothing to hide. When everyone else had gone upstairs, he remained on the couch, flipping through channels. He was considering going to bed when Mrs. Hubbard marched into the

living room and approached the couch, carrying a duffel bag
that she dropped to the floor. Then she tossed his car keys on
the side table.

"You're leaving," she said. "There's enough in there to see
you through the day tomorrow. After school, you can come back
for the rest. I'll be the only one here. I'll even pack your things
for you, but if I ever find out you've been talking to my son—to
any of my children—I *will* call the police."

Nathaniel worked his jaw, trying to find a way out. "I don't
know what you're talking about."

"You know damn well what I'm talking about!" Mrs.
Hubbard hissed, keeping her voice down. "Don't you try to deny
it, because I saw more than enough with my own eyes!"

"You don't understand," Nathaniel said. "We love each
other."

She responded with the words that he'd been dreading. "We
trusted you! We took you in to protect you! This is how you
repay us?"

Shame mixed with panic, making it hard to think. "I didn't—
We both— Caesar and I—" He couldn't find the right words to
express what they felt for each other, how they were happier and
stronger now, but only when they were together. If she took this
away it would damage them both. She couldn't want that. For
him maybe, but not her own son. "Please," he managed.

Mrs. Hubbard's features remained hard. He'd never reach
her. Nathaniel would talk to Mr. Hubbard instead, insist on
calling him immediately, because he would be on Nathaniel's
side. And if not? All those proud words, the supportive grip on
his shoulder, would withdraw. Mr. Hubbard wouldn't want to be
his father any longer. The idea would revolt him. That rejection
would hurt just as much. "Don't tell your husband."

Mrs. Hubbard's eyes widened at this request. Then her
expression became severe. "Leave now, and maybe I won't need
to."

Nathaniel felt unstable as he stood. Once he'd picked up the
duffel bag and keys, he nearly ran, as if fleeing the scene of a
crime. He tried to remain calm, to remind himself that everything
was okay. They were close enough in age to be legal, and their
love was a good thing, even if Mrs. Hubbard didn't see it that
way. She followed him to the door and shut it behind him, not

slamming it, but he did hear the locks click. He glanced down at his keys and wasn't surprised to find one missing. Then he went to his car, drove half a block, and pulled over. With shaking hands he reached for his phone, needing to contact Caesar, to tell him what had happened. That's when he saw the last text message he'd sent earlier in the evening, mocking and unbelievably naïve.

we'll be fine.

Nathaniel shook his head and tossed the phone into the passenger seat. He stared at it for a moment, then at the place he had briefly called home, before driving away.

Chapter Eight

"You've got to be kidding me."

Nathaniel spun around, and not for the first time. He'd been doing so continuously, searching the confusing halls of a school that wasn't his, all for one person. And now a familiar face had found him instead, but this wasn't good news.

"Don't tell me," Steph continued. "You enrolled here just to be closer to him."

Nathaniel nearly snapped at her, but he was tired. Last night he had driven around aimlessly before ending up at Rebecca's house. She had snuck him into her room and listened patiently as he explained and agonized over what had happened. Around three in the morning he finally took pity on her and suggested they go to bed. She might have managed to sleep, but Nathaniel had laid there motionless, stewing over everything in his mind, trying to find a solution. "I need to talk to Caesar."

Steph made a face. "Can't it wait until you're both home again?"

"I don't live there anymore," Nathaniel said, his voice hoarse. "And not by choice."

"His parents found out?"

Nathaniel nodded. The bell rang, the crowds in the hall dispersing. Soon no students would be left at all, and someone in authority would notice him.

Steph hugged her books closer to her chest, seemingly unbothered by class having begun. "He's gay, isn't he? When we broke up, he said he was bi, but if that were true... I thought he loved me."

"He does," Nathaniel said with a resigned sigh. Getting kicked out of the school seemed inevitable now. "He never stopped talking about you."

"Then why—"

"I don't know. Because I'm a guy and he had never been with one before? I'm sorry about what happened. It sucks that you got hurt."

He was turning away when Steph spoke again. "He has a wrestling meet tonight. Half an hour after school. In the gym."

Nathaniel wanted to thank her, but a teacher was approaching, informing them in chastising tones that the bell had rung. Steph disappeared into a nearby classroom. Nathaniel hurried down the hall toward the nearest exit. Once safely in his car, he checked his phone again. Nothing. Nathaniel had texted Caesar first thing in the morning, and many times since, but with no reply.

He kept checking the phone and sending texts between his own classes. Nothing came in response. The hours dragged on, Nathaniel struggling to keep his eyes open. When the school day ended, he rushed over to the Hubbards. He didn't really care about the clothes and other things left there. Maybe the lack of sleep was making him paranoid, but he felt if he didn't make an appearance, Mrs. Hubbard would realize he was out looking for her son instead.

When she answered the door, Nathaniel's belongings were behind her in the entryway. She stepped aside so he could collect them, watching him carefully.

"How long has this been going on?" she asked.

Nathaniel ignored her, grabbing a suitcase and setting it outside on the patio. Then he went back for a cardboard box.

"You owe me an explanation," Mrs. Hubbard said. "When did this start and… Well, I certainly don't want details, but how far did it go? Further than what I saw in the yard yesterday?"

Nathaniel picked up his dumbbells, made sure he had nothing more to gather, and looked her in the eye. "Who cares? It's over now."

He turned his back, bracing himself for shouting or worse. Instead all he heard was the door shutting quietly behind him. Good. He hoped she believed him. Nathaniel loaded his car and gunned it all the way to Caesar's school. The gym was near the entrance, the door propped open. Nathaniel hovered in the doorway. Mats were set up in the center of the room. A group of guys in singlets and headgear had gathered around an older man who was guiding the action and lecturing. Caesar was among the wrestlers, hands on his hips as he nodded at something the coach was saying. Seeing him sent a longing straight to the center of Nathaniel's being. He stared, hoping to attract Caesar's attention, searching for signs that he too was devastated by what had happened.

The coach noticed him, which made Nathaniel uncomfortable. The man's attention soon returned to the proceedings, but an adult was aware of his presence now. Standing in the doorway made Nathaniel feel conspicuous. He glanced to the bleachers, where a handful of students sat. That's when he noticed a head full of curly dark hair. Steph was watching him. She pointed, seemingly to herself, but the gesture became more curved, like he was supposed to look behind himself, so he glanced over his shoulder. In the hallway was another set of doors adjacent to the gym. When he looked back at Steph, she nodded enthusiastically.

Okay. Nathaniel turned and pushed his way through the new doors and found himself in a locker room. He stopped to listen, not detecting anyone else. That was good. If he could get Caesar to meet him here, they would have enough privacy to talk. Was that Steph's plan? Or was she setting him up to get busted? The hallways felt like public areas. The locker rooms were not. He could imagine what Mrs. Hubbard would say to the police if he was caught. He'd be branded a pervert or a—

"What are you doing here?"

Nathaniel turned at the sound of that voice. He answered Caesar by grabbing his shoulders, pulling him near, and kissing him. To his relief, Caesar responded as he always did. For once, he was more interested in talking.

"What's going on? You weren't there this morning, and for some reason I'm grounded from my phone. Did my mom... Did she see?"

Nathaniel nodded grimly. He led Caesar deeper into the locker room, choosing the aisle farthest from the door. Then he explained everything that had happened, bracing for the backlash. Caesar might push him away, deciding the risks outweighed their feelings for each other.

Instead he looked worried, but at least he took Nathaniel's hand. "What are we going to do? How are we going to see each other? It'd be easier if I had my license already, but that's not until—"

"September," Nathaniel said.

"Right, and by then you'll be gone."

"I'll figure something out. I promise."

Caesar frowned. "But how? We barely managed when we lived together."

"I'll get a place of my own," Nathaniel said.

Caesar brightened. "Really?"

"Yeah. I'm not going back home. I'll find an apartment. Then you can come stay with me." Nathaniel thought about this and chewed his lip. "We'll have to lay low. For a little while."

Caesar squeezed his hand tighter. "We can't see each other?"

"No," Nathaniel said, his chest aching with emotion. "We can't. You need to convince your mother that we're through. Otherwise, every time you spend the night with a friend, she'll wonder if you're actually with me."

"True." Caesar sighed. "How long will that take?"

"I don't know." Nathaniel thought of all the text messages he had sent, realizing that Mrs. Hubbard probably read them. "Does your mom know your pin number?"

"For my phone?" Caesar shook his head.

"Good. When you get it back, delete everything from me. Here." Nathaniel pulled out his phone and released Caesar's hand so he could place it there. "Take this. It's on vibrate. I'll call you. That's how we'll stay in touch. Okay?"

Caesar nodded glumly. "This sucks."

"I know." Nathaniel listened to make sure they were still alone. Then he leaned forward and kissed Caesar, trying to put enough into it to tide them both over. "How are you getting home after the meet? I could give you a ride."

Caesar shook his head. "Mom is picking me up."

"Then I better go." Nathaniel didn't move. Not yet. "We're going to make this work. I promise. No matter what I have to do, I'll make sure we don't fall apart. Okay?"

Caesar nodded, steeling his jaw, but his watery eyes betrayed him.

"Don't cry. Promise me that you'll stay strong."

"I promise."

"Say it like you mean it," Nathaniel said, forcing himself to grin.

Caesar copied him. "I promise!"

"Good. I love you." Nathaniel kissed him once more. Then he stepped back, leaning against one of the lockers. "Better get back to the meet before someone comes searching for you."

He seemed unwilling to go, so Nathaniel looked away, as if no longer interested. After a moment, Caesar slunk down the aisle and around the corner. Only when he heard the squeak of the swinging door did Nathaniel rest his head against cold metal and exhale. He didn't stand there feeling sorry for himself. Not for long. He had a promise to keep.

Shakespeare had once described time as a tyrant. To Nathaniel time felt more like a slave driver, spurring him on with promises instead of a whip. Promises that life would get much worse if he didn't complete his task, that Caesar would be lost to him forever if Nathaniel failed to change nearly everything. Over the coming months he tore his life down and rebuilt it so they could be together. High school graduation came and went, an unwelcome distraction that he barely acknowledged. Nathaniel went home despite his resolve not to, only showing up there to sleep, shoving the dresser in front of his bedroom door when he did so. Other times he slept in his car. He took showers at a truck stop more often than not. This was uncomfortable and inconvenient, but helped motivate him to get his own place. And he did, but that also came with a sacrifice. When he broke the news to Rebecca, Nathaniel expected her to be hurt that he wasn't going to Yale after all. Her anger surprised him. She called him stupid. Quite a few other names too. And she cried, but mostly in frustration. He told himself it had all been worth it, which was easier to believe as August approached, because now all the pieces were in place. The shape of his new life was complete. He moved in to his new home. All he needed to do now was to welcome his first guest.

Caesar. Nathaniel paced on the sidewalk, looking at his phone and trying to use his thumb to wipe clean the screen. Or maybe he was stroking the device, because in a way it had become synonymous with his boyfriend. They didn't see each other often. Quick rendezvous at the mall or other places Caesar hung out with friends. Group events where Mrs. Hubbard was convinced her son would be safe. At most they managed an hour alone together before Caesar's friends wanted to move on. Nathaniel had no desire to go with them. He only wanted Caesar, and felt increasingly frustrated by how difficult this became. The movie night was the best—Nathaniel's eighteenth birthday, Caesar's friends disappearing into the theater without him so they could spend nearly two hours alone together in the car. That had been nice, although the desperate groping and taking turns going down had left him feeling sleazy.

In addition to these encounters, they texted as much as possible. Caesar had his own phone back and had returned Nathaniel's, making it easier to maintain their connection. In theory. Lately those texts had become stilted. Conversation became stagnant when they weren't making new memories together. They could only reminisce about the past so many times. Today that would all change. The sound of a car made him look up. He didn't recognize the vehicle, but the passenger was familiar. As was the driver, a guy with short buzzed hair—one of Caesar's close friends who had recently earned his license. Nathaniel kept his cool as the car pulled over and Caesar hopped out. He watched as his boyfriend took in the surroundings— the University of Houston campus. Was he happy? Impressed? Nathaniel didn't like that he was having a hard time reading him. Maybe it was Caesar's new look, the shorter hairstyle, the dark locks barely reaching his eyebrows, or—

"Did you forget your glasses?" he asked.

Caesar smiled bashfully, touching the space above his eyes as if to push up frames that were no longer there. "Contacts," he explained.

"I liked the glasses," Nathaniel said. Then he opened his arms. "But you look nice."

They hugged, which felt much too platonic. The car that had dropped off Caesar drove away, Nathaniel determined to correct the awkward introduction. "You look hot. Good enough to eat."

He snapped his teeth shut just inches from Caesar's mouth, then covered those lips with his own. Caesar reacted, pressing against him. The chemistry was still there. They still had it.

"How much time do we have?"

Caesar took a step back. "Mom thinks Kurt and I are at a boat show. How long do people usually hang around those things?"

"Hours," Nathaniel said with a smile. "Hours and hours. Sometimes they stay overnight."

"I wish," Caesar said wistfully. "I just need to text Kurt when I'm ready. He met some new girl from around here who thinks he's in college." He turned and nodded at the uninspiring dormitory towers behind them. "Is this what I think it is?"

"Come see."

Nathaniel didn't exactly strut into his new home. Moody Towers, as it was called, was far from luxurious. Everything felt rundown—the community area by the entrance, the rattling elevators, the narrow hallways, and finally, the tiny dorm room they would have all to themselves. Or should have. The long room was furnished with what appeared to be couches on both walls. These pulled out to become beds during the night, although they passed plenty of rooms where these weren't tucked away. Luckily his roommate was tidy. That's about all they had in common, since Mr. Jung was a small, gray-haired Korean man who apparently couldn't speak English. Nathaniel found this highly suspect, since the man was always sitting prim and proper on his couch, reading English books.

Like now.

Nathaniel sighed. "Mr. Jung, this is my boyfriend, Caesar. Caesar, this is my roommate, Mr. Jung."

A shrewd eyebrow rose above thick glasses before Mr. Jung resumed reading.

"Nice to meet you," Caesar tried.

Nothing. They stood in awkward silence, Nathaniel hyper-aware of their limited time slipping away. "I told you I needed the room to myself this afternoon," he said. "I'm pretty sure you agreed."

Still nothing.

"Can't you go read downstairs? Or get something to eat? I just need a few hours."

Mr. Jung said something in Korean that didn't sound friendly.

"Sure," Nathaniel said, pretending to understand him. "I'd be happy to give you a hand." He swiftly slid an arm beneath Mr. Jung's legs, wrapped the other around his torso, and picked him up. Mr. Jung started protesting immediately, but Nathaniel was nearly twice his size and had no trouble carrying him to the hall and setting him on his feet. Then he shut the door and locked it. He waited just long enough to make sure Mr. Jung didn't have his keys with him.

"You stupid piece of shit!" a voice shouted. "You open the door or I'll call the police!"

"Just a few hours," Nathaniel said cordially. "Otherwise I'll make your life hell." He turned around and smiled at Caesar. "I *knew* he could speak English!"

Caesar managed a smile, then glanced around the room and sat on one of the couch beds. After a little more shouting, Mr. Jung went away. Not exactly the best start to their romantic day together. Nathaniel walked to the windows, trying to salvage the moment. "Come see the view. It's really nice from up here. Lots of green."

Caesar remained on the couch. "What happened to Yale?"

Nathaniel turned around and crossed his arms over his chest. "Yale can wait. I enrolled here so we can be together."

"Yeah," Caesar said. "That's cool. But I'm a junior now and… In two years, do you expect me to enroll here?"

"I'll kick Mr. Jung out permanently. We can be roommates." This attempt at humor failed, so Nathaniel sat down and took Caesar's hand. "I know this place sucks. It's the best I could do on short notice. I'm lucky to have gotten it. Next year I'll find something better. Maybe even next semester. When you do graduate, I'll transfer to Yale."

Caesar looked at him like he was crazy. The words he chose were a lot more gentle. "Think that'll work?"

"I'll make it work." Nathaniel bumped shoulders with him. "This way we can still be together. You'll get your license next month, so sneaking away will be easier."

"Unless my mom puts a GPS tracker on the car," Caesar joked. He glanced around the room again, which was barely bigger than the private bathroom he had at home. He seemed to make his peace with it, because he regained some of his humor.

"Why is your roommate called Mr. Jung when he's so damn old?"

Nathaniel snorted. "I'm wondering what he's going to do with a degree. Practice medicine in a nursing home and be a resident at the same time?"

Caesar took his hand and squeezed it. "I missed you."

All the yearning Nathaniel had felt during their time apart gathered in his chest. "Yeah," he managed.

"Did you miss me?" Caesar asked with his trademark naughty smile. He slid his hand up Nathaniel's leg to his crotch and found his answer there.

On the off chance that Mr. Jung really intended to call the police, Nathaniel decided to make the best of their privacy while they still could. They weren't patient enough to turn the couch into a bed, but they used it like one anyway. Only afterwards, when they wanted to hold each other, did they convert it so they had more room.

"I can't believe you did all this for me," Caesar said.

Nathaniel tried to interpret his tone—if he meant it in a good way or not—but decided not to concern himself. "When I fall in love, I don't mess around."

"I guess not!"

"Besides, we made a promise. Remember?"

"Yeah."

"Good."

Caesar, head resting on Nathaniel's chest, looked at him with eyes like sunshine. Maybe it was a good thing those glasses were history. "Got anything to eat?" he asked.

"Mr. Jung has candy bars. He hoards them. Does an inventory count every day, like I'm a thief."

"Oh. Can I have one?"

Nathaniel grinned. "Absolutely."

"How's college life treating you?"

The image of Rebecca was highly pixilated, and at times it froze completely, but he was glad to hear her voice. He adjusted the angle of the laptop screen so he could see better before he answered.

"Nobody told me I'd be so freaking busy."

Rebecca smirked. "I did. Remember when my cousin had that nervous breakdown? She's still working fast food."

"Which place?"

"KFC."

"Ask her to send me an application."

"You'll be fine," Rebecca said. "How hard could the University of Houston be? It's not... oh, I don't know—"

"Yale?" Nathaniel finished for her. "Go ahead, rub it in."

"It's not too late," Rebecca said, all teasing gone from her voice.

"I like it here," Nathaniel lied.

"Fine. Hey, give me tour of your dorm room!"

"Sure. Won't take long." He picked up the laptop and turned it around, walking along his side of the room so Rebecca could see it all. Then he did the same with the other half, ending with Mr. Jung, who was sitting on his couch, feet pulled close so he could clip his toenails. He didn't look up as Nathaniel filmed him. They had reached a tacit agreement to ignore each other completely.

"Very nice," Rebecca said when Nathaniel was seated again at the small desk.

"Let me see yours."

"Okay."

A few minutes later, he regretted asking. Her room was barely bigger then his own, but she had it to herself. She took him next into the living room, then the bathroom that was used only by her and three roommates. Nathaniel's dorm had a community bathroom down the hall that resembled the deepest pits of Hell. She finished by showing him the kitchenette in one corner of the living room.

"Is that wine?" Nathaniel asked.

"Yep. One of my roomies is old enough to buy it." Rebecca poured herself a glass before returning to the privacy of her room.

"I hate you," Nathaniel said when she toasted him and took a sip.

"Why? It's not like your roommate isn't of legal age."

He glanced over at Mr. Jung, who continued pretending he didn't exist. "So, have you been sneaking any hot guys into your room?"

"Nope." Rebecca frowned. "I used to blame the lack of action on my small-minded peers, feeling certain college would change that. I can't blame high school anymore, so I guess the problem is me."

"You're gorgeous," Nathaniel said. "Guys are probably too intimidated to come up to you. Maybe try asking them out instead."

"Eh. What about you? How goes the cradle-robbing?"

"We don't get to see each other that often. Caesar got his license, and his parents bought him a car for his birthday—"

"Of course they did."

"Yeah. But I still don't see him that much. Part of that is my fault. Sometimes I raise my head from the books and I'm surprised that entire weeks have gone by."

"I know the feeling." Rebecca sighed. "Just look at how long it took us to talk. We never would have let that happen before."

"True. When I do get to see him, it's never for long. We're always watching the clock. Privacy is an issue too. And then lately… I don't know."

Rebecca leaned forward. "What?"

"It takes him a lot longer to answer my texts. His replies are shorter. He even cancelled on me last weekend."

"He's fifteen years old," Rebecca said. "He has the attention span of a hummingbird."

"Sixteen," Nathaniel reminded her. "But yeah, maybe you're right."

"At least think about transferring up here. You'd still be able to see him on holidays."

He glanced at the date in the corner of the screen. The holidays were coming up. She was right. When Christmas break came for both of them, he and Caesar would have plenty of time to see each other. "You're the best!" he said.

"I am?"

"Yeah."

Rebecca took a hearty swig of wine. "You worry me."

Nathaniel grinned, still excited by the prospect. "Trust me, sometimes I worry myself."

As he waited in the hotel lobby, Nathaniel was reminded of when he'd first invited Caesar to his dorm. Half a year ago already. He shook his head, scarcely believing how fast his life was whizzing by. He wished for a simpler time, a Christmas from long ago when he was still little, when Dwight wasn't so cruel and the days leading up to the big day each seemed like a small eternity. Back then he wished he could speed time up. Now he wished it would slow down. Especially once Caesar arrived.

Nathaniel glanced around, feeling jittery and excited. At first he'd been irritated to learn that Moody Towers was closed for the holidays. He didn't like the place, but he considered it home and didn't appreciate being booted out against his will. Most students returned to their families. Nathaniel had booked a hotel room for a week. Nothing fancy, but after being cramped up in a glorified closet with Mr. Jung for half a year, it sure felt luxurious.

The lobby doors opened and Caesar walked in wearing a bemused smile. "You seriously got us a room?"

"Yup! Merry Christmas." Nathaniel hugged him, and instead of letting go, started dragging him backward through the lobby.

Caesar laughed. "I don't need convincing! Get off!"

"That's the idea."

Once they were in the elevator, Nathaniel kissed him and

kept doing so until the doors opened again with an electronic ding. He took Caesar's hand and led him down the hall to his room. *Their* room.

Once inside, Caesar laughed again. "Why are there two beds?"

"I booked a double. I thought it meant the room would be twice as big." Nathaniel shrugged. "Feels like a palace compared to Moody Towers."

"I like it," Caesar said, hopping up on one of the beds—in his shoes—and bouncing a few times. "This one's mine."

"Not if I can help it."

Caesar landed on his butt and reached into his jacket. "I got you something."

"I did too." Nathaniel went to the small table set by the windows. "Don't expect anything amazing. I could barely afford this place. Technically I can't. I'm counting on my parents giving me money."

"Better hope you don't get a fruitcake."

"That's what I got you!" Nathaniel said, grabbing the present. It clearly wasn't though. The wrapped gift was too flat. Caesar handed him one that was long and narrow. Nathaniel guessed what it was even before he pulled away the paper. A watch. A really nice one! He liked that. To him it symbolized time. Not just more, which he felt he needed, but the promise of time they would spend together.

Caesar had opened his present too, holding the frame in his hand and looking puzzled. "Yale?" he asked.

"I had Rebecca send me a postcard. We're still going there together. I'm busting my ass to make sure my grades are perfect. It'll happen."

"Oh." Caesar tried to appear enthused. "Thanks."

Nathaniel smirked. "A framed postcard is a stupid present. Open the back."

He watched as Caesar did so. Once he removed the black cardboard rectangle, the frame's true image was revealed. He and Caesar, sitting on a couch together, both more than a little tipsy. Their shoulders were touching. Caesar was talking as Nathaniel stared at him and smiled. A lot of love could be seen in that expression.

"Wow. Who took this?"

"Remember that dorm party on the fifth floor?"

"Yeah! Of course!"

"One of the girls there is really into photography and was snapping photos. Did you notice her?" Caesar shook his head so Nathaniel continued. "I ran into her later, and she mentioned a photo of us that she liked. There it is. It sucks having to hide it, but I figured your parents…"

"It's a cool idea," Caesar said. "Way more creative than what I got you. Speaking of which, what time is it?"

Nathaniel humored him by checking his new watch. "Just a little past five." When he looked up, he saw that Caesar wasn't joking. "Why does it matter? We have all night. Right?"

Caesar grimaced. "Dinner with my family."

"Are you coming back afterwards?"

"It's Christmas."

"That's my point!"

Caesar sighed. "It's a big day for my family. We always spend it together. I only managed to slip away because they think I'm at Steph's."

Nathaniel tensed. "Why Steph?"

"To give her a present."

"No, I mean why not Kurt?"

"Kurt is my friend."

"Steph isn't?"

"He's straight. Giving him a present on Christmas would be kind of gay." Caesar laughed.

Nathaniel didn't. "So they think you're at your girlfriend's house?"

"I'm starting to wish I was!" Caesar said in exasperation.

"Sorry." Nathaniel took a deep breath. "I was looking forward to finally spending lots of time with you."

"I'm sorry too," Caesar said. "It sucks."

"Yeah. At least we still have the rest of the week."

Caesar remained quiet. And very still.

Nathaniel clenched his jaw. "What now?"

"I'm taking a trip to Colorado with my family. There's no getting out of it."

"You're not fucking serious!"

"Sorry."

"I told you I was getting this room! Why didn't you say anything?"

"I didn't know." Caesar kicked at the carpet. "My dad surprised my mom. She kept saying she wanted to see the snow. It's his Christmas present to her."

Nathaniel groaned. Then he started pacing the room, trying to find some solution. Cancel his reservation and get a hotel in Colorado wherever Caesar's family would be? Of course there Caesar couldn't pretend he was out visiting one of his friends. "Fuck!"

"I'm sorry!"

"It's not your fault," Nathaniel said, trying to calm down. "So let me guess. We've got an hour?"

"Yeah. Maybe I can stay a little longer."

"Great." He pinched the bridge of his nose and turned to face him. "What do you want to do?"

The answer wasn't surprising. Sex. Nathaniel went through the motions. Caesar was his usual self—talking, asking, suggesting—like an enthusiastic orchestra conductor setting the tempo for a different kind of arrangement. Nathaniel remained silent, except when Caesar reached for the condoms and lube. Then he said no, ignoring the look of disappointment that so perfectly mirrored his own. Afterwards in the shower he defrosted somewhat, washing Caesar's back and wishing this hour could stretch into the many he had hoped for.

"I feel like I'm ruining your life," Caesar said as he was pulling on his shoes.

"Don't be ridiculous," Nathaniel said, sitting next to him on the bed.

"I'm serious."

"I just wish you'd make more time for me. That's all."

Caesar shrugged helplessly. "I don't see what else I can do."

Nathaniel exhaled. "I've told you before. Tell your parents you're staying the night at Kurt's house and come see me instead."

"And what? Cuddle up between you and Mr. Jung? I hate your dorm."

"Gee, thanks."

"I do," Caesar said. "I'm not trying to be mean, but it's hard to get into the mood there."

Nathaniel looked at him. "Seriously? Your love stops if the environment isn't right? This is more than just sex to me!"

"I know. I don't mean it like that. But being there reminds

me of how you should be in Connecticut. That was the plan. That was the promise."

"Which changed because I wanted to be with you."

"I didn't ask you to do that."

Nathaniel scowled. "What's that supposed to mean?"

"I feel like it's my fault! And if you *had* asked, I would have told you not to stay. You need to be *there*, not here at some crappy college."

"There's nothing wrong with the University of Houston! I like it there. Yeah, my living situation sucks, but that will change."

Caesar sulked. "It still won't be Yale."

"You're such a fucking snob!"

"What am I supposed to do if they don't let you in? Have you thought of that? It won't be easy. I asked my dad if transferring to Yale was possible. I didn't mention you, but even he laughed like there wasn't a chance. My parents aren't going to let me throw away my education."

"You think that's what I'm doing?" Nathaniel growled. "And hey, if you really think I'm destroying my life, the least you could do is bother answering my texts. What's up with that?"

Caesar looked away.

A pit opened in Nathaniel's stomach. "There's a reason."

"It's hard," Caesar muttered. "You're not around, so it gets confusing."

"Who?"

"Nobody. But it kind of feels like we can't really be together, so maybe we should wait."

"What?"

Caesar looked at him, eyes pleading. "I'll keep the promise, but since neither of us can fulfill it right now, maybe it would be easier if we waited."

"Easier? You think us being apart—not talking, kissing, screwing, *not anything*—would be easier?"

Caesar got off the bed. He reached for his jacket and stood holding it rather than putting it on. He gazed downward, like he was thinking very carefully about his next words. Funny that it ended up being just one little sound. "Yes."

"Fuck you."

Caesar looked up, his expression hurt. "I'm sorry."

"Fuck you," Nathaniel repeated. "Leave."

Caesar started to but hovered in the doorway. Nathaniel rose and pushed him into the hall so he could slam the door. Then he returned to the bed so he could punch the mattress, over and over again. He noticed then the photo frame he had given Caesar, the one with the postcard from Yale. He picked it up, ready to throw it against the wall and smash it into pieces. He couldn't. Instead he sat on the bed, removed the back of the frame, and stared at a tiny slice of time, one that was soon dotted with tears.

The knock on the door came an hour later. Nathaniel answered it without harboring any false hopes. His mother stood there wearing an apologetic expression.

"Is he already here?"

Nathaniel frowned. "No."

"Oh. I know you have a romantic evening planned, but it's Christmas, which made me think room service might not be available. So I brought you these."

She lifted the two plastic bags, one in each hand, the outline of Tupperware containers in both.

"Thanks." He took them from her, set them aside, and stepped forward for a hug. Once his mother was in his arms, he didn't feel like letting go.

"What happened?" she asked.

"Can you stay?" he asked, releasing her. "Please. Just for dinner."

His mother looked concerned. "Of course. Whatever you need." Then she brightened. "I have presents! In the car. You probably think you're too old, but you're not. Help me carry them in?"

Nathaniel managed a smile and a nod.

It wasn't the best Christmas, but his mother's presence made it a lot better than it would have been. The next day he called Rebecca at her parents' house. She stayed with him for the rest of the week. He thought about cancelling the reservation to save money, but after one night of sharing a carton of ice cream with her while watching bad holiday specials, he decided the expense was worth it. They were both tired and needed to recharge. His heart was weary, inside and out. He didn't know that was possible. If his heart wasn't broken, it was exhausted. Strange how love could be so empowering, could make getting up every morning worthwhile, could provide endless energy to make the other person happy. What he never expected was to be presented with a bill at the end. The time had come to pay, and after scraping clean the deepest vaults of his soul, Nathaniel found he had nothing left to give. He was destitute.

Interlude

A soft ticking was the only sound in Marcello's office. Nathaniel had never noticed it before, had to turn to locate the source of the sound—a small gold clock on the desk. Normally this room was so full of life—debates over new business ventures, the popping of champagne bottles, or even the classical music Marcello put on when trying to impress others with his refined taste. In truth he preferred disco. Nathaniel had walked in on him once while he was shaking his considerable bulk to the Bee Gees.

Even this memory couldn't make him smile. He turned back to the couch, where Kelly sat perfectly still. He was good at that. While telling his story, Nathaniel had shifted constantly, unable to find a comfortable position, before rising to pace the room. Not Kelly. He remained motionless, listening with undivided attention. No interruptions, no questions, not even facial expressions that hinted at his thoughts. Maybe this was a skill he'd learned while modeling. Or maybe he was quietly awaiting the perfect opportunity to pounce. Lord knows Nathaniel had seen him do so many times before.

"How am I doing?" He swallowed against the words, hating how desperate they made him sound.

Finally Kelly shifted, stretching out his arms as he frowned. "I'm sorry about your family life. I had no idea."

"I came to terms with it long ago."

"That may be," Kelly said, "but I can only imagine how different my life would have turned out had I been raised in an environment like that." His brow knotted, his lips moving slightly as if he had more to say. Then he gave a barely perceptible shake of his head.

"Don't hold back," Nathaniel said. "You never did before."

"It doesn't seem appropriate to challenge you on any of this, considering what you've been through."

Nathaniel walked back to the couch and flopped down. "I'm pretty sure I've got it coming. Hit me."

Kelly cocked his head. "It's just that I *know* I asked you about your family. Many times. I don't remember you avoiding any questions, but I also don't remember hearing anything like I did tonight."

"Does 'I was never close to my father' sound familiar? Or how about, 'We don't have much in common. I was always a mama's boy.' I found ways of telling the truth without spelling it out. I had plenty of practice before we met."

Kelly's frown deepened. "You said something once about not spending time with your brother because you always ended up butting heads."

"Literally, on a few occasions. Once in the eighth grade when he found out I had borrowed his bike."

Kelly's jaw flexed, and something in those brown eyes flashed. "Do you have a current address for him? I wouldn't mind paying him a visit."

Nathaniel shook his head. "Let karma finish the job instead. His life has been one miserable event after another."

"The way you tell it, so has yours. I hate that. It's not what I wanted for you. Give me a time machine and screw any paradoxes, because I wish I could go back and be there for you."

Nathaniel felt a rush of affection that he quickly tried to tame. "I wish it had been you instead of him."

"Me instead of Caesar? Maybe I'm getting soft, but he was just a kid. Fifteen—even sixteen—is really young."

"We were both young," Nathaniel said. "I don't hold any of that against him."

"You might have both been young, but only you were dealing with problems any adult would struggle with. Did you ever tell Caesar the full truth?"

"No," Nathaniel said. "He never knew about my dad hitting my mom, or how long my brother abused me. He asked me once what we were fighting about, like a temporary feud had us at each other's throats."

"How did you answer that one?"

"I claimed I stole Dwight's paper route."

Kelly didn't laugh. Not until Nathaniel did, but their amusement only banished the tension momentarily. "It's getting late," Kelly said, looking toward the elevator doors.

Nathaniel didn't move. "I've never told anyone the full truth. Not before tonight. I'm not finished."

Kelly appeared hopeful, which was puzzling until he realized why. As painful as his past might be, it didn't excuse what Nathaniel had done. Kelly wanted to forgive him, sought a reason to do so, but he was no fool. Three years was a very long time to suffer an injured heart. Somehow Nathaniel needed to justify that, and only the truth would suffice. That was fine, because the truth was all he had to offer.

"Want me to make some coffee?" Nathaniel offered.

"How much more could there be?" Kelly asked.

"A lot. And it only gets more complicated."

Kelly snorted. "Is that even possible?"

"Jason Grant."

Kelly's expression became guarded. "What does he have to do with any of this?"

"I'll tell you. But first, coffee?"

Kelly stared a moment longer. Then he nodded at the bottle on the table. "You better pour me a real drink."

Nathaniel leaned forward, picked up the wine bottle, and considered the label. Then he held it up. "Château Coupvray 1974. Do you recognize it?"

Kelly shook his head. "Should I?"

"It was dark that night. We'll get there." He grabbed the corkscrew, opened the bottle, and carefully poured. When they were both holding their glasses, he raised his slightly, but any sort of toast seemed inappropriate. He considered a declaration of love, just in case he never got the chance again. Instead, he settled for one word.

"Ready?"

Kelly looked him straight in the eye and nodded. "Ready."

Part Two
Houston, 2006

Chapter Nine

Fear is a cavity that rots the soul, every waking instance tainted by decay. For an individual escaping the oppression of fear, the world seems transformed. Borders cease to exist, the horizon filling with limitless possibilities. Nathaniel had a taste of this when he first moved in with the Hubbards, but one fear was soon replaced by another. No longer fearing his brother's unpredictable hate, he had instead feared Caesar's unpredictable love. One person he had hoped to escape from, the other he had hoped would never leave.

Now, nearly two years later, Nathaniel rarely entertained hopes and fears. Being free from both had allowed him to grow strong. He still had plans for the future and felt optimistic about his prospects. Only his methods had changed. Hopes were too passive, fears too crippling. Action was the only way forward. He had begun that process when turning his life upside down for Caesar, and while that hadn't panned out, Nathaniel had taken from the experience a blueprint for his future. Action led to movement, movement to change, and the change he sought was strength of body—so he continued to work out. Strength of mind—which he found in his studies. And strength of heart—which wasn't so easy. The best way to temper the heart is through repeated use of it, a prospect Nathaniel tried not to entertain.

The silent lulls late at night were the hardest. That's when he felt most alone. His living situation had improved. He had a private bedroom in a shared apartment, but in the darkest hours of the day, when standing at the window, he wished for more: a friend like Rebecca, who always made time for him, or maybe someone new who Nathaniel could love back. Hell, he even found himself missing Mr. Jung and his snoring. But mostly when he stared up at a black sky that seemed to reflect the emptiness inside him, he thought of only one person.

Caesar. The name was on the display of his cell phone tonight, Nathaniel tracing the letters with his thumb. He sometimes wondered if the number still led anywhere. Caesar's life wasn't a complete mystery. Nathaniel had seen photos of him on his high school's wrestling site. Just two, one blurry with motion, the other a profile shot of him grabbing some other guy. Neither was satisfying, but the photos still made Nathaniel yearn. A little more online snooping revealed a MySpace page that included a few cocky comments and a not-so-becoming profile pic. That page was never updated. While not much, these things proved Caesar was still out there, had survived their breakup.

Nathaniel snorted and shook his head. Of course he had. Taking a swig of his beer, he turned from the window and set the bottle on the nightstand, intending to do the same with the phone. Instead he walked the room, ended up back at the window, and sighed. Then he looked down at the phone, his fingers moving, typing out words and hitting send before he could second-guess himself.

I never forgot you. I never will.

He held his breath for a minute, finishing his beer in the next. Then he sat on the edge of his bed and stared at the phone's display. The digital numbers at the top seemed sluggish, changing much too slowly. Time continued to trudge by until Nathaniel tossed the phone onto the mattress and went to the bathroom to get ready for the night. When he returned, he ignored the phone as he got undressed. Only when he started to pull back the sheets was he forced to pick it up.

A new message. A reply! His breath caught in his throat as he read it.

I never stopped loving you. I never will.

Nathaniel felt torn. There they were, after all this time: the perfect parting words. Much better than how they had left things so long ago. No anger, no hurt. Just a bittersweet recognition of what they had felt for each other before they said goodbye.

But why should they? All the reasons they had failed were fading into history. His pulse raced as he tallied a mental list. Privacy? Nathaniel had plenty of that now. Parents? Caesar was nearly eighteen, an adult. His life would soon be his own. Yale? Nathaniel had been working hard to get there and still wasn't sure it was possible. Maybe he just needed a little extra motivation. What else remained in their way?

A nagging suspicion, that's what. An unanswered question. Nathaniel chewed his lip, slid between the sheets, and turned his back to the nightstand where he had set the phone. Half an hour later he rolled over and grabbed it, texting back.

A promise is a promise.

* * * * *

They met in a café downtown. Nathaniel chose the location carefully. The dining area was small, not big enough to escape the daylight streaming in from the front windows. The menu offered mostly soups and sandwiches, and from his experience, the staff was eager to get customers in and out quickly and efficiently. In other words, an environment not conducive to romance. Dinner out on a Friday night? Nope. Lunch on a Sunday afternoon would have to do.

The nagging suspicion was to blame. As was Nathaniel's determination to remain strong. This resolve was tested as he sat by the window, watching the flow of pedestrian traffic. That's when Nathaniel saw him, standing on the corner and looking up and down the street, no doubt searching for the right address. His skin was tan despite the early spring, his naturally highlighted hair had grown out again, tumbling down in waves that covered his ears and helped frame his pointed chin. No ponytail or glasses, although the uncertain expression reminded Nathaniel of when they had first met. Student and tutor. By the end of their time together, the tables had turned.

He watched as Caesar started off in the wrong direction before backtracking. Nathaniel considered his body. Was he taller? Perhaps a little. His shoulders were broader, his frame still lanky, although the loose T-shirt revealed arms and a neck that were meatier and nicely toned. Nathaniel looked him up and down as many times as he could, making sure not to do so when Caesar finally entered the café. His head swiveled around, searching for him, so Nathaniel helped by standing. Then those amber eyes lit up. Recognition. Affection. Joy. Caesar hurried forward, arms starting to open wide. Nathaniel cut this short by extending a hand.

Caesar noticed and looked reprimanded before accepting, his hand sliding softly into Nathaniel's and staying there. "Wow!" he said.

"You sound surprised." Nathaniel resisted a smile. "Didn't think I'd be here?"

Caesar sputtered something, laughed nervously, and tried again. "You look… Wow."

Nathaniel pulled his hand free and used it to gesture at the table. "Sit down. You're late. I'm hungry."

Caesar grinned as he sat. "I forgot how bossy you could be."

"Me?" Nathaniel challenged.

"Yeah, you," Caesar said, still beaming at him. "Oh man, it's so good to see you again!"

This took him aback. Nathaniel had imagined this encounter as a trial for them both. Each would have questions or accusations. Instead Caesar appeared genuinely happy to be here, his excitement contagious. Nathaniel found himself wanting to put his elbows on the table and lean forward, just so they would be a few inches closer.

The waitress provided a welcome distraction. Nathaniel ordered first, giving Caesar little time to glance at the menu. Not that it mattered, because he didn't even bother.

"Do you eat here on your lunch break?" he asked the waitress, eyes shining up at her.

"Me?" The waitress looked panicked, like it was a pop quiz. "Yes?"

"And do you have the same thing every day?" Caesar asked.

The waitress tittered. "Usually."

"Then that's what I'll have. If it's your favorite, it must be good."

The waitress blushed, scribbled something on her notepad, and after another glance at Caesar, twirled and walked away.

"I see you've only gotten worse," Nathaniel grumbled.

"Meaning?"

The nagging suspicion. But he wasn't ready to ask. Not just yet. "So how are things?"

"Same ol'."

Nathaniel waited patiently for Caesar to expound. Instead, he seemed content to leer at him. Nathaniel scowled.

"You're like a fucking minotaur," Caesar said. "How often do you work out?"

"Often," Nathaniel said. "In fact, I'm thinking about taking a walk right now."

"All right, all right," Caesar said. "It's the weather. It gets me worked up. It's been nice lately, huh? Way warmer than usual at this time of year."

"We're really going to talk about the weather?"

"Oh. Uh. No?"

"Then try again."

Caesar sighed. "My life. Okay. I wish I had something interesting to report. Things are finally returning to normal at home. Like how they used to be before you and I got caught. I told you my parents went on lockdown, especially my mom. She's always been a little controlling, but man, did she go overboard. Last year they finally started taking in male foster kids again, although none have stuck. We're getting a new one in a few weeks."

"You're still not talking about yourself," Nathaniel pointed out.

Caesar's shoulders slumped. "What am I supposed to talk about? The people I've dated? The trip I took up to Yale for an interview? Both of those things make me feel like a jerk. You don't care about my friends or high school gossip. I don't know what you want to hear from me."

Nathaniel realized he didn't either, but the answer was just beneath the surface. "Are you okay? Have you been happy?"

Caesar locked eyes with him. "Yeah. I guess. It's not easy living with all the stupid shit I've done, but there's not a lot of choice. I fucked up."

The waitress returned with their drinks, Caesar not looking at her this time. Instead he kept his gaze on Nathaniel. Once she was gone, he spoke again.

"I'm sorry. I know that probably doesn't mean much to you, but it's the truth."

Nathaniel saw the sincerity in his eyes, nearly taken in by it. He needed to compose himself before he could travel further down that road. But he supposed a temporary treaty wouldn't do any harm. "To answer your question, I work out every other day or so."

Caesar blinked. Then he perked up. "It's paid off because you've got a rockin' bod! The beard scruff is killing me. Your boyfriend must feel like the luckiest guy in the world."

Nathaniel raised an eyebrow to show he saw through this ruse. "I wouldn't be meeting you if I wasn't single. Don't read into that. I just know better than to meet an ex-boyfriend when already in a happy relationship."

"What's the worst that could happen?" Caesar asked innocently. Then he laughed. "You're probably dying to know if I'm single."

"Nope."

"Well it just so happens— Hey!"

Nathaniel cracked a smile. "Please tell me," he deadpanned. "I can't wait to find out."

"I'm single."

"I refuse to believe it! The great Casanova is all by himself?"

"Tragic, isn't it?"

"Yeah," Nathaniel said, allowing himself to sound serious. "It sort of is."

Their food arrived, Caesar flirting with the waitress again, but this time winking at Nathaniel once her back was turned. He shook his head, pretending not to be charmed by this, when in fact he was.

"What about you? How many college guys have had their hearts broken by Nathaniel Courtney?"

"Fewer than you might think. As in zero."

Caesar waited for the punch line, looking concerned when none came. "Zero?"

Nathaniel shrugged "I've been on a few dates." Very few, mostly just to prove to himself that he wasn't scared of love, which was like standing close to the aquarium glass to disprove a fear of sharks. "I get a lot of women asking me out. The guys weren't really my type."

"You can't wait for them to come to you," Caesar said. "Ever hit the bars? You're twenty-one now, right?"

"Not yet, so no bars. Although I rarely have trouble buying beer. Must be the scruff."

Caesar's eyes lit up like it was Christmas.

Nathaniel chuckled. "You like to drink? Never mind, I remember you chugging that fruity stuff. You barely managed to keep it down too. What was it called?"

"Boone's," Caesar said, puffing up his chest, "and I'll have you know that I drink beer with the big boys now. At least when I can get my hands on it."

"I'm not buying you any."

"Oh come on!" Caesar said, sounding like a pouty child.

Nathaniel shook his head, enjoying himself a little too much. And why not? As Caesar had said, what's the worst that could happen? Nathaniel had survived a broken heart before. He could do so again.

They spent the rest of lunchtime reminiscing, trading stories they both knew while squabbling over the small details of who had said what or what happened when. Nathaniel prolonged the experience by ordering coffee, Caesar opting for a slice of pecan pie. Afterwards they strolled outside, the afternoon cooler now. Caesar shivered, rubbing his arms to warm himself.

"It's too early in the year for just a T-shirt," Nathaniel pointed out.

Caesar turned to face him. "I was hoping to impress you with these." He flexed briefly. "But you've got me covered in that department."

I've got you covered with *these arms,* Nathaniel could say. Then he would step forward and embrace Caesar, reminding them both that he had done so long ago when lost in the woods together. Only one thing held him back. Time to face the truth. "Where's your car?"

Caesar nodded. "Over there."

The vehicle was the same one Nathaniel had last seen him driving, a silver sedan, like his future as upper management was already certain. Caesar had taken care of it, or at least was a good driver, since the car had no scratches or dings. "Let's get inside so you can warm up."

Caesar nodded eagerly, digging in his pocket to unlock the doors. Once they were inside, Nathaniel noticed the faint smell of Caesar's cologne mixed with that of the air freshener. He soaked in more details: the map on the floorboard with a muddy footprint on it, the sports bag in the backseat with wrestling gear sticking out of the top, the loose change filling the ashtray. Being here felt intimate. Not exactly like being in his bedroom again, but close enough to make Nathaniel want to be. He glanced over to find Caesar wearing a slightly questioning expression, as if to say, *Want more?*

Nathaniel broke eye contact. "When things ended—when you left me—it wasn't just your parents or my situation. Was it? There was someone else."

Caesar was quiet.

Nathaniel pressed on. "Steph?"

"I didn't cheat on you."

"But you left me for her."

"I also left her for you," Caesar pointed out. Then he sighed.

"The timing was bad. We should have waited. Steph and I *never* last. We've tried enough times to know better, but neither of us really accepted back then that it wasn't going to work. I love her. I really do. But we're not meant to be. If I had figured that out before you and I got together, then maybe…"

"What?"

Caesar shrugged. "I like to think you and I would still be together now. That we would have been together all this time."

Nathaniel wondered if that was possible. He couldn't imagine being the one to leave, not unless Caesar had given him good reason. Such as loving someone else, even if nothing happened physically. Caesar had once asked him if emotional betrayal was worse than the physical kind. Nathaniel wasn't sure, but if love was good, then could there ever be too much of it? He certainly didn't blame Caesar for loving Steph. She had always taken the high road, remaining mostly civil when he had replaced her, and even helping him when she had nothing to gain. Steph was a good person. Caesar was right. Only the timing had been bad.

Nathaniel felt a hand touch his and jerked it away instinctively. "You and Steph had your chance," he said. "It didn't work out. The same could be said for us."

Caesar shook his head. "We were interrupted."

"Our relationship reached its natural conclusion. I couldn't hold your attention."

"That's not true! I swear it's not."

"Then why aren't we still together? If we were meant to be, how come we didn't survive a little bad timing, huh?" Nathaniel exhaled and reached for the door handle. "It was good seeing you again."

"I don't want it to be the last time," Caesar said hurriedly.

Nathaniel hesitated, then leaned back. "I don't want it to be either. But I'm not making the same mistakes. That's not who I am anymore. You know what happens to clay when it stops being pummeled?"

"What?"

"It hardens."

Caesar considered him. "This probably isn't the best time to make a dirty joke, is it?"

Nathaniel glared. "You're an idiot."

"I know." Caesar sighed. "At the moment, I'm painfully aware of the fact."

"Good. That makes me feel better. Friends?"

Caesar nodded. "Friends."

Walking around the Yale campus was both invigorating and depressing. The air was thick with history, many of the buildings hundreds of years old. Spring break had just begun, meaning most students were gone, but Nathaniel could imagine the long lawns filled with reclining bodies or the sound of footsteps rushing along stone walkways. He breathed deeply and turned in a slow circle. Yale resembled a collection of great cathedrals and charming parks. The University of Houston had some nice architecture and interesting sculptures here and there, but this... This was *Yale*!

"You've got the fever," Rebecca said, taking one of his arms. "What did the admissions advisor say?"

"That they get over a thousand transfer applications a year."

"And I bet very few of them are handed in personally."

Nathaniel grimaced. "I think it's going to take more than that. More than an impressive GPA. She asked why I hadn't filled out the section on awards and recognitions."

"Oh."

"I don't think she was impressed. She made sure to point out—twice—that only twenty or so transfer applications a year are successful."

"Ouch."

"Yeah."

Rebecca perked up. "Still, I'm sure you charmed her more than you realize. You've always been oblivious to how much women like you. *And* when they're flirting with you."

"Are you flirting with me now?"

"A little." Rebecca squeezed his arm affectionately, then dragged him over to a bench. "When do you find out?"

"May."

"I'll make sure to send flowers. Of the congratulatory variety. Or maybe a trophy. You deserve one. It'll happen. You've got this!"

Nathaniel laughed. "We'll see. So how have things been with you? Any luck?"

They asked this question often, both of them understanding what it meant. Sadly, the answer rarely varied.

"Not really." Rebecca sighed. "Well, kind of."

"Yeah?" Nathaniel turned to face her better, one arm resting along the back of the bench.

"I let a guy feel me up." She shot him a glance before continuing. She looked good, still a beanpole but lately her red hair was cropped short. Nathaniel thought she resembled a young Annie Lennox. "We went on a date, but it was just coffee. I'm not even sure that counts. Afterwards he took me to the stacks—"

"The stacks?"

"You know, the library—which has a notorious reputation."

"The library," Nathaniel repeated in dry tones. "Notorious."

"Yup! I kind of figured that's why we were there, but part of me was hoping the guy really liked to read. Anyway, he dragged me down one of the aisles—the botany section actually—and barely bothered to kiss me before he got all handsy."

"You let him? Did you like it?"

"At first, because let's face it, I'm probably the last virgin on campus. But then I realized I didn't know his last name, and I started wondering if this was just him trying to cross 'sex in the stacks' off his list. Maybe he didn't like me at all, and to be honest, I wasn't sure I liked him. Once his hands moved lower, I called it off."

"And then?"

"I found a really interesting book on the Allium family. Did you know that garlic has both antibacterial and antiviral properties?"

Nathaniel just stared at her.

Rebecca groaned. "I'm hopeless!"

"No, you're smart! I don't want your first time to be with some idiot who treats a cup of coffee like an admission ticket to your pants."

"That would be dreadful," Rebecca said without conviction. Then she shook her head. "No, you're right. I'll just keep waiting and hoping, all the while feeling pathetic."

"You're not pathetic," Nathaniel said. "And if you are, then so am I. I haven't had sex since Caesar."

Rebecca bit her bottom lip. "Is that why he's back in your life?"

"No. We're just friends."

"So you're not going to get back together with him? Or at least hook up?"

"Nope. We've hung out a few times, and it works. I won't pretend there isn't tension between us, but I'm trying to be a good role model for you. Although I might let him feel me up in the stacks."

Rebecca laughed, then shook her head. "Don't you find it tragic that neither of us is getting laid? Aside from all the studying and degrees, isn't that what college is about?"

"That's just the Hollywood version."

"It's not. You should hear some of my friends talk." Rebecca nudged him. "You know what we should do? This is going to take you right back to high school, so bear with me. I say we go shopping and buy a bunch of men's clothes for me. A fake mustache too. Then we'll head back to my place, make sure the room is really dark, and I'll send my cousin in to pleasure you."

Nathaniel smirked. "This would be the cousin I've never heard of? Or met?"

"Yeah, him. Just keep your eyes closed tight. No peeking."

Nathaniel chuckled. "I wish it was that easy. If I could do that for you, I would."

Rebecca kept a straight face. "You sure? Last chance. I'm totally willing to take it up the butt for you."

"I'd rather you find a guy who recognizes just how awesome you are."

"Yeah, me too." She patted his arm. "I'd also settle for having my best friend here with me."

"I'm trying my damndest." Nathaniel gazed across the campus, noticing a guy with a quarterback's build. He supposed most gay guys would find that alluring, but for him, well-built guys triggered bad memories. "Did I tell you that my brother is getting married?"

"Ugh! No."

"Yeah. He even sent me a wedding invitation."

Rebecca looked concerned. "He has your address?"

"No, my mom hand-delivered it. It's a completely harmless invitation, but still… Just getting it reminded me of one of those serial killer letters where they spell everything with magazine cutouts."

"I already feel sorry for the woman deluded enough to marry him."

Nathaniel frowned. "It's worse than that. She's pregnant."

Rebecca closed her eyes briefly in sympathy. "We can only hope she'll come to her senses. Maybe she'll leave him at the altar."

"Or I could leap up during the whole 'speak now or forever hold your peace' part. I can drum up so many reasons that it'll be a sermon."

"Tell me you're not going!"

"My mom is pushing for me to be there. Pushing hard."

"Then the battle is already lost."

"Yeah. I think she sees it as a chance for all of us to make amends. Wanna be my date?"

Rebecca smiled. "I've been waiting a long time for you to ask me that question, and much to my surprise, the answer is no. I don't think I could stomach seeing someone tie the knot with that monster." She took his hand. "Just watch yourself, okay?"

"Trust me," Nathaniel said. "I'll be playing this very carefully."

"I love weddings!"

Nathaniel turned to face the person who made this declaration, which was a bad idea, because he instantly felt tempted. The gray suit Caesar wore framed his body well, accentuating the narrow waist and broad shoulders. "Exactly how many have you been to?"

"I have a lot of cousins," Caesar said, eying the decorated tables. White seemed to be the theme, whether cotton, lace, or silk. "Oh, and an uncle who has been married four times. No kidding. I've been there for three of them. Today though, *that* was magical."

Nathaniel maintained his puzzled expression. At the church they had sat in uncomfortable pews watching as a small woman made foolish promises to a leering beast. All he'd been able to imagine during the ceremony was Dwight throttling her frail body until it snapped like a twig.

"You didn't think so?" Caesar asked.

"I found the whole thing overwhelming."

"Weddings make you nervous?" Caesar bumped shoulders with him. "Is that why you asked me to be your date?"

"I asked if you were interested in free food." He gestured at the reception. "And here we are."

"Geez, when did you lose your sense of humor?"

Around the time you dumped me, Nathaniel wanted to reply. Before he could, Caesar took his hand and led him forward. His bitterness receded, like waves pulled back into the sea. Hell, even the sand had dried out in the sun, because this felt good. Having Caesar at his side, feeling the touch of his hand…

"Nathaniel plus one," Caesar said to the wedding coordinator. Once they were shown to their seating assignments, they ignored them in favor of wandering around the small hall. Nathaniel kept part of his attention on the entrance, waiting for the bride and groom to enter. Once they did, he would make sure to stay far away from Dwight at all times.

They were at the buffet when his mother arrived. She wasn't alone.

"Hey, Mom," Nathaniel said, sparing the briefest possible nod for his father.

Star hugged him, squeezing Nathaniel like a giant teddy bear. Then she turned to Caesar. "Do my eyes deceive me?" She opened her arms. "Talk about a blast from the past! How are you?"

"Hi, Mrs. Courtney." Caesar grinned bashfully. Then he extended a hand to Heath. "I don't think we've met before."

Heath stepped forward to accept his hand, but his eyes were on Nathaniel. "It's really great to see you both."

The buffet became Nathaniel's sole focus as he loaded a plate with crab salad and a few deviled eggs.

"The decorators did a great job," Caesar said. "I was just telling your son that I'm sort of an expert on weddings." He paused, probably hoping Nathaniel would join the conversation, but nothing mattered more to him right now than the buffet. "Uh, anyway, this is one of the nicest receptions I've been to."

"It just so happens," Star said with pride, "that I micromanaged the hell out of it. Come see the pillars of balloons before one of the kids starts popping them."

Nathaniel looked up in panic as his mother's voice faded away. She was taking Caesar with her, leaving him alone with—

"I really am glad to see you," Heath said. "I know you've needed your space to get things figured out, but these last few years haven't been easy on me. When you become a parent someday, you'll understand. It hurts to be away from your child."

Nathaniel dropped his plate on the table, the spoon taking a spill and clattering noisily on the floor, a deviled egg tumbling after it. "You think that's what this is about?"

Health showed his open palms. "If it's not, then please talk to me. I'm your father."

Nathaniel turned to face him, wanting to shout, but the child inside of him hesitated because this man really was his father. So was Victor, but that person hadn't raised him or taught him to ride a bike or taken him to see Santa Claus at the mall every year.

"I love you," Heath said. "Can't we work this out?"

"Can't you stop hitting mom?"

Heath's expression became pained. "I've made mistakes. I'm not perfect."

"Neither am I, but you don't see me hitting anyone."

"Besides your brother." This was stated calmly, without accusation. "I know you had your reasons, and I'm sorry your mother and I didn't realize them sooner. The men in this family have short tempers. That's a trait we all need to work on." His father opened his arms, as if expecting a hug.

"Seriously?" Nathaniel said. "You think you can treat Mom like a punching bag and expect me to forgive that?"

"I've only made that mistake on a few dark occasions. And not since you saw the bruises on her arm."

"Good. Maybe me staying away is the right idea."

Heath dropped his arms and sighed. "Please. Isn't there anything I can do? Don't ask me to leave her, because I truly do love your mother. But if there's some way of regaining your trust—"

"Go to counseling," Nathaniel said. "Not just one session either. Get your head fixed. Then we can talk."

"All right. I'll do that."

This took him aback. "I'm serious. I'll have to hear from your therapist. I'll make sure he knows the full truth. Unless he says you're a changed man, we're through."

"I'm serious too," Heath said. "I'll get counseling, not just to please you, but for your mother's sake." He opened his arms again. When this didn't work, he extended a hand.

Nathaniel took it, and not reluctantly, because he really wanted to believe his father would follow through. If his mother was safe, if Nathaniel could strike that fear off his list, then his life

186

would be perfect. Nearly. He looked across the room to where Caesar was patiently suffering a lecture on table settings. His attention was drawn away again by Heath, who was talking about Yale and how proud he was, even though Nathaniel still hadn't been accepted. He responded, making small talk to show that peace was possible. But he still didn't intend to have a relationship until his father fulfilled his side of the bargain.

The front of the room erupted in applause, signaling the arrival of the newly married couple. Nathaniel slipped away, fetching Caesar and pulling him out one of the side entrances and into fresh air.

"What are we doing?"

"Smoke break," Nathaniel said.

"Neither of us smoke."

"No, but it's a handy excuse."

"Oh." Caesar glanced through one of the windows at the increasing chaos inside. "Everything okay? You looked a little tense when talking to your dad."

"We never really patched things up."

"Seriously?" Caesar whistled. "I figured that would all be ancient history. I know he's not your biological dad, but—"

"It's a little more complicated than that."

Caesar nodded, hands in his pockets as he kicked at the ground. "You ever find out more about Victor?"

Nathaniel shook his head. "Sometimes I think about going back to Warrensburg and asking around. Somebody must have known him, right? Then again, I'm not even sure what I'd ask."

"What do you want to know?"

"Anything. Stories to flesh out the picture."

"Your mom must have a few of those."

"Yeah, but she was in love with him."

Caesar shrugged. "So?"

"Love is like a dream. People often wake up from it and realize they've been with a stranger the entire time."

Caesar raised his head. "Where'd you read that? A fortune cookie?"

Nathaniel smiled. "I wish. It's sage advice. Might have saved me some heartache."

"Back when I ruined it all?"

"Yup. Exactly."

Caesar strolled closer. "Maybe you've got it wrong. Maybe you wake up from the dream to realize it's all true. I didn't understand how much I loved you until I was dumb enough to throw it all away."

"You suck," Nathaniel said evenly.

"I know. But at least you like that about me."

By now Caesar was standing very close. That is until someone really did come out for a cigarette. Then he leapt away.

"Old habits die hard," Nathaniel said with a smirk, "but I don't think you have to worry about your parents here. Where do they think you are?"

"Bowling," Caesar said, eying the new arrival as she wandered toward the parking lot.

"In a suit?"

"They aren't paying much attention right now. They've got their hands full with the new guy. Another foster kid. He's in your old room, actually."

Nathaniel frowned. Despite how things ended, he still remembered his time with the Hubbards fondly. "I hope he lasts longer than I did."

Caesar snorted. "I don't think he will. The guy refuses to go to church or put on the doofy clothes my mom buys for him. He's not exactly trying to fit in, although to be fair, my mom is way worse ever since... You know. Hey, speaking of which, think you can get me a six-pack of beer?"

"Why? Hoping to knock back a few with your mom?"

"No, with Jason. The new guy. I want to get him drunk. I figure he's earned it for all the crap he puts up with."

Nathaniel shrugged, his stomach growling. "I'll see what I can do." He moved toward the door, music escaping when he opened it. At the front of the hall, a DJ bounced around behind a turntable, and while no one was dancing, the floor was filled with people standing in close-knit groups so they could talk. The buffet was another hotspot, a huge crowd swarming over it.

"If you want to prove your love to me," Nathaniel said, "you'll dive in there and get me some crab salad. And some crackers, but only the whole wheat kind. Something to drink too."

"And where will his majesty be?"

"At our table."

Caesar performed a little bow, then left to elbow his way into the crowd. Nathaniel took a seat, feeling at peace until someone did a double-take and sat next to him.

"Hi, Nate!" A dainty hand reached toward him, the nails perfect, a lace sleeve extending down the wrist. "I've been dying to meet you! I'm Sheila."

She made a beautiful bride. Even her stomach, which was curved, only made her seem radiant, more—quite literally—full of life. Her eyes sparkled as she patiently waited for him to accept her invitation. He took in the brown hair that was pulled back except for a single curl down one side of her face, the shine of her lip gloss, and the genuinely happy expression.

Nathaniel felt stunned, and as he took her hand, he also felt sad, because he could see her future. "Only my family calls me Nate."

Sheila's eyebrows rose a little. "I am family. Now, at least. It's official!"

"Right! I didn't mean it that way. I just don't like being called Nate."

"Oh, okay. Nathan?"

"Nathaniel."

"Nathaniel. Gosh, I wish I had a longer name. 'Sheila' seems so simple now."

"Be grateful that you don't." He looked her over again and shook his head. "Wow. I have a sister-in-law!"

"It's crazy, I know. Our families are merging together, and so much is changing." She put a hand over her belly. "You're going to be an uncle."

Nathaniel stared at her. Then he swallowed, not understanding why his eyes stung. Excitement? Dread? Both, most likely. "Do you get along?" he blurted out. "I know how hotheaded my brother can be."

"Dwight?" she waved a hand dismissively. "He's a pussycat."

"A pussycat," he repeated. Then he laughed at the sheer absurdity of the idea. "Seriously?"

"Yeah! I know it's hard to imagine the boy you once raised hell with as being a gentleman, but he is."

Raised hell with? That was one way of putting it. "Okay," Nathaniel said, deciding not to enlighten her. What choice did he have? To start telling her horror stories in the hope of scaring her off? It was a little late for that. Besides, maybe she really had tamed Dwight. He doubted it, but maybe.

"I know you're busy with college—" Sheila said, pausing to add "Yale!" like she was excited for him, "—but I hope to see you around more. Come crash at our place during the holidays. It'll be more fun than being stuck with your parents."

"I don't think my mom will allow it. Doesn't matter that I'm twenty years old. Not unless you want her sleeping over with me."

Sheila laughed. "You're not kidding. All she does is talk about you."

"Really?"

"Yes."

"What about Dwight? Does he mention me much?"

"Worried I know lots of embarrassing stories?" Sheila's expression was reassuring. "No, all he ever talks about is the big game, which apparently refers to whichever is on that day, regardless of the sport."

"You're safe with me," Nathaniel said. "The only thing I like about the Super Bowl is the commercials."

"Me too! Oh, we have to hang out sometime. Maybe a little of your gayness will rub off on Dwight. That would make my life easier." She put a hand over her mouth in shock. "Was that offensive?"

Nathaniel chuckled. "I took it as a compliment."

"Good." She patted his hand. "You won't have any trouble with my family. Not at all. Most of them vote Nader."

He laughed again, his response cut short when the DJ announced the first dance of the evening. Sheila gave him a peck on the cheek before hurrying off to perform her duties. He watched with fascination as she coaxed Dwight onto the dance floor, and at the way he held her carefully as they swayed. Seeing his brother capable of so gentle a gesture was a serious mind fuck.

People could change. He believed that, although he usually didn't consider his brother a human being. In Nathaniel's mind he had long ago transformed into a monster. Maybe Sheila was his Belle, the power of her love banishing the beast. And maybe an absence of love had cursed him in the first place. Nathaniel had to admit there were times he felt himself growing callous, the defenses he had erected around himself feeling more like a prison. He didn't want to exchange places with his brother, to become so full of bitterness and rage. The alternative meant leaving himself unguarded, his tender heart vulnerable to Cupid's arrow. But surely that was better than turning to stone.

Caesar approached the table, drawing his attention. His hair was mussed, his suit ruffled, and a big white smear marred one lapel. "That was barbaric," he said, setting a plate on the table.

"What happened?"

"I was going for the last of the crab salad when five thugs jumped me. Barely managed to fight them off."

Nathaniel repeated the question. "What happened?"

"I slipped on a deviled egg and fell face first. You think banana peels are bad? Who the hell drops an egg on the floor and just leaves it there?"

Nathaniel held back a grin. "The good news is that I forgive you."

"For?"

"Everything. All of it."

Caesar's eyes went wide. "Seriously?"

"Yeah. Except…"

Caesar looked concerned. "What?"

"You forgot my drink."

Caesar groaned, turned, and headed toward the buffet again. Behold the power of love!

Chapter Ten

Nathaniel walked as he often did these days—head down, one thumb in constant motion over his phone. His appreciation for technology grew each day. Previously he'd only been interested in the latest home theater advances, wishing he had more money to spend on high definition equipment or maybe a nice surround sound system. But much could be said for the magical little device in his hand. At the moment he was between classes and sending thinly veiled flirtations to Caesar. Later, when they were both out of school, this would continue. Caesar might be sitting at the dinner table, his parents just a few feet away, and Nathaniel could safely continue communicating with him. The cell phone had become their lifeline, their way of being together until—

He shoved the fantasy aside, surprised when his phone rumbled and a text message came through.

Stop bragging about what you saw in the locker room

it was impressive! Nathaniel texted back.

Probably a shower, not grower.

Nathaniel laughed. *are you in class?*

Nope. Little boys' room.

in a stall? with your pants down?

You're pooping with me.

gross.

Kidding. Tell me more about the locker room guy.

Nathaniel rolled his eyes, but he was tempted to see how worked up he could get Caesar. *save it for the bedroom.*

It's more fun in public. With someone else. Remember?

Nathaniel fought down a grin. *come see me.*

Soon.

no, right now.

Sunday. Family is in church then. I'll be visiting this hot guy I used to mess around with.

Nathaniel stopped walking, looking around the campus with a goofy expression he was glad Caesar couldn't see. *this pleases his majesty.*

I'll see you in court, Caesar texted back. A few seconds later, he sent another. *That was supposed to sound royal.*

I get it. back to class.

Nathaniel eyed the phone a moment longer, feeling a strange urge to give it a parting kiss. Instead he shoved the device in his pocket. That was the downside to technology. He and Caesar were still friends and nothing more, but when they connected this way, caution went out the window.

More and more, he was okay with that. Nathaniel looked forward to every reunion, hoping it would be the one when they finally gave in to temptation. Except lately Caesar seemed hesitant, as if something was holding him back. During one sleepless night, Nathaniel thought he discovered the reason why. They had made a promise to be together. Caesar's future was at Yale, not the University of Houston. Regardless of any potential they might have, they would still say goodbye at the end of summer. Unless Nathaniel could do the impossible. So far he hadn't heard from the admissions committee. He needed help, but asking for it would mean returning to the past. And putting himself at risk.

Nothing ventured, nothing gained. So went conventional wisdom, but Nathaniel was certain the opposite was equally feasible: Everything ventured, everything lost.

A hotel bar. Nathaniel didn't choose the location. He supposed for someone who travelled a lot, a bar seemed an appropriately neutral meeting place. He didn't feel like he belonged there, so he waited in the lobby instead. Every time the glass doors slid open, Nathaniel tensed, reminded of when he had waited for Caesar a few years back and the resulting heartbreak. Eventually he refused to look, sinking into the chair and staring at nothing until a familiar voice pulled him back to the present.

"I didn't recognize you at first. You're a man now."

Nathaniel looked up at Mr. Hubbard, feeling more like a boy. Caesar's father appeared much the same. Still the gray hair at the temples, the salt and pepper mustache, and the business-casual golf clothes. He didn't smile, but he did extend a hand. Nathaniel stood before he shook it. "Thank you for agreeing to meet me."

Mr. Hubbard released his hand to clap him on the shoulder. "I always felt bad for letting matters end the way they did. We should have spoken, so at the very least, I wanted a chance to correct that."

A promising beginning. They strolled together toward the bar where they sat on neighboring stools, Mr. Hubbard leaning toward him with a conspiring whisper. "Old enough to drink yet?"

"Still a few months shy," Nathaniel said.

"Close enough." Mr. Hubbard raised his hand to get the bartender's attention. "A couple of beers for my son and me."

Son. Mr. Hubbard only called him that to comply with Texas law, pretending to be his guardian so he could buy him alcohol. Regardless, the term made Nathaniel yearn for a time when that seemed a real possibility. In reality, he had one father he had never met and another he had rejected. Mr. Hubbard might have been the father he would have chosen, had he not messed it all up.

"I'm sorry," he murmured.

Mr. Hubbard heard him and took a deep breath. "I wanted you to love my son. That was my intention. But not like that."

"I know."

"You're not the first man to struggle with such feelings. Lord knows you won't be the last." Mr. Hubbard paused, watching the bartender finish tapping their beers. Only when the glasses were set before them did he continue. "I like to believe that events didn't progress beyond what my wife saw that day. Affectionate behavior bordering on the inappropriate. If it led to more, I need you to tell me now."

"No," Nathaniel said, shaking his head adamantly. It wasn't a lie. He was refusing to answer the question, but he knew Mr. Hubbard would misinterpret it as confirmation of what he wanted to believe—that his son had been confused and nothing more.

"Caesar was young," Mr. Hubbard said. "So were you. Old enough to know better, perhaps, but still young enough to be forgiven."

Nathaniel hesitated. He was willing to do a lot for Caesar or he wouldn't be sitting here, but he wasn't about to start denying who he was. What he had done, yes, but he wouldn't be shoved back into the closet. "It's not just a phase for me," he said. "That I fell in love with your son wasn't puberty-induced confusion. I'm a gay man, and I feel absolutely no shame in that."

Mr. Hubbard appeared surprised. Then he nodded and reached for his beer, placing his hands on it without pulling it close. "I want you to know that if Caesar's tutor had been a young woman who we invited into our home, and history ran the same course, she also would have been asked to leave."

"Then you better keep an eye on him," Nathaniel said, "because I remember him flirting shamelessly with every woman he came in contact with."

This seemed to cheer up Mr. Hubbard. He lifted his glass and waited for Nathaniel to do the same. Then they clinked brims before taking their first sip. Or first gulp as it turned out. More followed, accompanied by conversation. Mr. Hubbard asked Nathaniel about his family, how that situation had developed, and his life at the University of Houston—the perfect segue for what Nathaniel wanted to discuss.

"My life got off track," Nathaniel said. "Two years ago. Because of everything."

"Considering how many difficulties you were facing, I'd say you managed to stay the course."

"Not as much as I would have liked. As you know, I'd been accepted into Yale. I passed on that for reasons I felt were justified at the time, but now I'd like a second chance."

"Have you sent an appeal?"

"To the admissions committee, yeah. I haven't heard anything back, even though I maintain a near-perfect GPA. I know competition is fierce and there aren't a lot of openings. My gut says I'm not going to get in, but I thought—" He exhaled. "There's no easy way to ask this."

Mr. Hubbard emptied his glass, staring at it as he thought. "You know what always stuck with me? When Constance—Mrs. Hubbard—when she told me why you were no longer living with us, she said that you asked—no, that you *pleaded* with her not to tell me. Why is that?"

"Because I respect you," Nathaniel said instantly, swallowing against the sudden emotion. "I knew I was breaking a promise, even before it happened. I knew how disappointed you would be, and didn't want that to happen. I really didn't, so I fought against my own feelings. And I failed. Even if you say you can't help me or won't, I'll always be grateful that you took me in, tried saving me from a bad situation. I just wish I had repaid your generosity by being a better man."

Mr. Hubbard looked over at him, expression somber. "You're already on your way to being a great man. Who am I to stand in your way? I'll make a few calls and see what I can do."

Nathaniel shook his head, but only because he was overwhelmed. "How can I ever repay you?"

Mr. Hubbard raised his hand, signaling the bartender. "You can start by buying the next round."

"Did you get that keg I asked for?"

Nathaniel gestured Caesar inside. If money made the world go round, alcohol kept the gears greased. How ironic that he had so recently bought Mr. Hubbard a drink. Now he had bought one for his son. A large one. He crossed the common area to his private room and knocked on the metal barrel there. Caesar squatted next to the keg, eyes lighting up as if it were treasure.

"I want that thing wiped down," Nathaniel said. "Make sure my fingerprints aren't on it. And if you're stupid enough to get caught—"

"I won't squeal," Caesar said.

"I shouldn't have done this. A keg is too much."

"It's to celebrate graduation!"

"Which is still weeks away."

"Close enough," Caesar said, standing again. "Thank you."

Nathaniel shrugged. "This is the last time."

"For real? If you think I'm not drinking in college, then you're crazy. It's not like you'll be there to chaperone me anyway." Caesar's grin faltered. "Sorry. Dumb joke."

Nathaniel didn't take it personally, but instead felt this proved his theory. The separate paths ahead of them were the only issue keeping them apart. "We made a promise."

"I know."

"Do you think you'll get into Yale?"

"If I don't, I'm as good as dead."

Nathaniel nodded, then walked to the small desk. He picked up a letter that had arrived barely a week after his meeting with Caesar's father at the hotel bar. Was the timing coincidence, or did Mr. Hubbard really have that much influence? Nathaniel fingered the torn edge along the top of the envelope before he turned around. "What if we tried to keep that promise?"

Caesar eyed him for a moment, then sat on the bed. "I'm not sure that's possible anymore."

"Why? Because at the end of summer, you'll be flying to Connecticut?"

"Assuming I get into Yale."

"Is there really any doubt?"

Caesar averted his eyes.

"There's something you aren't telling me."

Caesar exhaled. "I got accepted."

"What?" Nathaniel grinned. "That's great! Why didn't you say so?"

"It felt like bragging. I still feel shitty because you got accepted once, and not because of who your father is. You gave all that up for me, and then I..." Caesar shook his head.

Nathaniel moved closer. "I still love you. You know that, right?"

Caesar's eyes widened. "After what I did?"

"Love is either a curse or a blessing, depending on how the other person feels. So I guess I'm asking. Which is it?"

"You know how I feel," Caesar said, looking pained. "I just don't have the right to say it. Not now."

"You don't need to because love never goes away." Nathaniel sat next to him on the mattress. "Do you still love Steph? Honestly. Do you love her more than a friend, even if that's all you can be to each other?"

Caesar nodded.

"And have you loved other people since?"

"Yeah, and that's why—"

"It doesn't matter. We can't control who we fall in love with, so what sense is there in placing blame?" Nathaniel stood again and started pacing, fearing the answer to the next question. "What I want to know is who you love most. Out of everyone you've ever loved. Tell me now, because two years ago I turned my life upside down for you. I'm about to do so again, and you might think the truth will hurt me—"

"It's you." Caesar's voice was hoarse. "I know it's you. But it's not that simple."

Nathaniel exhaled in relief before he spun around. "I met with your father."

Caesar blinked a few times. "You *what*?"

"I needed a favor." Nathaniel held out the envelope. "A promise is a promise."

He watched as Caesar unfolded the letter, his eyes darting around it as he scanned the information there. "My dad did this for you?"

Nathaniel frowned. "Hey, I busted my balls for the last two years to make this happen! For me, and also for you. Just in case."

Caesar glanced up, looking amused. "You always did have great balls."

"You sure? The memory cheats." Nathaniel stepped closer to him. "Maybe you should double-check." There it was again, a flicker of uncertainty. "Yeah, you hurt me. It happens. All I care about is being with you and keeping that promise. So decide. Right now. It's your move."

Caesar set aside the letter, bit his bottom lip, and stared at him with a pleading expression. Nathaniel offered his hand. He pulled Caesar to his feet once he took it, their bodies almost touching.

"Decide," Nathaniel repeated. He kept his eyes open, remaining motionless as Caesar leaned near. Only when their lips touched did he react by kissing back, grabbing Caesar and squeezing him tight. The kiss intensified. Nathaniel felt like he'd been holding his breath for all these years, finally able to suck in sweet oxygen once more.

Caesar broke the kiss with a gasp, leaned back a little, and grinned mischievously.

"What?" Nathaniel asked.

"I need you to let go of me so you can take off your shirt."

Nathaniel released him. Caesar walked backward until he bumped against the bed. Then he flopped onto it, reclining on his side, elbow bent and head propped up on his hand as he watched Nathaniel peel off his shirt.

"You really do look like a prince," Nathaniel said, flexing casually. "Just don't forget who I am."

Caesar laughed. "What do people say during chess? No wait, it's checkers." He rolled onto his back and grinned. "King me."

Nathaniel sauntered forward and did just that.

The celebration of their reunion was short-lived. Getting perfect grades was more crucial than ever, Nathaniel not wanting to jeopardize his good fortune with a less-than-perfect GPA. Focusing on his studies wasn't easy, not with visions of Caesar traipsing through his mind. Nathaniel did his best, wishing for more time, patience, energy... Ironically, when he and Caesar did meet, they reverted to their old roles. Nathaniel helped tutor him, and Caesar studied hard to end his high school education on the highest note possible.

The effort was exhausting, enough that he felt like throwing it all away, just for one night when he could focus on what mattered most. With this in mind, he lay in bed, thumb moving over the keys of his phone, digital text expressing his equally intangible emotions.

sick of class. sick of studying. sick of everything.

Caesar's response came soon after. *Does everything include me?*

no im not sick of you.

That's good, because if you were, I'd send tons of these :(:(:(

that would break my heart.

Then meet me. If you still want to.

of course I still want to. when and where?

Sunday, noon, campus library

Same place as last time, which probably meant more studying. He sighed and texted back. *ok ill be there. sweet dreams my lonely prince*

Sleep well my handsome king. And then another. *I love you.*

I love you too.

Just knowing they would see each other again lifted Nathaniel's spirits when Sunday arrived. He woke, showered, and treated himself to a real breakfast—not just the Pop-Tarts he sometimes wolfed down. Then he walked to the campus library, which was beginning to feel like a second home. Once he had been impressed by the multi-story wings filled with endless rows of books, or the main hall that was open to the floor above. His wonder had long ago faded to apathy. Nathaniel trudged back and forth to multiple departments to get the books he needed and those he was sure would help Caesar. He returned to the main hall, travelling up to the second floor and choosing a table near one of the rails. From here he could see the entrance on the first floor. He arranged his books and tried to focus but couldn't. His eyes kept returning to the entrance, waiting for his prince to arrive.

Once Caesar walked in, Nathaniel hid behind a book. When his phone rumbled, he pulled it out so he could see.

Where are you? This place always confuses me.

i'm the minotaur, Nathaniel texted back, *this is my maze. come find me.*

He saw Caesar frown at the message, then look exasperated and head into one of the wings.

colder, he texted

Caesar returned, standing in the main hall. Then he looked up. Nathaniel quickly ducked behind his book again. Too late. He heard footsteps on the stairs, the rhythm pausing on the top step. Then, a few moments later, the book was ripped from his hands. Nathaniel maintained a bored expression, not registering surprise or moving in the slightest. Caesar laughed, then leaned across the table to nuzzle their noses together. Nathaniel grimaced at this cuteness, so Caesar moved in for a kiss. Just a peck. A taste of what they would do later in Nathaniel's dorm room. Unless they found privacy here first.

He felt someone watching them and turned to see a younger guy standing there. His hair was messy and nearly covered his eyes, his expression slack-jawed in disbelief. Probably some yokel from the sticks who thought guys shouldn't kiss guys, but that fornicating with farm animals was perfectly fine. Nathaniel glared to frighten him away. The kid didn't move. Caesar made a frustrated noise and turned to see what the interruption was. The kid groaned, sounding like an animal in pain. What was he going to do next, drop to his knees and pray for their immortal souls?

"What are you staring at?" Nathaniel snapped.

"I know him," Caesar murmured. "He's my foster brother."

Nathaniel peered at him again, trying to age down the features. "Peter?"

Caesar shook his head. "No. This is Jason. The new one."

"Ah." Nathaniel didn't know why Caesar had brought him along, but he must be trustworthy or he wouldn't be here. From what Caesar had told him, Jason didn't see eye-to-eye with his would-be parents. Nathaniel stood and walked up to him, offering his hand. "In that case, it's nice to finally meet my new baby brother."

He thought the sarcasm was apparent, but Jason still seemed confused when he spoke. "You're a Hubbard?"

"No more than you are. How's my old room?"

Jason's face twisted, a number of emotions playing out before he settled on anger. He glanced at Caesar before glowering at Nathaniel defiantly. "Your old room is about to become available again. Feel free to move back in!" Then he turned and stomped off, heading toward the stairs.

"Jason! Jason!"

Nathaniel spun around, watching as Caesar called after him, pain etched across his features. Almost unwillingly, Nathaniel reinterpreted events. Caesar hadn't brought Jason along or he would have seen them arriving together. Jason's reaction hadn't been revulsion or disapproval at witnessing two men kiss, the emotional intensity closer to jealousy. Or betrayal. Nathaniel moved to the rail, looking down at the first floor where Jason paused briefly in front of the entrance, shaking his head as if chastising himself for being so stupid.

Nathaniel felt like doing the same. Then he addressed Caesar. "Aren't you going to chase after him?"

Caesar struggled within himself, breathing in and out through his nose before he answered. "No."

Nathaniel looked to the entrance again, but Jason was gone. "Tell me this was one-sided, that his reaction was based on unrequited love and nothing more."

"I'm not going to lie to you," Caesar said.

"Didn't you already?"

"No! I tried telling you, but you said I couldn't help what I feel. You said you wouldn't blame me for that."

Nathaniel huffed, feeling more like a minotaur than ever. Or just a bull, because he felt like charging. "How far has this gone?"

"Too far. I've been meaning to break it off. He just showed up in my room one night and... I had no idea, but I liked him. Jason is a good person, and I didn't want to hurt him, or you, and I figured if I could just make it to Yale, then everything would play out naturally."

Nathaniel remained motionless, picturing his old room, then Caesar's, and all the risks they had taken in both. That had felt special to him. And now... He turned to face Caesar. "Funny how history repeats itself."

"Yeah."

Nathaniel took one of the books off the table and flung it at him, Caesar hopping backward to prevent it from hitting his legs. "No, it's not fucking funny!" He took another book and threw it. This time it thunked against his target's chest. "I needed to know this!"

Caesar looked hurt, more by his intent than the physical pain. "I'm sorry!"

"What good does that do? What's going to happen if he goes home and tells your parents about us?"

"He won't," Caesar spluttered. "I know he won't!"

"You don't know shit! You don't think your dad can undo

what he's done? What about us, huh? Why do you have to ruin *everything*?"

Nathaniel swiped an arm across the table, sending the rest of the books flying. Heads were peeking around the aisles to see what the commotion was. He rounded on them, almost snarling. Instead he bared his teeth, kicked at one of the books, and made for the stairs. Caesar kept up with him, remaining a few steps behind, maybe in case Nathaniel swung at him. He wouldn't though. As pissed as he was, he wouldn't let himself turn into Dwight. Once was enough.

Caesar remained silent until they were outside. Then he began to plead. "Just let me explain. Please. Don't shut me out. Please!"

Nathaniel's head was throbbing along with his heart, his veins, his blood. He felt like a bomb ready to explode. "One hour," he said. "My place. No promises."

That's all he managed. Caesar nodded dumbly, which for some reason made him even more angry, so he turned and headed for home.

Caesar told him everything from beginning to end, a story about an aloof kid his parents had taken in. How Caesar ignored him at first, before discovering someone who was at times sweet and vulnerable, at others impossible and stubborn. Jason Grant. He became a part of Caesar's life about the time Nathaniel had reached out from the past. Caesar found himself between two men, one who insisted on only being friends, the other who he thought was straight. Until he found Jason in his room one night.

Caesar spent an inordinate amount of time describing how much he cared for Jason, the conversations they shared, the near scrapes they had gotten into, even intimate details, which seemed cruel at first. Eventually Nathaniel understood. Caesar wanted him to know that he loved Jason. This wasn't a casual affair. In fact, it wasn't an affair at all.

"We've been together a few months." Caesar sat on the floor, his back pressed against the bed. Nathaniel sat across from him in a small office chair, arms crossed over his chest like a bandage to seal the wound. "I didn't cheat on you to be with him. I cheated on him to be with you."

"That doesn't make me feel any better," Nathaniel grumbled.

"Nothing I can say will," Caesar said wearily. "I hurt you

again, and the fucked-up thing is—what I said two years ago? I think I was right. Until we can be together, we shouldn't have tried. We're so close to Yale. To everything being perfect."

"I know."

"We should have waited."

"And then what?" Nathaniel challenged. "You'll finally settle down? Right. Sure. Up until the next temptation—probably some young lawyer—attracts your attention and you stray."

"It's not about conquest. Or sex. I wish it was because then I could get it out of my system." Caesar hung his head. "I don't know what's wrong with me. Maybe I fall in love too easily."

Nathaniel thought of his speech, how he had promised he wouldn't blame Caesar, and maybe he didn't. Not for this. Feelings came unbidden. But other issues remained unresolved. "You know what pisses me off? You're incapable of shutting your mouth in the bedroom, all we've done recently is text for hours on end, and when we're together, it's rare we ever share a silent moment. And yet, somehow you never managed to mention this guy that you're dating or all these feelings you supposedly have. I'm starting to think it's all bullshit. Maybe you're not secretive *or* sensitive. Maybe you're just hollow."

Caesar raised his head, looking more defiant. "Sounds like someone I know."

"Because I don't like talking about my past?"

"Or your present! At least it was back then. Whatever happened was bad enough that you came to live with us, and I *still* don't know why because you hid it all from me."

"Not all of it," Nathaniel said, shaking his head wearily. "I was trying to spare you."

"That's exactly why I didn't tell you about Jason."

Touché. Nathaniel looked away. "What now?"

Caesar was quiet. "I'm surprised you're open to suggestions. I love you. I know you probably don't believe that—"

"If I didn't, you wouldn't be in my room right now."

"And I love him," Caesar said, his voice sounding choked. "But not as much as I love you. So when I leave here, I'm going home and telling him the truth. He deserves to hear it."

"And if he forgives you?"

"He won't. It's over. I'll stay away from him. From you too. When we start our new lives at Yale, I can only hope you'll give me one more chance."

"No," Nathaniel said. He let the pain remain on Caesar's face for a moment, hating the sadistic pleasure this gave him because that's not what love should be about. "You won't stay away from me. Not with summer so close. You'll take every opportunity you can to be with me. Then, in Connecticut, we'll continue, but without having to hide."

Caesar stared briefly before he nodded, but he looked too exhausted to smile. They had talked for hours without food or drink. The sun had gone down, and what they both probably needed was fresh air and a good meal, but not together. Not before the sacrificial lamb had been slaughtered.

"Go home." Nathaniel stood. "Do what you have to do."

Caesar got to his feet and wavered there uncertainly, probably wondering if some affectionate gesture would accompany his departure.

"Go!" Nathaniel snarled. Then he turned his back, remaining motionless until he heard the door shut behind him.

Nathaniel finished pouring out his heart, trying to summarize the whole messy situation, which meant talking nonstop for almost half an hour. He looked across the restaurant table questioningly, wishing Rebecca was there instead. Ever since he and Caesar had started meeting again, she had been depressed about not having a relationship of her own. Calling her to whine about his situation seemed especially heartless, which is why his mother was sitting across from him looking bewildered.

"Well," she said. "Hm."

"That's it?" Nathaniel said. "You're always asking about my personal life. That's all you have to say?"

"I'm glad you opened up to me. I'm just not sure I understood it all. Who cheated on whom?"

"That depends how you look at it. We made a promise years ago, but in this most recent round, Jason got there first."

Star still looked confused.

"Caesar cheated, that's all you need to know."

"Kick him to the curb?" she tried.

Nathaniel shook his head. "Not going to happen. I've already gone through the worst. I'm not giving up now. Otherwise it's all been for nothing."

His mother brushed a lock of blonde hair behind one ear.

"This isn't a game of odds. Lightning *does* strike twice, no matter what anyone says. That you've been hurt isn't a guarantee of good times ahead. Often it's the opposite."

"I suppose you would know."

"Yes, I would! I'm through denying it. The counseling sessions are going great, by the way."

"That's good," Nathaniel said. "You have no idea how glad I am to hear that. I want to forgive Dad. You know that, right? I want to believe he can change."

Star nodded. "I know. He's working hard to prove himself to us both."

Nathaniel studied her. "Maybe I'm the one in denial, but the more I think about it, the less certain I am that Caesar did anything wrong. He should have told me about Jason sooner, but I don't blame him for having feelings. Our hearts don't switch off just because we love one person. That's not how it works."

His mother's expression said he was being foolish. "You sound like your father."

"Really?"

"I mean Victor."

"Wow! Really?"

"Yes. Don't sound so excited. He was always going on about things like this." She made her voice sound deep. "'People don't stop wanting other people.' How many times did I hear that? Or, 'By giving ourselves one label, we deny all the other things we could have been.'"

"He said that?" Nathaniel asked. "Wait, is it true?"

"Honey, it's double-speak for 'I don't want a relationship because I want to screw around.'" This revelation didn't make him happy, and that must have shown on his face because she lightened her tone. "He liked getting philosophical, and I always gave him a hard time about it. That's all."

"Were there other women? Was he screwing around on you?"

Star turned her head toward the center of the restaurant, watching a family being seated. For a second she looked more like a lovesick teenager than a grown woman. "Not another woman. Another man."

Nathaniel stared until she met his eyes again. "Victor was gay?"

"Obviously not," she scolded, "or you wouldn't be here."

After a moment of tension, they both laughed. "Seriously?" Nathaniel asked gently. "He was bisexual? Do you think that's why I'm gay?"

"Who knows how these things work? I wouldn't trade you for the world or change a thing about you." His mother smiled. "Looking back, I'm grateful to him for being so fearless about who he was. When you came out—of the closet I mean, not from me—"

"Mom!"

"Sorry. But when you told me you were gay, having known Victor made it easy to accept. In a way, it was like meeting an old friend again, because you *are* like him."

This made him smile. "So who was this other guy? Do you know where he lives?"

Star shook her head. "His name was Jace. I don't remember a last name. As eager as he was to get out of Warrensburg, I doubt he ever returned there. When Jace left for college, that was it between him and Victor."

"Were there other guys? Or girls?"

"Victor got a little funny toward the end. He mostly kept to himself. The last time I saw him, he was on his own. I was scared for him and we got into an argument. Or at least I got upset. He kept his cool as always, lecturing me about how people might want other people, but that they don't need them. I argued that human contact is just as important as food and water, and that going without—" Star took a deep breath, pressed a finger to the corner of one eye and then the other. "—that going without was like committing suicide. I really wish I had chosen my words better."

"That was the last time you ever saw him?"

His mother nodded, busying herself with her purse even though she didn't seem to have a specific goal in mind.

Nathaniel pressed on. "How come you didn't tell me sooner? About his sexuality, I mean."

"Because he was always so vague about it. About everything really." She laughed, as if this was more amusing than frustrating. "He couldn't be pinned down most of the time. You were so sure of yourself, gay and proud, right out of the gate. Telling you that Victor was bisexual would have meant explaining who your biological father was. At the time, I figured you had enough to deal with."

"And when I finally found out?"

Star exhaled. "Once again, I worried about overburdening you. Should I have? Would it have made a difference?"

"No," Nathaniel admitted. He frowned and considered the coffee cup sitting before him, the wisps of steam growing weak as it cooled. "Does love always involve so many secrets?"

Star took a deep breath and sighed. "Not when it's done right."

Nathaniel leaned back and thought about it all. "I know you'll probably hate this question, but if I told Victor about my situation with Caesar, what do you think he would say?"

Star gave this serious consideration. "He'd lecture you about how concepts such as commitment and infidelity only get in the way of natural feelings, none of which can or should be denied. Then he'd probably ask you to buy him some cigarettes. Or to give him a ride somewhere."

This caused her to laugh. He joined her, amused by the sensation of having just received advice from both of his biological parents. Maybe Victor was right. If feelings were natural, and especially if they couldn't be denied, how could they ever be a betrayal? Nathaniel just wished his own feelings weren't so hurt.

People don't stop wanting other people.

As the summer progressed, Nathaniel sought the truth of this statement. Rather than pay the excessive rent on his dorm room, he returned home. Dwight no longer lived there, having started a new life with Sheila in a one-bedroom apartment. When he did visit, usually to load up on food or whatever else he could grab, an increasingly huge Sheila was with him. Somehow her presence kept Dwight in check, although Nathaniel still went on the defensive anytime he was around.

Mostly Nathaniel prepared for his new life in Connecticut while considering the wisdom of a man he had never met. Caesar still wanted other people. No doubt about it. As for himself, Nathaniel wasn't so sure. He searched himself for any indiscretion, any sign that Caesar hadn't been his sole interest since they met. He even flirted with a clerk at a mall clothing store and popped into a few gay chat rooms as if on the prowl, but these things didn't move him. He already had a boyfriend, and despite all his imperfections, he loved Caesar deeply. If personality traits could be inherited or learned, then Nathaniel's views on relationships came from his mother: loyal to a fault.

He put more faith in her advice too. Lightning does strike twice. Chances were good that Caesar would mess up again, and unless Nathaniel really could be more like his biological father, that betrayal would hurt like hell. He tried to understand how love worked for people like Caesar and Victor, hoping to soften the blow. He still wasn't prepared when the inevitable happened.

The men of the Hubbard house took a hunting trip every year. Nathaniel had once been invited before falling from grace, although he didn't regret missing out. Part of him couldn't help worrying, which was silly, because Jason and Caesar lived together. From what he understood, they avoided each other like the plague these days, but a cabin in the woods was a different environment. Less supervision, more privacy. He couldn't help but wonder, so he texted Caesar at every opportunity. Then, one morning, the responses ceased. Late that night a text came that had him chewing his nails.

Everything is fucked. Lay low. No texts no visits. I love you! I'm sorry.

He lost sleep trying to decipher this message. The first part only told him that disaster had happened. But in what form? Maybe Jason had finally taken his revenge, revealed that Nathaniel and Caesar were seeing each other. Or maybe Mr. Hubbard had discovered an unlocked cell phone full of their texts. That would explain Caesar's plea to stay low and not to text. No visits? Nathaniel didn't know where the cabin was. Had they returned home? The declaration of love was nice, but the last part worried him most. *I'm sorry.*

He had a few theories about that one, none of them pleasant.

Nathaniel waited three days for the truth to arrive. It was preceded by a text that simply said, *Your place, five minutes?*

He responded in the affirmative, then paced up and down the driveway. When Caesar's car arrived, the passenger seat wasn't empty. Steph didn't appear pleased.

"I needed my parents to see me leaving with her," Caesar explained when he stepped out of the car. He didn't smile. His face was gaunt, which made Nathaniel's stomach sink. Just how bad was the situation? "Can we talk inside?"

Nathaniel scowled. "You're going to make her wait in the car?"

"We don't have much time."

That news didn't make him happy. He led the way inside to his bedroom where they were less likely to be disturbed. Once there he turned to embrace Caesar, but found a restraining hand on his chest.

"You need to hear everything first," Caesar said.

Nathaniel nodded glumly, already knowing what was coming.

"My parents caught me," Caesar said, voice strained. "My little brother, Peter. He came into the room one morning, and I was... Jason was hurting. Emotionally. The hunting trip was a disaster. You should have seen him. He was so messed up, so traumatized, and he begged me and I knew I shouldn't but we.... I made him promise it would never happen again. So in the morning, I was holding him. That's when Peter discovered us."

Nathaniel glowered. "Did you do more than just hold him?"

Caesar looked away. "We were both naked. If you need details, I'll tell you."

"No." Nathaniel considered the nearest wall and thought about punching a few holes in it. He'd been preparing himself for this eventuality, but the news still stung. "So now your parents suspect the truth about you. That's why you told me to stay away."

"No," Caesar said, meeting his eyes again. "Now they know the truth because I told them. Not just about me, but you. They don't know that we're together now—if I can even still say that—but I told them how much I loved you. They can't pretend anymore that you were abusing your position, leading me down a path I didn't understand. Your name has been cleared."

"Until your father finds out that I've been seeing you behind his back, even asking his help getting into Yale, just to be with his son. You really think he'll give his blessing after learning all of that?"

"No. They're acting crazy. They sent Jason away."

"Good."

"Not good!" Caesar said, his voice rising. "It's completely fucked up! Jason was starting to fit in! Think how much it hurts that you never got to meet your real father. Then pretend that your mom died when you were little and you had no grandparents to save you. Instead you get thrown into some stupid home and bounce from family to family, never fitting in.

When you finally find one that clicks, you fall in love with their screwed-up son and are punished by being cast back into the wild. He doesn't have anyone anymore! Not even me."

Nathaniel watched Caesar wipe at his eyes, trying to make sense of his own emotions. On one hand, he felt betrayed. Logical or not, that's how he felt. On the other, Caesar clearly loved Jason, wanted more for him, sympathized with his plight. But all of that was out of Nathaniel's control. What could he say? What could he do?

"I love you," Caesar said, "and I'm sorry I ruined everything. Not just for you. My family is miserable, you must hate me, and Jason—" He shook his head. "I deserve to lose you. This is my punishment. I feel like I'm dying inside, but I hope that feeling never stops, because it's what I've got coming!" He thumped his chest once, lips trembling. "I wanted you to hear the truth from me in person. I owe you that much. I'm sorry."

Caesar turned and walked out the door. Nathaniel let him go. He stood there and tried to imagine what his future held now, what Caesar was returning home to, and how Jason probably felt he had neither future nor home. Then he hurried from the room and out of the house. Caesar, who had opened the car door, looked at him in surprise, but not with hope.

"I'm still going to Yale," Nathaniel said. "Maybe it can be a fresh start. For us both."

Caesar clenched his jaw, nostrils flaring as he fought back tears. Then he nodded. Nathaniel held his gaze before he turned and went inside. Once he closed the door behind him, he pressed his back against it. *People don't stop wanting other people.* Perhaps he had misinterpreted what Victor had been trying to say, because right now, despite all the emotional pain and logical reasons to let go, Nathaniel couldn't. He still wanted who he wanted.

Chapter Eleven

Nathaniel waited. Doing so allowed him to test the convictions of his heart. Moving to Connecticut provided ample distraction, as did acclimating to a new campus, the awe Nathaniel felt for Yale replaced by intimidation. He soon overcame this though and found his stride. That's when waiting truly became a challenge. He wanted to see Caesar. They had exchanged a few texts, during which Nathaniel admitted he wasn't ready to risk getting hurt again. He didn't ask Caesar to wait for him, since that seemed unlikely, but he hoped.

The holidays were nearing, finals the only roadblock standing in the way of Christmas cheer. That's when he decided he had waited long enough. His feelings hadn't changed. The love he felt for Caesar hadn't diminished, so he drove over to Caesar's dorm unannounced, carrying a potted plant. The pulse in his neck was beating as he found the right door and knocked, not knowing what he would discover.

A disheveled college student in need of a haircut, as it turned out. One who seemed to be suffering from sleep deprivation. Caesar's eyes went wide as he opened the door and tried to make himself more presentable. Then he gave up and grinned sheepishly. He might be a tired mess, but as far as Nathaniel was concerned, he still looked gorgeous.

"Housewarming present," he said, thrusting out the potted plant. "A few months late." He glanced over Caesar's shoulder at a cramped and disorganized room. "I see I was right to buy the smallest plant possible."

"Yeah," Caesar said, standing sideways to offer a better view. "My dad calls this the authentic Yale experience, which means slumming it here like he did."

"Roommate and all," Nathaniel murmured. "My how the tables have turned. I don't suppose he's a sour old Korean man?"

"Chain-smoking head-banger," Caesar said. "He just went out to buy more cigarettes."

"How long do you think he'll be?"

"Five minutes?"

Nathaniel leaned forward and said in a husky whisper, "I probably won't last longer than three."

Caesar's face registered surprise, then hunger. "Me neither. I haven't… not since you."

That's all Nathaniel needed to hear. He stepped forward. Caesar moved backward. Once inside the room he shut the door, glanced around for a clear surface for the plant, and gave up. Instead he set it on the floor. "You have a tie you can hang on the doorknob?"

"Yeah," Caesar said, kicking at one of the piles of laundry. "Uh, where did I see it last?"

Nathaniel sighed, grabbed one of the small dressers and lifted it, setting it in front of the door.

"Okay," Caesar began. "That should—"

Whatever else he had to say was cut short by Nathaniel's kiss. After a moment of gentle passion, they scrambled at each other's clothes, only unzipping or unbuttoning enough to gain access to what they needed most. They lasted longer than three minutes, but not by much. They had just finished when the door banged against the dresser, followed by an irritated knock.

"I don't suppose you have more privacy at your place?" Caesar asked, redoing his jeans.

Nathaniel checked his appearance in a small mirror, wiped at his mouth, and turned around. "Come see for yourself."

A few minutes later, after a very awkward introduction to Caesar's roommate, they were in Nathaniel's car, whizzing past old Yale buildings and onto the highway.

"You live off campus?" Caesar said, already sounding envious.

"Rebecca insisted. One of her roommates stole money from her the first year, the next she found someone's naked boyfriend passed out in her bed."

"And that was a problem?"

"He barfed before passing out. All over himself and the sheets."

"Ugh."

"Yeah." Nathaniel hit the turn signal and veered toward an exit. "Her parents agreed to help her get an apartment, so they pay for half."

"And you pay for the other. Did you get a job or something?"

"No. My parents are paying my half." His father had insisted. True to his word, he kept up with the counseling sessions, and from what Nathaniel's mother said, those had worked wonders for their relationship. Nathaniel had spoken with the therapist on the phone to verify this and had grudgingly agreed to a family session some day. In the meantime, a tentative peace had been made. Part of him still resented what Heath had done; the rest still loved him as a parent.

"Man, the tables really have turned." Caesar's tones were playful. "I never thought I'd see you mooching off your parents."

"Don't make me turn this car around! So how are you holding up? The first semester is rough, huh?"

"Is it that obvious?" Caesar flipped down the visor to check himself in the mirror. Then he sighed and flipped it up again. "I don't know if I'm cut out for this. Sometimes in class, it's like the teachers are speaking another language. In at least one class the teacher really is. I think."

Nathaniel chuckled. "You'll be fine."

"I don't know, man. My grades are pretty dire. If I don't pull it together for finals…"

Nathaniel glanced over at him. "That bad?"

Caesar nodded glumly. "Yeah." Then he perked up. "Maybe you could tutor me! We're starting over, right? Let's go back to the beginning."

"I need all my energy to keep up with my own studies," Nathaniel said. "Sorry."

"I figured." Caesar slid a hand over to take his. Then he squeezed. "It's good to see you again."

Nathaniel grinned, keeping his eyes on the road as he turned left into a dingy apartment complex. It wasn't much, but compared to the dorms, it was pure luxury. "You'll do fine," he said. "You just need to slow down and let yourself recharge."

"You probably shouldn't invite me in," Caesar said. "Once you do, there's no way you'll get me back to that dorm."

"You're not living here." Nathaniel parked and unbuckled his seatbelt. "If you promise to behave, I *might* let you spend the night. Come on."

They had a basement apartment, the windows small and high. Rebecca often complained about the limited light. He preferred it, since the gloom was better for watching movies. He showed off his home theater to Caesar as he gave a tour. The plasma television's picture was becoming diffused with age and the surround sound system consisted of mismatched speakers from thrift store stereos, but at least the couch was nice because he and Rebecca had invested in a new one. The kitchen was fully equipped, even though neither of them really cooked, and their small bedrooms were on opposite sides of the living room, ensuring privacy.

"It's so clean!" Caesar said, eying the bathroom longingly before Nathaniel flicked off the light. "You sure I can't move in?"

"From what I've seen, you'd probably trash the place. What happened to your room?"

"We had a party the first week and never found time to clean up afterwards. At least the plastic cups are gone now, but only because someone was doing a study on mold cultures."

Nathaniel grimaced. "And to think I just had my mouth all over you. Maybe you should take a shower."

"Maybe you should join me."

The front door opened before they could pursue this idea. Rebecca came in, carrying a twelve-pack of Coke. She noticed Caesar right away and was gracious about his presence. Of course she had fair warning. Nathaniel had claimed his sole purpose in going over there was to drop off the plant and say hello, but she knew him better than that.

"I've got caffeinated sugar," she offered. "Perfect cure for freshman fatigue."

"It *is* obvious!" Caesar groaned. "How old do I look? Forty? Fifty?"

Rebecca laughed. "You look fine. It's a given, that's all. I've got more carbs in the car if you want to help me carry them in. You don't have to worry about putting on weight. The constant anxiety burns more calories than you'd think."

Caesar went to help her. Nathaniel joined them, but only after pausing for an 'aha!' moment. Problem, meet your solution! Once they were back inside and putting plastic bags on the kitchen counter, he casually said, "You'll get used to the grind soon enough. Just look at Rebecca. She has a near-perfect GPA and still manages extracurricular activities, such as the, uh... what's that crazy long title again?"

"The Residential College Math and Science Tutoring Program," Rebecca said proudly.

Nathaniel nodded. "That's the one. Too bad they couldn't work in a catchy acronym somehow."

"Wait," Caesar said, looking hopefully to Rebecca. "You're a tutor?"

"Yes." Rebecca saw his desperation. "Oh. I already have a full allotment of pupils."

"Officially," Nathaniel said helpfully. She shot him a glare that he combated with his best puppy-dog eyes. "Just a little help to get him through his first finals. You remember how terrifying those were."

"Fine," she said. "You'll owe me! Both of you. What can you offer in return? What are your talents?"

"I'm good at wrestling," Caesar said, clearly grasping.

"I'm just easy on the eyes," Nathaniel said, flexing his pecs.

Rebecca nodded. "Fine. A private mud wrestling match, just for me. I hope you boys are willing to get dirty!"

Nathaniel and Caesar exchanged a heated glance. Then Nathaniel nodded. "I think that can be arranged."

Christmas lights, enough to surround a house in a warm cozy glow and chase away the dark of winter, but these weren't lining the roof. Nor were they in the yard, strapped to wooden cutouts of Santa and his reindeer. Nathaniel's mother always chose instead to fill the interior of their home with lights of every color and variety. A string of elegant golden bulbs wove among the branches of the Christmas tree, reflecting off the glass ornaments. Flickering flames came from a group of scented candles on the coffee table. Clusters of colorful paper lanterns hung in each corner, while a net of tiny white lights draped the front window, like little snowflakes trapped in time.

And that was just the living room. Nathaniel sat on the couch, letting his eyes unfocus, creating a natural kaleidoscope. Then he breathed out a contented sigh. Christmas music played from the kitchen where his father worked on his famous gravy. His mother had rushed out after some forgotten necessity. Nathaniel was content to sit and do nothing. No college, no housekeeping, not even a boyfriend. He and Caesar were dating again, exclusively, and things were going well. Nathaniel still insisted they keep their distance over the holidays. Caesar had always claimed that the timing had been wrong, that they should have waited until they were in Connecticut. Maybe the environment in Houston was a contributing factor too, although as tranquil as Nathaniel felt now, that was hard to imagine.

The front door squeaked open.

"Hey! Look who it is!"

Nathaniel tensed at the sound of his brother's voice. They didn't see each other often, and even then Nathaniel managed to keep his distance. He turned in his seat, surprised by Dwight's dark beard that made his blue eyes more striking. Part of him wished that married life had given his brother a large belly or bags under his eyes, but he was still as handsome as ever.

"Hey, stranger!" Sheila was right behind her husband, a small bundle strapped to her chest.

Nathaniel gave a cordial nod before turning back around. Maybe he should help Dad in the kitchen. Or find out where his mother had gone and join her. Or hell, he could make a run for his room and barricade the door. Instead he forced himself to take a deep breath. His brother was standing in front of him, taking off his jacket while rambling on about the Yale Bulldogs and some game he had seen. Sheila was at his side, cheeks still red from the cold. She was smiling at him, approaching cautiously, holding out something small and squirming for him to take.

"Your nephew has been waiting a long time to meet you," she said.

Nathaniel opened his arms, despite fearing he would drop or somehow break this delicate creature. Sheila helped him, showing him how to support the head. Nathaniel got the baby settled in the crook of his arm. The kid had his brother's eyes, but his sparse hair was a much lighter shade than Dwight's. Nathaniel had seen plenty of photos already. Sheila sent him emails all the time, and while he glanced at the pictures she sent, they had never made much impact. Now, holding the child in his arms, feeling the soft skin, a tiny hand wrapping around one of his fingers, he finally understood.

"Hey there," he managed.

Sheila sat next to him, bending over her son. "Do you know who this is, Arthur? That's your Uncle Nate! Yes it is!"

"Nathaniel," he corrected automatically, already knowing it was hopeless. "He's ridiculously tiny."

"He'll be a big guy," Dwight said, sounding self-assured. "A real scrapper. Runs in the family, right?" Nathaniel wasn't sure if that was a reference to their past, but his brother didn't seem too interested in him. Instead he looked around. "Where's Dad?"

"In the kitchen."

Dwight went to find him, leaving them alone. Nathaniel tried talking to the baby more, but of course got no response. Then Arthur started crying, at which point he was handed back to his mother.

"Always hungry," she said, reaching for the buttons of her sweater. "Um, would it bother you if…"

"No!" he said hurriedly. "Wait, do you want me to turn around? I can leave the room."

"Only if you want," Sheila said easily. "Some people have a problem with breastfeeding, so I tend to ask. Not that I care about the answer."

Nathaniel shrugged. "Go for it. What could be more natural? Hell, I might have a little for him if you're running low." He squeezed at one of his pecs, and she laughed. "So did you choose the name?"

"Your brother did. Why?"

"It's just… Uh."

"Nerdy like an aardvark in glasses? I know, but when you grow up with a name like Dwight, I suppose you lose perspective." She adjusted the baby so he'd be more comfortable. "I like to think of him as a little king."

"When he gets old enough," Nathaniel said, "I'll have to make him a pint-sized version of Excalibur."

He glanced down at Arthur and noticed again how small and frail he was. An old fear stirred in his stomach. "How are you and Dwight doing?"

"Fine. Starting out is never easy and babies are expensive, so money is tight. We manage. Your parents have been wonderful, thank goodness, because mine are useless."

"Oh. Is that where you just came from?"

"No!" Sheila laughed humorlessly. "Hanging out in a smoky bar isn't my idea of a pleasant Christmas Eve. They'll probably still be there in the morning too."

Nathaniel felt uncomfortable with her candor, but he supposed they were family now. "Sorry."

"It's fine. I got used to it while growing up, but not enough to accept their lifestyle as normal. Or acceptable. How's college?"

"Stressful," he answered distractedly. "So you and Dwight are getting along okay?"

"Yes! You're obsessed." Sheila cocked her head. "You asked something similar at our wedding."

He shrugged, trying to play it off as nothing. "Just looking after my sister-in-law. My brother can be a pain in the butt sometimes."

She continued watching him, as if he was being transparent. "I know he was rough on you when you were little. He told me."

Nathaniel clenched his jaw a few times. "Yeah?"

"Yes. And he regrets it. Give him a chance. You'd be surprised how much he's grown up. Even in just the last year."

Nathaniel looked toward the kitchen. His father had once asked him for a second chance. Nathaniel had given it grudgingly, but it seemed to have paid off. His parents' relationship was better now. Maybe he could do the same for his brother.

The front door opened again. His mother came in looking disheveled. "Three different stores were out of eggnog!" she declared. She held up a carton. "And I made it four!"

Nathaniel and Sheila laughed together. Heath appeared from the kitchen with his son in tow, and the evening became a whirl of noisy conversation and abundant food. Nathaniel struggled to remember the last time they felt like a real family. Tonight they could have had their own sitcom on television—the innocuous adventures of a picture-perfect family enjoying the holidays together.

This made him long for Caesar. Everything was going so well that maybe holiday magic would be enough to keep their relationship safe, even in this old battleground. As the evening wore on, Sheila retired with the baby. Then his mother and father. Although Nathaniel never would have let it happen before, he found himself alone on the couch with his brother, each of them taking swigs of beer while watching National Lampoon's *Christmas Vacation*.

"I swear I have every single line of this movie memorized," Dwight said, proving it by speaking aloud with Cousin Eddie.

Nathaniel tried doing the same for the next, botching it and causing them both to laugh. "I guess I'm rusty," he said. They snorted again, because the line he had gotten wrong belonged to a character named Rusty.

They finished their beers at the same time, like synchronized drinkers. Dwight swiped Nathaniel's empty bottle and stood. "Another round?"

218

"Yeah, okay." He ignored the television, watching his brother leave the room. People could change. He just never thought it would happen. Sheila must be a miracle-worker.

Dwight returned with two cold bottles, handing him one and toppling onto the couch. They focused on the screen until the movie reached one of the boring heartwarming scenes.

"It's really cool that you're making something of yourself," Dwight said. "Mom can't shut up about it."

A warning light went off in his head, but Nathaniel told himself he didn't need it anymore. "I'm just studying. Look at you! Family man! Supporting your wife and son."

"Sheila earns more than I do," Dwight said, "which makes maternity leave a fucking nightmare. I told her it would be smarter if I stayed home to take care of the kid."

"I really like him," Nathaniel said, trying to steer the conversation toward the positive. "Arthur's going to be an amazing man. I can tell."

"Yeah?"

"Yeah."

"Thanks."

Dwight put an arm around Nathaniel's shoulders, but with the couch in the way, it ended up more around his neck. He pulled Nathaniel closer, squeezing tightly, which wasn't very comfortable. He ended by roughing up his hair and patting him on the side of the head. None of this was gentle, but they were guys and they had been drinking. Nathaniel took another swig, then another, knowing the credits were close and wishing they would hurry the fuck up. The moment they rolled, he stood.

"I'm going to crash. You should too if you want Santa to show up."

Dwight didn't laugh. He just looked at Nathaniel as if he were being stupid, which he supposed he was for still standing there. He raised his beer, mumbled good night, and headed for his room. Once inside it, he locked the door. Then he sat on his bed, telling himself not to worry. It wasn't necessary. Nothing had happened. Just a rough but affectionate gesture. Right? He made sure the door was locked, despite being certain. Then he turned off the light and got beneath the covers, still wearing his jeans and T-shirt. He lay facing the door, listening to the sounds of the house. Occasionally his eyes would start to close, but he'd feel a jolt of fear again and they would open wide.

-tap tap tap-

Nathaniel jerked upright. Dwight was at his window! Wasn't he? Seemed weird that he wouldn't try the door first. He had never come through the window before. Nathaniel swung out of bed, peering through the dark.

"Hurry up," a voice hissed. "I'm freezing my candy cane off out here!"

Nathaniel grinned wildly and went to the window, opening it and knocking the screen out of the way. Then he practically dragged Caesar inside.

"What are you doing here?" he asked, not caring about the answer.

Caesar nodded to the bedside clock. Five minutes past midnight. "Merry Christmas," he said a little tentatively. "You're not mad?"

Nathaniel grabbed his hand and guided it to a certain area of his body. "Does this answer your question?"

Later, when they were wrapped in each other's arms, Nathaniel considered how much he had worried about them being together here. Houston had seemed threatening enough, but now, in a room that normally harbored so many bad memories, Nathaniel felt safe. And happy.

"Where are you going?"

Nathaniel paused on his way to the front door, glancing at the kitchen where Caesar and Rebecca stood. Lately they had been spending more time together and not always to study. He wasn't disturbed by their friendship, but when they spoke in perfect unison—*that* was a little creepy.

"I'm heading out to the lecture," he answered.

"But it's Saturday," Rebecca complained.

"So?" Nathaniel checked his watch and sighed. "I thought you were tutoring him."

Caesar looked to her hopefully. "Can we? I have a paper due on Monday that I'm totally screwed on."

"But it's Saturday!" Rebecca repeated. "Please don't make it a boring one."

"Come to the lecture," Nathaniel said. "It won't be boring. Did you read the flyer?"

"I thought you were joking. It's some business thing, right?"

"Flyer," Nathaniel said pointedly.

"Fine." Rebecca dragged her feet on the way into the living room—Caesar following like a duckling—and picked up the single sheet of paper from the coffee table. "Marcello Maltese? Sounds like a circus performer."

"He's a media tycoon. Mostly photography, but I've done some digging, and he's got a production company on the side. As in movies."

Rebecca and Caesar both responded with the same disinterested expression.

Nathaniel glared. "It's just my dream. No big deal. I guess we could get drunk and play pool instead."

"Okay!" Rebecca said. Then she rolled her eyes. "Go to your lecture. Caesar and I will crash a party or something."

Caesar grimaced. "I really need help with that paper. Seriously."

Rebecca sighed in resignation.

"I'll make it up to you," Nathaniel said. "Hot date, just me and you. We'll leave the brat at home."

"Hey!" Caesar complained.

Nathaniel didn't have time for more banter, wanting to arrive early to the lecture hall to secure a seat up front. After a round of hugs and kisses, he headed out. He reached the hall early enough that not only did he get his seat, but he grew bored while waiting for the lecture to start. He began to regret his decision. Hanging out at a pool hall sounded like fun. Then the lights dimmed, and a thin figure walked across the stage to the podium. A spotlight switched on, illuminating a guy who might have been a student. His brown hair was styled neatly to the side, his glasses thin gold frames. He stood in silence, eyes sweeping across the audience. Then he spoke.

"Salesmen understand the importance of making a good impression, but for true success, all that matters is making a memorable impression. Ladies and gentlemen, Marcello Maltese."

The lights were switched off completely. Nathaniel could barely make out the thin man retreating to the black curtains at the back of the stage. Then music blared, the sort of jazzy horns that might introduce the Academy Awards. At the same time, from the side of the stage, flashes went off in a frenzy, as if paparazzi were waiting in the wings, their cameras illuminating a rotund man with short graying hair who gracefully strode to the podium. Then he raised his hands. All at once the music and camera flashes stopped and the normal overhead lights returned.

"Who am I?" he asked in a pleasantly husky voice, holding up a finger to stop any reply. "Not just my name, but what am I known for? No doubt some here tonight were dragged along by a friend, or were looking to escape their tiresome roommate. Let's hear from you." Someone must have raised their hand, because Marcello pointed to the audience. "Very well, who am I?"

"I don't know, but you must be important!"

"That's precisely what I would have you believe. And for the record, I'm only important to those who stand to make money off me. Tonight that includes you, because if you listen carefully to what I have to say, you might find my success contagious. Now then, the rest of you. Who am I?"

He raised his hands like a conductor, most of the students saying his name in unison. "Marcello Maltese!"

The man grinned in response. "Now that's an introduction you're unlikely to forget!"

Nathaniel felt amused, but hoped there was more to the evening than just show.

"Let me pose another question to you," Marcello said. "I promise I won't place the entirety of the evening's entertainment on your shoulders, but allow me to put forth a scenario. The best hamburgers in the world can be found in Denmark, in a small town forty miles outside of Copenhagen. There a former farmhouse functions as a restaurant, but the farm remains, sustaining free-grazing cattle and produce that will decorate the burger. The thinly sliced bell peppers, the leaves of rocket, the soft seeds of mustard—all of it quite literally made on location. Every item needed for these exceptional hamburgers is grown or raised or milled right there on the farm. Culinary giants in every food industry have made pilgrimages to this farm and returned forever changed by the experience. There is, I assure you, no better burger in the entire world. Much skill and effort is required, but I'm certain all the hard work is worth it. After all, what could be better than being the best? That's the riddle you must solve. What is more important than reputation?"

The audience was silent.

"The question wasn't rhetorical," Marcello said. "This isn't a lecture, it's a conversation. Now then, what is more important than reputation?"

Nathaniel, feeling ridiculous, raised his hand as if in a classroom.

Marcello noticed him and nodded. "Go ahead."

"Recognition."

Marcello appeared interested but not completely satisfied. "Recognition?"

"Yeah. Brand recognition is more important than reputation."

"Well done! That is absolutely correct. We've all heard of McDonald's. We've all stuffed their miserable greasy offerings down our throats in an effort to banish hangovers. All of us have entered their establishments on more than one occasion and will likely do so again. And yet they spend millions of dollars on marketing every year. Why? So that future generations will continue to treat them as a household name or—better yet—to take over the language we use, replacing common nouns with registered trademarks: Band-Aid, Kleenex, Q-Tips, Coke."

The lecture continued this way, although it quickly became laced with dubious morality. Marcello spoke of techniques to gain both reputation and recognition, such as reviving companies that had failed centuries ago so organizations could claim to have been in business for hundreds of years. Or staging publicity stunts similar to his introduction to fool people into assuming significance, even before a company had produced a single item. His argument was that people took the world at face value. Marcello felt that should be exploited as much as possible. During the lecture, he posed more questions, but Nathaniel refused to answer them because it made him feel silly.

Until the end, at least, when he couldn't resist. He got that one right too and felt good about himself as Marcello ended the lecture. Surprisingly, this was done without the use of smoke machines or pyrotechnics. Instead he simply thanked everyone for their attention, then waved over the thin man with glasses. Marcello whispered to him, pointing twice to the audience. Unless Nathaniel was mistaken, one of the people pointed to was him.

He stood, but didn't hurry to leave. The thin man hopped off the stage, ran up to him and placed a hand on his arm. "I'm Kenneth," he said, already looking elsewhere. "Stick around for a minute, okay?"

Nathaniel nodded. The stage was empty now. Marcello

had disappeared behind one of the black curtains. Most of the audience filed out the exit. Kenneth stood next to it, gesturing emphatically to a young girl who shrugged apologetically and turned to leave. Kenneth stared after her. When he saw Nathaniel watching him, he smiled. The guy was cute in a bookish sort of way. He strolled over, offering his hand.

"I hope you're smart enough to appreciate being vetted."

"Why would I go to an animal doctor?" Nathaniel said, putting on a blank expression.

Kenneth appeared concerned for a moment. Then he grinned. "Almost had me, but your answers to Marcello's questions were much too sharp. Care to meet him?"

Nathaniel shrugged. "Sure."

He hoped this act wasn't seen through, because he felt more than a little nervous. Ignoring the stairs at one end, Kenneth climbed on stage and turned to offer Nathaniel a hand. His eyes were sparkling when Nathaniel took it, and despite being thin, he didn't have much trouble hoisting him up. Then he led the way to the wings. Nathaniel paused, noticing a tripod rigged with numerous lights, no doubt the source of the imaginary camera flashes. He was fingering the equipment with interest when a voice startled him.

"The theater department set that up for me," Marcello purred. "I love universities. Where else can you find labor willing to work for little more than a pitcher of beer?"

Nathaniel turned to face him. Marcello was sipping from a bottle of water, his face still flushed from giving the lecture. Up close, Nathaniel's original impression became even stronger.

"Have you ever seen *The Maltese Falcon*?" he asked, unable to help himself.

"Doesn't ring a bell," Marcello replied.

"I just thought… With your name and everything. Never mind." Nathaniel felt his cheeks burn. He had thought this might be a good way to jumpstart a conversation about film, and eventually Marcello's production company, but now it just seemed awkward.

Marcello didn't seem concerned either way, his attention on Kenneth instead. "Where's the other one?"

"She wasn't interested in sticking around. Medical student."

Marcello frowned. "I'm less concerned with what she intends

to do with her life than what she'll actually end up doing. The two rarely correlate."

Kenneth exhaled impatiently. "What did you want me to do, handcuff her?"

"No matter," Marcello said, turning to Nathaniel again. "Let's talk about your intentions. Why are you here tonight?"

"To listen to your lecture."

"Yes, but you only did so hoping it would enable you to achieve some goal. A dream, perhaps? Am I right?"

Nathaniel nodded.

"Excellent! Come, sit with me." Marcello led them past audio and video equipment to a canvas folding chair. He sat down, then smiled pleasantly. Apparently "sit with me" meant standing and watching him get comfortable because no other chairs were available. "I always find it wise to begin with the basics," Marcello said, looking expectant.

"Nathaniel."

"Very good. Tell me, Nathaniel, why are you studying so tirelessly at Yale? What is your goal in being here?"

"I'm aiming for an MBA-JD."

"Is that some sort of boy band?"

"It's a type of degree," Kenneth snapped. "Business and law."

"Ah." Marcello leaned forward. "And what will you do with so many letters?"

Nathaniel risked the truth. "I'm interested in starting my own production company."

"As in film?"

"Yup. I figured you might have some advice for me."

"I mostly deal in photography," Marcello said dismissively.

"But you have your own production studio," Nathaniel pressed. "Your company makes movies. Right?"

Marcello exchanged a glance with Kenneth, then leaned back again. "I suppose some department might dabble in such. It's so hard to keep tabs on everything. Tell me more about you. Why the film industry?"

"As you said, for college students the real question is what we'll do with our lives. When considering the decades of work ahead, I figured it was smartest to go with my passion. I've been fanatic about movies since I was a kid. I don't see that ever changing, and since that could make the daily grind bearable—"

"You decided to pair the two." Marcello nodded as if understanding. "But why not acting or directing? You must have a screenplay on your person somewhere, one that you wrote. Everyone does these days. Where is it?"

Nathaniel smiled. "I don't write. I do okay with a camera, but I struggled through enough art courses in my first year of college to realize I'm meant for more practical work. I know a good movie when I see one, so I thought I'd give production a try instead."

"How refreshing to hear," Marcello said. "There are far too many artists in the world these days. Everyone is writing a book or pitching ideas to Hollywood or describing the content of their cell phones as photography. Don't even get me started on YouTube. I don't mind creative impulses, but soon there won't be an audience left. The world will just be performers, stumbling around each other and impressing nobody in the process."

"I disagree," Nathaniel said. "Technology has paved the way for independent productions along all spectrums of art. The world is a more interesting place because of it."

Marcello narrowed his eyes shrewdly. "And yet you wish to be in a position of deciding what is of value and what isn't. From what I understand, the gatekeepers are all dead and the rabble has come pouring through. Do you really think you can sort them out?"

"That's not my goal. I want to help a select group bring their vision to life, but that doesn't mean denying others that right. Art inspires art. David Lynch's movie *Blue Velvet* was partially inspired by the song of the same name by Bobby Vinton. Then in the eighties, a metal band called Anthrax recorded *Now It's Dark*, which is inspired by Lynch's movie. A world full of artists can create for each other. And before you think I've got my head in the clouds or shoved up my ass, I assure you that I'm stone-cold pragmatic. I'm willing to deal with hard facts so that true art can happen."

Marcello considered him anew. "*Blue Velvet* is a Tony Bennett song. Bobby Vinton merely covered it, but I suppose that only proves your point. A world full of artists..." He chuckled as if amused by the idea. "I'm on vacation for the next week, enjoying the hospitality of this fine university. That doesn't mean work ceases while I'm away. Perhaps during my stay, you'd be willing to assist me with a few tasks? We can put that pragmatism of yours to the test. Some of your idealism too."

Nathaniel grinned. "Where's my pitcher of beer?"

Marcello's dark eyes twinkled in response. "I'm sure Kenneth would be happy to accommodate you in that regard. I have an appointment, otherwise I would happily tag along. You're a strapping young man. See if you can't help me out of this rickety old thing."

Nathaniel took his hand but he barely needed to pull. Marcello was more agile than he appeared. His palm was warm but dry, and after a gentle shake and a cordial nod, he wandered toward the nearest hall. Once he was gone, Nathaniel turned to Kenneth.

"Is he always like that?"

Kenneth sighed as if exhausted. "Trust me, usually he's worse."

"But it's Sunday!"

Nathaniel's expression pleaded with Rebecca to be patient. She stood between him and the front door as if to prevent him leaving. "This is a big opportunity."

"I know, but we've hardly seen each other lately."

"We live together. Besides, you're the one with so many extracurricular activities that you don't get home until ten most nights."

"On the weekdays, but you're right. I'm a horrible friend."

"You're not. I'll only be busy this weekend." He grimaced. "And the next."

Rebecca put on her best pouty face. "I miss you."

"I miss you too. Now how do I look?"

She straightened his tie, gave him a hug, and brushed at the crinkles in his suit. "Knock 'em dead."

"Thanks."

"Break a leg."

"Uh-huh."

"Kick their asses!"

"Feeling violent?" Nathaniel asked, but he offered her a peck on the cheek on his way out the door. He was standing by his car when another pulled up beside it. Nathaniel glanced over and groaned.

"Hey!" Caesar said, his head appearing over the roof of the car.

"Didn't you get my text?"

"Yeah, but I thought we'd have time for... You know."

"We don't."

Caesar closed the car door and walked over to him. "A kiss at least."

Nathaniel complied.

"When will you be finished? We could —"

"It's going to be a long night. That's what I was told."

"Oh."

Another sad face. Sometimes being loved was such a burden. Not that he would trade it for the world. An idea occurred to him. "Hop in your car and follow me."

Nathaniel drove to the nearest shopping center and pulled up to the liquor store. He motioned for Caesar to wait as he rushed inside. When he came out, he was carrying a bottle of wine. He got in the passenger seat of Caesar's car and handed him the bottle.

"What's this?"

"Rebecca's favorite wine," Nathaniel said. "Swing by there later today and surprise her. She's feeling lonely. Take care of her for me, okay? And none of that homework crap. Just be her friend."

Caesar nodded. "Okay. How about a keg while we're here?"

"Nope."

"A quickie?"

"Not a chance."

"Some inappropriate groping?"

Nathaniel grinned, gave Caesar a kiss worth remembering, and went back to his own car. With that miniature crisis taken care of, he could focus on the work ahead. He was looking forward to it. Drinking with Kenneth last night had been interesting, but not enlightening. Kenneth enjoyed talking about himself. Nathaniel now knew more about him than he cared to: born and raised in Richmond, came out when he was eighteen, went to Virginia Tech nearly ten years ago where he was vetted by Marcello in a similar fashion — except according to Kenneth, he had answered *every* question posed to the audience. Correctly. Nathaniel never would have guessed the guy was in his early thirties. He aged well and flirted a lot, but Nathaniel's relationship with Caesar had given him plenty of practice in deflecting such behavior.

He hoped their session today would focus more on actual work and less on Kenneth's life story. They met in an office on campus that the university was allowing Marcello to use. The big man was nowhere in sight, which was disappointing, but Nathaniel soon found himself preoccupied by the project.

"We're selling cologne," Kenneth said, pulling up a sales pitch on his laptop. "What better way to do so than with pigs?"

Nathaniel, sitting next to him, glanced over at the screen to see he was serious. "Oh."

Kenneth nodded sympathetically. "Exactly. You want to support creative types? This is the sort of madness you need to rework into a logical process. Luckily, this concept isn't so bad." He clicked a few times, bringing up a rough storyboard. "You have a pig farmer, covered in mud and shoveling manure out of a pen. He's filthy, as is the barn and the huge hog he's tending. The farmer checks his watch, notices his lack of time, and sprays on his trusty cologne. Magic happens, and we see the farmer looking clean and handsome. The barn is full of nice fresh hay, and the hog has been replaced by an adorable piglet. All this happens just in time for the arrival of his beautiful date, who will appear at the side of the frame here. The photographer is pushing for six sequential photos, but I want it done in four so the details remain sharp in the magazine."

"Wait," Nathaniel said. "This is for a print ad? I figured it would be a commercial."

Kenneth shook his head. "We don't make commercials."

"But you have a production studio. If you're going to all the trouble of setting this up, why not sell both to the customer? They get a print ad and also a commercial they can put on television or online."

Kenneth peered at him. "Where did you hear about Marcello's production company?"

"It came up during one of my online searches."

"Can you show me?" Kenneth pushed the laptop toward him. Nathaniel didn't see why it mattered, but when he finally found the site, Kenneth bookmarked it and sighed. "Marcello has his hobbies, which he likes to keep discrete. For the sake of the company."

"What do you mean?" Nathaniel pried. "What sort of movies is he making?"

Kenneth's expression became ambiguous, but only just.

"Seriously?" Nathaniel said, feeling let down.

"Let's focus on the task at hand," Kenneth said, returning to the storyboard.

What followed was hours of planning. Would they do location scouting or recreate a barn interior in a studio? They settled on the latter, which then became an issue of finding the materials and the hay. Who would they get to play the farmer and his date? Who could provide both the hog and a piglet? Then came scheduling, not just of the models in the advertisement, but lighting technicians, photographers, set dressers, and even someone from the American Humane Association to supervise treatment of the animals. Every little detail had to be considered and planned, which was exhausting—but interesting too, like a jigsaw puzzle that had to fit together just right.

"The photos should be taken in reverse sequence," Nathaniel said. "It'll be easier to dirty up the place than clean it again."

Kenneth smiled in a way that showed he'd already thought of that, but he seemed impressed. "Look at the time," he said, noticing a clock on the wall.

Ten at night. To Nathaniel it seemed only a few hours had gone by. They weren't even close to being finished.

"There's still tomorrow," Kenneth said, chuckling at his transparent panic. "Let's call it a day."

"Okay," Nathaniel said. "I guess I should be getting home."

Kenneth shook his head. "I owe you a pitcher of beer. You didn't think last night was supposed to pay for the week, did you? I'll even throw in dinner. How about that?"

Nathaniel's stomach grumbled. He grinned sheepishly. "Sounds like a yes to me."

They spent another hour at a restaurant, then moved to a nearby bar. The workday might be over, but they kept talking about it, hashing out ideas and issues that needed to be researched the next day. It was nearing one in the morning—Nathaniel's head spinning—when they stumbled out of the bar. Kenneth called a taxi, which drove to Nathaniel's apartment first. They were parked outside, the vehicle idling, when Kenneth leaned over.

"Maybe we could both get off here," he suggested.

Nathaniel shot him an apologetic expression. "I've already got someone."

"A boyfriend?"

He nodded.

"Just my luck," Kenneth said. "Ah well. Take an aspirin and drink some water before you pass out. We've got a lot to do tomorrow."

At least he had taken it well. Nathaniel tried to be quiet as he entered the apartment, ignoring the advice Kenneth had given him and going straight for his bedroom. Caesar was there, curled up on top of the bed. Rather than disturb him, Nathaniel kicked off his shoes, used the blankets from his side of the bed to cover Caesar, then crawled in beside him despite still wearing his suit. A few minutes later he shrugged off the jacket and nestled up to Caesar for warmth before finally falling asleep.

Chapter Twelve

Hitting the new Tex-Mex place tonight. Join us?

Nathaniel read this text message on the sly, hoping Kenneth wouldn't notice. He kept his response as short as possible.

No. Sorry.

He set aside the phone, trying to focus on the task at hand. A moment later, the phone started vibrating.

"Make it quick," Kenneth said with a hint of irritation.

Nathaniel grabbed the phone and hit the button to answer it, but he didn't speak until safely in the hall. "What?"

"I'm not going to say that it's Friday," Caesar said. "But it's Friday."

"I know. Just have fun without me, okay?"

"You can make this one. Rebecca isn't free until eight, so it'll be a late dinner. We're going to mock how 'authentic' the food is. Tex-Mex in Connecticut. Can you believe it?"

"I'm sorry," Nathaniel said.

"What if we wait until nine?"

"No. I'll make it up to you somehow. Both of you, I promise. I gotta go."

He hung up before Caesar could respond. He felt guilty but went back inside the office and lost himself in the work. At least he tried to, but as the hours went by, the numbers blurred together and began to resemble little fajitas and margaritas.

"I realize budgeting isn't exactly fun," Kenneth said, "but you haven't been the same since that phone call. Bad news?"

Nathaniel chose his answer carefully. "Peer pressure."

"Ah. You understand the general principle of what we're doing here, right? It's not that I can't handle the work on my own. I usually do."

"I definitely understand it all," Nathaniel said, sounding hopeful.

Kenneth smiled. "All right. Go have fun."

Nathaniel checked his watch on the way out the door. It was nearly eight now, which meant he had time to join them. He hurried to his car and cruised across town to a mall parking lot, where some failed grill had been turned into a little piece of Texas. In theory, anyway. He could already spot cheesy decorations through the windows. Was that a stuffed armadillo? Wearing a little sombrero? The locals were clearly eating it up, in more than one way, since parking was scarce and several people were gathered outside, waiting to be seated. He spotted Caesar and Rebecca on his way across the parking lot, sitting together. Next to them on the bench, the electronic coaster that signaled their table was ready flashed with lights but went unnoticed. Caesar was distracted, pointing briefly at Rebecca's face. She brushed at it self-consciously while Caesar laughed and shook his head. She wiped the other cheek, Caesar shaking his head again before reaching out and rubbing her chin with his thumb. His hand remained there, even when his thumb stopped moving. Then he dropped his hand and leaned forward. Rebecca did the same.

Nathaniel halted, the toe of one shoe scuffing against the pavement. He stared in disbelief, watching two sets of lips meet that were never supposed to. His best friend. His boyfriend. Rebecca pulled away first, laughing at Caesar, who still leaned toward her, remaining stubbornly in place until she returned for another peck. And another, which turned into a more impassioned kiss.

A car horn honked, Nathaniel illuminated by headlights. He turned to glare at the driver, then looked back at the couple on the bench, who had noticed him. Nathaniel strode forward, his steps matching the drum of his pulse. His vision narrowed to one person who was standing up now with an apologetic expression Nathaniel had seen much too often. Once that expression had moved him. Now it enraged him, made him want to snap Caesar's neck so the muscles in his face would go limp, wiping it from existence. Indeed, he found his hand on that neck, Caesar skittering backward over gravel and carefully planted bushes until his back hit the building. Nathaniel didn't have any words for him, just a growl as his fingers tightened. Caesar's eyes went wide, his spluttered explanation lost as he struggled to breathe.

"Nathaniel!"

Two arms grabbed his, pulling ineffectively. He looked over and saw someone he had turned to for comfort countless times. Red hair and a sprinkling of freckles. His loyal friend and confidant. That made her betrayal even worse because she had done the one thing that could hurt him most.

Why? What sense did any of this make? What good was love if it couldn't keep the darkness of the world at bay? Instead it was the source of the worst pain imaginable. He released Caesar, vision blurring as he turned away. He shrugged off Rebecca when she pulled on his shoulder, ignored her tears and apologies as he stomped back to the car. He even pushed her aside when she tried to stop him from getting inside. Then he pulled out of the parking lot, ignored a red light when turning onto the main road, and pushed the gas pedal down as far as it would go.

Nowhere to run. No best friend to turn to for comfort. No boyfriend to hold him and whisper soothing words. Even Nathaniel's home was contaminated, since both people would be waiting there, ready with explanations he could already predict: Rebecca had finally found someone willing to give her affection. Caesar had felt neglected or had simply fallen in love with her because his bleeding heart tended to leave a mess everywhere he went, staining the world with its excessive sympathy.

Nathaniel gunned it out of the city, by some miracle not getting pulled over for speeding. He kept driving until the lights behind him faded and he was cruising through darkness. A country road somewhere, gravel grinding beneath the tires when he pulled over to the side and started crying. His head ached from searching for a solution, for anything to make the pain go away. He even considered forgiving them both, just so he wouldn't be alone. So he would have a home again. Eventually his thoughts and tears both exhausted themselves. He crawled into the backseat and fell into a fitful sleep. When a tractor rumbling by woke him in the morning, he drove back to campus, arriving hours early at the office where he was to meet Kenneth. Neither Rebecca nor Caesar knew exactly where that was.

"Hey, extra points for punctuality!" Kenneth said when he arrived. He slowed as he unpacked his laptop. "Must have been some party last night. You look rough."

"I didn't go home," Nathaniel said.

"I remember those days. Can't say I miss them. Still, you better pull it together by tomorrow. Marcello wants to meet with you."

"I don't care."

Kenneth stopped what he was doing to focus on him. "No? Most people are eager to get into his good graces. They treat him like a god among men."

Nathaniel shrugged moodily. "Takes more than a couple of flashbulbs and some cued music to impress me."

He expected a reprimand for this remark. Instead, Kenneth seemed pleased. "We don't have to jump right in. Wanna grab breakfast?"

Food sounded good, but... "I don't want to be seen in public."

"Wow. Okay. Assuming the FBI isn't about to bust down the door for crimes you committed last night, I'm guessing you're avoiding someone. The boyfriend?"

"Ex-boyfriend," Nathaniel corrected.

Kenneth digested this news. Then he perked up. "Take-out it is! You wait here. I'll be back in a jiffy with some sensational breakfast burritos. Coffee?"

"Yeah. Thanks."

Once he was gone, Nathaniel pulled out his cell phone. He had turned it off after the first text message came in last night. Since then he had resisted the temptation to turn it back on. Tossing it aside, he went to the nearest men's room to clean up as much as possible. Kenneth returned not long after, remaining quiet while they ate. Only when they both had full stomachs did he speak.

"Want to talk about what happened?"

Why not? Nathaniel didn't have anyone else he could turn to. He kept the story as basic as possible. His boyfriend had cheated on him with his best friend, who was also his roommate. A triple whammy. That was too simple though, so he launched into his history with Caesar. Kenneth listened patiently, giving his opinion once Nathaniel was done.

"Doing the same thing over and over again and expecting a different outcome. That's the definition of insanity. I'm not saying you're crazy, but you'd have to be to give this guy another chance."

"This is the third time," Nathaniel said, nodding his agreement. "He's hopeless."

"But you're not. You're too smart to waste your time with a loser like that. Handsome too. You'll have no trouble replacing him."

The thought made his stomach turn. A life without Caesar sounded empty. Imagining someone taking his place was impossible. "I think I'm done with relationships for the moment."

"Wise decision. You know what would cheer you up?"

"What?"

"More budgeting!"

"Seriously?"

"I also took off early last night. We've got catching up to do."

Nathaniel started work grudgingly, and even though Kenneth had been joking, he soon felt better losing himself in a world of numbers, logistics, and problems that could be solved with a quick phone call and the right amount of money. When lunchtime rolled around, he declined the offer to take a break, not wanting those unpleasant emotions to catch up with him again. By evening, he was disappointed when their tasks came to an end. For more than one reason.

"What about tomorrow?" he asked.

Kenneth shut his laptop and shoved it inside the carrying case. "As I said. Marcello wants to see you. After that we have a flight back to Austin."

"Take me with you," he joked.

"Now there's an idea." Kenneth appraised him. "I have a feeling you're going to turn down a pitcher of beer, since that would be in public. What if we hide out in my hotel room instead? I'll grab a twelve-pack on the way, and we'll see how much damage we can do."

The man was flirting with him, maybe making an outright proposition, but Nathaniel didn't care. He knew it would hurt Caesar, and that was motivation enough. "Better make it a twenty-four pack."

"I love your job," Nathaniel said, tapping an arrow key to move through a document they had put together. His thoughts were warm and disconnected, his emotions reduced to a dull ache. He pushed the laptop back a little, bumping one of the room service plates. He looked over at Kenneth, ready to apologize, but he seemed amused.

"Why don't you come work for me?" Kenneth said, his slurred words bumbling into each other. "Be my personal assistant."

Nathaniel stood to grab another beer, noticing that Kenneth needed one too. He twisted the caps off two bottles and held one out. "I'm not going to Yale so I can become someone's glorified secretary."

"Well excuse me," Kenneth replied playfully. "God forbid you start on the ground floor!" He stood up—swaying a little—so he could accept the bottle, but reached instead for the buttons of Nathaniel's shirt, undoing the top one. "Okay then. How about I give you my job?"

Nathaniel set the bottles on the table, so his hands were free. He used them to stop Kenneth from progressing further. "Wouldn't you be out of a job then?"

"Nope. I'm going to *be* the boss."

Nathaniel snorted. "Then won't Marcello be out of a job?"

Kenneth smiled. "Exactly." He pushed aside Nathaniel's hands so he could work on the next button.

Once again, Nathaniel stopped him. "What do you mean?"

"That's my business," Kenneth said, sounding frustrated.

Nathaniel examined his face. He seemed serious, and if he really was going to be in such a position... Of course it was tempting, but this could also be a ruse to get him into bed. Only one way to find out. Nathaniel tore open his shirt, shrugging it off and flexing in the process. Kenneth's eyes lit up. He reached out a hand, which Nathaniel caught.

"Empty promises aren't going to get into my pants," he said. "Tell me what you've got planned."

"You want in on this?" Kenneth asked.

"You want this?" Nathaniel replied, guiding his hand downward. He wasn't hard, but Kenneth seemed impressed by what he felt. Nathaniel stepped back, breaking physical contact. "I'm interested in a job, and not just in a sexual way."

Kenneth leered at him, then reached for the two beer bottles. He handed one to Nathaniel before taking a swig from the other. Then he sat in front of the laptop. "You wanna know what kind of movies Marcello makes? Give me your best guess."

"Porn."

"Right. Gay porn. I don't know if that would cause much scandal, since the modeling industry is hardly chaste. Most brands don't care where their photo stock comes from, and the general public isn't aware of the various studios. All of it is too behind-the-scenes to interest the media. 'A company you've never heard of is doing something you might not like.' Who cares?"

"What's your point?" Nathaniel said.

A flicker of irritation crossed Kenneth's features, but his eyes travelled over Nathaniel's body again. "Marcello doesn't like to share his power. Or get his hands dirty. Hard work is beneath him, meaning that I've been the one running the company for nearly a decade now. It's because of me that profits have been on a steady rise, but guess who reaps all the benefits?"

"Sounds like a shitty deal," Nathaniel said.

"I want him out of the way, that's all. He's old. He's made his fortune. Now it's time for someone else to have their chance."

"I'm guessing Marcello wouldn't agree with you."

Kenneth looked up at him and laughed. "No. Definitely not. That's why…" He clicked the mouse a few times. "Meet the star of his next movie."

Nathaniel leaned closer to the screen and instantly wished he hadn't. The guy was hot as hell, his skin olive-toned, his eyes hazel, his hair dark. He could have been Caesar's cousin. The resemblance was enough to make his heart ache.

"How old would you say he is?" Kenneth asked.

Nathaniel swallowed. "I don't know. Nineteen? Twenty?"

Kenneth nodded happily, pulling up a scan of a driver's license. He tapped the screen, drawing attention to the date of birth.

Nathaniel did some mental arithmetic. "Sixteen? That kid is going to be in a porno?"

Kenneth grinned. "Yes, he is."

"And Marcello is okay with that?"

Kenneth clicked again. The image stayed mostly the same. All except for the year of birth, putting the license's owner well within the legal age range. Kenneth leaned back in his chair, seeming satisfied with himself.

"Kind of harsh," Nathaniel said carefully. "Won't Marcello be a registered sex offender? They'll throw him in prison."

Kenneth sighed impatiently. "People like Marcello are too rich to do time. But yes, he'll be a registered sex offender. Trust me when I say he has enough land that he won't need to inform the neighbors. He'll step down from Studio Maltese to avoid scandal, passing control over to me. Even keeping his name on the business would threaten the little empire he's built. He'll retire, which at his age he should have done already. Then I'll take the company higher than it's ever been. The only question is: Are you coming along for the ride?"

Kenneth turned in his seat, reaching for Nathaniel's belt.

This time he didn't meet any resistance. Nathaniel's head was swimming with what he'd just learned—with all that had happened recently. On the screen he could still see a scanned driver's license, the photo in one corner showing locks of brown hair and an innocent expression. He closed his eyes, imagining Caesar's face there instead. At first he appeared happy, eager to see him again. The slurping noise changed this expression—Caesar devastated, crying when he found out what Nathaniel had done and who he had been with. He deserved exactly that. Nathaniel opened his eyes. He reached for the laptop screen and shut it. Then he grabbed his beer, chugged it down, and kept on gasping, even once it was empty.

Nathaniel felt dirty. His throat burned, his mouth tasted of stale beer, and the sheets tangled around his waist were suffocating and damp with sweat. He raised his head, squinting against the morning light. Kenneth was lying next to him, back turned. Nathaniel checked the clock, then rose quickly and hopped in the shower, realizing he hadn't bathed since the day before. He drank directly from the hot water spray as he stood under it, trying to ignore thoughts on the periphery of his mind. Memories of having sex with Kenneth, of plans to force Marcello out of the company, and the ugly events that had led Nathaniel here. Caesar. Rebecca.

He reached for the soap, engrossing himself in the cleansing process to a ridiculous degree. Time to flip the switch once more. Shut out all those unwelcome emotions. He must have been out of practice, or maybe it was his hangover, because he still felt like shit once finished with his shower.

Wrapping a towel around his waist, he returned to the room. Kenneth was up now, sitting on the edge of the bed, hands covering his face.

"You all right?" Nathaniel asked.

"Nothing a little codeine can't cure," came the muffled response. He dropped his hands when the phone on the nightstand chimed. Kenneth picked it up and read the screen. "You have an appointment with Marcello in ten minutes. He's in the buffet downstairs, perhaps literally."

"Do you have anything I can wear?" Nathaniel asked.

"He's going to offer you an internship. Who cares how you look?"

"I've been in the same clothes for two days. I don't want to make it three. Do you think I should even go?"

Kenneth exhaled irritably. "Why wouldn't you?"

"Last night you offered me a job."

"Oh." Kenneth looked over at him, his expression softening when he took in the bare chest and skimpy towel. This didn't help Nathaniel feel any less dirty. "You better go. To maintain appearances and such. Don't fuck this up. I hope you can act natural."

"I won't. And I can."

"You'd better."

Kenneth rose and stretched. Seeing him naked brought back memories that weren't pleasant. Not because what happened last night didn't feel good or hadn't been consensual. The problem was that Kenneth's body wasn't familiar, didn't belong to someone he loved. In fact, Nathaniel wasn't sure he liked this man at all.

Kenneth strolled over to him, morning wood still at full mast. He pointed to it, then the carpet before him. "Why don't you take care of this for me?"

"Maintaining appearances," Nathaniel reminded him, trying to hide his revulsion. He walked around him, picking up his clothes from the floor. He could feel Kenneth glaring, but eventually heard the bathroom door close. Nathaniel hurried to get dressed, repeatedly glancing at the clock. The shower was running when he checked the room for the last of his belongings. That's when he noticed the laptop.

Nathaniel stood there a full minute, weighing his options. Even if Kenneth could be trusted and wasn't just using him for sex, Nathaniel wasn't okay with landing a job in such an unscrupulous manner. The business world was cutthroat, but surely this was a step too far. Marcello couldn't be as lazy as Kenneth made him out to be. Otherwise he wouldn't have achieved so much. Nathaniel didn't owe loyalty to either man. He could just walk away and let them get on with their war. The only problem was that one side didn't know he was supposed to be on the battlefield.

He grabbed the laptop and left the room, the door automatically locking behind him. His heart was racing as he waited for the elevator doors to open, which seemed to take an eternity. Once downstairs he asked the front desk clerk for toothpaste and a toothbrush, then went into the public restroom to make use of them. He set the laptop on the counter next to the sink, eying it warily while he brushed. Finally he went to the buffet, spotting Marcello with little difficulty.

"Ah! There you are." The large man waved him over to his table. "Help yourself to a nice coffee. One of the omelets too. I can see this week hasn't been easy on you."

"We need to talk," Nathaniel said.

"Human beings can go their entire lives without speaking. Bodily sustenance cannot be ignored. Go on now, I insist!"

Nathaniel took the laptop with him, which probably looked ridiculous, especially when he used it as a tray for his coffee and eggs. Not that Marcello seemed to notice when he returned. He was happily nibbling on a pastry while glancing around at other diners.

"Could you imagine if every meal was so communal?" he commented. "At a buffet we take from the same pile of food, like a pride of lions tearing apart a freshly caught gazelle, rubbing elbows while shoveling more food onto our plates. A shame then that we don't dine at the same table. That would bring the concept full circle."

"Listen," Nathaniel began.

A ringtone interrupted them, an electronic version of ABBA's *Dancing Queen*. Marcello set down his pastry and reached for his phone. Nathaniel wanted to grab it first, but it was too late.

"Kenneth! When are you— Hm? Why?" Marcello looked across the table at Nathaniel as he listened. "Yes, I'm by myself. Why would he steal your laptop? Oh, a petty thief. I see! Well, I think he would have found me by now, if that was his intent. No doubt he's headed to the nearest pawn shop. Are you coming down for breakfast? The police? Perhaps you're right. You better stay in your room until they arrive, just in case he has further mischief planned. I'll do the same and return to my room immediately. Okay. Goodbye."

Marcello put down the phone, laced his fingers together on his belly, and gave Nathaniel a frank expression. "Well? What's this all about?"

"Give me a second and I'll show you." Nathaniel shoved his plate aside so he could open the laptop. Once the computer was roused out of sleep mode, he found it still on the same image of a driver's license. He turned it around so Marcello could see.

The man sniffed, as if not particularly interested. "How careless of Kenneth not to have a password screen. This machine contains confidential information."

Nathaniel huffed impatiently. "Do you make adult movies?"

"Yes. What of it?"

"Is this guy going to be in one of them?"

Marcello's eyes flicked to the screen and back again. "Blackmail?"

"Not yet. And not from me. Look at the date of birth. Now watch." Nathaniel hit the arrow key, going back and forth a few times to highlight the difference.

For once Marcello looked surprised. He leaned forward, mouth agape. "Which is his true age?"

"Take a guess. Kenneth is hoping to force you into early retirement, and by force, I mean he intends to get the police involved." Nathaniel took a quick sip of coffee and stood. "I don't want anything from you. I thought you should know. That's all." He turned to leave.

Marcello cleared his throat. "Has it occurred to you that Kenneth might have called the police, knowing they would find us together? All he has to say is that I asked you to steal the laptop so I could destroy the evidence. The altered image could have been crafted by me to get an underage actor into one of my films. Not as damning as his original intentions, if what you say is true, but a decent contingency plan nonetheless."

Nathaniel stared at him. "So what do we do?"

Marcello closed the laptop and gestured at it. "Return it to him. Convincingly."

"How?"

"How indeed. I don't suppose you could disguise yourself as a maid and slip into his room? Purely in the spirit of adventure. I don't see how it would really assist you."

"This is serious," Nathaniel said.

"I know," Marcello said. Then he nodded at the lobby. "Off you go."

Nathaniel grabbed the laptop and hurried back to the elevators. On the way up, he decided that he needed to get caught, but not by the police. He knocked on Kenneth's door and heard him moving behind it a moment later.

"I can't find Marcello," Nathaniel said. "He's not downstairs."

The door swung open. Kenneth looked him up and down and noticed the poorly concealed laptop behind his back. "What are you doing with that?"

"Oh." Nathaniel made sure to look uncomfortable. "I thought I might need it. For taking notes."

"I know what game you were trying to play. Give it to me!"

Nathaniel took a step backward.

"I called the police!" Kenneth said. "They'll be here any minute."

Nathaniel sighed, as if defeated. Then he held out the machine. "You wouldn't have given me the job, would you?"

Kenneth snatched away the laptop. "Now you'll never know!" The door slammed shut. Nathaniel made sure to look despondent, figuring Kenneth would gleefully peer through the keyhole to catch his expression. Then he rode the elevator back down to the lobby, where two police officers were standing at the front desk. They noticed him and walked in his direction.

"Great," Nathaniel muttered.

"Oh good, you're here!" Marcello swept past him, shaking hands with both officers. "I'm so sorry about the false alarm. I left my laptop in the dining room. When I returned upstairs, I assumed this young man had—" He turned and waved a hand at Nathaniel dismissively before addressing the officers again. "Oh, I am getting old! I turn fifty this year, you know."

The officers exchanged weary expressions.

"I'm sorry about the wasted trip," Marcello continued, "but it doesn't have to be. Why don't you take a well-deserved break and enjoy the buffet?" The concierge squeaked in protest, prompting Marcello to add, "My treat! A coffee at the very least."

That seemed to do the trick. He escorted the officers toward the dining room, returning a moment later. "He has the laptop?"

Nathaniel nodded. "What are you going to do?"

"To Kenneth? A severance package of three-months' salary and a glowing letter of recommendation."

"Seriously? The guy wanted to get you arrested!" Lowering his voice, he added, "You would have been a registered sex offender."

"I do hate registering for things," Marcello admitted, "but it's best in such situations to resolve matters quietly. Besides, no doubt one of my competitors will hire him, hoping to undermine my studio. My own version of a Trojan horse, if you will. Won't they be surprised when Kenneth betrays them too. On that note, I should probably get to my room, just for appearances, but I was wondering if you would consider working for me. After all, a job vacancy is opening, and you did train with the former occupant."

"I still have another year of college."

"Ah, but an MBA-JD can be earned AI—Accelerated Integrated—which only requires three years of study. You're nearly there. I could pull some strings."

Nathaniel stared at him. "Last time we met, you acted like you didn't understand what any of those letters meant."

"You'll find one of the easiest ways of manipulating others is by playing the fool."

"So your whole persona is an act?"

Marcello smiled. "Those most blessed in life *are* fools. No acting required. What do you think of my offer?"

Nathaniel hadn't had time to think, but he already knew the answer. "No. Most of my world fell apart a couple of days ago. Knocking down the rest doesn't sound very wise."

"Have it your way." Marcello reached into his suit and produced a business card. "If ever you should change your mind, I am in your debt. Do not underestimate the value of that statement."

He handed the card to Nathaniel, then walked to the elevators with a careless gait, as if nearly being framed for a heinous crime was part of his daily routine. Nathaniel watched him leave, then went outside to the parking lot, both accepting and dreading one fact: It was time to go home.

Nathaniel returned to an empty apartment, which wasn't surprising, since they all had classes to attend. But for him, his first order of business was a change of clothes. Once he'd stripped down, he found himself longing for a second shower. More water to wash away the experiences of the night before. He left the light off in the windowless bathroom, standing beneath the hot stream in perfect darkness. Then he let himself ache inside and out. His skin burned from the heat, his head throbbed from too much alcohol, his stomach felt tight with hunger, and his chest… That pain was only emotional, but at the moment it sure felt physical. Kenneth was easy enough to forget. Everything Nathaniel had been avoiding by turning to him wasn't.

When the hot water started to run out, Nathaniel turned off the faucets, went to his room, and put on comfort clothes: a worn-down cotton T-shirt, a soft hoodie that zipped up tight against his torso, and jeans with too many holes to be presentable. Then he fed himself, standing at the kitchen counter and unceremoniously eating a sandwich. Afterwards he returned to his room, shut and locked the door, and waited. He tried to brace himself, but when the knock came in the early afternoon, he still wasn't ready.

"Nathaniel?" Rebecca said through the door. "Are you okay?"

He clenched his jaw. What a question!

"Can we talk? Please. I'm worried about you!"

He threw open the door. "If you gave a shit about me, you wouldn't have—" The words caught in his throat, so he found new ones. "Fuck you!"

Rebecca flinched. "I'm sorry."

"Oh, okay." Nathaniel said, expression incredulous. "That fixes everything. What now? Want to catch a movie together? Or hey, how about we head out for some Tex-Mex? I know the most romantic place!"

He wanted her to fight back and get defensive so he could keep shouting, wound her, make her share his pain. Maybe he had already succeeded because she started crying.

"I'm a horrible person," she said.

Nathaniel crossed his arms over his chest. "Yeah, you are. How long has this been going on? No, I can guess that. How *far* has it gone? That's what I want to know."

Rebecca averted her eyes.

"Congratulations," Nathaniel said coldly. "You finally lost your virginity. I hope it was everything you dreamed it would be."

He slammed the door, went back to his bed, and pounded the mattress with his fist. It didn't make him feel better, but it siphoned off just enough anger to allow him to cry a little. He rubbed at his eyes harshly, focusing on the pain, which wasn't difficult to do. A few minutes later, he heard the door behind him open.

"I was lonely," she said. "Not because you were busy. I've been lonely since high school. I wanted what everyone but me seems to have."

"You wanted what I had," Nathaniel said. "Now you've got it."

"I don't think I do. He loves you."

"He doesn't know what love is," Nathaniel spat. "Don't talk to me about him. Understand? We're through!"

Rebecca's eyes went wide. "Do you mean you and Caesar? Or you and me?"

"Both!" he shouted. "Do you really think I'm going to be your friend after this? I trusted you with *everything*. More than I've trusted anyone else. Maybe I can't kiss you or fuck you, but I gave you everything I could! And what did you do?"

"I'm sorry," Rebecca whispered.

"I don't care. Remember how I always felt in Houston, how I was scared to go home because I didn't want my brother to hurt me? Guess what? I'm right back there again. This is my home, and I no longer feel safe because you hurt me in a way I never dreamed possible. I'd rather live with Dwight. Seriously! I'd rather get the shit beat out of me every day than spend another second here with you."

"I'll move out," Rebecca said, her voice shaking.

Nathaniel turned his back on her. "I can't afford the place alone. Neither can you. Caesar can move in and I'll find somewhere else. Hell, maybe I'll take his stupid dorm room."

"I don't want to live with him," Rebecca said. "I don't even know if I want to see him again."

"You'd better!" Nathaniel spun around. "You'd better be so fucking in love with him that you lose control when he's around. Otherwise it makes what you did even more screwed up." He looked at her questioningly, his chest heaving. "Well? Do you love him?"

Rebecca shook her head. "I don't know."

"Get out."

"Nathaniel—"

"Get. Out. Don't speak to me, don't even look at me. Until I figure out where to go, I'm a ghost." His voice cracked. "I'm dead and buried."

Rebecca was on the verge of tears again, so he stood and

marched toward her. He wouldn't have done anything, would have stopped short had she stood her ground. Thankfully she stepped back enough that he was able to slam the door and lock it. Then he returned to his bed, lay flat on his stomach, and covered his head with his arms, willing this all to be over.

Nathaniel left the room a changed man. He had barely slept during the night, but he felt strangely rested. In the dark of his room he had gathered all the pieces, all the shattered fragments of his identity and emotions. Then he put them back together again, but not in the same order. He assembled for himself a suit of armor, cold and impenetrable. No matter what he still felt inside, the fire was now contained within a furnace. He did this to survive, because he knew the worst was yet to come.

Over the next few days he walked around the apartment as if nothing had happened. He relaxed on the couch and watched TV or ate his bowl of cereal while sitting there in the morning. Rebecca tried talking to him on more than one occasion, but it didn't matter. She was no longer of any consequence to him. Nathaniel had been wrong: He wasn't the ghost, she was, and he had exorcised her from his heart. That left only one.

Wednesday night. Rebecca was off playing tutor. Nathaniel sat on the couch looking at the TV, a six-pack waiting for him on the coffee table. Music videos were on the screen, but the volume was turned down completely, mouths moving without making a sound, bodies shaking to a rhythm he couldn't hear.

Someone knocked on the door. He ignored it. When a key scratched into the lock and the door opened, he didn't show any surprise as Caesar came in and stood there uncertainly. Nathaniel refused to look at him, even though his presence caused barely-healed wounds to tear open again.

"Rebecca is worried about you," Caesar said.

No words, no matter how carefully chosen, would have made a difference. But starting with *her* name was the worst possible strategy.

"I'm worried too," Caesar added. He shut the door and came a few paces closer. "I'm sorry. I know it doesn't matter. I hurt you, and I don't deserve to be with you."

"You aren't with me," Nathaniel murmured, attention still on the television.

"Fair enough. I just…" Caesar's voice faltered. "I wish there was something I could do. I don't want you to be hurt or messed up just because I am. I want you to be okay, and I guess staying away is my only option, but I want you to know that I love you. Anyone would be crazy not to. Someday you're going to meet an amazing man, and he's going to be really nice and appreciate you and not make stupid mistakes like I did. He's going to love you, and it's going to be perfect because that's what you deserve. I'm going now, but I wanted to say thank you for loving me. I'm just sorry that—"

"I didn't love you." Nathaniel turned his head, making eye contact for the first time. "I never loved you. When we first met, I needed somewhere else to live. That didn't work out, but you suck good dick, so I kept you around. When I was bored, you were there."

"That's not true," Caesar said, shaking his head. "You just want to hurt me."

"I just want you to leave," Nathaniel said calmly. "Once Kenneth started blowing me, I realized I could do better. And I have." His smile was cold. "A few times."

"Okay," Caesar said, lip trembling. "I guess I deserve that, but I still—"

Nathaniel grabbed the remote and cranked up the volume until it was maxed out and the overwhelmed speakers were vibrating with crackling sound. He resumed staring at the screen, keeping his attention there until from the corner of his eye he saw Caesar turn and leave. Then Nathaniel lowered the volume and turned off the television. A moment later he threw the remote at the wall. Then he grabbed his first beer, twisted off the cap, and leaned back, bringing the bottle to his lips.

Nathaniel walked the paths of Amistad Park, retracing his steps over and over again. The Yale-New Haven Psychiatric Hospital was just across the street. As mind-bending as the past few weeks had been, he was tempted to check himself in. These days he often explored new sections of the campus, lingering in areas like the Medical Center because of the reduced risk of running into anyone he knew. The sun was setting and once again, Nathaniel dreaded the idea of going home. So often Rebecca would show up, trying to make peace or pretend nothing catastrophic had happened. On one occasion Caesar had been waiting for him in the parking lot, but Nathaniel brushed by him like celebrities did paparazzi. He kept his composure in these situations, but each challenged his resolve to remain stoic.

He hated the apartment. Hated the familiar areas of campus. Hated anywhere memories had been made with Rebecca and Caesar. This was another reason why he wandered to unfamiliar locations these days, but lately even that wasn't enough. He didn't want to return home. And yet, that's exactly what he desired most. Nathaniel dug his phone from his pocket, selected a name, and stopped pacing until he heard a familiar voice.

"Hi, honey!" his mother said. "How are you?"

"Fine." Nathaniel tried to keep his tone steady. "Spring break is next week."

"I'll bet you're excited. You're under a lot of stress. I can hear it in your voice."

"Can you fly me home?" he blurted out.

"For spring break?" Star asked after a moment's hesitation. "Wouldn't you prefer Miami? Or maybe Las Vegas?"

"I want to come home. I could take my car, but the drive is crazy long and I'll be on my own."

"Did something happen? Are you okay?"

"Yeah." Nathaniel started pacing again. "Just homesick. The airfare can count as my birthday present."

"It's a little early for that." His mother tried to laugh, but her concern won out. "We'll fly you home. Let me grab a calendar and you can tell me your dates."

The knowledge that he would soon escape made the remaining time bearable. When taking the train to the Newark airport, he braced for the worst, fearing something—anything—would keep him from boarding his flight. But he made it, watching from his cramped window seat as Connecticut sank away and disappeared beneath the clouds. Then he exhaled, feeling more at ease than he had for weeks.

By the time he landed in Houston and was standing at the luggage carousel, he wasn't exactly grinning at his fellow passengers. At least he felt secure, like he could let down his guard, which made it all the more ironic that a guard stopped him just as he was leaving. Or an officer of some sort.

"Would you mind setting down your bags?" the man said.

He smiled reassuringly, raising the leash he was holding. "Just a training exercise."

Nathaniel looked down at a… dog? The creature was the right shape and size, but was missing chunks of fur all over its body, some sort of rash filling in the bare patches. Its blue eyes were clear and alert, but other than that, the animal appeared contagious. Currently it was sniffing his suitcase.

"Please, sir. The bag."

Nathaniel shrugged and set the duffel bag on the floor. The dog hopped over to it excitedly, tail wagging as it circled and sniffed.

"There's half a sandwich in there," Nathaniel said without much interest. "Feel free to confiscate it."

"No, it's fine. Come along, Bonkers." The officer tugged on the leash, but the dog was still interested in the bag. So interested that he lifted a leg, and a yellow arc of urine soaked the cloth.

"Hey!" Nathaniel shouted.

"Bonkers!" The officer yanked, dragging away the dog, who didn't stop peeing for a few more seconds. "I'm sorry!"

"It's fine," Nathaniel grunted.

"There's a restroom just over there," the officer said, picking up the bag and moving in that direction. "We'll get this rinsed off, and it'll be like new!"

Nathaniel sincerely doubted that. He followed the officer and the dog, who bounded along happily. Once in the restroom, the officer was wetting paper towels in the sink when the dog broke loose, scurrying around the restroom and bumping into a man at the urinal, triggering another pee-related accident. Nathaniel snorted and tried not to laugh. He stepped on the leash so the dog couldn't escape out the door.

"No good deed goes unpunished!" the officer said, shaking his head. "He's not the right breed to be a sniffer dog, but one of the local shelters asked us to help train some of their problem cases. Better than them being put down, but of course they didn't give us any of the smart ones. God forbid!"

Nathaniel bent over and took the leash. Bonkers wagged his tail and jumped on him, probably hoping to knock him over, but Nathaniel was a lot bigger than the dog. The beast bounced against him ineffectually, then strained against the leash to reach the nearest urinal where he tried to drink the water.

"I think he might have brain damage," Nathaniel said.

"That would explain a lot. Here." The officer thrust out Nathaniel's bag. Now it was even wetter, with shreds of paper towel stuck to the damp parts.

"Gee, thanks." Nathaniel offered the leash in exchange. "This belongs to you."

"Not for long. He's going back to the shelter where he'll meet his maker. At least he'll get two weeks of vacation before he has to face reality."

"I know the feeling," Nathaniel replied.

They left the restroom, the officer walking off in a different direction, perhaps in search of his next victim. Nathaniel glanced over his shoulder at the dog, who was looking back at him, tail wagging. He might be the ugliest creature ever, but the eyes were youthful, the open mouth like a goofy smile. Was he still a puppy? Nathaniel felt a pang of sympathy, knowing how life could deal shitty cards at times. Then he turned and left the airport, already spotting a familiar car pulling up to the curb. A second later, his mom hopped out of the passenger side and ran to embrace him. He was home again, and this time, it sure felt good.

Chapter Thirteen

Hollow. Nathaniel spent the better part of two weeks trying to fill the void inside. Often this meant sitting around the house watching movies, letting the plight of each character supersede his own. His mother seemed to sense his situation and tried to help by dragging him out for shopping or lunches, even insisting once that they both needed makeovers. This meant a trip to the stylist for a haircut followed by a pedicure. Nathaniel didn't enjoy the experience, but didn't act as despondent when around his mother. That he saved for when he was alone in his old room, stretched out on the bed, staring up at a blank ceiling.

In a strange sort of way, he did find contentment. Moping around his parents' house was better than the emotional mess he'd left in Connecticut. But of course Thomas Wolfe was right. You can't go home again. Not without being reminded of why you left in the first place.

Dwight was coming over for dinner. It would be too public for any sort of trouble. Nathaniel wouldn't share a few beers with his brother afterwards. Not this time. Dwight managed to surprise him anyway. He barged into the front room, voice loud as he greeted Nathaniel, breath acrid from alcohol.

"Hey, it's the college graduate! Mom's golden boy."

Nathaniel didn't risk correcting him. He remained perfectly still when Dwight ruffled his hair, reassured that his parents, Sheila, and the baby were present. Only when Dwight threw an arm around his neck, pulling him down into a headlock, did Nathaniel react. He pulled free and shoved. Hard.

Dwight stumbled away, his features twisting up in rage. There it was again, after all these years. His family would finally meet the monster! Nathaniel didn't cower. He felt hungry for confrontation, wanting to punch out some of his frustration.

"Boys!" their father shouted. "No roughhousing!"

"Roughhousing?" Nathaniel spat. "Because that's all this is, right? I'll be in my room!"

His family gave him privacy, which he spent pacing, trying to figure out what to do. He couldn't stay here. Nathaniel knew that already. He'd be fine until spring break was over, but he hated the idea of returning to Yale. The entire experience had been soured. Even if he found a new place to live, the thought of being on campus and running into certain people made him miserable.

A knock on the door caused him to spin around defensively. Dwight? Then again, so what! Part of him was still itching for a fight. He threw open the door and found a much smaller figure standing there.

"I brought you dinner," Sheila said.

He caught a whiff of the mashed potatoes and fried chicken and took the plate from her. "Thanks. Come on in."

Sheila examined the room as she entered, then sat on the corner of the bed. Nathaniel nudged the door shut with his foot, joined her on the mattress, and wasted no time in eating.

"I knew you'd be hungry," she said. "Just like your brother. You Courtney boys sure like to chow down!"

He glared at the mention of Dwight.

"I know," Sheila said with a sigh. "He's been having a rough time lately."

Nathaniel chewed and swallowed. "I hope you didn't let him drive."

"Of course not. He doesn't have a choice."

"Meaning?"

"They didn't tell you?" She stood and walked to a bookshelf that was mostly empty now, except for some old decorations his mother had brought in. Sheila touched a ceramic bird, fingers tracing the intricate pattern of its feathers. "Dwight got arrested a few weeks back for driving while still a little... Um."

"Drunk driving," Nathaniel said.

Sheila nodded. "He spent five days in jail and was fined enough to clear out our bank account. His license is suspended for six months too, but despite all that, I was happy. I honestly thought this would be his wakeup call." She turned to face him. "I should have known better. I've seen it all before, thanks to my parents, but I thought... I love your brother. When I was little I always wished I could change my parents. Make them better. Maybe I saw them in Dwight and thought I could finally be the little girl who fixes the world." She shook her head. "He needs help. I'll make sure he gets it."

Nathaniel finished another bite. "You know," he said eventually, "for someone who grew up with alcoholic parents, you sure seem well-adjusted."

Sheila appeared unconvinced. "Is that what you see when you look at me? Well-adjusted people don't marry an equally dysfunctional version of their father."

"We all marry our parents," Nathaniel said. "Figuratively speaking."

Sheila scrunched up her nose. "I always hated that idea."

"Yeah, me too."

"Do you think it's true?"

"I hope not." They shared a laugh before he continued. "What I mean is that you seem happy. You had a rough childhood. I did too, but you seem way more together than me."

"You're not happy?"

He shrugged, not wanting to answer the question.

"I was loved," Sheila said. "Maybe not by my parents. Not in the way I wanted to be, but I had Missy."

"Missy?"

Sheila nodded and took out her phone, navigating screens and finally holding up an image of a beagle sitting in the grass. "There's no better cure for a broken heart than a dog. Anytime I was hurt, she was there. The nights when my mom and dad didn't come home, I wasn't alone because Missy was with me. She loved me unconditionally. I still wanted normal parents like my friends had, but I never felt unloved." She put the phone back in her pocket, looking sheepish. "Sounds stupid, doesn't it?"

"No," Nathaniel said firmly. "It doesn't."

"As soon as Arthur is old enough, I'm getting him a puppy that he can grow up with. I already love him with all my heart, but I want him to have that same comfort. Anyway, what's all this about you being unhappy?"

Nathaniel started to shake his head. He preferred the pain to remain buried. Why speak of it? Then again, Sheila had always been open with him. "I broke up with a guy I'd been in love with for years. I think I still am."

"Then what got in the way?"

Nathaniel started talking. At first he tried summarizing the situation, and as shocking as "my best friend was sleeping with my boyfriend" sounded, it still didn't evoke all the despair he had gone through, so he kept speaking, delving into more detail than necessary.

"You can always start over," Sheila said. "Build yourself a

new life. I know it can be difficult to see the way forward right now, but there's nothing holding you back. Reinvent yourself. Make the world what you want it to be."

Nathaniel felt a nostalgic pang. It was good having someone to confide in again. He missed Rebecca. She had given him so much. Maybe he hadn't given enough in return.

"You okay?" Sheila asked.

"Yeah. I just had a non-angry thought about Rebecca, that's all."

"Maybe you should forgive her."

He shook his head. "We'll never be friends again."

"Fine, but you can still forgive her. Even if she never finds out. You'll feel better if you let go of that anger completely."

Nathaniel considered her with fresh perspective. Pretty, intelligent, and caring. "Where's my brother?"

"Sleeping it off in his old room. Why?"

"Because I'm seriously thinking about proposing to you. Let's run away together. We'll elope."

Sheila laughed. "Considering what an ass he's been lately, I'm tempted to take you up on that."

They talked a little longer, Nathaniel getting to know her better and listening to stories about Arthur that made her cheeks grow rosy. For once he believed the kid was going to be all right, because however much fury coursed through his brother, Sheila possessed twice as much love. When she heard Arthur crying, she left to tend to her son.

Nathaniel considered her advice. Build a new life. He could do that. Even if he walked out of the house right now and lived on the streets, he would be setting the past firmly behind him. Of course he wasn't too keen on sleeping under a bridge. A job would be nice. Hadn't he been offered one recently? He pulled out his wallet, searching for Marcello's business card. Then he remembered using it as a bookmark on the plane. Nathaniel stood, grabbing the duffel bag from one corner and wincing at the stench of urine. Then he laughed, remembering how the smell had gotten there.

Bonkers the dog. What a stupid mutt. He was probably tearing apart some poor tourist's backpack right now. Unless the officer hadn't been kidding about sending him back to the shelter. If so, Bonkers had probably been put to sleep. Nathaniel couldn't imagine anyone adopting such an ugly or ill-behaved creature. He swallowed, surprised by the lump in his throat. Then he opened the bag, digging around until he found the book. And the business card. He considered everything he needed before he dialed the number.

"Marcello," a voice said by way of introduction.

"Nathaniel," he replied. "Do you remember me?"

"I never stopped thinking of you," Marcello purred. "To what do I owe this pleasure?"

"Is that job offer still open?"

"Funny you should mention that. Kenneth just left our employ today."

"You let him stick around that long?"

"Of course! I didn't want to alert him, not before my computer specialists finished searching for more nasty surprises. And we found a few. Yes indeed. Now that his fangs have been pulled, Kenneth has been set loose, free to slither off to browner pastures."

"You still need someone to take his place?"

"Ah."

"Ah?"

"Naturally I've been planning ahead. I have some very impressive résumés on my desk. And if I'm not mistaken, you're still preoccupied by Yale."

"Fuck that place," Nathaniel said. "And everyone there too."

"What a novel idea! You know, perhaps you should reconsider your verbal demeanor. I've never had a potential employee use such language during a job interview."

"Is that what this is?" Nathaniel blanched. "I figured it was already too late."

"You did good work," Marcello said. "It's hard to separate precisely what you accomplished while working with Kenneth, but the results were of a higher caliber than usual."

"I'm willing to work even harder," Nathaniel said. "I promise."

"The position is more complicated than you might imagine."

"I can handle it."

Marcello chuckled. "Such hubris. Enjoy it while you can. I haven't sounded so certain about anything since my thirties. I'm afraid, however, that I must consider what is best for the company. Youth has its drawbacks as well, such as a lack of experience. Perhaps I can find you a position as a personal assistant or—"

"You said you were in my debt," Nathaniel pressed.

"Do you really feel now is the appropriate time to play that card?"

"I'm desperate."

There was a pause on the line. "You helped me at a time when I didn't know I needed it. I'd be remiss not to return the favor. If worse comes to worst, we can agree to part ways."

"Will I get a three-month severance package too?"

"Avoid extorting me and I might make it six."

Nathaniel's breath felt short. "So I've got the job?"

Marcello hesitated. "I'm not usually one for public service announcements, but from what I understand, it's cool to stay in school. Student loans are dreadful. At the very least you should finish the semester and earn a degree."

"I'm not going back to Yale," Nathaniel insisted. He glanced at the business card. "Austin has a university. I'll finish my degree there. Eventually."

"Then you're willing to relocate?"

"Totally. Except…"

"Yes?"

"Money is a little tight right now. I'll need a place to stay."

"Then you can be my guest until you find your footing."

"No," he said without thinking. It didn't take him long to understand his aversion to the idea. "I've never had much luck living with other people. I need to be on my own."

"And you expect me to buy you a house?"

"Works for me," Nathaniel said, "but I was only hoping for an advance so I could find an apartment."

"A rental?" Marcello sounded amused. "How practical! I've always said that renting is like dating. No sense in proposing to the bank before you're ready to get ravaged by them on the honeymoon."

"I'd be in your debt," Nathaniel said.

"Literally, when I'm interested in obligations of a more abstract nature."

"I did save your entire company."

Marcello chuckled. "Then the company will save you. I'm

sure we'll find a way of making the apartment tax-deductible. Please don't tell me I need to go grocery shopping for you. Or worry about the furnishings."

"No. I can handle all that."

"Very well," Marcello said. "You have my email address. Send me any information you find relevant. I'll respond with your new address, once I have it. Everything else can be handled in person. Can I expect you to report to work next week?"

"Yes," Nathaniel said, head spinning. He couldn't believe this was happening! He would need to return to Connecticut to collect his belongings. As soon as this phone call was over, he'd contact the airline, then start packing. His eyes shifted to the duffel bag and remained there. "Just one more thing. Make sure the apartment allows animals. Please."

"You have a pet?"

"I might have a dog. I'm not sure yet."

Nathaniel called the airport first, but not to change his flight. Instead he asked about the drug dog program, which resulted in an awkward conversation that led nowhere. He was transferred a few times, and eventually put on the line with someone who seemed to think he was seeking exploitable knowledge. When he continued rambling on about a dog missing most of its hair that had severe behavioral problems, he was accused of being with the press. The call ended fruitlessly.

Then he turned to the Internet, but the shelters he found were closed for the day. He tried calling a few numbers regardless, picturing Bonkers being led toward an electric chair, a red phone outside the room ringing just in the nick of time. Nathaniel didn't have any luck. He gave up for the night and went to find his parents, telling them the good news. He had a job! Of course they didn't see it that way. Not only was he dropping out of Yale, but he didn't know how much he'd be earning or if he would have benefits. He didn't share their concerns, still high from making such a brash decision.

The next morning he felt less certain but set aside his fears to continue his quest. If the officer hadn't been lying, and dogs only had two weeks before they were put down, then Nathaniel was cutting it close. He called five different shelters, but none of the employees he spoke to recognized the description he gave. He also asked about the drug dog program with no luck. He became convinced the officer had made up the whole thing, but decided to try one more shelter before calling it quits.

"Ugly as hell," he said. "Most of his hair has fallen out, or maybe it never grew in the first place. I don't know. Has some sort of rash. He kind of looks like roadkill."

"When did your dog go missing?" the woman asked, sounding hopeful.

"He's not mine. I just met him at the airport." Okay. That sounded crazy.

"Was he sniffing bags?"

"Yeah!" Nathaniel said. "That's the one! Is he still there?"

"I'm afraid not. He didn't make it."

"Oh." A pit opened up in Nathaniel's stomach. "I'm sorry to hear that."

The line was silent a moment. *"We* still have him. Is that what you mean? He's not at the airport anymore. He flunked out of the sniffer program, so they sent him back."

"He's alive?" Nathaniel asked, feeling happy.

"Yes! Did you want to adopt him?"

"Oh." He pictured all of his possessions covered in dog pee. "Kind of. I just don't want him to die."

The line went silent again. "Maybe you could come visit us at the shelter so we can see... So you can visit Bonkers and get a second impression."

She probably thought he was completely nuts and wanted to verify that in person, but he accepted anyway. The shelter was open most of the day, so after a shower and a quick breakfast, he drove there. He had more doubts on the way. Even a well-behaved dog would be a handful. The new job would demand most of his attention. Then again, if he was the dog's only hope, how could he possibly turn his back?

The woman at the shelter, Mary, was short and chubby, her cheeks red from exertion. She seemed to be the only person working there. After answering three phone calls and accepting a cat that a family no longer wanted, she led him to the back. The floors were hard and beige. Fluorescent lights hung from the ceiling. Down one long hallway with a drain in the middle was a series of cage doors separated by concrete walls. Most of these spaces were filled, the air loud with the sound of barking.

Nathaniel grimaced openly at the environment. "Can't you do better than this for them?"

"Money," Mary said. "I play the lottery every week hoping I can buy land and give these babies a proper home. Until then we look for other solutions. Not just homes, but training programs, like the one at the airport. Or another for service animals. Here we go."

They stopped at a cage. The animal inside sat on a blanket, preoccupied with licking his own junk. Bonkers. The dog stopped licking and looked up when the cage door rattled and opened. Nathaniel's first impression had been correct. The poor thing looked like he had been run over by a lawn mower. Bonkers didn't seem to mind. He hopped up, paws skittering on the slick floor, tail wagging. Mary blocked the doorway long enough to get a leash on his collar. Then she moved aside so they could be reunited.

Nathaniel wasn't sure if Bonkers recognized him, since currently he was going from cage to cage, sniffing the other dogs. Mary suggested they take him outside where he would calm down, but once in a fenced-off yard, all he seemed interested in was running back and forth and peeing different places.

"He's still a puppy," she said fondly. "Usually they are the first to get adopted but..."

"He's ugly," Nathaniel supplied.

Mary laughed. "Eye of the beholder. I think he's a sweetie."

"What's wrong with him?" Nathaniel asked. "His fur, I mean."

"Food allergy is my guess. It isn't fleas or mites. We had him dipped, but it didn't help. Diet is the main suspect. Lord only knows what they put in most dog food. I'd feed him BARF if I could afford it."

"Gross!"

"It's an acronym." Mary tittered. "I only remember what the last two letters stand for. Raw Food. As in meat. You'd be surprised how many animals benefit from that."

"Couldn't you try it just for a week?"

"Money," Mary repeated. "It's a large expense, especially for an animal that won't be around much longer. Not my policy, I assure you. Just the cold, hard facts."

Bonkers chose that moment to finally notice Nathaniel,

running circles around him and bucking like a horse. This threatened to tie them both up, so Mary dropped the leash. Nathaniel stepped out of the circle and picked the leash up again before the dog could flee. Soon he was yanked forward, the dog taking him for a walk instead of the other way around.

"His allergies are why he was given to us," Mary said, keeping up. "He's purebred—Siberian Husky—but that often leads to complications like these. Happens a lot. People want a beautiful dog, no matter how inbred, and they're willing to pay a pretty penny to get it. When the animal starts to have problems, they suddenly can't find the cash for those veterinary bills. Funny how that works. They have no problem finding us though."

"That sucks," Nathaniel said.

"Do you have pets already?" Mary asked.

"No."

"Any experience with them?"

"Nope."

"Do you have a suitable home?"

"I'm not sure," Nathaniel admitted. "Does that mean I can't have him?"

Mary hesitated, watching as Bonkers started kicking with his hind legs, showering them with grass and dirt. "As long as you can pay the adoption fee, he's all yours!"

Nathaniel felt like he was trying to communicate with an alien species. Getting the dog to slow down enough to pay attention was the first challenge. After a number of walks that felt more like a tug-of-war, and a huge bowl of dry kibble, Bonkers finally settled down on Nathaniel's bed. That was good. Nathaniel still didn't know if the dog remembered him. He did sniff the duffel bag and look back at Nathaniel with something that resembled a smug expression, but he was probably just reading into things.

Getting down on his knees so they were eye level, Nathaniel tried asking. "Remember me?"

"Pant pant pant," was the only response.

"I saved your life today. That makes us tight. We're best buds now."

More panting.

So far so good. "I know we've both been through a lot. The people who were supposed to love you failed. They let you down.

The same happened to me. Now we're starting over. Together. There's something we've got to talk about though. Your name. It's really *really* stupid."

The dog stopped panting and cocked his head.

"Mary thinks you're not even a year old. That's pretty young, so I'm hoping you haven't gotten too attached to it. Do you really want to be called Bonkers your entire life?"

The dog resumed panting, as if he wasn't concerned either way.

"If you're leaving it up to me, I was thinking Zero. That's a movie reference. Tim Burton, not Mel Brooks. Am I making sense?"

Somehow the dog managed to look embarrassed for him.

"Think of it this way: We're both starting from scratch. From zero. That makes it more poetic. See?"

The newly christened Zero rolled over on his side, as if exhausted by the conversation.

"Yeah, I agree. It's getting late."

Nathaniel rose to turn off the light. Then he got undressed. He peered at the bed through the gloom, remembering a time when it had been occupied. Now it was again, but he would rather have Caesar there instead. So much for dogs being the best cure for a broken heart. He sighed, then got between the sheets. Not long after, he felt the dog stir. Zero crawled near and flopped over again so their backs were pressed against each other. Then he exhaled as if content. A few moments later, Nathaniel did the same.

A new life. With nothing to weigh him down except what he could fit in his car. Nathaniel flew back to Connecticut at the end of spring break, spending one more night in his old apartment. He packed everything he could into boxes. The next day, when Rebecca went to class, he loaded the car with clothes, his movie collection, the television, his surround sound system, and enough pots, dishes, and utensils for one person. He even managed a few lamps, but that still left the couch and bed. Both were a lost cause. He and Rebecca had gone halfsies on the couch, which had set them back hundreds of dollars. He considered the couch carefully, then took off all the cushions and shoved them in the car, because fuck her.

Then he began the long drive to Texas, pulling over at a rest stop to sleep at around midnight. The vehicle was so stuffed that he couldn't even recline his seat. This at least prevented him from sleeping in. He was on the road again at five in the morning, finally arriving home in the late afternoon. Zero seemed happy to see him, which was progress. Nathaniel unpacked enough to free the passenger seat, making room for the dog.

"Are you sure?" his mother asked as she watched him work. "I talked to your father. We can get you your own place in Connecticut. It's not too late."

"This is what I want," he said, even though he wasn't certain. Maybe it was all a big mistake, but doing something crazy made it easier not to *go* crazy. "This is what I need."

"What if the new job doesn't work out? What will you do without a degree?"

"Live off the land," he said easily.

This seemed to worry her even more, but she didn't try to talk him out of it again. Not even the next morning when they said goodbye. Once on the road, he felt liberated. Zero had his head out the window for much of the drive, perhaps basking in the same freedom. Their lives were their own now. No treacherous friends or lovers, no heartless owners. Just the open road and an address Marcello had texted him. Their new home.

When they arrived at the apartment complex in Austin, he let Zero out to pee, then put him back in the car. No sense in letting the new landlord discover that a feral beast was about to move in. He reported to the complex's office and learned that everything had been taken care of. The leasing agent walked Nathaniel through a one-bedroom apartment on the third floor. Nothing luxurious. It was barely bigger than his old place minus one bedroom, but he did appreciate the balcony that overlooked a green lawn. Soon it would be dotted with Zero's calling cards.

Once the keys were placed in his hand, he moved in. This process didn't take long. He hung the clothes in the closet or placed them folded on the floor. An unzipped sleeping bag went in the bedroom, extra blankets on top. A laptop plugged into the dining room corner was his new office. The TV was set up on the living room floor, a Blu-ray player off to one side. He arranged the couch cushions across from it so he'd have somewhere to sit. Until he got a few paychecks, most of his home life would take place on the floor. At least the kitchen was fully equipped. He had just enough money to go grocery shopping, which he planned to do soon. First he sat down on his makeshift couch, Zero crawling on his lap and trying to initiate a play fight. Nathaniel pushed him away to glance around at undecorated walls and rooms so empty that a faint echo answered him when he spoke.

"Home, sweet home!"

"Male escorts," Nathaniel said, not hiding his irritation.

"A gentleman's club," Marcello repeated patiently.

Nathaniel pinched the bridge of his nose. "Fine. Where exactly is this club full of gentlemen? Because from what you described, we send boys out like taxis to please any old geezer with enough cash to afford them."

"Taxi boys," Marcello said musingly. "I like that!"

"I'm serious," Nathaniel said.

"Perhaps it's more of a gentleman's network. Better?"

"No!"

The week had started so well. Marcello had greeted Nathaniel enthusiastically outside a drab studio the size of a warehouse. After ushering him inside and up an elevator to the second floor, Marcello presented Nathaniel with his own corner office. This meant two of the walls had windows, illuminating the wooden desk. A small table and matching chairs sat to one side, a bottle of champagne and two glasses waiting there. They had toasted each other, chatting idly before Nathaniel signed a number of contracts. He wished he'd read them more carefully, because after days of pouring over accounts, he was realizing what he'd gotten into. Now he was on the top floor, an addition built on the flat roof that consisted entirely of Marcello's spacious office. Granite floors, comfortable couches, a wet bar against one wall, and a view of Austin's distant skyline. Nathaniel had found the place elegant the first time he'd been there. Now it seemed decadent. Marcello seemed completely at home, sitting behind an antique desk in a high-backed chair that made him resemble a Bond villain.

"Do you have a moral objection to prostitution?" Marcello asked. "Some people struggle with loneliness and frustration, others with financial difficulties. If two consenting adults find a mutually agreeable solution to these problems, who are we to judge?"

"You paint a rosy picture," Nathaniel said. "How many prostitutes do their job willingly? How many are beaten or forced into the situation because of human trafficking?"

"Which is exactly why it should be legalized and heavily regulated. Governments create the shadows they force people into, then waste our tax money persecuting those very individuals. Wouldn't that effort and expense be put to better use protecting sex workers and legitimizing their profession? That would generate tax revenue instead of wasting it, lining the coffers of—"

"Okay, okay," Nathaniel said, waving him into silence. "I don't want to argue. But from a practical point of view, why take a risk like this? Hell, why didn't Kenneth expose your escort service if he wanted to oust you?"

"Because there is nothing illegal about it. My agency simply helps like-minded people meet for a night out on the town or a cozy dinner at home. What happens during these dates is none of my business, not that I mind hearing details."

"It's a risk. You and I both know what's really going on. I can't imagine anyone who doesn't, law enforcement included." He pushed an account summary across the desk. "It doesn't even generate that much revenue. Not compared to your legitimate business. So why bother?"

"Why not?" Marcello said, gesturing grandly. "I refuse to subject myself to the backward values of the current century. For me such issues are as controversial as women being allowed to vote or black and white people sharing the same drinking fountain. Such restrictions were once the law of the land, but legality by no means made them morally sound. Would you like a list of all the countries where homosexuality is still illegal? Would you prefer the men in those places not take a risk, not fight for change, and instead live within the confines of laws that punish them for their natural feelings and urges?"

"Of course not," Nathaniel muttered.

"We look back at the past decades and shake our heads in disgust at the conservative values that infringed on personal liberties. Future generations will do the same when reflecting upon our time. I'm merely ahead of the curve."

"Which brings us to your porn movies."

"My film division," Marcello said, smiling pleasantly.

"Porn isn't forward-thinking. It's a trashy remnant of the past. Aren't you concerned about the reputation of your company?"

"You disappoint me. In my lecture at Yale, you yourself acknowledged that recognition trumps reputation. The name 'Studio Maltese' is synonymous with media production. I work hard to keep it that way. As I'm sure you've noticed, the other divisions are owned by limited liability companies that themselves are— Well, suffice to say, even I barely comprehend all the smoke and mirrors."

"I wanted to ask you about that, because those different divisions all make regular payments to one person." He tapped a reoccurring name on the accounts. "Who is this?"

"The CEO."

"I thought you were the CEO."

Marcello winked in response.

Nathaniel leaned back. "*That's* your real name? No wonder you don't go by it."

"I know little about my biological parents, but clearly they had atrocious taste."

"But if you chose your name… Come on! You must have seen *The Maltese Falcon!*"

Marcello stared hard at him. Then he chuckled. "As a boy. Almost every single day after school when it aired in a local cinema. That story resonated with my very soul. So many people determined to get what they want, no matter how much they are forced to sacrifice. How inspiring!"

"You know it's a cautionary tale, right?"

"All good stories are. I've since tracked down the magazines the story first appeared in, and a first edition copy of the novel. Oh, and I might just own the Maltese falcon itself."

Nathaniel sat upright. "You mean one of the actual film props?"

Marcello smiled mysteriously. "I appreciate your concern for the reputation of my company and the well-being of others. I have no doubt you'll become a valuable asset. Perhaps though, you'll consider setting aside your judgment. That will relieve you of a burdensome weight. Here." Marcello opened a drawer and took out a shrink-wrapped DVD that he slid across the desk.

Nathaniel took it. The cover showed two young men staring longingly at each other. His eyes scanned the title. Then he snorted. "*Love is the Hottest Season?*"

"One of my personal favorites that this studio has produced. The most popular seller too. You should at least have a passing familiarity with our products."

Nathaniel blanched. "You want me to watch your porn."

Marcello smiled. "Adult romance. Porn is a trashy remnant of the past, or so I'm told. And yes, I do expect you to watch that. Unless you have more engaging plans this weekend. Is there someone special in your life?"

"No." Nathaniel frowned and considered the cover again. "I don't suppose you have it on Blu-ray?"

Establishing a routine took little time. Nathaniel's first order of business when he returned home was to let Zero take care of *his* business. For all his behavioral problems, Zero didn't need potty training. Not unless duffel bags were involved, apparently. Out in the yard, Nathaniel would try exhausting him with exercise, which meant chasing him around like an idiot. Once they were both panting, they went upstairs for dinner. When first arriving in Austin, Nathaniel had planned cheap meals, buying ingredients in bulk and cooking in the largest pot he owned. Chicken and rice. Canned tuna and pasta. Cheep cuts of beef and potatoes. These dishes lasted for multiple nights. In the morning he had a bowl of oatmeal; at lunch he ate a sandwich he had brought from home.

Zero lived off the same food once his kibble ran out. Not the oatmeal or sandwiches, but whatever dinner Nathaniel made, twice a day. He didn't seem to mind. In fact, his skin had cleared up considerably and a light fuzz—like a teenage boy's facial hair—covered most of his bald patches.

"You're growing up!" Nathaniel joked as they settled down for another movie night. As Zero cuddled up next to him, Nathaniel noticed the fur felt less coarse. Maybe this diet was a good idea, even if they could afford kibble again. After three weeks of work, Nathaniel had finally received his first paycheck and had decided to splurge on fast food. Zero got his own quarter-pounder with cheese. Greasy burgers probably weren't healthy for either of them, but having money again—and a respectable sum at that—had him in the mood to celebrate.

For him this meant sitting on stolen couch cushions with a dog and rewatching old movies. That might appear sad from the outside, but Nathaniel looked forward to this ritual every day. When it came to fulfilling companionship, a dog was ideal. In most areas. When the synth-powered credits to a John Hughes film rolled, he regretted choosing the movie because for a comedy, it sure had romantic moments. This made him question if an essential piece was still missing from his life. Or maybe he was just horny. His eyes drifted to the copy of *Love is the Hottest Season* that Marcello had given him. He had ignored it previously, but now his curiosity—and hormones—got the better of him.

First he took Zero outside to potty, then shut him in the bedroom. Nathaniel, despite the lecture he'd given Marcello, had nothing against porn. He had indulged in his fair share. Blood was rushing to all sorts of areas when he put in the disc. Twenty minutes later, he got up and let Zero out. Not because he was finished, but because so far the movie was sweet. The story was about two guys who meet in high school, both closeted and harboring secret feelings for each other. Fate separates them, but they meet again in college. Only toward the end of the film do they confess their feelings. And more.

The sex scene was graphic, except the motions weren't mechanical. Most gay porn followed a tired formula: mutual blow jobs, one guy getting rimmed and fucked, followed by the money shot. Usually a facial. The sex in this movie felt more spontaneous, as if the actors had been allowed to ad lib their performances. In fact, he could believe they had fallen in love during filming and were genuinely eager to be together. The story had so much emotional buildup that Nathaniel felt more moved by the performances than turned on by the sex. Of course that didn't stop him from shutting Zero in the bedroom once the film was over so he could rewatch the sex scene and relieve himself.

Afterwards he felt haunted by the story. The movie had been low budget, sure, but the heart of it rang true. Love could survive separation, could remain strong over the years. He had once experienced that himself. Part of him wanted to again. Not with Caesar. Nathaniel wasn't foolish enough to open himself to that sort of pain again. But maybe someday he'd meet someone special.

These thoughts were on his mind when he reported to Marcello's office Monday morning. The big man was behind his desk, scowling at the computer screen, but his expression brightened when Nathaniel spoke aloud a key line from the movie.

"Don't run away from love. Chase after it."

"You watched it!" Marcello said, transparently pleased. "What did you think?"

Nathaniel sat down across from him, nodding slowly. "I have a newfound respect for what you do. I've never seen a movie like it before."

"You will," Marcello said, sounding confident. "Those cheesy porn movies of days gone by, they were ahead of their time. Sex is much more erotic when framed by a real world situation, even if it involves a mechanic spilling motor oil on his crankshaft. The human mind responds to stories."

"You're right," Nathaniel said. "Usually with porn I don't care about the guys. All that matters is how good they look. Even then I'll skip ahead to the best parts. Afterwards I never think of them again. The guys in this movie… I was really excited when they were finally able to be together. I was happy for them. And for myself, for getting to watch."

He laughed, Marcello joining him. "I do love a good plot. I keep pitching a new idea to my writers for a superhero movie. It's similar to Spider-Man, except instead of shooting webs from his wrist, they come out of his—"

"That newfound respect is plummeting," Nathaniel interrupted.

"I wouldn't have it any other way. Not all of our films are so romantic, but they have their fans. Have you ever wondered why people obsess over celebrity sex scandals? We get to see their breasts, a flaccid penis, or maybe a shaky home recording, and the Internet explodes with excitement. Seems ridiculous when you consider the hardcore material just a click away. Celebrity sex tapes are more enticing because we know who they are. We know their stories. And yet we judge these people harshly when they are caught. It's ridiculous. Most celebrities I know are shameless exhibitionists, their audience wanting to see them naked and going at it. Once again we enter the realm of mutually beneficial agreements between adults. My movies will never take their place among classic films, but in the future Hollywood will stop beating around the bush—so to speak—and give audiences what they want. Fifty years ago, films were forbidden to depict a kiss lasting more than three seconds. Progress marches along no matter who stands in the way. The good old days are straight ahead of us. I just hope Hollywood gets more comfortable with male nudity while George Clooney is still around."

Nathaniel laughed. "Or how about Joseph Gordon-Levitt? I'd commit serious crimes to spend a night with him."

"Was that a risqué comment?" Marcello pretended to be scandalized. "And here I was beginning to think you didn't possess a libido!"

"Hey, I might not be as open as you about this stuff, but I'm still flesh and blood."

"I was only teasing. I know you are. Kenneth shared enough details to convince me of that."

Nathaniel grimaced. "That's not who I am."

"No?"

He looked away and shrugged. "Maybe it is. I don't know. I prefer to actually like the guy. The same as in your movies. When you care about the other person, even if it isn't love, it's much more satisfying."

Marcello eyed him for a moment before smiling warmly. "Was I ever as young as you? Was I ever so innocent?"

"I doubt it."

"As do I. Satisfaction comes in many forms, as I'm sure you'll discover, and what you desire sounds rather noble. Are there any candidates?"

"I'm still recovering from the last one."

"He will be much easier to forget when someone has taken his place, believe me. You can either stew on old memories or simmer up new ones."

"I'm not ready yet."

"You sound just like a good friend of mine. Handsome as can be, hopelessly single, and absolutely impervious to my advice. Whenever the topic of love comes up, he mutters those same words." Marcello made his voice deeper, sounding more like a jock. "I'm not ready yet. I still love him."

"I do," Nathaniel said defensively.

"And you always will, so stop letting that hold you back and find some other miserable fool who needs to move on." Inspiration struck Marcello. "My goodness! What a pair you would make!"

"No," Nathaniel said immediately. "I'm not interested."

"You haven't even seen him yet." Marcello focused on his computer, clicking the mouse repeatedly. "These photos are old. Nearly eight years. Still, you'll get the idea."

He turned the monitor so Nathaniel could see. The photos were professional, two shirtless guys with their arms around each other. Both were good-looking, one of them especially so. Nathaniel stared.

"The one with the dark hair and silver eyes," Marcello prompted, poking at his keyboard to cycle through the images. "What do you think?"

"These aren't photoshopped?" Nathaniel asked, mouth watering a little.

"No, these are scans of the raw negatives. Ah, except for this one. It was touched up for publication."

The guy in question now appeared annoyed, probably due to the tongue jammed in his ear. "Wow."

"I'll take that as a yes," Marcello said. "His name is Tim Wyman. I'll give you his phone number and you can—"

"No!" Nathaniel said, feeling panicked.

Marcello blinked. "Why not?"

"He looks like my age in these photos. How old is he now?"

Marcello clucked his tongue. "So picky! Very well, here's a more recent one." After more clicking, he brought up a new photo, this one taken at an evening party, the flash too strong. Tim was wearing a suit, standing next to Marcello and looking just as handsome with clothes on. One of them appeared gleeful, the other exasperated.

"Are you grabbing his ass?" Nathaniel asked.

"Indeed I am. I know it's difficult, but tear your eyes away from me and consider him. You'd make such a handsome pair!"

Nathaniel was tempted. He'd be crazy not to be. But he still felt tender, his wounds barely healed. He pushed away from the desk and stood. "I've got a lot of work to do."

"Keep him in mind," Marcello said. "He's not going anywhere, believe me! Not unless one of us drags him there kicking and screaming."

Chapter Fourteen

Three months. Days filled with work, nights filled with movies, weekends filled with road trips or hikes—Zero at his side. The dog had blossomed like a Chia pet. Whether it was relief from stress or food allergies or some mystery of body chemistry, Zero's empty patches of skin had filled in with thick fur, silver on his back, white on his legs and belly. The woman at the shelter had claimed Zero was a Siberian Husky, but Nathaniel hadn't believed it until now. The dog looked more like a wolf these days, having gotten taller and beefier. But he was still every bit a puppy on the inside.

Nathaniel, on the other hand, felt he was losing his hair. The mirror proved otherwise, but working for Marcello meant more than just scheduling events, worrying about budgets, and balancing the books. Nathaniel had to answer to Marcello's every whim. This was never anything trivial, such as brewing him a cup of coffee or fetching his dry cleaning. The tasks were more involved, such as when Marcello wanted a humidor installed in his office. A simple box wouldn't do. The humidor needed the capacity to store one hundred cigars—presumably just in case a small army dropped by—and Marcello wanted it filled with a wide enough variety to please even the pickiest connoisseur. He also needed it to be on prominent display so it would, as he put it, "intimidate those intelligent enough not to smoke, and charm those wise enough to value camaraderie." Whatever that meant. So Nathaniel not only had to shop for a humidor, haul it through the building and install it, but also learn about a pastime he cared nothing for so he could stock it with the right cigars. Marcello feigned ignorance about what was needed until the very end, when he mentioned a variety of cigar Nathaniel had overlooked.

Many weekends and nights were spent researching surveillance equipment, foreign policies, or even ballroom dancing, just to cater to Marcello's latest impulse. If Nathaniel was honest with himself, he loved it. His life was rarely boring. He was much too busy to dwell on the past. At times he felt like he was still in college, stuffing his brain with knowledge, but now he was getting paid for the privilege instead of the other way around. Nathaniel was happy.

Mostly. Occasionally while at work, he would open the file

folder with Tim's old modeling photos and check him out, trying to imagine touching that handsome face. Or even having a simple conversation. As the weeks flew by, this became something of an obsession, so he decided to do something about it. One way or another, he needed to purge this temptation from his system.

"Remember that one guy?" Nathaniel said during one of his many visits to the upstairs office.

"Yes," Marcello said confidently. "I've never met a man that I haven't remembered for one reason or another. I suppose Thailand might be the one exception, since I indulged too much and blacked out, only to wake up feeling chafed in the strangest of places."

Nathaniel pressed on, the only way of keeping a conversation on course with Marcello. "The one with the silver eyes. The model."

"Ah! The fabulous Mr. Wyman. Is this what I think it is? Has the time finally come?"

"You don't have to smile like that," Nathaniel grumped. "Is he still single?"

"Tragically so." Marcello reached for the phone. "Let's see what we can do about that!"

"Wait!" Nathaniel said, reaching across the desk to stop him. "Nothing fancy. Not even a real date. I just thought it might be fun to hang out."

Marcello nodded. "Understood. There's a wonderful little bed and breakfast outside San Antonio. I'll see if they still have the weekend free."

Nathaniel glared. "Dinner and a movie."

Marcello looked pained. "Please! Anything but that! How about a nice cabaret? I know of one where the boys on stage put fruit in their—"

"Dinner and a movie," Nathaniel repeated firmly. "No reservations needed. We'll grab something from the food trucks before the movie."

"And when is he allowed to pick you up for this dream date?"

"I'll pick him up," Nathaniel said. That way, if the guy turned out to be a jerk, Nathaniel wouldn't be dependent on him for a ride. "Saturday. Around seven."

"In the morning, no doubt. That should wring the last drops of potential romance from this encounter."

"At night is fine," Nathaniel said, standing to leave. "Text me if he says yes. If not, don't bother. Doesn't really matter to me."

Except it did. Nathaniel spent the rest of the day periodically checking his phone, stomach churning. Marcello was probably getting his revenge, making Nathaniel squirm. Or maybe Tim had said no. Nathaniel was just coming to terms with that possibility when a text finally delivered his answer. One little word that made him feel both excitement and dread.

Yes.

Nathaniel drove to West Lake Hills, the car's air conditioner cranked up to keep him from sweating. When he found the right address and pulled into the driveway, he wished he could dunk himself in an ice bath. Ahead of him was a separate garage, which was hardly noteworthy. The house to the left had him intimidated. Size wasn't everything, but a house this large signified money.

Nathaniel was already late, so he stopped gawking and got out of the car. He was heading up the walkway when the front door opened. Even framed in light, features cast in silhouette, he could see that time had been kind. Nathaniel couldn't help but compare Tim to the old modeling photos as the man shut the door behind him and strode forward, offering a hand. Black hair, no longer gelled into spikes but natural and brushed to one side. The same piercing silver eyes. A handsome smile that seemed genuine, if not completely certain. The body still impressed, even when hidden beneath a black dress shirt and gray slacks. Nathaniel preferred a slimmer build, but at least Tim was a few inches shorter than him. Then again, most guys were. They made contact, the palm of Tim's hand soft and warm as they shook. The smile widened.

"Nathaniel! Nice to meet you."

"Yeah," he replied, grasping for words and finding a few that didn't make much sense. "Blind date, huh?"

"I guess it is," Tim answered smoothly. "Not totally though. Marcello kept sending me photos of you. And a video, which was weird, because you were just sitting at his desk talking. No audio either."

Surveillance equipment. The very system Nathaniel had installed. "Marcello can be a little weird at times."

"Brother, you ain't kiddin'!" Tim's smile wavered. "So you work for him? He was a little vague about the details."

"I do." Nathaniel nodded at the house. "But if I'd known that being a model paid so much, I would have applied for that job instead."

Tim's smile disappeared. "You're one of his escorts, aren't you?"

Nathaniel scowled. "I'm not an escort!"

Tim matched his expression. "I'm not a model!"

After staring each other down, they both laughed.

"Let's start over," Tim suggested. "I'm an old friend of Marcello's. Everything you see behind me I inherited. I don't have the discipline to be a model or much of anything else."

Nathaniel took a deep breath. "I'm… You know what? I don't think I even have a job title. I just do whatever Marcello needs me to."

"You have my sympathies," Tim said. "Wanna tell me all about it on the way into town?"

That's exactly what they did. Nathaniel was grateful for such an easy topic. In truth, him talking about his work probably bored Tim to tears, but the guy acted interested, and even asked questions that helped prevent awkward silences. By the time they pulled into a parking lot filled with colorful trailers, Nathaniel felt more relaxed.

"What are we eating?" Tim said as they got out of the car.

"Ever heard of Torchy's Tacos?"

"Yeah! Tacos from a trailer. Sounds awesome!"

If he was being sarcastic, Nathaniel couldn't tell. They walked along the trailers, each converted to serve food. The interiors were filled with everything needed for a kitchen. Each trailer had a window used by workers to take orders and hand out food, customers eating their meals on nearby picnic tables. Not exactly luxury dining. As they took their place in line, Tim seemed cheerful enough.

"I love the food trucks," he said. "Haven't tried this place yet, but everyone raves about it. What do you usually get?"

Nathaniel barely heard the question. Instead he considered the guy talking to him: handsome, gay, and willing to go on this date. His teenage self had dreamed of nights like this, before feeling foolish for entertaining impossible fantasies. Guys didn't fall in love with other guys. But they did. Caesar had proven that. He had also taught Nathaniel many things he had never wanted to learn, and that made it hard to let go and enjoy this moment.

"Have you ever cheated on someone?" he blurted out.

Tim considered him in silence, then turned his attention to the menu posted beside the ordering window. Nathaniel felt his face burning. When Tim looked back, his expression was sympathetic. "What was his name?"

"Who?"

"People don't ask questions like that unless someone has done a serious number on them."

Nathaniel exhaled. "Caesar. He was my first... everything."

"I get it." Tim's laugh was ironic. "I know all about those."

"Really?"

"Yeah. Benjamin was mine. If you're waiting to get over yours, I've got some bad news. It doesn't happen."

"Oh." They shuffled forward a few steps as the line shortened. "Did he cheat on you?"

"When we first met, I cheated to be with him. Later on, I tricked him into cheating. Sort of." Tim's brow furrowed. "Listen, you need to know who I am. I get that. But before I drag out every skeleton from my closeted days, I at least want a free meal. You're paying, by the way."

"Fair enough," Nathaniel said. "To answer your original question, the fried avocado tacos are life changing."

"Sounds vegetarian," Tim said with a shake of his head. "I need meat. I'm a growing boy."

They talked food until it was their turn to order, and despite what Tim had said, he insisted on paying. They found two free seats at the end of a bench, comparing notes on Marcello as they ate. When finished, Tim patted his belly contentedly and sighed.

"All right," he said. "Here's the deal. I'm sort of an asshole. Less so than I used to be, I hope, but still an asshole. When I first met Benjamin, we were in high school and I was struggling with my identity. Not just in regard to my sexuality. I was messed up about all sorts of things. I had a girlfriend at the time, so that's strike one against me, although I did leave her for him. Wait, does that count as two strikes?"

Nathaniel laughed. "I don't think so. Caesar left his girlfriend for me. Felt sorry for her, but I wasn't complaining."

"Okay," Tim said with a nod. "Just one strike. Unfortunately I didn't get my shit together in time and ended up ruining what Benjamin and I had together. I thought it was all over until college, when we met again. Great news, right? Not at all, because by then Benjamin had met this amazing guy. If you really need the details, I'll give them to you, but basically I forced them to break up. I wouldn't call that cheating. Using deceit to wreck a happy relationship might be worse though, so strike two." Tim paused. "This is the part of the story where you get up and walk away."

Nathaniel stayed where he was. "What happened after that?"

"The truth came out and they got back together." Tim frowned, crumpling one corner of the foil wrapper left from his taco. "We met a third time. Fate had nothing to do with that. I went looking. I was in a bad relationship, which only made me miss him more. At first I just wanted to see him again, not to mess with anything. I needed help, and he gave it to me because that's how Benjamin is." Tim's smile was sad. "We actually managed to be friends for a while. That's all we could be, because that perfect guy of his was smart enough to marry him. But I couldn't stop feeling what I feel, and even though this time I didn't try to ruin anything, loving him made it impossible for us to be around each other. Strike three. I'm out."

"Doesn't count," Nathaniel insisted. "You didn't do anything wrong. Loving someone and not acting on it isn't cheating."

"Sometimes being a distraction is enough. At least I bailed in time. They're still out there somewhere, living a fairytale life together. I guess that's my consolation prize, knowing that he's happy."

Nathaniel considered him, then shook his head. "You're way more generous than I am. I don't want Caesar to be happy. I have fantasies where we meet again in twenty years, and he's completely miserable."

"And where are you in twenty years?" Tim asked. "With me? With anyone?"

Nathaniel looked away. "I don't know. I try not to think about it."

"You can't love with stuff like that in your heart," Tim said. "It gets in the way."

"I have my reasons. Just imagine that you and Benjamin

had made it to college and were still together, despite all the curveballs that life can throw. You're perfectly happy together, or so you think, and then he cheats on you."

"That's rough," Tim said.

Nathaniel sighed, returning his attention to his date. "I'm simplifying it too much. Caesar and I had all sorts of problems, but I'm not letting myself get hurt again."

"I'll hurt you," Tim said easily. "If given a chance. I can't promise I won't because it's inevitable. I'll try my best to avoid it, but I don't think it's possible to love someone without hurting them in the process. You can't shine a light without casting shadows. Ugh. Don't make me get cheesier than that."

Nathaniel managed a laugh, but he quickly grew serious again. "Are you sure?"

"If there's an exception to the rule, I've never witnessed it." Tim crumpled the foil into a ball and successfully tossed it into the nearest trashcan. "Put it all behind you. That's the best you can do. Brooding won't help. I've tried that. It won't change anything. Set it all aside as much as you can and move on."

"Is that what you're doing?" Nathaniel asked. "Is that why you're here tonight?"

Tim leaned back and laughed. "Busted! I'm here because I know Benjamin would want me to be. If I ever meet him again—and I don't think that's going to happen—he'll make a sad face if he finds out I've been alone for all these years. Not that I'm totally alone. He made sure of that."

"Meaning?"

Tim looked embarrassed as he reached into his pocket and took out his phone, holding it up for Nathaniel to see. Behind all the icons of the main menu was an image of a bulldog with its head cocked. "I'm one of *those* people."

Nathaniel whipped out his own phone and brandished it. "I'm one of those people too."

"Nice!" Tim said. "That's a Husky, right? What's her name?"

"Zero, and he's a nightmare on four legs. What about yours?"

"Chinchilla," Tim said. "She's my little Mexican princess."

"I thought bulldogs were British."

"She's got a Mexican soul," Tim insisted. "Breed has nothing to do with it."

They talked dogs, the conversation becoming much more

lively. As they made their way to the movie theater, the topic of ex-boyfriends was mostly forgotten. Only when a computer-generated rat filled the screen, running around a kitchen while cooking, did Nathaniel's attention start to wander. Maybe Tim was right, maybe it *was* time to let go of the past. What easier way to do so than moving on? He reached into the dark, finding Tim's hand, their fingers intertwining. And it felt wrong. Caesar's hands were longer, his fingers thinner, and while Nathaniel didn't truly want to feel them again, he also didn't want to get used to a new pair of hands that—chances were—he'd have to forget again too. What were the odds that the guy sitting next to him was the right one, that any relationship could survive all the trials and temptations of life? If Nathaniel kept trying, kept searching, maybe eventually he would find the right guy, but that meant having his heart crushed over and over again. How much of him would remain when he finally found his soul mate? Would he still have any love left to give?

He moved his hand away, reaching for his drink. Even after he sucked on the straw, he didn't set it down again. He made sure his hand was occupied for the rest of the movie. Afterwards, he drove Tim home. They discussed the movie on the way, Tim talking about another man from his past who had loved to cook and how much he missed that. They had that much in common. All either of them had for company were faithful animal companions and memories of other people.

"Do you want to come inside?" Tim asked when they pulled into his driveway. "Meet the dog?"

Nathaniel hesitated.

"That's not code for us sleeping together," Tim prompted.

Nathaniel laughed nervously. "Okay. Just real quick. I need to get back to Zero before he has an accident."

Chinchilla met them at the front door. Tim led the way through a sprawling first floor to a backyard, complete with swimming pool, so she could go potty.

"Does she like the water?" Nathaniel asked.

"No!" Tim said. "Bulldogs can't swim. I mean they *can* if they have to, but there's a good chance they'll drown. They don't do well with running either, which sucks because I like to jog. Occasionally I'll let her run with me to the end of the driveway and back. She thinks it's a big deal."

Nathaniel laughed.

Tim's sparkling eyes met his. He must have seen something there because he grew somber. "We've been really honest with each other so far," he said. "That goes against all conventions for the first date, but since we've already broken that rule, there's no sense in stopping now. So what do you think? You and me. Are you feeling it?"

Nathaniel considered the question. "I like you, and I'm sure you've never ever heard this before, but you're smoking hot."

"Thanks," Tim said, but he didn't smile, already guessing what was coming.

"I'm too messed up. I'm not willing to take any chances. You're right that I need to put the past behind me, and that's what I plan on doing. But that doesn't mean I'm open to the future."

"I understand completely," Tim said. Then he grinned and winked. "Quickie?"

"I can see why you and Marcello are friends," Nathaniel said. "I think I'll head home before you manage to seduce me."

"Smart move." Tim walked him back through the house and stopped on the front porch, but neither felt any tension. They both knew there wouldn't be a parting kiss. "If you ever need a sympathetic ear or just someone to dog sit, give me a call."

Nathaniel nodded his appreciation. "You'll regret that offer when you meet Zero, but thanks."

"Take care of yourself."

"You too," Nathaniel replied. "And remember, if you do meet Benjamin again, you've only got two strikes. That last one didn't count."

Tim laughed. "I'll keep that in mind."

"Is everything prepared for the charity ball?"

Nathaniel glanced up from his desk in surprise. A visit from Marcello was rare. Usually Nathaniel was summoned to the office upstairs. His boss glanced around the room, as if confused by the small space. Or maybe he was looking for a wet bar that wasn't there. He came prepared though, an open bottle of champagne in one hand.

"I couldn't find the damn glasses," Marcello said, settling down in a chair.

"That's because I hid them along with the champagne. I don't know how you managed to sniff one out and not the other."

"I've been told that I have a gift."

"And soon you'll have a shortage. Those are for the ball."

"I'm not the slightest bit concerned," Marcello said, waving a hand vaguely. "You always take such good care of my balls."

Nathaniel grimaced. "Yet another mental image I'd like to carve out of my brain."

"Speaking of balls," Marcello continued unabashed, "Tim will be at this one. You know that, right? I don't want any jealous behavior because he's moved on."

"We went on one date two years ago," Nathaniel said.

Marcello blinked. "Has it been so long? Where does the time go?"

"In there," Nathaniel said, nodding at the open bottle.

"Then we better get it out again." Marcello took a hearty swig. "I need a favor. Are you busy?"

"I need to get the guest list approved so the invitations can be sent out today. Otherwise there won't be anyone at the charity… event."

"Excellent," Marcello said as if not having heard him. He set the bottle on the desk. Apparently he was staying. "I need you to do some research for me. Find out everything you can about a certain individual."

Nathaniel sighed and grabbed a pen. "Does this person have a name?"

"William." Marcello made a face and patted himself down until he located his phone. Then he read from the screen. "Townson."

"Okay," Nathaniel said. "How soon do you need this?"

"I can wait," Marcello said. Then he leaned back, looking around the room pleasantly.

Nathaniel glared at him. When that didn't help, he started typing on his computer. "What are we looking for?"

"He's secretive about his past. That's very frustrating to a young man I met recently. Bright as a spark. In fact, we need to discuss some of his ideas soon. For now, I'm eager to play Cupid, and as I said, this William isn't very forthcoming about himself."

Nathaniel paused in his searching "Maybe he doesn't want anyone to know about his past."

"What difference does that make? Come on, what can you tell me?"

Nathaniel focused on the task. Twenty minutes and one

champagne bottle later, the printer next to his desk was whirring out the essential documents. He handed these to Marcello, who flipped through them. "Well well," he said musingly. "Nasty business. Still, I see no reason for hiding what was essentially an accident." He sat upright. "Did you see his boyfriend? How striking!"

Nathaniel's eyes flicked back to the monitor. The newspaper article was about a car wreck, the two victims still in high school. One was William Townson, who appeared to be the consummate boy next door. The other was Kelly Phillips, whose sly smile looked like it could cut through steel. He was indeed very fetching. Judging from the comments found on one site, the two were dating openly, which led to all sorts of ugly speculation about what exactly had caused the accident. "The kid lost a leg. It would be a miracle if his face made it out unscathed."

"That's not always a bad thing. Did you have a chance to see Tim's scar? I think he likes to show it off. Why else would he walk around his house shirtless when he knows I'm peeping in the windows?"

"It was one date," Nathaniel reminded him. "Our clothes remained on."

Marcello peered at him. "I understand the words, but you're not making sense."

"Anything else?" Nathaniel asked pointedly.

"One of these articles is just an excerpt. Do you think you can track down a copy of the paper? I like the cheap and tawdry feel of newsprint."

Nathaniel sighed. "I need a raise."

"Done. Maybe we should look into this Kelly Phillips. Put him in front of a camera and see if he's always that photogenic."

"If he is, it's bad news for the guy hoping to hook up with William."

Marcello shook his head. "Nonsense. Love is a revolving door. The only trick is timing when you step in."

Nathaniel scowled. "I have a lot to do."

"Of course! Thank you for your help. You've been very kind."

Nathaniel watched him leave. Then he looked back at the newspaper article—at Kelly—before he closed the browser window and got back to work.

* * * * *

Nathaniel enjoyed organizing charity events. Over the past few years, he had watched Marcello spend ridiculous amounts of money on cars, clothes, and vacations. He binged on food and drink, engaging in frequent illicit activities, as if unaware of his own mortality. And yet this pattern of indulgence extended to charities as well. All of Marcello's questionable personality traits were balanced out by his drive to help others less fortunate than himself, which quite frankly included almost everyone else on the planet. Arranging these events could be a logistical nightmare, but Marcello always swept in and became directly involved. Nathaniel had once seen him talk a contributor into changing his generous five-figure donation into six figures instead.

Nathaniel looked forward to each such event, but this one was difficult. The concept had him intrigued: a shut-in to support those who were unable to leave their homes due to illness or disability. Nathaniel had worked with the production wing to create films that helped expose their plight. That had been fun. Dealing with building codes or health and safety regulations invoked by shutting a bunch of rich guys in a ballroom for one hour—that wasn't so enjoyable. Nor was replacing the caterers when they pulled out at the last minute, or this stupid request of Marcello's to allow William and his suitor to sneak off together during the shut-in. They would be masquerading as waiters, which seemed ridiculous and unnecessary. Nathaniel intended to put them to work regardless. He wouldn't allow them to stand around being idle.

"Is everything going according to plan?" Marcello asked.

Nathaniel looked up from his list. The kitchen was a buzz of activity with him in the center like a queen bee. Or like someone who just had a hive fall on his head. "The lead bartender informed me—now instead of yesterday—that one of the deliveries didn't arrive. So it's either an evening of virgin cocktails or I need to run to the store."

"No need," Marcello said. "You can raid my private pantry. There should be sufficient supplies there to get us through the night."

That would save time. Marcello's home was a few turrets short of palatial. Who else had a ballroom and professional kitchen in one wing of their home? The first time Nathaniel had visited he had gotten lost. Literally.

"Do you have a moment?" Marcello said, gesturing to one of the hallways.

"No. I need to play drill sergeant to these waiters." All around them were shirtless men dressed in formal slacks and bowties, most of them socializing instead of preparing for duty. One was currently rolling a joint, which set his teeth on edge.

"Tim will take over from here," Marcello said. "He's on his way. I figured you have enough on your plate, and he's very experienced in such things."

"At playing waiter? I know he runs the Eric Conroy Foundation but—"

"He volunteered often in his youth. Just wait until you see him shirtless in person. It's absolutely breathtaking. Time for that later. Come along!"

Nathaniel followed Marcello grudgingly down a hallway and into a sitting room full of books. The only thing stopping him from calling it a library was the existence of one elsewhere in the house.

"You've been an absolute blessing," Marcello said. "I didn't hold back when you first came into my employ, and you've met every challenge with absolute ferocity. You're twice the man Kenneth ever was. Much easier on the eyes too."

"Thanks," Nathaniel said, "but if this is you trying to seduce me…"

"I wouldn't dream of it," Marcello said, stopping at a table and spinning around. "The best cake is the one you never nibble on. Speaking of which…" He gestured at a table, where a cupcake was burning with a single candle. Next to it was a bottle decorated with a red ribbon. "Happy birthday!"

Nathaniel was speechless.

Marcello smiled. "You didn't think I forgot, did you?"

"To be honest, I forgot myself!"

"Here, make a wish before the frosting gets singed. I had to run down the hall after lighting it. I almost passed out."

Nathaniel, still overwhelmed, scrabbled for an appropriate wish. *More of this.* That would do. He liked his life. Plenty of challenges, none of them emotional. What more could he want? One thing came to mind as he blew out the dangerously low candle, but he quickly shoved it aside.

"No doubt you're watching your carbs," Marcello said, eying the cupcake longingly.

"Knock yourself out," Nathaniel said. He picked up the bottle of wine instead, jaw dropping once he read the label. "I know how much this costs!"

"Prove it," Marcello said playfully.

"Upwards of one thousand dollars."

"Correct! You know, it really is astounding how much you've learned in the past few years. Nobody comes by such things naturally, no matter how much they might pretend to. I've spent decades sampling an unimaginable number of spirits, just to familiarize myself with the subject."

"Alternatively, you can just memorize the names and descriptions." Nathaniel continued to study the bottle, unable to imagine ever drinking it. "I appreciate the gesture, but I think I'd rather have the money."

Marcello chuckled. "I thought you'd say that, which is why you'll find another little treat on your next paycheck."

"Thank you," Nathaniel said, looking up. "Not for the money or the wine. I like both, but thank you for trusting me. I was naïve when I asked for this job. You could have started me out in some lowly position or ignored me completely, but you trusted me with—well, *everything*."

"Oh I still have a few secrets," Marcello said, "and if I remember correctly, at the time I owed you a favor. I did see potential in you though. Loyalty too, which is a truly rare commodity. Working with you has been an absolute pleasure. Of all the assets this company has, you are my most treasured."

Nathaniel felt moved but did his best not to show it. "You sure this isn't just you trying to get into my pants?"

"As I said…" Marcello lifted the cupcake and took a bite.

Nathaniel considered the bottle fondly, appreciating what it symbolized more than the actual contents. "Thank you," he murmured, setting it down again. "Now it's time for me to keep proving myself to you."

"Excellent! Don't forget about our young lovers tonight. When the shut-in starts, William and Jason will be venturing into the house alone. They know where to go. If you see two waiters sneaking around, don't sic that dog of yours on them."

"He's out back," Nathaniel said. "I won't forget."

He returned to the kitchen, and while Tim had clearly set the waiters in motion, not everything was up to Nathaniel's standards. He barked orders, telling men to stand up straight or pull their pants up over their underwear lines or in the case of one vaguely familiar face, to stop poking at the *hors d'oeuvres*. He was blond, pale-skinned, and had an impressive physique, but tonight that didn't count for much.

"William, right?"

The guy looked up in surprise and smiled. "Yeah!"

Nathaniel didn't return the gesture. "Why are you touching the food?"

"I'm trying to figure out what it is."

"Brandade de Morue au Gratin," Nathaniel said. "You need to tell the guests what you are presenting them with when offering it."

"Brandy morey gray tong?"

He sighed. He might not be fluent in French, but this job had forced him to learn how to pronounce most words. *"Brandade de Morue au Gratin."*

"Brandaddy de morey gratin?"

Nathaniel was seriously tempted to tell the guy to fuck off and go wait for his lover. Instead he repeated himself until William got the pronunciation right. Then he took him by the shoulders, turned him toward the ballroom, and gave him a gentle push. After making sure no other waiters were loitering around, Nathaniel went into the ballroom to greet guests and make sure everything was going smoothly.

He spotted Tim, a tray of champagne glasses balanced expertly on one hand, his smile just as sparkling. He would stop, hand out drinks, flirt, and move on. Perfect. At least Nathaniel wouldn't have to worry about him. He stopped by the stage, checking the audio equipment. Then he made his way to the back of the room to confirm that the digital projector was properly primed. He berated the technician there, just to make sure he knew his job, then moved through the crowd, stopping to speak with some of the bigger names while keeping an eye on refreshments moving around the room. When he noticed more empty glasses than filled, Nathaniel took one of the younger waiters by the arm to stop him.

"The champagne is running a little dry," he said. "Better get another tray from the kitchen."

The kid looked up at him with huge eyes, as if he was being chastised by a stern parent. Or maybe it was recognition, because there was something familiar about that face. If they did know each other, it wasn't well enough for them to stand there gawking. "Did you hear me? We need more champagne. Marcello will be asking for money in half an hour, and we want everyone feeling generous."

The young waiter worked his jaw, finally managing to speak. "I'm not old enough to serve alcohol."

"Oh, sorry. In that case just head to the kitchen and let them know. Tell any waiters on your way too. All right?"

The kid nodded. "No problem." Then he pivoted and headed toward the kitchen. Nathaniel watched him go, the familiarity nagging at him until an older man extended a hand toward him. One of their more generous contributors. Nathaniel tried to put the matter out of mind and focus on playing host, but when he risked another glance toward the kitchen, he saw Marcello speaking with the young waiter. The conversation seemed more involved than just the champagne shortage. What were the names of the two star-crossed waiters? William, obviously, but who was the other?

"I'd like to make a donation before the actual shut-in," Nathaniel's conversation partner was saying. "I haven't stayed up this late since my sixties!"

This reminded him to focus on the true priority of the evening. Nathaniel accepted a check, issued a tax-deductable receipt, and escorted the man outside to his car. When he returned inside, Marcello was on stage, announcing the shut-in. The waiters were swarming toward the kitchen, taking the food and drink with them. One whole hour without snacks and booze. How would any of them survive? Once the room was clear of staff, Nathaniel locked the doors personally, then nodded to one of the technicians, who lowered the lights.

He looked toward the stage, where Marcello and Tim had just finished speaking about the cause. The digital projector switched on. Nathaniel watched to make sure the edges were aligned and the image wasn't skewed. Everything looked good, so he allowed himself to relax by leaning against a wall. That didn't last long. A motion to his immediate right caught his eye, someone yanking on the kitchen door. He sighed. There was always one person who couldn't wait to break the rules.

"Can I help you?" he asked, pushing away from the wall.

The guy was slender, his skin dark, the hair buzzed close to his head. Whoever he was, he barely spared Nathaniel a glance before he started yanking on the door again. "I need out."

"Didn't you hear the announcement?" No response. "Hey, are you listening to me?"

The guy stopped pulling on the door long enough for Nathaniel to size him up. His features were striking. Enough so that he could be a model. This thought brought a name to mind: Kelly Phillips. Marcello had mentioned him a few times, bemoaning that Kelly wasn't interested in becoming a model. Now, in person, Nathaniel could understand his boss's agony. The shadows seem to lie across Kelly's face contentedly, having found the most beautiful place to rest.

Nathaniel's heart didn't swell with desire because his brain had put the pieces of Kelly's sad story together. This wasn't difficult, considering he'd been in a similar situation once. Some claim the truth can set you free, but Nathaniel had felt shackled by it ever since he saw Rebecca kissing Caesar. Love was cruel. Only a lucky few spent their entire lives without learning that truth. He often wished someone had kept him from discovering it.

Nathaniel stepped sideways, putting himself between Kelly and the exit.

"Even if this door wasn't locked, it leads to the kitchen, which is off limits." He threw the kid an excuse to walk away with his dignity intact. "Are you looking for the restroom?"

"Yes," Kelly said.

"Other side of the room."

Kelly lifted one of the two crutches supporting him, the kind that attached to the forearms. "Is it handicap-accessible?"

Nathaniel glanced down, noticing that one pant leg was folded and flat just above the knee. "I don't know. I'm sure you'll be fine."

"I need support bars mounted on the wall," Kelly insisted.

Then he kept rambling about everything else he required, playing up his handicap, but Nathaniel wasn't buying it. "I'll support you."

Eyes widened in response. "What?"

"I'll accompany you to the restroom, and if need be, I'll hold you up."

Kelly's jaw dropped. "Do you have any idea how offensive that is?"

"I don't care. You're not getting through this door." Time to cut through the bullshit. "What is it that you really want?"

Kelly sighed. "There's someone in there that I need to talk to."

"Need?"

"Yes! Need!"

Nathaniel snorted. "Trust me, there isn't anyone you need."

"Oh really. How would you know that?"

"Because I've put a lot of thought into the subject. Hold on."

He took the keys from his pocket. Part of him was tempted to toss them to Kelly and look away. Instead he unlocked the door and slipped inside, shutting and locking it before he could be followed. Then he sighed. William and his lover were off doing who knows what, while Kelly was left clawing at a closed door, wanting to see with his own eyes what he already knew in his heart.

Nathaniel felt sorry for him, which he didn't like because pity was a useless emotion that never helped anyone. But maybe something else could. He hurried from the kitchen, down the hall to the small reading room. He grabbed his birthday present, then snagged two glasses on the way back. When he opened the door again, he almost expected to be attacked with crutches. Instead Kelly looked him over, noticing the wine.

"What's this supposed to be?" he asked.

"Come find out." Nathaniel locked the door and gestured for Kelly to follow. Then he walked toward the back of the room. When he reached an empty table and pulled out a chair, Kelly wasn't far behind. Nathaniel sat across from him, working on getting the bottle open using the pocket knife he carried. While the knife had its own corkscrew, this was hardly the way to treat such an expensive wine. Then again, today was his birthday, and Nathaniel intended to enjoy himself a little. He poured two glasses.

"I'm not old enough to drink," Kelly said.

"Oh no," Nathaniel deadpanned. "I hope I don't lose my job over this."

"You could be arrested. Believe me."

"So be it." Nathaniel pushed one of the glasses toward him. "Drink up."

Kelly stared. "What kind of a bouncer are you?"

"I'm not a bouncer. My name is Nathaniel, and I'm the coordinator of this event. Are you enjoying yourself?"

"No."

"Good. Now shut up and take a drink so I can have one too. Otherwise, you'll think I'm rude."

Kelly continued to stare, but now with a hint of amusement. Finally he picked up the glass and held it aloft. "Here's to not getting what you want."

Nathaniel nodded his approval and took a hearty swig. The wine, despite its price tag, still tasted like wine. He turned his attention to the front of the room, judging how far along the presentation was. Then he started doing mental calculations on how much each glass of wine would cost, then each sip.

"It's great what you're doing here," Kelly said to get his attention.

Nathaniel looked at him, noticing the half-empty glass, the wine having placated him somewhat. He wished he could say the same, because he couldn't stop wondering what Kelly hoped to achieve by catching his boyfriend in the act. Nathaniel could find out, but he'd have to do so coyly. "And what is it that you're doing here? Are you someone's date?"

"No," Kelly said with a shake of his head. "I'm not rich either, so don't try hitting me up for money."

"Then I ask again, why are you here?"

"It's a mystery," Kelly said, playing with the stem of his glass. "I'm afraid you'll never find out. We'll share this drink together, go our separate ways, and that will be the end of our story."

Was he flirting? That might make him feel better, so Nathaniel decided to play along. "Fair enough. Of course the drink isn't over quite yet." He refilled Kelly's glass, then his own. He returned his attention to the presentation, but whenever he looked at Kelly, those eyes were still on him. He found that amusing and more than a little flattering. He believed in his own convictions though. He didn't need anyone else these days.

"So what about you?" Kelly asked, making conversation again. "Are you someone's date?"

Oh boy. "I already told you, this is my job."

"Yes, but it's not like you can't bring your boyfriend along. If I was dating you, I'd insist on coming just for the free food.

Except for those fish things. Those were gross."

"*Brandade de Morue au Gratin*," Nathaniel said.

"Exactly." Kelly made a face, sliding his glass over so it could be topped off again. "Whoever put those on the menu needs to be fired."

"I put them on the menu."

"Oh!" Kelly's eyebrows shot up. "Well maybe not fired. Um…"

"It's perfectly fine," Nathaniel said, pouring roughly one hundred and fifty dollars into Kelly's glass. "I was disappointed too. We had to switch caterers at the last minute. I won't be using them again. And for the record, if I had a boyfriend, I wouldn't bring him here. Topless waiters, rich old perverts, and bouncers who ply underage boys with booze. Not the most wholesome of environments, is it?"

He tried a smile. Kelly responded in kind, which had more of an effect on Nathaniel than he cared to admit. Unable to handle much more, he nodded at the video that had just started.

"Watch this one. It's good."

When Kelly turned to do so, Nathaniel stared at the back of his head and wondered how William could be so foolish. Maybe there was more to the story than he knew, but in addition to the handsome face, Kelly had tenacity and pride. Sure he was slugging back the wine, but he wasn't crying into the glass. Then again, the crutches leaning against the table testified that Kelly had probably overcome worse.

Nathaniel forced himself to watch the video, which he had personally directed, working with a local woman who had severe agoraphobia. She had been eager to help, even suggesting different ideas, including one he liked so much that he ended the video with it. He watched the scene play across the screen and felt just as moved as he had when they filmed it.

"That last shot," he said, "the soil passing through her gnarled old fingers… Beautiful stuff."

Kelly turned to face him again. "You like photography?"

"Something like that." The time to collect donations had come, and that was of greater importance than trying to prevent a broken heart. "I'm afraid our time together is over."

"My glass isn't empty yet," Kelly said, still flirting.

Nathaniel no longer had time for it. He picked up his

own glass and drained it. Marcello and Tim were back on stage, making their plea. "I have to help collect donations," he explained. Then the lights brightened to their normal level and his resolve wavered, because Kelly now wore a vulnerable expression. Nathaniel felt for him, he really did. Tonight he had only delayed the inevitable. Kelly would find out the truth soon enough. That would hurt, but he would survive the experience.

Nathaniel stood. "You'll be all right."

"Yeah," Kelly said dryly. "Just fine. Especially if you leave the bottle."

"Not a chance." Nathaniel swiped the wine bottle and turned away, but part of him didn't want to leave. He could at least say goodbye properly, which was funny because they hadn't had a real introduction. He spun back around. "You never told me your name."

"Kelly."

Nathaniel pretended to mull this over, as if weighing the pros and cons. "Well, Kelly, I'd say it's nice meeting you, but I guess this is goodbye."

"I guess so." The vulnerable expression remained a moment longer. Then Kelly smiled, exposed now in the full light of the room. Nathaniel had no choice but to stare. The kid should be on the cover of a magazine. Or in the arms of someone who wouldn't take him for granted. Maybe he would get there eventually. Some hearts bounced back quicker than others. Just not Nathaniel's. He turned away, already searching the crowd for a heart more generous than his own.

Nathaniel had a pocket stuffed full of checks when he returned to the kitchen, unlocked the doors and sent a platoon of waiters out to wine and dine the benefactors. Next he made sure the tables nearest the stage were cleared away so the band could resume and dancing could begin. All of this forced thoughts of Kelly out of his mind. That is, until he saw a young waiter standing in one corner of the kitchen, wearing a dreamy expression. No doubt he was still reeling from his little tryst with William. This made Nathaniel want to snap, which to his surprise, he did.

"Why are you just standing there?" he snarled, moving toward him. The young waiter appeared shocked, and for the briefest of moments, defensive, which finally helped Nathaniel make the connection. Grow out the messy hair until it covered his eyes, make those cheeks bright red with indignation, and the face became much more familiar. Jason Grant. Former foster son of the Hubbards. The guy who nearly ended his relationship with Caesar all those years ago. "Oh. I didn't recognize you before!"

Jason appeared twice as panicked. "You didn't?"

"No, sorry," Nathaniel replied, realizing that he was walking into a very awkward conversation. He quickly switched tracks to avoid it. "Marcello said two waiters would be sneaking around his house. You're one of them, right?"

"Yeah."

Jason freaking Grant. Of course it had to be him. Funny how history repeated itself. Instead of Nathaniel and Caesar getting caught up in a love triangle with him, now there were two new players. "How did everything go?"

Jason visibly relaxed and nodded slowly. "Good. Better than I expected, actually."

"So lucky. There's nothing like young love." Nathaniel tried to look caught up in the moment. This was his chance to help Kelly and bring these ridiculous games to an end. "If I can offer some advice... Don't let it stay hidden. Love is like a flower. It needs to be out in the open where it can get fresh air and sunlight. Secrets can be fun, but eventually they'll smother what you have together." He made a face. "Did I really just compare love to a flower?"

Jason laughed. "Yeah, you did."

Nathaniel shook his head shamefully. "Anyway, you get my point, right? If you like this guy, you'll both have to come out or whatever the issue is. That's the only way you'll make it."

"I'll keep that in mind." Jason searched his features. No doubt about it. He recognized Nathaniel too. "So what about you? Anyone special in your life?"

He meant Caesar. Jason wanted to know if their relationship had survived the test of time. "No." Nathaniel swallowed against the pain. "No, I think I'm done with all of that. I have better things to do with my time. If love is a flower, then someone ran over mine with a lawn mower a long time ago."

Jason's expression became sympathetic. Or was it pity?

"Not that I'm bitter," Nathaniel said hurriedly. "I'm just

more interested in my career right now. Speaking of which, Marcello didn't say anything about you slacking off. Grab a tray of cocktail wieners and be sure to laugh when these guys make all the obvious jokes."

"Yes, sir!"

Jason saluted in jest and flashed a smile, but it couldn't compare with the one Nathaniel had seen earlier in the evening. He hoped Kelly's smile would survive learning the truth, and that he would prove stronger than Nathaniel had when facing the same rite of passage. Love might be cruel, but life itself could offer alternative paths that were just as satisfying. He wished he had taken the time to tell Kelly that, to explain how he had built a new life for himself, one where he could no longer be hurt. Nathaniel returned to the ballroom with that thought in mind but found his Cinderella had already fled, leaving behind an empty wine glass instead of a slipper.

Interlude

The air conditioning in Marcello's office kicked in, filling the room with a gentle hum. Kelly leaned forward to pick up his wine glass, sipping from it before considering the contents thoughtfully. "We met on your birthday," he murmured. "I had no idea."

"I never thought it worth mentioning." Nathaniel grunted. "As much as I've missed you over the years, I still have standards. So if you're expecting a cheesy line about how you were the best birthday present I've ever gotten, you can forget it. Even if it is true."

Kelly looked up and smiled. "I'll take that as a compliment, especially considering the caliber of presents you've gotten before. A thousand dollars for a bottle of wine? That's crazy!"

"You don't like how it tastes?" Nathaniel asked, nodding at his glass.

Kelly stiffened and sat upright, holding the glass with added caution. "*This* is the same wine?"

"You've got about—" Nathaniel narrowed his eyes in concentration. "—three hundred dollars swishing around in your stomach right now."

Kelly set down his glass carefully. "I wish I could pee it back out into my bank account."

"Is money tight? I can help. Seriously."

"No." He shook his head. "I appreciate it. Including what you tried to do the night of the charity ball. I thought back on it sometimes, once I learned the truth. Occasionally I wished you had let me pass through that door so I could have caught them in the act. But you were probably right. Seeing them together would have been more traumatizing, making it harder to recover from."

"You did though," Nathaniel said. "I was so proud when I heard you reached out to Marcello. You didn't need my advice or my protection. You've always been smart and strong. You bounced back, started modeling, and damn-near became a household name. I don't know if you understand just how close you came to that."

Kelly shrugged. "That sort of fame never appealed to me. Being an Olympic star would have been nice. These days I'd like my photography to gain recognition, but getting famous just because I look good in the right lighting and under layers of makeup? Not for me."

"You always look good."

Kelly shook his head in disagreement. "I'm flattered you think I'm strong, but it was Jason Grant who pushed me to contact Marcello. Did you know that? I grew to like Jason, once we got to know each other. I understand why William fell in love with him. The same reasons Caesar did, I imagine. I know Jason will always be a homewrecker to you and me, but I think that's because he didn't have a home of his own. He was placed in foster care at a very young age, and from what he told me, he never stayed in one place for long. He wasn't oblivious to the consequences of his actions, but considering how little stability his own life offered, it's not surprising he bumbled into ours and knocked things over."

Nathaniel studied Kelly critically. "Have you gone soft on me?"

Kelly snorted. "No. If Jason ever puts the moves on someone I love again, I'll break his damn fingers. Then I'll drive him to the hospital myself, because I really do like the guy."

Nathaniel chuckled, refilling their glasses. He hoped such forgiveness extended to him, but perhaps not. Even before Nathaniel set down the bottle, Kelly fidgeted and stood.

"Where are you going?" Nathaniel asked.

"Bathroom break. And then home."

Home? He watched as Kelly walked toward a door in the far corner of the room, getting tenser by the second. Neither of them could leave, but what concerned Nathaniel is that Kelly wanted to. After a rush of pipes and the trickling sound of a sink, Kelly returned and spoke words that sent panic racing to Nathaniel's stomach:

"It's getting late."

"We're stuck here," Nathaniel reminded him.

Kelly shot him a look. "How many times have you dealt with building codes? What happens if the elevator breaks down, which apparently it has, and Marcello drinks too much, passes out, and sets himself on fire? It would serve him right considering how manipulative he's being, but I'm assuming there's a contingency plan in place."

Nathaniel remained silent.

Kelly shook his head in response and headed for the nearest window. "There's a fire escape and—so help me—if these windows are on lockdown or whatever, I *will* throw a chair through one."

Nathaniel stood. "I'm not done."

"I know the rest of the story," Kelly said, spinning around. "I was there."

"You don't," Nathaniel said. "Especially at the beginning, when I was holding back my feelings."

"I can guess! You were scared of getting hurt again, but I slowly lured you in, and everything was great until—"

"Cancún."

Kelly blinked. "What?"

"Cancún. You remember?"

"Of course. The first time we travelled together. It was a nice trip."

"It was more than that."

Kelly shook his head in confusion, not remembering the significance.

"That's what I'm trying to tell you," Nathaniel explained. "You need to hear my half of the story. The highlights. I need you to know how I feel about you."

Kelly sighed. "I already know."

"You don't! What the hell is 'I love you' worth anymore? People throw it around like they're saying 'good morning' these days, but I'm not fucking around. I *love* you, and you're not going to understand what that really means unless you sit down and listen."

Kelly raised an eyebrow. Then, with a cool expression, he returned to the couch and sat. "I suppose it would be a shame if the wine went to waste." He left his glass where it was though and leaned back to consider him. "Cancún," he prompted.

Nathaniel shook his head. "We need to go back further than that."

"How far?"

"To the first time I saw you naked."

"I definitely remember that night."

"Don't be so sure," Nathaniel said. "It wasn't night. It was day. But only just."

Kelly's smile was subtle. "This should be good. Let's hear it."

Chapter Fifteen

Jason Grant was a troublemaker. Nathaniel regretted going easy on him during the charity ball. Not only had Jason once messed up his romantic life, but now he was meddling in Nathaniel's professional life as well. Admittedly, Jason's involvement hadn't come unsolicited. Losing three international clients in one year had caused a crisis of faith for Marcello, and so he had sought advice from the bottle, retired professionals, strangers on the street, and eventually a teenager. The solution? Jason felt the studio needed to start producing spontaneous photos. The sort of sloppy images people slapped a meme on before posting on the Internet. No careful lighting. No makeup crew. Professional photographers need not apply. Just little moments captured in time that struck a chord with the masses.

The idea possessed a certain modern sensibility, the obvious fault being that a professional studio couldn't sit around waiting for life to happen. Planned spontaneity wasn't possible, and yet Marcello expected Nathaniel to try. This meant waking up annoyingly early and collecting their new star model—from his parents' house. He hadn't realized just how young Kelly was until that moment. Nathaniel took him to a pancake house for breakfast, feeling like an uncle whose nephew was visiting for the weekend. Kelly didn't seem to share this impression. The kid kept grinning at him like they were on their first date, but at least he'd snapped at the incompetent waiter who failed to give the kitchen their order.

Now they were standing outside in the parking lot and facing the impossible. Nathaniel had taken a few photos of Kelly trying to appear grown up by forcing down coffee, but that wasn't enough. They still had the entire day ahead of them. Spontaneity on demand. Kelly knew the assignment and agreed that it was nonsense, but seemed more optimistic about finding a solution.

"I could spread myself out on the hood of your car," he suggested. "Or wait, maybe I should just do it instead of talking about it."

"Won't make a difference," Nathaniel said. "Would still come across as contrived."

"In that case, you should drive me home so I can play video

games with my brother. That's what I'd be doing if it weren't for this assignment."

Nathaniel considered him. "Maybe you've got the right idea. Video games are boring, but what else would you do today? It's Sunday. Church?"

"Sort of. I have a gay youth group every couple of weeks. There's one this afternoon."

Nathaniel shook his head. "I can't see that being exciting. Unless I'm wrong. I'm picturing an AA meeting except with nervous gay teenagers instead of tired old alcoholics."

"Pretty much. You're probably way above the age limit anyway. How old are you? Thirty?"

Nathaniel glared at him. "Twenty-three. How old are you? Twelve?"

"Eighteen."

"Great." Not much of an age difference, but enough that their lifestyles were completely different. "So what else do nervous gay teenagers do for fun?"

Kelly shrugged. "Hang out with my friends, usually at their place or in my room. Or at the mall."

"Gosh, if that's your idea of a good time, I'd hate to hear about your bad days."

Kelly's eyebrows came together, but not in offense. "Actually, you're on to something." He walked around the passenger door. "Come on."

Once in the car, Kelly started giving directions. Nathaniel hoped the idea was good, although even a bad idea was welcome at this point. After twisting and turning through the streets of Austin, they arrived at a high school. In the height of summer, the place felt desolate—just a large brick building, an empty parking lot, and the overzealous landscaping of buzzed grass and spindly trees. The scene was bleak, which appealed to him, but Kelly had another destination in mind. He led the way to the side of the school. Keeping up with him wasn't easy. Kelly didn't let crutches slow him down. Nathaniel hadn't paid much attention to the missing leg, which in the darkness of the charity event had barely been evident, but he knew Marcello hoped to capitalize on its absence. Not in an exploitative way exactly, at least no more so than the norm in this business. Success required not riding the crest of the current wave, but being the force that drove it forward. Marcello wanted modeling to become more inclusive. An amputee would draw attention and generate discussion, but most of all, it would prove the world craved more than images of plastic perfection. The truth of that remained to be seen, but the response from Kelly's initial photo shoots had been promising.

Kelly led them to a running track—a giant oval of maroon material separated into lanes by white lines. Nathaniel waited to see if Kelly considered this environment ironic, or if he was a proud disabled athlete eager to show off his abilities. Instead he led them to the bleachers, taking a seat higher up so they had a decent view. There they sat and watched a middle-aged man try to jog away the flab. Kelly remained silent. Withdrawn.

"What's the story?" Nathaniel asked.

"Same as Icarus when he flew too close to the sun." Kelly's expression showed longing, his almond-shaped eyes focused straight ahead. "If you delight in something too much, the gods punish you for it. Icarus got his kicks flying, and I got high off running."

Nathaniel followed his gaze. "You were on the track team?"

"Fastest guy in school. I even planned on making a career of it, Olympic dream and all that. Sounds arrogant to say it now. I probably would have learned a hard lesson when meeting the pros, but I would have preferred that to this."

A sob story? That's why they were here? "Huh."

"That's it?" Kelly's head whipped around. "That's all you've got to say?"

Nathaniel shrugged in response. "You don't strike me as the self-pitying type."

"I'm not." Kelly looked forward again. "I used to be, but not anymore. Now I just miss it. I sit here because it's as close as I can get. I even wondered if I should be some sort of coach, you know? Professional boxers always have an out-of-shape dude telling them how to punch. You don't have to be the champ to make a champ."

"Is that something you're interested in doing?"

Kelly shook his head. "Not really." He continued to stare at the track with a hint of longing and an air of resignation, still dreaming of a future that would never be.

Nathaniel could relate to that. Who hadn't carefully made plans, only to discover that fate had different intentions? "I left the flash in the car," he said. "I'll be right back."

He walked away, retreating to a safe distance so he wouldn't be seen. Then he raised the telephoto lens. The angle was perfect. An athletic guy sitting on the bleachers, rounded shoulders beneath the maroon T-shirt that hung off his slender frame, the arms nicely toned. Kelly looked like an athlete who had been sidelined, the reason why hinted at by the singular leg protruding from the long basketball shorts and the crutches propped up on his other side. Nathaniel captured this image with the camera. Then he zoomed in to focus on Kelly's face, snapping a few just for himself, because he found himself fascinated: the thick lips, the fine curves of his nose, the eyebrows that could communicate so many degrees of expression, especially mild irritation and questioning amusement. Both were better than the sorrowful mask he wore now, similar to the one Nathaniel saw often enough in the mirror. He lowered the camera, no longer comfortable with the situation, and hurried forward to break the spell of loneliness. For them both.

"Got some good photos of you," he said.

Kelly turned his head and nodded. "I figured."

"You knew?"

Kelly's eyes sparkled. "I know that a flash is nearly useless in broad daylight. Especially when you're using a telephoto lens. What's the maximum range on that thing? Three hundred millimeters?"

"Five."

"Impressive."

Nathaniel stared down at him. "It felt sleazy as hell, taking photos of you looking sad. Too exploitative."

Kelly shrugged this off, grabbing his crutches and pushing himself up to stand. "I wouldn't have brought you here if I had a problem with it. I thought we'd go to a shoe store next, followed by a dance club." He flashed white teeth, startling against his dark skin. Before the day was through, that smile definitely needed to be captured on film.

They travelled next to the wilds of Texas. Sort of. The nature preserve had trees, blue skies, and dirt paths. Kelly navigated just fine along these, only slowing when Nathaniel suggested they cross a field to a place where the light had caught his eye, but he did well enough. Nathaniel decided not to concern himself further, since Kelly was clearly comfortable in his own mobility. This was proven when they approached a tree. Kelly grabbed a low branch and let his crutches fall to the ground. He performed an impressive pull-up, his shirt lifting to expose the bottom of enviable abs. His waist was narrow and defined enough that two angled lines began at the hips and plunged tantalizingly into his shorts. Nathaniel raised the camera and snapped photos, already feeling Marcello patting him on the back in congratulations. Kelly positioned his foot against the trunk, kicking against it so he could grab another branch. Nathaniel raised the camera as Kelly continued to climb higher.

"Care to join me?" he asked once he stopped.

"Not sure the tree would appreciate my weight," Nathaniel replied.

"Excuses, excuses," Kelly taunted. "You're too old and feeble. Admit it."

Nathaniel shook his head, slung the camera around his neck, and grabbed the same branch Kelly had started with. He did a set of pull-ups, slow and deliberate. He might not have a six-pack, but he had maintained his upper body strength. He glanced up to see Kelly looking impressed, then swung his legs to hook another branch with his feet, but he chose one too high up, leaving him hanging horizontally. Kelly started laughing, which would have been annoying if his face wasn't such a beautiful sight. Nathaniel let his legs drop, jumped to the ground, and grabbed the camera again.

"I feel like I escaped from a bear," Kelly said. "There's no way you're getting up here."

"Lucky for you," Nathaniel said. "I'm getting hungry again."

"Have some pine cones." Kelly twisted one off a branch and tossed it at him.

Nathaniel didn't bother dodging. The photos were too important, even if he got pelted. Kelly was either merciful or a bad aim because none of the pine cones even came close. Until the fifth one bounced off the top of his head.

Nathaniel lowered the camera and glared. "Bears *can* climb trees," he growled. "Especially when provoked."

Kelly smirked. "Seeing is believing."

"I'll bide my time. You have to come down eventually."

"I don't want to," Kelly said wistfully. "It feels too good."

"Being able to move around without these?" Nathaniel asked, nudging the crutches with his foot.

"More than that," Kelly said. "The ground has always been my enemy. I bet most runners want to fly. I always did. It feels possible when you're going fast enough, like you're about to outpace gravity and leave the ground. The same when you're up here." He grabbed a nearby branch and let himself flop forward until swinging from it. "Almost like flying."

"Well you're not, so be careful." He watched Kelly's foot find another branch so he could climb down. Then he grabbed another and let himself swing freely, his waist now at eye-height. Most people could probably safely drop to their feet, but that would prove challenging for Kelly. Nathaniel waited, not wanting to be presumptuous with an offer of help.

"Um," Kelly said. "I might not have thought this all the way through."

That was his cue. Nathaniel stepped forward and wrapped an arm around Kelly's waist. Through the nylon mesh shorts, he could feel the warmth of another body. He tried to ignore everything he came into contact with as Kelly slid down his torso and was held there briefly until he balanced himself against the tree.

"Let's sit down," Kelly suggested. "I need to cool off."

"Okay."

Kelly grabbed Nathaniel's arm without asking, trusting him to hold it stiff so he could lower himself to the ground. His touch felt significant in a way it shouldn't, and as Nathaniel sat next to Kelly, both of them with their backs against the tree, he realized how rarely he made physical contact with other people. When he did it was business-related handshakes or hugs from his mother. God, that was sad!

He wondered if Kelly also considered their touches electric, but then again, it hadn't been so long for him. Probably. Hell, Kelly and William could have patched things up, but Nathaniel was too much of a romantic pessimist to believe that. Still, he should at least confirm his theory.

"So how are things?" Nathaniel asked, and even though he was continuing a conversation that had begun two months ago, Kelly had no trouble picking up where they left off.

"Someone once told me that I don't need anyone," Kelly said.

"And?"

"Turns out the guy was full of shit, because I'm single and constantly wishing I wasn't."

Nathaniel snorted. "Did he also mention there's a difference between wanting and needing?"

"Maybe. I was a little distracted at the time. He wasn't completely wrong though. He told me I'd be all right."

Nathaniel rested the back of his head against the tree. "And are you?"

Kelly thought about this. "I figure everyone is messed up in some way. It's impossible to get through life without going a little crazy, right?"

"Some are nuttier than others, but yes."

"In that case I fit right in, so yeah, I'm okay."

They sat under the tree, content with silence as the sun climbed high above. Eventually Nathaniel's stomach growled, so he suggested they head back to his place. Zero needed to be fed, and since that involved cooking, eating there before getting back to work was most practical. Kelly seemed a little too excited by the invitation—less so when they arrived at Nathaniel's apartment and Zero knocked him down. Regardless, he spent most of the time asking Nathaniel about himself.

As flattering as that was, Nathaniel firmly drew a line, not wanting to discuss the past. He resisted the urge to lecture Kelly on why he refused to date. Once they got to know each other, Kelly would reach the obvious conclusions on his own. Eventually. For now he was still eager to please, seeing potential in Nathaniel that wasn't truly there. He even insisted on doing dishes. Nathaniel was too tired to argue, the food having made him groggy, so he stretched out on the couch with Zero and only meant to rest his eyes briefly. He ended up falling asleep. When he woke, Kelly was sitting at the dining room table waiting for him. Embarrassing, but Nathaniel's nose soon informed him of the good news. "Do I smell coffee?"

"Coming up!" Kelly said, rising. "If you're tired we can call it a day."

"Nope." Nathaniel shoved Zero until he slid off the couch with a grumble. Then he sat up. "We have to hit the pool before it gets dark."

"The pool?"

"Yeah. Marcello wants a swimsuit shoot. He didn't tell you?"

Kelly poured coffee into a mug. "No. I don't have a swimsuit."

Nathaniel sighed. "That was probably intentional. How do you feel about nude photography?"

The steady trickle of coffee became a splash, Kelly swearing a second later and scurrying to find a rag. When he brought the mug into the living room, he set it down on the coffee table and stared at Nathaniel. "Nobody said anything about nude photography."

Nathaniel resisted a grin. "Comes with the territory. It's no big deal. You don't need to get hard or anything."

"Hard?" Kelly repeated.

"Yeah. A boner. Unless you want to, of course. It does pay extra."

Kelly's jaw dropped.

"I'm fucking with you," Nathaniel said, tossing one of the couch pillows at him.

Kelly deflected it easily, already glaring. "Give me that coffee back. I forgot to put rat poison in it."

"I'd still drink it for the caffeine." Nathaniel took the mug and demonstrated. "Seriously though, Marcello wants some typical poolside photos, and it'll look awkward if you're fully dressed. We can hit the mall on the way, pick out a few swimsuits you like. Deal?"

Kelly nodded. After a few more sips, Nathaniel decided to bring the coffee along, leaving immediately to take advantage of the remaining daylight and heat. They drove to the nearest mall, ducking in and out of stores, but Kelly seemed hesitant about the available options. Was he insecure about his body? If so, he had chosen the wrong profession. The quest for the ultimate swimsuit dragged on. They were walking through the mall when Kelly nodded toward the food court.

"My ex-boyfriend used to work at the juice place over there," he said. "He was one of the waiters at the charity ball that night. That's who I was trying to get to."

"Really?" Nathaniel said, playing dumb. "What was his name?"

"William."

He rubbed his chin theatrically. "Yeah, I definitely remember him."

"Really?"

Nathaniel nodded. "He did a terrible job."

Kelly smiled a little. "Seriously?"

"Yup. In fact, I wish he still worked here. I wouldn't mind getting back at him. We could make him jealous."

"How?" Kelly asked.

"By ordering a banana daiquiri with extra whipped cream."

"I'm not sure that would do it."

"When he put the drink on the counter," Nathaniel continued, "I'd take off the lid, set aside the straw, and dip my finger in it. Then I'd let you lick it clean."

"That doesn't sound sanitary," Kelly replied, but now he was grinning.

Nathaniel was flirting shamelessly, hoping to bolster Kelly's confidence. It must have worked, because at the next store he actually considered the swimsuits instead of dismissing them outright. Unfortunately, what he ended up selecting wasn't very inspiring.

"What do you think?" Kelly asked, holding up a pair of long swim trunks.

"I was thinking these," Nathaniel countered, showing him a much skimpier pair.

"Is that a thong?"

"Speedos. They'll show off your body, which is the whole point of a pool shoot. You aren't there to enjoy the water."

Before Kelly could reply, a sales clerk walked up, his big watery eyes looking them over, lingering on the crutches. The top of his round head was mostly bald, the trimmed beard compensating on the opposite hemisphere. "Can I help you with something?"

"We found what we need," Nathaniel said. "He's going to try these on. Right?"

Kelly sighed and nodded. "Fine."

"The dressing rooms are over there," the clerk said, pointing to curtained doorways on the far wall. "Do you need any assistance?"

"Nope," Kelly said, already heading there. "Thanks."

All three dressing rooms were occupied. While they waited, Kelly kept considering the skimpy swimsuit and making an unhappy expression.

"Worried about filling it out?" Nathaniel teased.

Kelly raised an eyebrow. "No."

Finally one of the curtains opened and a man exited, leaving behind pairs of crumpled jeans on the floor.

"Oh, excuse me," the clerk said, reappearing. He swooped into the small space and gathered up the pile of jeans. Then he stood just outside the door and smiled. "There you go! Wouldn't want you to trip and fall."

"Thanks," Kelly said tersely, heading inside.

The sales clerk grabbed the curtain and held it open. "Are you going to be okay?"

Kelly's eyes narrowed slightly. "I'll manage."

"There are courtesy wheelchairs in the customer service center downstairs," the clerk said. "If you wait, I can fetch one for you."

Kelly looked at the corner of the dressing room, where a small bench was attached to the wall. Then he returned his attention to the clerk, his lips curling into a smile, but one unlike any Nathaniel had seen so far. Kelly resembled a viper. "What's wrong with the seat in here? Do you think it needs wheels? Would that somehow make it easier to try on clothes?"

"No, but it's not a very big seat. I was telling my manager last week that there should be handicapped dressing rooms, just like there are restrooms. Nice and spacious with some bars on the wall and…" The man trailed off, misunderstanding Kelly's impatient expression. "Sorry. Should I run and get that wheelchair?"

"I'd rather you get a lobotomy, but there's no point. If you had even half a brain, you'd realize how offensive you're being."

"Offensive?" The clerk blinked a few times. "I was thinking of your convenience!"

"You were thinking that all crippled people belong in wheelchairs. Do I look like I have trouble getting around?"

The clerk set his jaw. "I was only trying to help!"

"If you want to help me," Kelly said, "you can promise not to reproduce. If you ever find someone stupid enough to mate with you, *please*, for the sake of mankind's future, don't do it."

"You're very rude!"

"And violent, so you might want to leave before I put the one foot I've got halfway up your ass."

The clerk spun around to face Nathaniel, but if he was seeking sympathy, he had chosen the wrong guy. A moment later he stomped toward the registers, cheeks red.

"That was harsh," Nathaniel said, leaning against the doorway. "I like your style."

Kelly batted his eyelashes innocently. "Just my little way of making the world a brighter place."

"You get stuff like that a lot?"

"Yes. Mostly from kids. One asked me the other day if I was a pirate."

"Did you bite his head off too?"

"No. Children are too young to know better, and frankly, there are worse things than being compared to a pirate. I might even dress up as one for Halloween. Speaking of which." He held up the swimsuits and shook them.

"Oh." Nathaniel grabbed the curtain, just as the clerk had. "I'm here if you need me. Just in case you fall or something."

"Asshole," Kelly said with a chuckle.

Nathaniel grinned and shut the curtain. He waited for it to open again, expecting Kelly to demonstrate how he looked in each swimsuit. Instead, after much rustling of fabric and a barely audible sigh, the curtain was pushed aside, revealing the same outfit as before.

"Maybe a pair of jeans," Kelly suggested hurriedly. "They can be tight. I know a brand that looks good on me. The photos will still be sexy. I can make them work, you'll see."

"Okay," Nathaniel said.

They went to a different store. Kelly knew exactly what he wanted. He was confident enough to buy them right away, asking the clerk to cut off the tags. Then he went to the dressing room to change so the jeans would loosen up before the shoot. Nathaniel had to admit they looked good. They showed off Kelly's package nicely, but it still wasn't the assignment they had been given. He was tempted to remind Kelly of this, but he'd grown quiet and reserved, confirming Nathaniel's suspicions: The guy had body issues.

They drove in silence to Marcello's home, which of course had a sprawling patio and a large private pool. This location had been used for numerous photo shoots, Nathaniel grateful that using it didn't require the usual paperwork or special arrangements. Just a certified lifeguard for insurance reasons. Today they would go without.

"Feels weird being back here," Kelly said as they wound their way through one of the living rooms. "At the time I didn't understand that someone actually lived here. Jesus! Is that a Ming vase?"

"If it's got cookie crumbs in it, yes."

"What?"

Nathaniel shrugged. "Marcello told me once he keeps cookies in his Ming. I always imagined it would be in the kitchen. Or next to his bed."

When they stepped out onto the patio, the sun was growing orange as it descended toward the horizon. Marcello's home was built on top of a hill, affording an impressive view of the city. This was useful in terms of light, since the trees were too low to cast interfering shadows, but they needed to act quickly.

"We don't have much time," Nathaniel said, unpacking the camera.

He worried that Kelly would need to be coaxed out of his shirt, but when he looked up, it was being stripped off. He raised the camera, snapping a few photos. Then he lowered it again, because Kelly had a nice body. Slender. A runner's build, even now. Arms ropey with muscle, tight pecs, and of course, those abs.

"This light won't last," Kelly said, lowering himself onto a lawn chair to remove his sock and shoe. "Keep snapping photos. You might get something good. Or maybe Marcello has a foot fetish."

"He has every fetish," Nathaniel said, raising the camera again. "He collects them."

Once down to his jeans, Kelly stretched out on the lawn furniture, but he wasn't being lazy. He had good instinct for body posture and his position relative to the camera, especially considering that yesterday was his first day in the studio.

"You sure seem to know a lot about cameras and light," Nathaniel said while taking photos.

"It used to be a hobby of mine."

"And now?"

"Try holding that camera steady while hopping on one leg."

Nathaniel didn't argue. Kelly was mostly stationary, but Nathaniel was ducking and dodging, moving around him to try different angles. He needed his full mobility and couldn't imagine working like this while trying to balance on crutches. He kept taking photos, appreciating the orange glow on Kelly's brown skin, but he was distracted by the mostly empty pant leg, which flopped around, getting tangled in an unappealing way.

Nathaniel stopped taking photos. "You like to swim?"

Kelly narrowed his eyes. "What do you think?"

"I've seen enough inspirational movies to know that people are capable of anything they put their minds to. I stopped making assumptions after watching *My Left Foot*. So again, do you like to swim?"

"I haven't really tried since the accident," Kelly said.

"I just need you in the water," Nathaniel said. "The shallow end will do."

"In my jeans?"

"It was your idea."

Kelly nodded. He stood and moved to the stairs leading into the pool. He waded in, crutches and all, keeping close to the wall. Then he raised them for Nathaniel to take.

"How's it feel?" he asked, setting aside the crutches.

"Warm," Kelly said. "Is this pool heated?"

"Could be," Nathaniel said, looking through the camera lens again.

Kelly glanced around, trying to figure out what to do. He inched along the wall to deeper water. Up to his neck.

"Move back," Nathaniel instructed. "Get your arms down."

Kelly did what he was told, the sun catching his brown eyes.

The shutter clicked and whirred, and as handsome as the resulting photos would be, Nathaniel didn't think they were getting anything special. "Listen," he said. "You know how they say you should make love to the camera? I need you to fuck it. Hard. Like you and the camera broke up, got back together again, and you still haven't forgiven it completely."

Kelly smiled but then grew serious. Bedroom eyes smoldered as teeth slid along his bottom lip. No come-hither expression, instead Kelly's look said I'll-come-to-you with a little bit of whether-you-like-it-or-not. Kelly moved forward again, placing his hands on the edge of the pool. Then he slowly raised himself, water cascading over his flexing muscles, weighing the jeans down so that one angular hip was exposed more than the other. Nathaniel was getting hard, but he ignored that. If these images were turning him on, chances are they would work for others too.

"Do that again," he breathed.

Kelly lowered himself and repeated the maneuver, this time the water pulling on his jeans enough that Nathaniel could see a line of hair that he knew was just a few tantalizing inches away from a much more enticing prize. From the way the wet denim cupped his package, he could imagine how big that prize would be.

The sun hit the horizon, the light becoming dimmer, the color still rich but too dark for the camera. Kelly must have noticed this, because instead of lowering himself back into the water, he turned and sat on the edge of the pool.

"These jeans feel like they weigh a ton. Did you get what you need?"

"Yeah," Nathaniel said, more aware now of his own arousal. He did a quick adjustment, hoping to conceal it. "I'll grab some towels."

Kelly just nodded. Had he noticed? Did it make him uncomfortable? Nathaniel walked to the house, keeping his back to Kelly. Only once he was in the dark interior did he turn around, feeling certain he couldn't be seen. Kelly watched the house for a moment, then scooted toward his backpack and took out the basketball shorts he'd worn earlier. He hoisted himself up onto the lawn chair, then swung around, facing away from the house. From the motion of his arms, he was clearly unbuttoning the jeans. Sure enough, he then lifted himself to tug them off his hips, giving Nathaniel a nice view of his ass. A bubble butt with curves that made his mouth water. Once the jeans were tossed aside, landing in a wet puddle, Nathaniel realized he was seeing Kelly completely nude, even if most of the details were obscured. Kelly turned sideways and leaned back to pull up the shorts, his most intimate parts already covered.

The amputated limb rose in the air briefly, the fabric tumbling down it before Kelly tugged the mesh-fabric over it again, hiding it from view. He shot a look toward the house as if concerned. Nathaniel felt like rushing out to reassure him, which would of course be hard to do without admitting he'd been spying. Instead he filed the issue away and went to fetch a towel. He checked the images on the camera display as he went: brown eyes smoldering with desire, orange light reflecting off beads dripping down dark muscle, and water sucking at jeans clinging to narrow hips. Nathaniel felt hungry, but he wasn't the slightest bit interested in food.

Marcello flipped through the photos from yesterday's shoot in a rare state of silence. Some of the photos he set facedown in a pile, rejecting them. To Nathaniel's surprise, these included all of the pool photos except for the one of Kelly removing his shirt. Face up in another pile were those he approved of—Kelly looking grossed out while trying to drink coffee or laughing in the branches of a tree.

"Sleeping on the job?" Marcello asked, holding up one.

Nathaniel leaned forward. The photo was of his apartment, him stretched out on the couch, Zero pressed up against his side. Kelly must have taken it while he was snoozing.

"Have you not seen these yet?" Marcello asked, reading his face.

"No. Just grabbed them from the lab. Any others like that?"

Marcello placed the photo between the two piles and resumed sorting. At the end, he shook his head. "That's the only one, which is a shame. The composition is promising. Do you suppose Kelly got lucky?"

"He used to dabble in photography until…" Nathaniel picked up on the double meaning and rolled his eyes. "Anyway, what do you think?"

"They have a certain charm," Marcello said. "I'd like to offer a selection in our catalog and gauge the response. More to the point, what do you think of Kelly? He's very photogenic. Should I offer him a full contract?"

Nathaniel leaned back and sighed. "Depends on what you expect from him. If you want a normal model, then sure. If you expect his amputation to be part of the photos, it'll take some coaxing."

"How so?"

"He doesn't like anyone seeing it. Kelly made sure to hide it from me. That's why he's climbing out of the pool wearing a pair of jeans."

Marcello stuck his bottom lip out in puzzlement. "I saw no such reservation from him in the studio. He seemed completely comfortable with his body."

"Really?"

"I have the photos to prove it."

Marcello reached for a drawer, but Nathaniel stopped him. "I believe you. Maybe he changed his mind."

"I assure you, we spoke quite openly about the issue before this trial period began. I don't leave much to chance, especially where emotions are involved."

"Then why—" A lurid smile cut him off. Nathaniel sighed. "You think I'm the problem?"

"Perhaps you've caught his eye."

"The swimsuit probably made him nervous."

Marcello tapped the photo of Nathaniel sleeping on the couch. "He could have posed next to you while making a face, or written something on your forehead, or snapped a photo right after jarring you awake. Instead the photo's perspective brings to mind an admirer, standing over the sleeping form of the person they long to touch."

"He barely knows me."

"Familiarity is rarely the heart's first concern. How does his desire make you feel?"

Nathaniel tore his eyes from the photo. "Feelings have nothing to do with it. He's got talent. I think you should offer him a contract."

His boss's theory was put to the test a week later. Nathaniel wasn't the least bit surprised to find himself organizing a downtown photo shoot for a low-profile client who normally wouldn't have merited a session outside the studio. Kelly would be the star of the day, posing in the middle of a crosswalk, surrounded by extras. The entire affair was over-budget before it began, but he knew Marcello would find some way of recouping his losses. The true purpose of the day was to put two chemicals together and watch for a reaction. Nathaniel had to admit he was curious. He already knew what he felt. Relationships were a bad idea. What Kelly felt was a mystery. In his mind, at least. Marcello remained convinced that Nathaniel had an admirer.

Not wanting to compromise the experiment, Nathaniel focused on his work. Kelly did seem eager to prove himself. Maybe his crush was on the job itself, and any nervousness he felt was about performing correctly, because once they began, Kelly's attention didn't waver from his task. No longing glances were sent in Nathaniel's direction. By lunchtime Nathaniel had already dismissed Marcello's theory. He had more important concerns, since a bureaucrat had called to inform Nathaniel that certain promises wouldn't be kept.

He hung up the phone, tempted to grind it beneath one foot, when he noticed Kelly standing there. "Better eat something," Nathaniel said. "That was the city. We've got less time than we thought. Lunch is only ten minutes today."

Kelly offered a sympathetic expression. "I'm not hungry."

Nathaniel glared at his phone before putting it away. Then he gave Kelly his full attention. "You're doing great. I've known pros who don't try half as hard."

"I won't either when I'm famous," Kelly said. "The crew will be forced to visit my bedside for photo shoots. What's the point of making your way to the top if you've got to keep working?"

"If you love what you do…"

"Good point." Kelly looked him up and down before appearing slightly panicked and scrambling for conversation. "How's Zero?"

"Good. Doing real good."

"Great," Kelly replied.

Nathaniel nodded. "Yeah." This was going nowhere fast. Ugh. Why did Marcello always have to be right about such things?

Without the support of his crutches, Kelly would no doubt be squirming. Instead he stared straight ahead, eyes unfocused. Then he blinked suddenly and blurted out "Dog dinner!" He winced visibly, then added, "Sorry. What I mean is, I thought maybe you and I could… Uh. What are you doing this weekend?"

Nathaniel tried not to laugh. He really did. "Dog dinner?"

Kelly got over his embarrassment enough to glare.

"I'm not doing anything," Nathaniel said casually. "Besides feeding Zero his breakfast. And his lunch. And his—"

"Shut up," Kelly said, laughing a second later. "What I meant to say, is that maybe we could take Zero to the dog park. Afterwards, we could grab a bite to eat. If you're not busy, that is."

A date. Nathaniel's stomach sank. But what could he do? Kelly had embarrassed himself by asking. Getting rejected now would be devastating. "No, I'm not busy."

His phone rang. Saved by the bell. Nathaniel made a big show of being irritated by the interruption, lifting the phone to his ear. Before he spoke, he decided that he could sacrifice one afternoon of his life before letting Kelly down easy. "Saturday," he whispered while covering the phone. "Dog dinner."

Kelly's eyes lit up, but he nodded coolly, turning toward the catering truck. Then Nathaniel spoke into the receiver. "I hate you."

"You love me," Marcello replied in his ear. "I take it things are going well?"

"A date. Saturday. Strictly platonic, of course."

"Naturally! Need any pointers? How long has it been?"

"The guy from Paris about a year ago. That was your idea too."

"I remember quite a bit of chemistry between you both."

"He couldn't speak English! And I don't speak French."

"Still, he showed you his baguette, didn't he?"

Nathaniel rolled his eyes. "What else was I going to do with him? Besides, it had been a long time since I'd had... a baguette."

"Everyone needs to eat," Marcello said innocently.

"Right. Just promise me this is the last time. No more pushing me toward this sort of thing. Promise me, or I'll cancel my date with Kelly."

Marcello sighed. "You have my word. Still, make sure you're prepared. It pays to be optimistic. A little butter for your bread and a plastic bag to wrap it in! Ha ha!"

Nathaniel hung up the phone, deciding not to eat lunch after all.

Chapter Sixteen

In and out. That was Nathaniel's plan. A trip to the dog park, a quick burger, and a small speech about how amazing Kelly was and how he'll make some less fucked-up guy happy one day. Then it was back to kicking ass at work and snuggling up to Zero while watching movies at night. Nathaniel glanced over at his passenger, a smell reaching his nose at the same time he saw Zero's pitiful expression.

"Roll down the window if you're going to fart," he said, pushing the buttons to bring all four down.

Zero whimpered in response.

"It can't wait until the park?" He sighed and pulled over. Kelly's house was in view, but Nathaniel couldn't allow Zero to take a dump in his yard, even if that would be an excellent mood killer. He grabbed a few baggies and left the car, letting Zero out the passenger side. Then Nathaniel stood and studied the clouds while business was conducted.

"Is that your dog?"

Nathaniel looked over just as a skateboard skidded to a stop. A teenager was watching Zero kick his hind legs in an effort to cover the evidence. "You think I saw some dog taking a crap and pulled over to enjoy the moment?"

"Can I pet him?" the teenager asked, unabashed.

"Knock yourself out." Nathaniel bent over, using one of the baggies to pick up the poop. Then he double-bagged it. When he was upright again, he saw Zero leaping circles around the teenager, who was laughing happily. Clearly a fellow dog-lover.

The teenager noticed him staring. "You here to pick up my brother?"

"That depends on who your brother is."

The teenager gave him a nice-try expression, which made the family resemblance unmistakable. "There aren't a lot of black people living in this neighborhood."

"How should I know?" Nathaniel said with a shrug. "I'm either a dick for making assumptions or I'm a dick for trying not to."

"Yeah, basically." The teenager flashed him a wry smile. "I'm Royal, Kelly's brother."

"How'd you know I'm here for your brother? Do all gay people look alike to you?"

"Yup." Royal squatted so he could pet Zero more. "Kelly said he was going to a dog park, that's how. Seems weird. Why would you bring your dog on a date?"

"He's the chaperone."

"Aren't chaperones there to make sure nothing fun happens?"

"Yeah. And it's not a date. I'm not interested in your brother."

Royal looked up at him. "Your loss."

Nathaniel sighed. "I mean I'm not interested in dating anyone."

"Right. Want me to look after your dog while you go on your date?"

"Is all of your family like this?" Nathaniel asked, feeling exasperated.

"More or less." Royal stood. "You better go. Kelly's waiting. Don't you fucking hurt him. He deserves someone who actually likes him. If you don't, you better pretend to until he realizes he can do better."

Nathaniel had thought going on a date would be the low point of his day. He hadn't counted on being lectured by a teenager. He opened the passenger door and whistled, his faithful companion ignoring him for his new friend.

"Dog park," Nathaniel prompted.

That did the trick. Zero climbed into the car. Royal continued on his way. Nathaniel made sure the dog was buckled in, then drove a few houses down and parked in the driveway. The home resembled those he had grown up in. Not rolling in money, but enough to stuff a mattress or two. The house didn't belong to Kelly but to his parents, whom he certainly didn't want to meet. That would only increase the feeling he was picking up someone way too young for him.

The second Kelly opened the door, Nathaniel jerked his head toward the car, then headed back that way. "You'll have to wrestle Zero for the front seat," he joked.

"I can sit in back," Kelly replied. "I don't want him to think I'm a homewrecker."

Nathaniel nearly stopped in his tracks. "You'd really do that?"

"Sure!"

This made him smile. "Thanks. But you're not sitting in the back. And why am I picking you up again? You don't drive?"

"One leg," Kelly said.

"Last I checked, that's all it takes. You know how?"

"Yeah."

Nathaniel held out the keys. "Perfect solution. You drive, Zero gets to stay where he is, and I'll sit in the back." Safely out of hand-holding range.

Kelly seemed a little uncertain, but nodded and accepted the keys. Zero greeted him by getting all up in his face, then stuck his head out the window in anticipation.

Nathaniel made sure Kelly knew where they were going and spent the rest of the drive white-knuckled and wind-blasted, suddenly finding himself in a race car. That's how Kelly drove, zipping along the road, the small print of Nathaniel's insurance policy flashing before his eyes. Would it cover a totaled car and medical care for all three of them? When by some miracle they arrived at the dog park in one piece, he swore Kelly would never drive his car again and tried not to feel dizzy while putting a collar and leash on Zero. Once that was done, they walked together across the green lawn, which would have been more pleasant if it wasn't a minefield of dog poop.

Kelly seemed unaware of the danger, sighing contentedly. "Peaceful, isn't it?"

"Yup. Very." But not for long. Nathaniel stretched out his arm and intentionally dropped the leash. "Watch this."

Zero sensed his freedom and launched forward toward a group of dogs and their owners. He brought chaos and destruction in his wake, jumping over dogs, snapping at the air, and weaving between legs as he was chased. Dogs were yapping, owners were shouting, and one man fell over in an attempt to free his ankles from a tangle of leashes. His work completed, Zero zipped off toward the pond and another group of dogs.

"I love that beast," Nathaniel said wistfully. "Come. Time to pretend this was all an accident."

Kelly shared his humor, laughing as they went to the first group of owners. Nathaniel whistled shrilly, and Zero raced over to sit at his feet, as if his previous actions had simply been a misunderstanding. *Clearly I'm a good boy. Just look at how well-behaved I am!* This act didn't fool anyone.

"You need to keep that dog on a leash!" an older man complained.

"He is on a leash," Nathaniel said helpfully.

"Then learn to hold on to it!" a woman said, wagging her finger. "I should call animal control!"

"My fault," Kelly interjected. "I was holding the leash, and well—" He raised his crutches, drawing attention to them. The tension dissipated almost immediately. Except for one straggler.

"You should enroll him in behavioral training."

"I agree," Kelly said, shooting a glance at Nathaniel. "He won't be getting any treats tonight, I promise you that."

Nathaniel started laughing as he bent over to grab Zero's leash. Having worn out their welcome, they headed toward one of the ponds. A few dogs followed, freshly indoctrinated members of the cult of Zero.

"So where did you find him?" Kelly asked. "A bullfight?"

"He found me. Or at least he chose me."

"How? Did he put a classified ad in the paper? '*Ill-behaved dog seeks unscrupulous owner.*'"

Nathaniel grinned. "Hey now, that dog is a saint! And my hero." He let his expression grow serious, stooping to free Zero from his leash properly so he could swim. "He saved me from a very dark place."

"What do you mean?"

He watched as Zero charged forward, head turning left and right to make sure he was being followed. The other dogs gleefully gave chase, perhaps feeling liberated by his wild behavior. Or maybe they had fallen in love with him as quickly as Nathaniel had. "Someone once told me that a dog is the best cure for a broken heart."

"And is it?"

Zero splashed into the water, the other dogs hesitating until Zero started barking orders. Then they followed him in. "All of us have an undeniable urge to be loved and to give love in return. In that regard, you can't do much better than a dog."

"I suppose," Kelly said, "although there are some comforts a dog can't provide."

Nathaniel glanced over at him. "Such as?"

"Zero probably gives a lousy foot rub."

Nathaniel chuckled. "Oh, you'd be surprised. When he's passed out in front of the couch, he makes a nice rug."

Kelly didn't look convinced. "I bet he can't cook you breakfast in the morning."

"He once tore into a carton of eggs I was unpacking from the store. That's pretty much scrambled eggs right there."

Kelly sighed dramatically. "I give up. I just wish I'd known you were already spoken for before coming on this date."

There it was, out in the open. The D word. The sooner he shot Kelly down, the better for them both. Still, he didn't want to burn this bridge completely. Kelly understood his sense of humor and was fun to be around. "I could definitely use more friends," he said gently. "Zero isn't the best conversationalist."

Kelly seemed to struggle with this. Then he shrugged. "Friends, pets, significant others… Whatever form it comes in, you can never have enough love."

Nathaniel looked over appreciatively. "Maybe you're right."

Kelly was mature for his age. More so than Nathaniel had been lately, since he was the one agonizing over one little date. Marcello wasn't poking them with a shotgun and pushing them toward the altar. They were just hanging out. Of course Kelly had used the word 'date,' which carried certain baggage, but so had Tim and nothing had come of that.

"So what were you thinking for dinner?" Kelly asked.

"Sonic. Or some other drive-thru so Zero can stay with us."

"How about we get Zero his burger and put him to bed early?" Kelly said in a bedroom voice. "Then you take me out for something less greasy." The smile that followed left little room for interpretation. He grimaced in response, causing Kelly to scowl. He looked so adorable when angry that Nathaniel couldn't help but laugh.

"Yeah, okay."

"You've got a thing for bad behavior, don't you?" Kelly teased. "If so, you're with the right guy. I'll give Zero a run for his money."

"I'll hold you to that," Nathaniel said. "We'll have an award ceremony at the end of the night to see who the winner is, although you've got some catching up to do."

He nodded to the water where Zero was trying to climb over another dog, dunking its head under the surface. The dog's owner fidgeted at the shore, making little whimpering noises.

"Want me to push her in?" Kelly murmured.

Nathaniel grinned broadly. "Nah. It's the thought that counts. This time, anyway."

"Or maybe I should copy Zero and convince some of these owners to follow me into the water."

"Now that I would like to see!"

Kelly nodded, as if willing to grant his wish. "Once they saw my crutches floating on the surface, they'd probably all jump in to save me. You could film it with your phone and we'd go viral. By morning I'd be on every news program in the country. Instant fame!"

"Better keep that idea from Marcello. He'll make you do it." Nathaniel whistled for Zero. "It's cool you have a sense of humor about it all."

"I don't always," Kelly said. "I still have my bad days. I can live without the Olympic dream, but I really loved to run. I miss how that used to feel. Even just watching Zero race across the grass like he does, I envy him because I used to revel in the same sensation."

"Don't you have options?" Nathaniel asked. "I saw a guy on TV missing both legs, and he had these sort of blades he ran on instead. Didn't look like he'd be easy to catch up with."

Kelly was nodding, already familiar with the concept. "Prosthetics aren't for everyone. After the accident, once I had enough time to heal, I tried an artificial leg and didn't like how it felt. They're heavier than you might think, and uncomfortable because of the way they ride up on you, especially for a transfemoral amputation. That means above the knee. The runners you see on television with the blades still have their natural knees, which is difficult to recreate artificially. So for me, it was a choice between lurching around with a fake leg or swinging along on my crutches."

"You seem to have mastered them," Nathaniel said. "I was having trouble keeping up with you the other day."

Kelly grinned. "I've adjusted to my situation. I don't even think about it. Only unusual circumstances remind me, like rude sales clerks. And, um, dating can be kind of terrifying. Most people want a guy with a complete set of limbs. Then there are the people *really* into amputations. I'm not sure how I feel about that."

"Might sound rude," Nathaniel said, "but I don't really care either way."

Kelly's eyes lit up. "That doesn't sound rude to me. In fact, that's the ideal response. Being politically correct doesn't mean fawning over someone because they have a disability or using clunky terms to describe who they are. It means not giving a shit about their differences and not drawing attention to them."

"For a white guy, you sure can empathize with what minorities go through."

"I'm not white," Kelly said, taking the bait.

"What? I didn't even notice! That's how politically correct I am."

"What you are is single," Kelly retorted, "and I'm starting to understand why."

They started walking along the shore, away from any potential victims. Zero had found a stick and was carrying it in his mouth, trotting along and looking proud.

"Bad jokes aside," Nathaniel said. "I don't even like the term 'politically correct.' It seems to imply that someone wants to be correct for political reasons, not because of their actual convictions. Common courtesy already covers not saying stupid things that will offend other people. A new convoluted term for other convoluted terms isn't a good idea. If you can't figure out if you should call someone black or African-American, don't call them either. In most situations there's no need."

Kelly shrugged. "I'm okay with it when people are describing how someone looks. Some people are blond, some people are skinny, and some people are black. What I don't like is when someone says 'I was talking to a black woman at the grocery store, and she mentioned that it's supposed to snow tomorrow.' Really? What does her skin color have to do with the weather? People wouldn't say a blonde woman or a skinny woman in such situations."

"Maybe it's sexist to even mention it was a woman," Nathaniel said.

Kelly thought about it. "It's definitely optional. Our language is probably to blame for making basic gender distinctions. I'm not a woman so I can't say if they find that as offensive. I'm guessing they don't."

"Want to find out?" Nathaniel asked. "For the rest of the day, we'll draw attention to gender as much as possible. 'Excuse me, woman, do you know what time it is?' Or 'Thank you for the menus, woman, but could you tell us about the specials?'"

Kelly shook his head. "You're determined to be offensive, aren't you?"

"Maybe I'm trying to scare you off," Nathaniel said, feeling brave.

Kelly looked him over. "You'll have to try harder than that, but only because you're hot."

Nathaniel smiled. "I'm no model. And don't worry. I'm not usually an asshole."

"Too bad," Kelly said. "I've had my fill of nice guys."

"Really?"

"Yes. The problem with a truly nice person is that they're nice to everyone, not just you. Most of the time that's endearing, but in some situations it hurts like hell."

"Yeah," Nathaniel said, thinking of Caesar. "Some people have a little too much love in their hearts."

"That they do," Kelly said.

"Too much salt, not enough pepper."

"Too much angel, not enough asshole."

After a pause, they both laughed.

"I promise you I'm no angel," Nathaniel said.

Kelly's smile was playful. "Prove it."

As the date continued—and even Nathaniel had to admit that's what it was—he found himself more and more eager to prove himself in any way possible. During dinner, Kelly very generously let Nathaniel ramble on about movies, having plenty opinions of his own, which was refreshing. Zero might be his movie buddy, but he never weighed in on his favorite directors or revealed what he thought about a film's plot. Kelly was intelligent and at times charming, squashing any qualms Nathaniel had about his age. He was damn fine too, and sitting across from him at a table for a few hours had the animal inside Nathaniel roaring to get out. As rusty as his dating skills were, he was certain the feeling was mutual. Kelly was sending all the right signals as they got back in the car, so Nathaniel made his move.

"You wanna come home with me?"

Kelly stared straight ahead. Then he looked over. "Yes."

Nathaniel smiled. "Good." His heart was thudding. He wanted nothing more than to start the car and get them to his place, but he had to be sure. "Listen, I don't want any mixed signals here. I'm good for a fling. That's about it."

Kelly shook his head, as if not understanding. "You think that's all I'm after?"

"I'm not sure, which is why I want to clear the air. I'm not the relationship type. I'd love to wake up next to you, but it wouldn't change anything. I'll make you breakfast—or maybe Zero will finally master scrambled eggs—and then we'll carry on just like before. Does that make sense?"

Kelly searched his eyes. "I want more."

More. A relationship and the wonderful honeymoon period where everything ahead of them was full of possibilities and love. But "more" also meant finding out who they really were, getting hurt, and wondering how they had been stupid enough to begin in the first place. Nathaniel couldn't do that. "Then maybe I should take you home."

Kelly's lips quivered, then settled into a firm line. "I guess you should."

Nathaniel started the car, the interior stuffy. Suffocating, like he couldn't breathe. Even rolling down the windows didn't help. He considered turning on music to drown out the silence, but part of him still hoped Kelly would reconsider or maybe find some magical words to change his mind, but neither of them spoke. Not until they were parked in front of Kelly's house.

"Thanks for the evening," Kelly said, the passenger door already open. "It was a beautiful fantasy."

Nathaniel stayed long enough to watch Kelly make his way to the house, his shoulders tense as he unlocked the door. The light inside was warm, and hopefully comforting in some way, because Nathaniel had gotten his wish. He had proven he was no angel. Just not in the way he'd hoped.

Anyone who felt sorry for Kelly was a fool. He had survived a crippling accident and an unhealthy relationship. No wonder then, that despite what had transpired between them, he kept his head held high at work. When Nathaniel approached him in the break room one day, Kelly demanded to know—in front of everyone—why Nathaniel was okay with sleeping with him but nothing more.

In the privacy of his office, Nathaniel tried to explain why. He was a broken man. He was weak. He couldn't handle getting hurt again. That's why he hadn't let anyone get close to him in years, not even as a friend. Nathaniel didn't have any, but now he was willing to take that one small risk. They could be friends. Not surprisingly, Kelly wasn't interested. Or at least he said he needed time to think about it, which sounded like a polite way of saying goodbye.

The obvious solution was to shove these feelings aside and focus on work, but Nathaniel found this impossible to do. The fashion world was falling in love with Kelly, which meant photos of him were constantly crossing Nathaniel's desk, his name popping up in email after email. When not at work, Nathaniel was horny as hell, but jacking off provided little relief. A marathon of Christopher Nolan's blissfully delirious early films helped, but once the credits rolled and the TV was off, Nathaniel struggled to find sleep.

Such as tonight. The steady patter of rain on the roof had slowed and stopped, the drops on the bedroom window reflecting distant lights. Nathaniel stared at these and wondered when his feverish need would finally break. That's when he heard the knocks, few but insistent. Nathaniel glanced at the clock. Then he swung out of bed, grabbed his robe, and went to the door. He looked through the peephole, recognizing a face that haunted his fantasies despite it being distorted by the fisheye lens. When he opened the door, he saw raindrops still resting like little diamonds in the dark hair.

"Kelly?" Nathaniel liked how that name felt on his lips. Zero chose that moment to run for the door, Nathaniel stopping him with a well-timed leg and ordering him to stay back. Once he complied, Nathaniel returned his attention to his unexpected guest. "Any idea how late it is?"

"Two in the morning," Kelly replied, radiating confidence. "I finished thinking. What we talked about, I reached a decision."

"Oh yeah?"

"Yeah." Kelly came closer. Just a few inches, but already Nathaniel felt his body reacting. "Just friends. Nothing more."

If that were true, he wouldn't have shown up at this hour. "Strictly platonic?"

"Strictly?" Kelly leaned forward. "I don't think so. How about no strings attached?"

Close enough. Nathaniel reached out, felt Kelly's short hair in the palms of his hands, brought his mouth to those thick lips so he could taste them. Their first kiss. If the night was generous, it wouldn't be the last.

"You're not going to make me drive home, are you?" Kelly said. "Any idea how late it is?"

"Two in the morning. I should be in bed."

Kelly's eyes smoldered. "I was hoping you'd say that."

Nathaniel stepped aside, clearing the way for Kelly to enter, but he only seemed interested in moving in for another kiss. Nathaniel was happy to reciprocate but couldn't concentrate, since Zero might try bolting out the door again. "The dog," he murmured.

"Oh, right." Kelly entered the apartment, stopping halfway down the hallway. Nathaniel shut the door and locked it, then moved past Kelly to the bedroom where an animal was blocking the way. "You're sleeping on the couch tonight," he said.

"You'd better be talking to Zero and not me," Kelly replied.

Nathaniel looked over at him. "That depends on how you do."

"Challenge accepted."

"Come on, mutt." Nathaniel bent over and pulled on Zero, who was already resisting. He never slept on the couch. Tonight would be different, unless he wanted to learn about the birds and the bees via a demonstration. Once he got the dog moving and Kelly entered the bedroom, Nathaniel followed. He shut the door and approached Kelly from behind, smelling the skin of his neck before kissing it.

Kelly turned in response, their lips meeting again, but kissing wasn't enough. Nathaniel brought their bodies together, the fluffy material of the robe not concealing his erection. He felt it throb against Kelly's warmth, wanted to press it even harder against him, and so he picked Kelly up. The crutches dropped to the ground, Kelly trusting Nathaniel's strength as he leaned back. He was tempted to topple back completely, falling to the floor just to feel Kelly's full weight on him. Of course that would hurt, so instead he took a few steps forward, dropping Kelly onto the mattress.

After scooting backward on the bed, Kelly propped himself up on his elbows, looking Nathaniel over with a lustful gaze, his eyes settling on the tenting fabric of his robe. He wanted a show? Seemed only fair considering how much of Kelly's body Nathaniel had already seen. He grinned, slowly loosening the belt and letting the robe fall open. Then he shrugged it off until it dropped to the floor.

With an expression of awe, Kelly gawked. Not just at his cock, but his entire body, even back up to his face a few times.

Nathaniel couldn't remember the last time he felt so appreciated. "You're making me feel like a piece of meat," he said, crawling onto the mattress and placing a hand to each side of Kelly's head. "And I mean that in a good way."

Kelly dodged an attempted kiss so he could reply. "Just as long as you don't expect me to compete with that thing."

"It's not a contest," Nathaniel said, "but I wouldn't mind judging."

Their lips met again, then their chests as Nathaniel lowered himself, feeling fabric against his bare skin, the idea of being naked around someone who was fully dressed oddly erotic. His pecs rubbed against a cotton shirt, his dick against denim. He kept kissing Kelly, but he wanted to feel their skin touch. Nathaniel switched to a sitting position and started working on the buttons of Kelly's shirt, then decided he didn't have the patience and tore it open instead, revealing a body smooth and dark.

"I'll buy you a new one," Nathaniel murmured, tugging off the remnants of the shirt. Then he let his fingers play along silky skin, tracing the curves of toned muscles. He'd stared at them so many times in photos, had even locked his office door while entertaining wild desires. Now those fantasies were coming true. Nathaniel leaned forward, licking Kelly's bottom lip and nibbling it gently. Then he slid off the mattress and onto his knees, reaching for the waistline of Kelly's jeans, wanting to rip them open so the bulge there could flex and grow. He had just worked the belt loose when Kelly grabbed his hand to stop him.

"Wait," he said.

Nathaniel noticed the insecure expression. "I told you it's not a competition."

"It's not that..."

Not insecure. Vulnerable, the way he had acted before and after the swimming pool shoot. He was worried what Nathaniel would think about his amputated leg. He moved his hands away from the jeans and leaned back. "If I had any doubts about what I wanted, we wouldn't have made it this far. Your move."

Kelly stared at him intensely, then unbuttoned and unzipped his jeans. Nathaniel was more than willing to do the rest, tugging them off. Kelly stopped watching, his head plopping down on the mattress so he wouldn't witness Nathaniel's reaction. This was the moment of truth. Claiming he was comfortable with the situation wasn't the same as dealing with it directly. The jeans slid off. Just above where a knee should be, the leg came to a rounded point and ended. No big deal. Nathaniel considered it briefly before returning his attention to removing the skimpy underwear. He hooked his index fingers around the red cotton near the hip and tugged them down and off. Then he climbed back onto the bed, running a hand up one of Kelly's thighs, letting his nose brush against the ebony skin of his balls, and tracing his tongue up the long pole before taking the brownish-pink head into his mouth.

Nathaniel wasn't content with this alone. As he continued to suck, he reached up and across those abs, felt Kelly's chest, returned south to caress his hips and stroke his legs. Anywhere he could reach, Nathaniel wanted to touch, and so he did, Kelly moaning his approval. Nathaniel's own body began to ache with need, so he stopped what he was doing and looked up.

Kelly raised his head to see why he'd stopped. "What?"

"I've been dreaming about those lips every night. Or at least right before bed."

Kelly's eyes became half-lidded. "What did you dream I'd do with these lips?"

"Stay right there and I'll show you."

Nathaniel climbed up, placing a knee to either side of Kelly's head and using one hand to point his dick downward. He rubbed the head of his cock across the closed lips, which opened in invitation. Nathaniel slid inside, the sensation overwhelming. Digital porn and a palm greased with lotion couldn't compete with this. Kelly's head was bobbing, but soon Nathaniel's hips were thrusting, deeper and deeper, but Kelly seemed able to take it, his nose bumping into Nathaniel's pelvis a few times. He found himself getting close, but he didn't want to finish yet. Not in this position.

Nathaniel rolled over onto his back. "Come sit on me."

"Condoms and lube," Kelly said. Then he added, "And a few more nights like this, because I'm not ready yet."

"That's fine," Nathaniel assured him. "That's not what I meant anyway. Come here."

Kelly climbed up and over, that gorgeous bubble butt of his settling down on Nathaniel's cock. He might not be ready emotionally, but when Nathaniel flexed it a few times, he could tell Kelly's body was willing.

"I love your face," Nathaniel said, grabbing Kelly's hips and grinding against him. "So many expressions." Then he shifted Kelly downward enough that Nathaniel could sit up. They were facing each other, Kelly in his lap, arms and leg wrapped around Nathaniel as they kissed. Their hands reached for the same area, bumping together before adjusting and pressing their cocks together. Nathaniel's was still wet from Kelly slobbering on it, but that wasn't enough for their hands to slide freely. He looked down, took aim, and spit, Kelly doing the same. Then they laughed at the absurdity of this. Their levity didn't last long. Nathaniel locked eyes with Kelly as they resumed pumping. He paced himself, not wanting it to end, watching every sensation play out on Kelly's face. More so than ever, especially in the throes of bliss, Kelly was beautiful. If only the camera could capture him now! Nathaniel wouldn't let that happen. This was for him alone. The handsome face became strained as he struggled to hold back the inevitable. Nathaniel thrust against him a few times, bringing their mouths together but not allowing them to touch. "Come with me," he whispered.

Kelly chewed his bottom lip and nodded, his expression shifting to need. Nathaniel pumped faster, still waiting for the right moment, but that face was so damn beautiful that he couldn't hold back. Hot white liquid splashed against the dark skin of Kelly's chin. Mere seconds later, Nathaniel felt more of the same covering his stomach, Kelly nearly howling in ecstasy. Nathaniel leaned forward to kiss him, mostly to shut him up before the neighbors could complain. They shared the same air, gasping against each other. When their breath slowed to mere panting, Nathaniel grabbed Kelly and fell backward, holding him tight. He didn't want to let go. Not ever. Eventually he sensed Kelly wasn't exactly comfortable and loosened his grip.

Kelly rolled off. Nathaniel's mind summoned up ghostly echoes of words he used to speak after such moments. Promises of love or jokes about what they had done or demands for more. Instead the room was filled with a heavy silence—his fault because he'd forbidden anything more than the act they had just shared. Maybe he had been wrong.

"Kelly—" he said, but his new lover was already sitting up,

groping over the edge of the mattress for his clothes. "What are you doing?"

"Just friends," Kelly said, sounding upbeat. "I'm totally cool with that. Don't worry. Besides, I sort of stole my mom's car and should probably get it back."

Nathaniel weighed this information. Part of him wanted more. Just a little affection, that's all. This could be the best of both worlds. A friend, and when needed, slightly more. "You're really okay with this?"

"Yeah!" Kelly said.

"In that case," Nathaniel reached out and grabbed him, dragging him back into bed, "friends have sleepovers too, you know."

"I suppose they do." Kelly's back was still to him, so Nathaniel couldn't see his expression, but he didn't sound despairing. "And I suppose when my mom finds both me and the car missing, she won't call the cops right away."

"Exactly."

"How about a towel? You're a human geyser!"

Nathaniel grinned. He did tend to make a mess. "Sorry. Be right back."

He wasn't sure how clean the towel in the bathroom was, and even though it would get much dirtier, he still wanted to present Kelly with something decent. He went to the hallway instead, Zero slinking along behind him on his way back into the room. Nathaniel pretended not to notice.

"The dog isn't sleeping with us, is he?" Kelly said with a hint of a smile.

"It's actually his bed." Nathaniel tossed him the towel. "Zero got a part-time job to pay for it and everything. If we're lucky, he'll let us share it with him. It's either that or the couch."

"I suppose we'll have to make do." Kelly finished wiping off and threw the towel back, Nathaniel finding one end still dry enough to use. Then he tossed it aside and flopped into bed, patting an empty space next to him out of habit that Zero soon filled.

"You sleep naked with the dog?"

"Don't worry, he's naked too. No collar, see? He'll let you wear it if it makes you feel more comfortable."

"That's all right." Kelly found something wet just above

his collarbone and looked at Nathaniel incredulously. When Nathaniel grinned shamelessly in response, he wiped it on the sheets defiantly. He considered the dog between them once more and sounded resigned as he got beneath the covers. "When in Rome..."

Nathaniel settled down, expecting a sense of warm satisfaction to lure him into sleep. That didn't happen. He found himself still wanting. His body had been satisfied, but his heart... Nathaniel reached over, stroking Zero's fur a few times before he let his hand settle there. Love. Just not the kind he was longing for. He listened to Kelly shift, surprised when fingers bumped into his. He didn't know if it was pure chance, if Kelly was petting Zero without knowing his hand was there or if Kelly had reached for him specifically. Either way, the need in Nathaniel rose up. Only when he allowed their fingers to weave together did it settle down again.

Chapter Seventeen

Marcello didn't play chess, not because he wasn't skilled enough to master the game. Nathaniel's theory was that the game was too simple for him. Or perhaps too convoluted, because while Marcello manipulated events with casual ease, he rarely utilized deception and deceit. Instead he simply gave other people whatever they desired. But first he made sure to convince them of what exactly that desire was. By no coincidence, this always coincided with his own needs.

Kelly was the perfect example. He had accepted the modeling contract on a purely temporary basis, since he was already enrolled in college and about to begin his first year. However, his summer job had attracted international attention, so delaying his education could be very profitable. Nathaniel knew Kelly wasn't enthusiastic about studying, mainly because he didn't know what career he wanted to pursue. Despite being professional and hardworking, Kelly wasn't passionate about modeling. Getting him to commit to either path could have been tricky.

Not for Marcello. He idly dialed numbers on his phone, creating an assignment for Kelly at one of the most beautiful places on the planet. Clients normally came to him, but Marcello was comfortable making propositions when needed, such as the one he made to Kelly.

College could wait. The world was calling! Fame and fortune were too, but they wouldn't stay on the line for long.

Check and mate. Kelly resisted the offer at first, but something had changed his mind. When they arrived at their hotel in Cancún, Nathaniel discovered what that 'something' was. One room. Nathaniel *knew* he had booked two, because he had made the reservation himself. He still had the email confirmation. When he tried to correct the situation, the desk clerk pointed out that the exclusive emperor's suite had already been prepared, an expense that would need to be paid for even if they didn't stay in the room.

They took the suite. Kelly seemed delighted. Nathaniel glowered at everyone in sight. He soon relaxed when discovering the suite had two separate bedrooms. Marcello probably envisioned them driven by temptation to visit each other in the night. His prediction would no doubt come true, which was frustrating because Nathaniel had stayed tight-lipped about the increasingly frequent sleepovers. They had an understanding: no talk of relationships, no sappy terms of endearment. He and Kelly conducted themselves professionally when at work, not even flirting behind closed doors. And yet Marcello seemed to know the truth anyway. This assignment—a business-class flight to Mexico, a stay in a luxurious suite, and a few days off after the shoot—was no coincidence. A honeymoon without the wedding.

Work came first. While on the way to their appointment, Nathaniel did his best to disregard Cancún's azure waters and ivory beaches. The tanned bodies in swimsuits were a little harder to ignore, as were the scents drifting from the restaurants they cruised by. Nathaniel usually felt an aversion to such places, preferring to travel further down the road to wherever the locals called home. For a tourist trap though, Cancún sure did sparkle.

Their destination was equally as ostentatious, leaving him puzzled. Nathaniel had expected a studio with minimal windows to control the light. Instead they parked in front of a resort. He leaned forward to argue with the taxi driver, explaining that they weren't tourists, but to no avail. The address was correct.

"Location shoot?" Kelly asked once they were out of the car.

"Maybe," Nathaniel said. "The emails I got were hard to understand. Very broken English in all capital letters." Bellboys rushed out to assist with their luggage, but all Nathaniel had with him was a laptop in its case. They still tried to take that from him until a glare sent them slinking away.

"Where do we go from here?" Kelly asked.

"Front desk, I guess." Nathaniel strolled inside, the interior full of fountains, sculptures, polished brass, and squeaky-clean floors. This made him long for a couch covered in dog hair. Which reminded him... "You sure your brother knows what he's doing?"

"I'm not answering that again," Kelly said patiently.

"Taking care of a dog isn't easy. What if he doesn't cook for him? I don't want Zero eating fast food. That's not healthy."

"We'll send him to fat camp as soon as we're back," Kelly said, nodding and smiling at the front desk receptionist as she rattled off a greeting. She asked for their names, as if they were checking in.

"We're here for the photo shoot," Nathaniel said. When she looked at him blankly, he exhaled, because he felt stupid just saying the name. "We're here to see the Lieutenant."

"Ah! Yes, of course. Just a moment please."

She picked up her phone, and when it clicked, loud party noises could be heard on the other end. She spoke in rapid-fire Spanish, listened for a response, and hung up.

"Just a moment please," she repeated, smiling at them nonstop until another person arrived in the lobby.

The man looked starved and exhausted, which meant he probably shared Nathaniel's occupation. No greeting was offered. He simply gestured for them to follow. Down a few hallways they reached the hotel ballroom. The space had been transformed by an explosion of clothing, which littered the floor, hung from racks, and stuck out of boxes and trunks. Scattered amongst these were little tables cluttered with makeup and mirrors. People were squeezed into any remaining room.

"Kelly Phillips?" their guide asked, leading them toward one corner.

"Yeah," Nathaniel answered for him, struggling to keep up. "I'm sketchy on the details. Do you have studio space set up somewhere, or is this an outdoor shoot?"

"Outdoor," the man said, pointing to open doors on the far side of the room. The light of a swimming pool shimmered beyond.

"Swimwear?" he asked. "The photos we were sent didn't look like—"

"Here is your technician," the man said, gesturing to a thin-faced woman with dark hair and eyes. "She can answer questions."

Nathaniel attempted to block the man as he left, but he slipped away into the crowd.

"This looks like a fashion show," Kelly said, as the technician pulled at his clothes with no regard for his privacy. All around the room, people were in various states of undress.

Nathaniel watched as the technician matched Kelly's skin tone before she started powdering his bare chest. "Hey," he said, trying to get her attention. "I need a schedule. When does the first shoot take place and what does it involve?"

She shook her head like he wasn't making sense, then continued her work.

"It looks like a fashion show," Kelly repeated.

"That's not what you're here for." Nathaniel spun around, searching for someone—anyone—in charge. Eventually he spotted a short Mexican man with a gravity-defying coif of white hair. He wore huge shades that concealed his eyes and a lavender version of a military uniform. That had to be him. The Lieutenant. A fashion designer and a would-be dictator judging from the way he was making the rounds and barking orders. He was coming toward them anyway, so Nathaniel waited until he approached.

"I think there's been some sort of mistake," he said.

"Ah, the Americans." The Lieutenant offered a smile that lasted a fraction of a second. Then he pushed past Nathaniel to face Kelly. "Have you seen them? I've made such wonderful things for you!"

"The outfits are beautiful," Kelly said, remaining motionless so the technician could apply makeup, but his eyes were on the rack of clothing to his right.

"This looks like a fashion show," Nathaniel said, borrowing Kelly's words as he elbowed his way between them.

"That's because it *is* a fashion show," the Lieutenant said, looking up at him.

"I thought we were here for a photo shoot."

The Lieutenant slowly took off his sunglasses and stared at Nathaniel. "There will be cameras. Lots of cameras. Taking pictures."

"While he's on the catwalk?"

"Yes! What, you thought he would be in a photo booth? Does he need passport photos made or something?"

Nathaniel was ready to growl a response, but Kelly intervened. "I've never been on a catwalk," he explained. "It might be a little tricky with my crutches."

The Lieutenant perked up. "Oh, no problem there! I have these for you!" He hustled over to the rack and pulled from the folds of clothing a pair of forearm crutches similar to Kelly's, but these glittered and sparkled, the highly polished metal covered in clear multifaceted stones. The Lieutenant pushed away the makeup technician so he could hand them to Kelly. "Here you go. Give them a try."

Kelly accepted them, but a shadow had come over his features and he was clenching his jaw.

Now it was Nathaniel's turn to intervene. "He's supposed to

be here for a professional photo shoot, not a circus performance using those ridiculous things."

The Lieutenant's face grew red. "I designed these myself!"

"Obviously," Kelly muttered.

"Listen," Nathaniel said. "There's been a misunderstanding, but if you'd like Kelly to model your *clothing* designs, we can grab a photographer and some lighting technicians and get set up somewhere. I'm sure a resort of this size has—"

"He's a model." the Lieutenant said. "Models go on the catwalk."

"He doesn't have any runway experience, and frankly, I feel like you're being exploitative. If you want him for his appearance, that's fine. If you want to pull some publicity stunt by—"

"Of course I'm being exploitative!" the Lieutenant shouted. "This entire industry is built on exploitation! You want diamonds because they sparkle? First you've got to wipe off the blood."

"He's not an object!"

"You don't think we have beautiful black boys in Mexico? Why do you think he's here?"

"To be respected as a model," Nathaniel shouted back, "not some marketing gimmick!"

"He can go home if you don't like—"

"That's exactly what we'll—"

"It's fine!" Kelly snapped. Both men turned to him. "I can handle this. Really."

"I'm glad one of you is professional!" the Lieutenant sulked before stalking off.

Nathaniel glared after him, then turned back to Kelly. "Are you sure about this?"

"Yes." Kelly gave a single nod, then the makeup technician descended on him again. "I'd feel worse if I ran away. I want to own this, make it mine."

"Okay." Nathaniel exhaled. "Whatever you want. I'm behind you all the way."

"Thanks. Do you think I'll have time to practice first?"

"Probably not. All you've got to do is have a shitload of attitude. Think you can manage?"

Kelly smirked. "That's a rhetorical question, right?"

"Definitely."

"Just don't fall in the pool," the makeup technician interjected.

"What?" Nathaniel asked.

"The pool. That's where the catwalk goes."

He wasn't sure what she meant, but he soon found out. Nathaniel walked to the end of the room and peered out the doors. The catwalk was narrow and transparent, which was bad enough, but it extended directly over a large swimming pool. One misstep would lead to disaster, a challenge for any model. Kelly had his work cut out for him.

The lights around the pool were low, the only luminance provided by narrow-beamed spotlights above and submersed lamps directly beneath the clear runway. This all changed when the first model stepped out from the doorway, camera flashes blazing. Blinding. Nathaniel barely paid attention to the model, noticing the water that had slopped onto the runway despite it being toweled off before the show. He sat front and center after bribing a member of the press to give up her seat. Nathaniel would be close, ready to dive in if Kelly fell into the water.

He watched impatiently as model after model crossed one leg over the other up the runway, hands on hips when they reached the end and turned around. Did they realize how lucky they were to move with perfect ease? To not need to compensate for a missing body part?

Kelly appeared. He did a damn fine job of slinking seductively down the runway, wearing an expression normally reserved for the bedroom. The gaudy crutches flashed and flared, reflecting the lights of the press back at them. The effect was surprisingly cool. The outfit was striking too, tailored for Kelly's amputated limb, thin chains hanging down where the rest of his leg should be. Nathaniel braced himself, ready to beat any laughter into silence. Instead he heard gasps of awe. As Kelly reached the end, his crutches forming an X as he paused, the cameras couldn't snap photos quickly enough. Nathaniel was even jostled as people tried to get a better angle.

He relaxed slightly, but each model had to make multiple rounds, which meant more chances for an accident. He watched as a stiletto heel slid off the edge of the transparent runway, the shoe grazing the water before the model caught her balance. The runway had been hard enough to see during the day, but now it must be nearly impossible, especially with so many lights flashing.

Kelly appeared again, this time wearing strange pants. One

leg was white, the other black, and as the cloth neared his knees, the two shades spiraled down to his foot, creating the illusion that humans were one-legged creatures. Kelly was nearing the end of the runway when one of the crutches slipped on the wet surface, causing Kelly to stumble but not to fall. No one missed this, the audience tensing, but Kelly's "I'm sexy as fuck" expression didn't waver in the slightest. He swiftly recovered and kept moving.

Nathaniel should have felt proud, and to some extent he did, but seeing his fear partially realized only made the subsequent rounds more grueling. Kelly seemed to be in his element regardless, his performance as exceptional as it was varied. He acted goofy and friendly during one appearance, which suited the outfit covered in flowers—an upside-down rose where his leg should be. Or fiercely angry when he appeared in an outfit made entirely of tight black netting.

The press was eating it up. Perhaps that's why Kelly closed the show, the final model on the runway. This outfit matched the crutches—silver and glittering—but the material only covered certain areas of his body, smooth dark skin providing a natural contrast. As Kelly reached the end of the stage and stopped, his expression became defiant. He didn't turn around. Instead he spread his arms wide until they were perfectly horizontal, muscles trembling with effort as he balanced on one leg. He held that position until the audience grew quiet in anticipation. Then Kelly released the crutches, letting them drop into the pool.

Nathaniel was on his feet in an instant, ready to leap across the water to catch him. Everyone rose with him, cameras clicking. Kelly turned with one graceful hop. Then he kept on hopping. Nathaniel froze, sending out silent prayers to any gods willing to listen. Kelly reached the far end of the runway and disappeared through the doorway.

Nathaniel pushed through the crowd, in spite of the large round of applause that came when the Lieutenant appeared on stage. The models reappeared next, but not Kelly. Had he fallen? In his anger, had he refused any offer of help and been forced to crawl back to his usual crutches? Or was he being lectured for disrespecting the Lieutenant's work? Nathaniel almost decked a security guard when he was stopped outside the ballroom and suffered an agonizing wait while the man confirmed via radio that he was allowed inside. Finally in the room, Nathaniel dodged around people to find Kelly.

He spotted a crowd circling one person. The Lieutenant, no longer on the runway basking in the audience's approval, was in the center. He had his arm around Kelly, squeezing him affectionately, grabbing a champagne glass and shoving it into his hand. Applause, smiles of admiration, cell phones held up to take photos. Nathaniel stopped and watched from a distance. Kelly was so happy that tears filled his eyes. Oddly enough, they matched Nathaniel's own.

Kelly was drunk in the most wonderful way possible. He kept laughing and speaking in funny voices, asking the same questions over and over after forgetting the answers. He stumbled out onto the wooden patio of their hotel suite that overlooked the ocean but offered a hot tub in case they were feeling lazy. Kelly obviously did, because he started ripping off his clothes, at one point spinning around dangerously while battling with his shirt.

"Easy now," Nathaniel said, grabbing him by the shoulders. He'd decided to remain sober, mostly because of situations such as these. "You've had enough brushes with water tonight, don't you think?"

"Nope. Hot tub. Right now."

When Kelly struggled with his shirt again, Nathaniel helped him take it off. Then Kelly started messing with his shorts.

"All of it?" Nathaniel asked.

Kelly's nod was exaggerated. "Naked. You too."

He was feeling silly rather than horny because he wasn't hard when Nathaniel helped him out of his underwear. That's more than he could say for himself as he stripped down, but Kelly was too distracted to notice as they both slipped into the tub. Kelly sighed, as if feeling relief, which raised a question Nathaniel finally felt brave enough to ask. Funny how alcohol could summon courage for the person drinking, and also for those who remained sober. He could ask anything he wanted and there was a fair chance Kelly wouldn't remember later.

"Does it hurt?"

Kelly looked at him, struggling to focus, but the question seemed to sober him up. Somewhat. "Stumpy? Noooo. It doesn't hurt. I'm lucky. No phantom tingles. No pain. Not physically anyway."

"Emotionally?" Nathaniel asked, searching his eyes.

Kelly took a deep breath. "You know about the accident, but

what about the details? They weren't in the newspaper. They don't print stuff like that!"

"Then tell me."

Kelly looked around, as if searching for another drink. When he couldn't find one he sighed. "William and I weren't a good match because he was too good and that wasn't good." Kelly didn't laugh. He shook his head. Then he looked at Nathaniel with pure adoration. "You can take it. I don't have to be some impossible ideal with you. I can be fucked up and bitchy and a mess, and you're like this stone wall that I can't break. I wasn't good for William. The only good I am is damaged goods." Kelly chuckled madly. "Damaged goods... That's so true."

Nathaniel made a concerned face. "Maybe we should call it a night."

Kelly seemed not to have heard him, his emotional pendulum swinging from manic joy to sudden sorrow. "He was breaking up with me. William. I loved him. More than anyone, and I'm sure he loved me too. I still managed to push him away. I ruined it all. It was raining and we were arguing and he said it was over. I wanted to hurt him and I guess I did because he turned the wheel and—" Kelly's voice squeaked. "You can't kill love. Not that way. It didn't change how I feel. It should have, but it didn't."

Nathaniel couldn't reassure him otherwise. He knew Kelly was right. People hurt you—the ones most capable of doing so—because you love them and they love you. They hurt you deeper and more permanently than anyone else can, and it doesn't change a damn thing. You keep on loving them, even if you leave.

"It doesn't hurt so much anymore," Kelly mumbled. Then he pantomimed peeling something and pressing it to his chest. "Band-Aid. You're my Band-Aid."

Nathaniel considered him a moment. Then he laughed. Kelly flipped him off, then started laughing too. They boiled in the hot tub a little longer until Kelly started nodding off. Nathaniel made him stand. Dizzy from the heat, he still managed to carry Kelly to bed, thinking about what he had said. Damaged goods. They both were, even if Nathaniel's wounds weren't as visible. Perhaps that's what made him want to take care of Kelly, to look out for him, so he wouldn't get hurt again. Nathaniel wondered if the feeling was mutual. Maybe Kelly had the same urge. Maybe that would be enough for them to not hurt each other.

If only.

After convincing Kelly to take two aspirin, chug a glass of water, and lie down, Nathaniel stood to leave but found a hand still gripping his own, tethering him to the bed.

"Time to sleep," Kelly murmured, face half-buried in a pillow.

"Let go," Nathaniel said, shaking him off. But he didn't walk away. He watched Kelly, certain he was finally sleeping just before he opened his eyes and smiled.

"Why are you naked?"

"The hot tub," Nathaniel said. "Remember?"

"Time to sleep," Kelly answered, closing his eyes again.

Nathaniel shook his head, then turned off the bedside lamp and slid between the sheets. Kelly made room for him, reaching out to thwack him with his hand.

"I didn't mean what I said," Kelly slurred.

"Go to sleep," Nathaniel whispered, not having a clue what he was talking about.

"I don't love William more than anyone else. Only back then."

"That's fine," Nathaniel said reassuringly. "Now sleep."

"I love you more than him."

Nathaniel's breath caught in his throat. He tried to respond, but too many feelings were rushing to the surface. One realization managed to rise above the chaos in the form of four simple words. He rolled them over in his mind, examining them to make sure they were true. By the time he was certain, Kelly was quietly snoring beside him. Nathaniel spoke his name aloud, just to make sure he was truly asleep. When no response came, he set the words free to fall on deaf ears.

"I love you too."

Being politically correct might mean not giving a shit, but being in love meant caring way too much. Nathaniel was on constant alert, making sure photographers were treating Kelly right, that he wasn't being worked too long without adequate breaks, that he was eating and drinking and sleeping and getting everything he needed from him. Physically, at least. Kelly didn't seem to remember his drunken confession, returning to the same unspoken agreement the next day. At work they would be professional. At night they would be together. And while travelling…

Nathaniel found letting go easier during their trips. Kelly celebrated each success with little additions to their repertoire: holding hands during a bus ride through Dublin, stopping to kiss while crossing one of Venice's canal bridges, hugging to stay warm while waiting for a taxi one chilly night in Milan. As long as they weren't in Austin, they allowed themselves almost anything. Except for words, which would only divide what they had together, dissecting it into different categories and restrictions. In Nathaniel's mind, he labeled what they shared as affection. Musicians sang about love tearing people apart, not affection ruining lives.

He began to yearn for each trip, worrying less with each as Kelly proved himself over and over to be fully capable of handling himself. One photographer had mistakenly referred to Nathaniel as Kelly's manager, to which he only snorted and shook his head. Nobody could manage Kelly, not even Marcello. Getting him headed in the right direction was possible, but what he would do once he got there was anyone's guess. Kelly had taken down models who thought they could bully him and won over egotistical monsters like the Lieutenant, who even half a year later kept begging Kelly to relocate to Mexico. Most recently on his birthday.

"Have you seen the size of this box?" Kelly said, dragging it into Nathaniel's office, one end of it pinned beneath his arm.

"Yes," he said, pushing aside the ridiculously huge bouquet of flowers that the Lieutenant had also sent.

Kelly managed to get the long box onto Nathaniel's desk, grinning at him as he sat. "So what did you get me?"

Nathaniel opened a drawer, then slid a flat rectangle across the desk surface.

"It's not very big," Kelly pointed out. "Not by comparison. Oh wow, those flowers! Are they from you."

"You know they aren't. You saw the card already." Nathaniel glared at the bouquet, trying to get them to wilt. Kelly laughed and opened the Lieutenant's present first. The contents were familiar. Jewel-encrusted crutches.

"Think these are real diamonds?" Kelly asked.

"They better not be!" Nathaniel grumped.

Kelly laughed again and read the enclosed letter, doing his best imitation of the Lieutenant's accent. "It pains me to give these, since they are part of myself, but you already have my heart. These will now join it. You have inspired me, my muse, and will continue to do so even from a distance. But really, Marcello can't afford to pay you what—" Kelly stopped narrating and scanned the rest. "Same as usual," he summarized.

"Don't show that to Marcello."

"But I love it when his face gets all red. Like a big cherry!"

Nathaniel sighed. "Might as well open mine. It can't compete with promises of untold wealth."

"And fame," Kelly said helpfully. He grabbed the present and unwrapped it. The frame was vintage, as was the content, a black-and-white photo of a man on crutches, one leg missing. The image was taken from behind; the man's artificial leg sticking out of his backpack. He seemed to be waiting for someone, his head turned slightly to look down the railroad crossing where he stood.

"Ernst Haas," Nathaniel said. "He did a series on returning prisoners of war. I just thought… The image is compelling. That's how it is whenever you're in front of the camera, but from what you've shown me of your own photos—the ones you used to take—the reverse is also true. You've got talent. I thought about getting you a camera or something, but I know you already have one, and this seemed a better symbol. Just don't give up. That's all."

"I love it," Kelly said, admiring the image again and chuckling a little. "Seems to be a theme this birthday. Crutches."

"I also got you a new cell phone, just in case this was a total bust." Nathaniel dumped the gift onto the desk without ceremony.

"Yay!" Kelly cried, setting down the frame and grabbing the box.

"Considering it has a built-in camera," Nathaniel said, "maybe the real theme is photography."

"Works for me!" Kelly said, grinning happily. "Now let's go see what Marcello got me."

Another assignment, as it turned out, this time in Vancouver. Canada was experiencing blizzards, but the shoot was indoors so the snow didn't matter. Not until they were hurrying from the hotel to catch their flight home when Kelly slipped on the ice and fell. No serious damage. Just a bruised knee and elbow.

It could have happened to anyone, but Nathaniel brooded over it all the way home. He'd been doing research, not because he wanted to change who Kelly was or try to fix him. That wasn't it at all. He wanted him to have the best quality of life, but it seemed disrespectful to even bring it up. Kelly had done his own research, had experience with a prosthetic, and had made his decision long ago.

Regardless, when a woman at the Austin airport assumed Kelly was a war veteran, Nathaniel couldn't hold back. He glared after the woman as she walked away, but Kelly took the encounter in stride.

"That was beyond awkward," he said. "I'm going to start wearing long flowing dresses to hide my secret shame."

"You've got nothing to be ashamed about," Nathaniel grumbled.

"It was a joke."

Nathaniel turned to him. "Aren't you sick of this?"

"Yes," Kelly replied. "Of course. What can I do about it? Become a scientist and develop a cure for stupidity?"

"You've got options."

Kelly raised an eyebrow. "Hate to break it to you, but I'm not doing this for kicks. The leg is gone for good."

"What about prosthetics?"

"You know I already tried that. We've talked about this. It was uncomfortable and—"

"—you gave up after a week. Or did you even make it that long?"

Kelly's lips tightened. "Tell you what, genius, why don't I saw your leg off above the knee and we'll see just how cozy a fiberglass shell crammed halfway up your ass feels. Then you can lecture me all day long about—"

"Shut up."

"—about how easy it is to pop on a peg leg and prance around the room. And if you think I'm changing who I am because the occasional idiot mistakes me for a veteran, and because *you* think I'm incomplete, you can shove it up your—"

"Kelly!" Nathaniel pleaded. "Shut. Up. Now! When have I ever said you were incomplete, or treated you as if you were helpless or anything but perfect?"

Kelly's nostrils flared, but he calmed down.

"News flash," Nathaniel continued, "I want the best for you.

If you were smoking, I'd be pressuring you to quit. If you started snorting white powder, or throwing your money away, or eating fast food three times a day, I would step forward and ask you to think about what's best for you. That's all I'm doing right now. You tried once while in the throes of trauma. Maybe it's worth another shot."

"I'm fine how I am," Kelly said. "Except for the occasional embarrassing assumption, I'm good."

Nathaniel grabbed one of the suitcase handles, leaving the other where it was. "In that case, pull your own luggage."

Kelly snorted and did just that. Both pieces of luggage had wheels, so he could roll his along without carrying it. He was forced to yank it with each swing of his arms, and while that couldn't be comfortable, he was managing.

"Good," Nathaniel said. "Now take out your phone and call your brother. We need to know if he's picking us up."

Kelly paused, reaching into his coat for his phone.

Nathaniel kept walking. "Come on, I don't have all day. Let's go."

Kelly glared defiantly and resumed walking. He pinned one crutch under an arm, freeing a hand so he could get at his phone. This forced him to hop, and with the luggage pulling on him from behind, he only managed a few steps before he stumbled.

Nathaniel reached out to support him, feeling horrible for putting him in this situation. Seeing Kelly vulnerable made his heart ache. "What if you were on your own and about to miss your flight?" he asked. "Or worse, what if some crazy asshole is chasing after you and you need to call the police? Homophobes are cowards by nature, and if they perceive you as an easy target..."

Kelly's eyes were fierce as they locked with Nathaniel's, but after a moment his features softened.

"If anyone comes after me," he said gently, "I'm probably faster on my crutches than I would be on a fake leg."

Nathaniel shook his head. "It's not just my stupid fears, and it's not about how other people perceive you. I don't know how to express it without it sounding trite, but there are times when I want to give the world to you. Everything good in life, I want you to have it. I think this might be one of those things."

Kelly sighed. "Have you done your research? Prosthetic legs are like buying a car. Past the hefty price tag, there's maintenance and repairs when things break, and even then it won't last forever."

"If money wasn't an issue..." Nathaniel prompted.

Kelly smirked. "There's not going to be a fake leg under the Christmas tree next week, is there?"

"I'm serious."

"So am I, and money is *always* an issue."

"Just for the sake of argument, if it wasn't, would you at least give it another try?"

"Yeah," Kelly said, "but—"

Whatever he was about to say was interrupted by Royal calling their names. Kelly's brother being here meant a certain dog was too. Zero leapt at him from behind, causing Nathaniel to stumble forward. He got down on his knees so he could hug the squirming mutt and kiss his furry face. Being apart always reminded Nathaniel how much he loved the dog. Separation could work wonders in that regard. He would experience that soon with Kelly, who would be returning to his parents' house, allowing them to decompress after being so close. All it would take is that one night apart, and Nathaniel would start missing him again. He glanced up. Kelly was talking with his brother, but he sensed Nathaniel's gaze and met his eye. Then he nodded, almost imperceptibly, agreeing to give it one more try.

Deceit plays a part in every relationship. Lately, Nathaniel had worked hard to make sure Kelly didn't know the truth. This new leg of his, state-of-the-art technology that they had travelled to Berlin to acquire, was a gift from Ottobock, the corporation that produced it. Kelly was taking part in a test program that Marcello's connections had gained access to. This was the story Nathaniel had concocted, and while most of it was accurate, the truth was much more expensive. Ottobock wasn't handing them a prosthetic leg for free. Marcello had offered to cover the expense, but Nathaniel insisted on paying because he wanted to do this for Kelly. He also insisted that fact remain a secret. The truth might make Kelly feel obligated to wear the leg, even if he hated it, and Nathaniel certainly didn't expect gratitude. If Kelly believed the leg hadn't cost a thing, he could accept or reject the new prosthetic without concern.

Nathaniel still expected a lot of bang for his buck. He needed this thing to make all of Kelly's dreams come true, so when they reported to the Competence Center—as Ottobock called the private consulting area of its Berlin headquarters—Nathaniel refused to sit. Instead he remained standing, occasionally flexing his hands into fists. If all of the company's claims were merely snake oil, heads would roll. That would be a shame because the German woman helping them, Inga, was very likeable.

Yesterday she had been welcoming and patient with them. Today she was helping attach Kelly's new prosthetic. This involved a plastic cup-shaped object that suctioned over the end of his stump. The prosthetic itself attached to this. Nathaniel had to admit it looked nice. He had done his research so wasn't surprised, but he was glad it didn't try to duplicate the appearance of a real leg, or resemble something the Terminator would lurch around on. Instead it was sleek and black, not unlike the guy now attached to it.

"Ready to stand?" Inga said, rolling backward on a small stool, balancing bars to either side of her.

This made room for Kelly, who was seated in front of her. "Okay," he said, flashing an uncertain smile. Then he stood. That was no miracle. Nathaniel had often seen him stand without his crutches. Kelly grabbed the balancing bars for support.

"One step at a time," Inga said in her lightly accented English. "Don't rush! You need to let the knee bend on its own. It knows what to do."

Kelly grunted, but not from effort. Nathaniel could read him well enough to recognize his impatience. He no longer held on to the balancing bars. Each of his steps seemed to take no effort at all. If Inga wasn't standing in his way and coaching him, Kelly would probably be sprinting by now. Nathaniel had been careful not to tell him, not to get his hopes up, but this prosthetic had been designed for the military, and soldiers needed to do much more than amble around.

"Stay patient," Nathaniel said.

"Yes," Inga agreed. "You must be patient. But I think you are ready."

Finally she set him free and rolled out of his way. She didn't seem poised to rescue him if need be, confident in the product. Kelly took a few steps, then his face lit up. After that he walked without a care in the world. At the end of the bars, he turned smoothly, doing a little jig as he walked the length again. No crutches, his long-fingered hands not forced to grip a plastic handle. Instead they waved in the air, Kelly acting silly in celebration. Nathaniel felt pretty damn happy too, which nearly had him crying. He swallowed against this, forcing himself to calm down. Even happy tears might send the wrong signal or make Kelly feel pressured to choose this as his new lifestyle.

Inga stood, holding out her hands. "Would you like to try without support?"

For Kelly the question was rhetorical. He kept walking past the bars, Inga backing up to keep pace with him until her back hit the wall. Then she laughed.

"Very good!" she said. "You're a quick learner."

"By the end of the day, I'll be running laps," Kelly joked.

"Jogging?" Inga asked, worried by the suggestion. "Not today. Maybe in a week, you can try."

"Not on this leg," Kelly said. "The Genium doesn't support running."

"*Icks tsfy*," Inga responded.

"I don't know what that means."

"Oh! I'm sorry. The leg you have, it's a... uh... X2."

"I still don't know what that means," Kelly said.

"The X2 leg is designed in cooperation with the United States military." Inga put an arm around him, leading Kelly back toward the bars. "Right now it is for soldiers, but in the future, there will be a civilian release too."

"But what you're saying," Kelly said, "is that I can run on this leg. The one I've got on right now."

Inga nodded. "Yes. Of course. Just not now."

"Not now because it hasn't been developed fully, or—"

"You must learn to walk," Inga said, sounding stern. "You must train. Once you have, you can run with the leg you are now wearing."

Kelly's head shot up, eyes searching him out. Nathaniel swallowed again and nodded. Kelly stared a little longer, grinning like Nathaniel had done something clever. He was still smiling when he turned back to Inga.

"Bear with me," Kelly said, "but when you say run, do you mean I'll dawdle along at a respectable rate, or that I'll be hauling ass like I used to?"

"*Mein Gott,*" Inga said to herself. "*Ist das so schwer zu glauben?*"

"Okay," Kelly said with a mad laugh. "That sounded irritated enough to convince me.

Nathaniel headed for the door. When two heads turned to him in confusion, he muttered that he needed to use the men's room. Once he was in the hallway, he pressed his back against the wall and exhaled, trying to get himself under control emotionally. What he felt wasn't pride or satisfaction for having done a good deed. He didn't even know if what he felt had a name because seeing Kelly happy, seeing him get the good things he deserved, felt like God had stepped in to correct his own mistakes. Nathaniel took no credit for that. Chance had led him to his current position in life. But he was grateful. To anyone out there listening, he gave thanks.

Kelly refused to sit. Even while riding the U-Bahn—the underground train that snaked beneath the city—Kelly stood, only occasionally grabbing a pole for support. He wasn't talking much. He kept his full attention on his body as he readjusted his sense of balance. Nathaniel couldn't imagine living through such an experience, but he assumed it was going well because Kelly kept flashing him a smile.

They arrived in Kreuzberg, just far enough from the center of Berlin to have local flavor. Winter wasn't tourist season in Germany, so they were mostly surrounded by natives who treated them like idiots for not being able to speak German, and often responded in English with an air of superiority. Nathaniel loved it. Finally he was seeing an authentic part of the country. They bumbled through alternative shops, were approached on the street by a strange person with an offer they couldn't understand, and stopped for a late breakfast at a burger place that didn't seem to offer any meat. They slowly made their way on foot to the East Side Gallery, where a section of the Berlin Wall stood as a memorial.

"I thought it would be bigger," Kelly said musingly. "As in taller. I'm pretty sure I could pole vault this sucker."

"Easy now," Nathaniel said. "You're not the Bionic Man."

"I might be. Seriously though. I was thinking it would be more like the Great Wall of China."

"Just try to enjoy the art," Nathaniel suggested.

They strolled the length of the memorial wall, each section covered in painted murals. The styles varied greatly, although most made a political statement of some sort. They stopped in front of one depicting two former Communist leaders kissing.

"Up against the wall," Nathaniel said, reaching for his camera bag.

Kelly smirked. "Sounds promising." He walked up to the wall and turned around. "Aren't there enough photos of me in the world already?"

"No. I need more."

"So these aren't for Marcello?"

"Nope."

"Then maybe we should take a selfie," Kelly said. "Try to recreate the art behind us."

Nathaniel considered him through the viewfinder, then lowered the camera. "Actually, let's swap places. My mom has been asking me to email some new photos."

"Oh."

Kelly stepped forward. Nathaniel met him halfway and handed over the camera. Then he walked to the wall and leaned against it, ignoring the hissed complaint from one of the locals. Kelly messed with the settings, absorbed in the process. Then he raised the camera, snapped a few photos, and walked diagonally to change his angle.

"Step away from the wall," he said. "I want to get a long shot."

Nathaniel did what he was told, even though he didn't enjoy having his photo taken.

"Try to look less miserable," Kelly suggested.

Nathaniel crossed his arms over his chest and scowled.

"Perfect," Kelly said, the shutter clicking. Then he lowered the camera, his face growing somber when he tried to hand it back.

"Hang on to it," Nathaniel said. "I'm sick of carrying it around." When Kelly's expression remained pensive, he added, "You okay?"

"Yes." Kelly's shoulders relaxed. "It's just intimidating when you run out of excuses to avoid doing what you've always wanted. I can take photos again. There's nothing holding me back now."

"You'll do fine," Nathaniel said. "The worst that can happen is you'll realize you're not talented enough to fulfill your greatest dream."

"Very encouraging," Kelly said, raising the camera and snapping another photo of him. "I'll be sure to remember that when I'm doing covers for *Time* magazine."

They grabbed a kebab from the nearest train station, then used the S-Bahn to explore the city, hopping off at different stops to look around. Nathaniel kept waiting for Kelly to say he needed a break, but his energy seemed limitless.

Today was a trial for them both. Nathaniel fell back a few paces, looking at Kelly from behind, wanting to be sure he hadn't done any of this for selfish reasons. Seeing him walk so effortlessly was different. Did he prefer it? Not really. He was grateful that life would be easier for Kelly now, but he didn't find him more attractive than before or any less so. Only the person mattered to him—the intelligent, sharp-tongued powerhouse of attitude. How Kelly happened to get around didn't matter. Nathaniel loved him either way.

He stopped suddenly. These feelings were hardly a revelation, but for once he didn't fight them, re-label them, or avoid their implications. He loved Kelly. All he needed to do now was say it out loud, but not here. Not on a sidewalk. That brought back memories of the past. Besides, the crowds were growing thick as people got off work, the light of the day fading.

Kelly noticed he had stopped and turned around. "What's up?"

"Want to go back to the hotel?" Nathaniel asked.

Kelly gave him a knowing expression. "I was hoping to do a little shopping first."

"Okay."

Kelly glanced around. "I need to sit down."

"You all right?"

"Yeah, just normal tired."

They decided to grab a beer, avoiding food since they were still full from the heavy lunch. Once they felt recharged, they slipped into a nearby department store.

"I need new shoes!" Kelly declared. "And maybe a nice pair of jeans. I won't have to fold one leg anymore! Oh my god! Do you have any idea how exciting this is?"

Before Nathaniel could respond, Kelly was practically

leaping through a retail paradise. He caught up with him on the escalators and took his hand, not to slow him down, but because it was the least of what he really wanted to do. Only part of his urges were physical. Most of all he wanted to be alone together so he could finally confess his feelings. Instead he found himself standing in a shoe department, Kelly trying on a good portion of the inventory and deciding on nothing. Then they took a trip to men's fashion, where Kelly assembled an outfit with expert skill. Nathaniel waited outside the dressing room, listening to him gasp happily or murmur in surprise as he dressed. Apparently the process had changed or whatever, but Nathaniel's patience was running out.

"You almost done in there?" he called.

"Come see."

Nathaniel yanked open the curtain to find Kelly staring at himself in the mirror. The lighting was becoming, not that he needed it. He stepped close to Kelly, placing hands on his hips, looking over his shoulder at their reflection.

"What do you think?"

"Handsome as always," Nathaniel said, placing a kiss on his neck.

"Thanks," Kelly said, "but I mean… I look normal!"

Nathaniel laughed. "Normal? I don't think so. You're the most beautiful man I've ever laid eyes on."

Kelly appeared flattered, playfully swatting one of his hands. "You're just saying that because of the new leg."

Nathaniel shook his head. "Take it off and throw it in the next dumpster you see. I don't care. Go back to your crutches if that makes you happy, or let me carry you anywhere you want to go. I'd do anything for you, Kelly. Absolutely anything, because I love you. You know that?"

The almond-shaped eyes in the mirror grew wide, Kelly barely managing a nod.

Nathaniel felt vulnerable. "Is that okay?"

Kelly spun around, placing hands on his chest. "Is it okay that I've been in love with you for a ridiculously long time?"

Nathaniel resisted a smile. "Since when?"

"Gosh," Kelly said, glancing off into the distant past. "Somewhere between the second and third glass of wine."

"At the fundraiser?" Nathaniel laughed. "That far back? Wow! Must have been some potent moonshine!"

"It was," Kelly said with a grin. "Seriously, I don't know when it happened, but I've been keeping it a secret because I was worried that—"

"Kelly," Nathaniel interrupted.

"Yes?"

"I need you to stop talking."

"Why?"

Nathaniel pulled him close, gently placed his forehead against Kelly's, and stared deep into his eyes. *I love you,* he tried to make that gaze say, and just in case the message wasn't received, he brought their lips together for a kiss. And another. There could never be enough. Nathaniel would have to find other ways, gestures of an infinite variety, to communicate what he felt inside, but he looked forward to each attempt. For now, a simple kiss would have to do. *I love you.*

Chapter Eighteen

Idealistic dreams were sent scattering by a knock on his office door. Nathaniel hurriedly gathered the photos of Kelly to turn them upside down. He had nothing to hide, but the last thing he wanted was Marcello prying into his personal life.

"What is it?" he grunted, hoping to sound busy.

The door opened revealing dark hair and silver eyes. "Hey!" Tim said. "Long time no see. You busy?"

"No!" Nathaniel stood and gestured for Tim to enter. They only saw each other sporadically. Tim didn't work for the studio, but since he and Marcello were friends, occasionally they bumped into each other in the hallways. Or during certain events, such as—

"The Eric Conroy Fundraiser is coming up," Tim said, shaking hands before flopping into one of the chairs.

Nathaniel sat down again. "I've already got the invite list ready."

"Cool. This year I'd like to get the artists directly involved with the people shelling out money to help them. I also want the patrons to see the actual art. The gallery is a little too small for what I'm thinking and, well, Marcello said you were the man to talk to. Unless he's trying to hook us up again. Ha ha."

"I have a boyfriend," Nathaniel blurted out.

Tim's eyebrows shot up. "I was kidding."

"I know," Nathaniel said, shaking his head. "Sorry. I'm still trying to wrap my head around it, which apparently means telling everyone I meet. Although if I'm honest, I think I've had a boyfriend for a long time. I just didn't realize it until recently."

Tim's grin was easy. "Believe it or not, I know *exactly* what you mean. Some guys lure you in nice and slow. You wake up one day and realize you're in a relationship. Or they straight up tell you. Remember on our date when I waxed nostalgic about that one guy? *The* one?"

"Ben," Nathaniel said. When Tim looked surprised he added, "Marcello talks about you two a lot. You found your way back to him."

"Yeah," Tim said, his smile getting even brighter. "Never thought it would happen, but it did."

"Congratulations." Nathaniel tapped his index finger against the desk, his leg jittering. "Aren't you terrified that you'll fuck it all up? Like now that you've got what you always wanted, you'll make one wrong move and ruin everything?"

"Every single day," Tim said matter-of-factly.

"And you're okay with that?"

"I don't have a choice. If it does happen… This guy you're with, is he patient?"

"No."

Tim laughed. "Okay, is he forgiving?"

Nathaniel thought about it. Kelly had been through a lot with William, but he never blamed the accident on him or obsessed over him falling in love with Jason Grant. When William came up in conversation, his memory was treated with affection. That relationship might have been a painful learning experience, but Kelly didn't seem to hold a grudge. "He's pretty forgiving. I think."

"There you go. Unless you do something unbelievably stupid, chances are you can work through it."

Nathaniel didn't feel much better. "What if I hurt him? Or he hurts me?"

Tim thought about this. "My grandma has a saying. It's in Spanish, because she's Mexican, but roughly translated…" When he spoke again, he sounded more like an old woman with a thick accent. "If you strike yourself while hammering a nail, you can either suck your thumb for the rest of your life or get on with building yourself a home."

"So basically, get over it."

Tim nodded. "That's what she would tell you, and believe me, you wouldn't want to argue with her. I tried once." He rubbed his arm as if he'd been punched there. "It didn't go so well."

Nathaniel's relationship with Kelly had come full circle. Or full oval, considering they were standing in front of a high school running track. The same one they had visited on their first date, as Nathaniel now thought of it. He had mentally rewritten much of their relationship, stripping it of distance and denial. He could admit now that they had been together a long time, getting to know each other emotionally and physically. And here they were again, except now Kelly's spirits were high.

"Are you sure this is a good idea?" Nathaniel asked.

Kelly glanced up from fiddling with the camera and tripod. "Why wouldn't it be?"

"Because you're supposed to work with a physical therapist before attempting anything like this, and I don't recall you going to any appointments."

"I go while you're at work," Kelly said, focusing on the camera settings.

"Really?"

"Yes."

Nathaniel narrowed his eyes. "You don't really have one, do you?"

"I have a therapist," Kelly insisted.

"Then what's his name?"

"What's *her* name," Kelly said, wagging a finger at him. "*Her* name is Allison Cross."

"That's the name of your counselor. Wrong kind of therapist."

Kelly fought down a grin. "How do you remember these things?"

"Because I like to imagine her being cross with you when you're being a duplicitous shit. Like now."

"Her technique is more of the kill-them-with-kindness variety. You should try it sometime."

"Not a chance," Nathaniel said. "I'm serious. I don't want you hurting yourself." He was tempted to add that he didn't blow thousands of dollars just for Kelly to break the damned leg while messing around, but that would give away his secret.

"I'll be fine," Kelly said. "If anything goes wrong, at least we'll have a series of photos to show the physical therapist. I'm sure that will be enlightening."

"So you'll go? You'll see a physical therapist?"

"Naturally." Kelly pushed one last button and stepped away from the camera. "But only if this doesn't work. I'm going to run again, no matter what it takes. Ready?"

"Just start slow," Nathaniel insisted. "Maybe a little speed-walking."

Kelly humored Nathaniel for the first lap, Zero running circles around them as if he too agreed. *Why hesitate? Now or never!*

After the first lap, Kelly stopped to adjust his leg, spared Nathaniel a sly grin, and said, "Try to keep up." Then he was running. Despite his boast, he wasn't going too fast. Not at first. Nathaniel easily kept pace, his full attention on Kelly, who kept looking down at himself as if taking stock. He seemed to be experimenting, his lope becoming longer or shorter as needed, his arms alternating between swinging and pumping. Whatever he was looking for, he must have found it, because he burst forward, Zero barking excitedly. They ran past the camera's location not once but twice, Kelly clearly intent on going for a third. As much as Nathaniel wanted to keep tabs on him, his exhaustion was increasing. He was considering heading for the bleachers when he saw Kelly looking at him, his face plastered with wild glee. Nathaniel was smiling back when a scuffing noise interrupted their perfect moment.

Kelly hit the ground, tumbling across the track and rolling to a stop. Nathaniel rushed over to help. Kelly flopped over onto his back, giggling like a child.

"You all right?" Nathaniel asked.

"I think I skinned my knee." Kelly pointed at the prosthetic leg.

Nathaniel shook his head and offered him a hand. Once standing, Kelly gazed out across the track and beamed in satisfaction.

"Keep grinning like that and people will think you've gone insane," Nathaniel teased.

"I don't care. That felt too damn good. Ready for more? I'll race you!"

"Only if you promise to slow down." Nathaniel was still trying to catch his breath.

"That was nothing. Just wait until I get my running blade. Then you'll really see fast."

"I'd rather see fast food." Nathaniel checked his watch. Breakfast seemed like ages ago. "It's past lunchtime."

"Save your appetite," Kelly said, leading them back toward the tripod and camera. "The party will have plenty of food."

"Isn't that tonight?"

"No, in just a few hours." The camera snapped one last automatic photo as Kelly reached for it and began disassembling the setup.

"Kind of early for a party," Nathaniel said.

"It's a birthday."

"For who? A little kid?"

Kelly jabbed the folded tripod at him so he would take it. "Geez, chill out, Mr. Nightlife! Things happen during the day too, you know. And for the record, it's Layne's birthday. He's a friend of mine from the youth group."

"Youth group. As in teenagers."

"Yes. Tons and tons of teenagers who are eager to meet you for the first time. Prepare yourself. You'll probably have to give everyone piggyback rides."

"Sounds like a real cool party," Nathaniel grumbled. "Super neato."

"Don't be a snob." Kelly turned to walk toward the car. "With all the travelling we've been doing, I haven't seen most of these people for ages. The youth group is important to me. They were there when I first came out and also after the accident. When William and I split up too. They're like a second family, one I've dated quite a few members of. Ha ha."

"You're not exactly winning me over."

Kelly ignored him. "They're awesome people. I'm already dreading being too old to attend meetings. Hey, speaking of old, I need you to buy some booze. As a present."

That was an unwelcome flashback. Kelly usually didn't ask him for such things. He enjoyed a drink now and again, but was content to let Nathaniel surprise him. Of course working for Marcello meant a glass of champagne was never far away.

"So this guy," Nathaniel said. "This birthday boy. Did you and he ever…"

"His name is Layne, and no." Kelly bumped their shoulders together playfully. "Don't tell me you're feeling jealous."

"A complete stranger hit on you yesterday."

"She wasn't my type. Very flattering though."

"All I'm asking is that you wear a bag over your head when in public."

Kelly smiled at the compliment. "Just stay close to me. You tend to scare away most Romeos."

"Deal."

They loaded the car with camera equipment and an ill-behaved dog. Once home again, they took a shower together. Kelly's new leg wasn't water-proof, meaning it couldn't join them, but he spent most of the shower in Nathaniel's arms. Once the water was turned off, Nathaniel suggested they crawl into bed to enjoy the afterglow, but Kelly went to the closet and started pulling out clothes. After they dressed and left the house, they made a quick stop to buy a bottle of booze and another to get wrapping paper, then drove to a suburban house set against untouched woods. The house's backyard was currently filled with a gift-covered table, a huge cake, and most ridiculous of all, an inflatable castle. Teenagers were bouncing around inside this like popcorn, making it rock back and forth.

"How old did you say this guy was?" Nathaniel murmured. "Please don't tell me I bought vodka for an eight-year-old."

"Welcome, welcome!" a voice said in greeting. Layne, most likely, since he was playing host. The guy was thin, his blond hair carefully blow-dried and styled, his body motions slightly exaggerated, like he thought he was on stage and needed to communicate to a broader audience. That might explain his makeup—powder, base, and just a little eyeliner—which was laughable, because he was much too adorable to need such things. "How kind of you to be here on my special day. My *very* special day."

"Eighteen is quite the milestone," Kelly said, stressing the age as if to reassure Nathaniel.

Layne gave the sort of nod that said *I hear you talking but I'm not interested.* Instead his eyes were all over Nathaniel. He obviously liked what he saw because his smile grew wider and he stepped forward for a hug. Nathaniel raised his arms above his head to protect the camera and the wrapped present he was holding. Layne grabbed his torso anyway and squeezed. "It's so nice to meet you at last! We've heard so many wonderful things, some of them about you. What's your name again? Oh, it doesn't matter. You're so warm!"

"Okay," Kelly said, trying to peel Layne off him. "Let go. Seriously."

"Fine." Layne released Nathaniel. Then he opened his arms to Kelly and gasped. "Oh. My. God!"

Kelly hopped from foot to foot. "No more crutches!"

Layne covered his mouth in awe. Then he took Kelly by the arm and guided him toward the party. "Everyone, look who's standing on his own two feet!"

Nathaniel eyed the crowd and felt asocial for not having so

many friends. Not even a fraction. Outside his professional life, he only had Kelly and a dog. Sort of sad when he thought about it, but he was happy. Kelly gave an impromptu speech, and the reaction he got showed that he was close to these people. Maybe he didn't see them often, but they were all comfortable around each other.

"I think it's fabulous," Layne said, looping arms with Kelly. He took hold of Nathaniel too and walked with them across the yard. "Speaking of which, did you bring my present?"

"You mean the bottle you're still three years too young to drink from?" Nathaniel shook the present they had gift-wrapped to disguise its form. A good thing too, considering Layne's parents had answered the door.

"That's the one!" Layne released them so he could take it. "This should liven things up!"

Kelly nodded toward the inflatable castle. "You might want to think twice about getting people drunk and shoving them in your ball pit."

"It's not a ball pit," Layne said patiently. "It's a bounce house, and it happens to be my most ingenious plan yet. Just imagine me and a handsome boy jumping around in that thing, bumping into each other and getting all handsy until he falls on top of me and... Well, paint your own picture."

Kelly chuckled in appreciation. "So who's the lucky guy?"

Layne nodded to one corner of the yard where three guys stood. Nathaniel looked without much interest. One was tall and pale, his hair crimson. The other two looked like brothers, their skin and hair dark. One wore a tank top, his rounded shoulders glowing bronze in the sunlight.

"Which one are you after?" Kelly asked.

"Any of them will do," Layne said with a wistful sigh. "Or all of them. I'm hedging my bets. I figure I'm tripling my odds by inviting all three here."

"Are they from the youth group?" Kelly asked.

"Imported. God bless the Internet!"

"Hungry," Nathaniel muttered, interrupting their gossip session.

"If you'll excuse me," Kelly said, patting his arm, "I have to go feed my man-beast."

Layne smiled at him longingly. "Have fun, you lucky bastard."

Nathaniel was led to the buffet, which offered everything he needed: food to satiate his bodily hunger, a focus so he wouldn't have to mingle, and an excuse to keep his mouth full so he couldn't respond to small talk. Kelly was already making the rounds, Nathaniel happy to remain alone and eat. His plan backfired somewhat when Layne's mother lit the candles on the cake, attracting more people to the buffet. The rest were called over by Layne, who made them watch and wait while he struggled to find the ultimate birthday wish. While this decision was being made, Kelly returned to his side.

"Did it work?" Layne asked once he blew out the candles. "Are you all madly in love with me?"

"Yes," the crowd moaned.

Layne appeared delighted until he spotted something in the distance. "My beautiful palace!" he cried. "It's shrinking!"

Kelly turned and snorted. Nathaniel followed his gaze. The multi-colored inflatable castle was drooping around the edges, one of the parapets already limp and lifeless.

"This is worse than the Hindenburg disaster!" Layne declared. "Oh, the humanity!"

"The air pump motor is still running," Nathaniel said to Kelly. "The connection probably came loose."

"Think you can fix it?"

He took one look at those hopeful, pleading eyes and puffed up his chest. "I'll try."

"Best boyfriend ever!"

Nathaniel sauntered over to the castle. Layne was trying to lift the parapet, as if that would help. Nathaniel went instead to the motor, crouching down beside it and trying to make sense of all the tubes.

"What have we got here?" a female voice asked.

Nathaniel glanced up. Bonnie. Kelly's best friend. They had only met a few times, but Nathaniel liked her. He thought of her as a plucky lesbian, but if he ever told her that, she'd probably get him in a headlock and make him apologize. She was a fraction of his size, but her spunky style and feisty personality more than compensated for her stature.

"You know anything about air pumps?" he asked.

"Yep." Bonnie hoisted up her belt like it was heavy with tools and squatted next to him. In a quieter voice she added, "Not a clue. I just wanted to avoid being drafted into food service."

Nathaniel glanced back to Kelly, who was dishing out cake, talking to each person as he handed them slices. "You guys are lucky," he said, returning his attention to Bonnie and the air pump. "I should have found myself a youth group when I was a teenager. When I first came out, everything that followed was anticlimactic. My parents didn't care, so no drama. I didn't know any other gay people, so no action of any sort. Basically I told the world I was gay, and it replied with a half-hearted shrug."

"Could be worse," Bonnie replied. "My mom created a profile for me on an online dating site, trying to get me hooked up with the right sort of guy. She figured I was confused and just needed a feminine boy, or maybe she was trying to confuse me. Either way, it was extremely misguided."

"I'm sure nothing came of it," Nathaniel said, checking various connections.

"Oh, I totally went for it. My mom offered to double my allowance, and I've always been a sucker for bribes. I actually found out about the gay youth group from one of my dates. He wasn't gay, despite being feminine, but his brother was queer enough for them both. Butch as hell too. Funny how the world works sometimes."

Nathaniel laughed. Then he noticed the problem, reattached a tube that had come loose and tightened the metal clamp around it. Brushing off his hands, he stood at the same time Bonnie did. "You should hang out with us more often," he said. "I know I've been hogging Kelly, but you're welcome at my place any time. I don't want to keep you guys apart."

Bonnie smiled. "Don't feel guilty. It's not your fault Kelly is busy being famous." She looked over at her friend. "These days he seems to find fans wherever he goes."

"No kidding." Nathaniel followed her gaze. "Did he tell you about the woman at the…" He trailed off, puzzled by what he saw. One of the guys Layne was hoping to seduce was standing in front of Kelly, lifting up his sleeveless shirt to reveal his torso. Even from here Nathaniel could see he was toned. Kelly was clearly taken aback, but kept talking to the guy even once his bare skin was covered again.

"Nothing to Hulk out over," Bonnie said. "You know you can trust Kelly."

When she placed a hand on his arm, Nathaniel was surprised

to notice how tense he was. In the distance, Kelly turned away, giving his full attention to cutting cake. This didn't seem to discourage the other guy, who leaned in closer and continued to speak, teeth flashing when Kelly eventually looked over at him again.

"Who is that?" Nathaniel grumbled.

"Rico," Bonnie said. "I don't really know him. He's from out of town. We can go over there. Introduce ourselves. I'm sure once he sees you he'll get the hint."

"Good idea."

Nathaniel walked toward them, watching as Rico continued talking to Kelly, who appeared slightly confused. Then Kelly wiped at a cheek self-consciously, Rico shaking his head and reaching out, as if to help. For one brief moment, Nathaniel was no longer in the middle of a teenager's birthday party. Instead he was in the parking lot of a Tex-Mex restaurant in Connecticut, Caesar reaching forward to wipe Rebecca's chin. Nathaniel had mentally replayed that scene countless times, agonizing over the kiss that had ruined two relationships at once. Now history was repeating itself, except Rico was no friend, that hand of his hooking behind Kelly's head. Their lips met, a growl escaping Nathaniel as he charged forward. He saw his boyfriend's eyes go wide in shock, his body stiffening before he tried to pull away to end the kiss. Nathaniel could definitely help with that. He reached them and used both arms to grab Rico around the torso, lifting him off the ground and flinging him to one side, sparing the table and cake. A shame, because Nathaniel would have loved seeing him roll through the food like the pig he was. Still, throwing him on the grass would make beating the living hell out of him a lot cleaner. At least until Nathaniel drew blood.

Rico rolled onto his back. Nathaniel pounced on him with his full weight, forcing breath to wheeze out of his lungs. Rico wouldn't need to breathe for much longer anyway, because Nathaniel was pretty damn sure he was going to kill the little shit. He pulled back a fist to punch, but someone grabbed his arm, slowing him enough that Rico was able to dodge. Nathaniel glanced over to find Kelly pulling on him, his expression pleading. Rico said something in Spanish and lashed out, popping Nathaniel on the chin. His jaw rattled painfully. Now Kelly's expression matched his own, his fury evident. He released

Nathaniel's arm, freeing him to slug Rico in the face with an ugly crunching noise. Rico touched his nose instinctively and saw blood on his fingers. Then he snarled, about to lash out again, but Bonnie skidded across the grass like a referee ready for the count.

She shoved Rico down with one hand and pushed at Nathaniel's chest with the other. "Break it up!" she shouted. "Come on, guys. You don't want to do this!"

Kelly pulled at Nathaniel until he got off Rico and stood. He braced himself for Rico to rise and continue the fight, but Bonnie was still holding him down. Layne rushed over to help, dabbing at Rico's bloody nose with a cheerful napkin depicting streamers and balloons.

Layne spoke and Kelly answered, but their words were lost on him. Nathaniel was too busy huffing, staring down at Rico and resisting the urge to stomp on his face until his head was buried in the ground.

"Come on," Kelly said, yanking on his arm. "Let's go."

Nathaniel stumbled along with him as they left the yard, walking around the house. When he saw the car, he picked up the pace. Kelly released his arm, going instead for his hand. Nathaniel knocked it away, not in the mood for tenderness.

This didn't please Kelly, who forced him to stop. "You *know* I didn't want to kiss him, right?"

Just the mention of it made his blood boil again. Nathaniel wanted to turn around and finish beating the hell out of Caesar. He winced and shook his head. No, not Caesar. Rico. But for a second he had seen Caesar on the grass, Rebecca holding him down and trying to stop the fight. Old ghosts. When would they cease haunting him? Nathaniel wanted them to finally fucking go away. Forever. He headed for the car again.

"I'm driving," Kelly said from behind him. "You're way too emotional right now."

Nathaniel dug in his pocket for the keys and tossed them over his shoulder. He waited by the passenger door until it unlocked, then slouched in the seat and covered his eyes with one hand. His head hurt, his temples pounding. When the car finally stopped again, they were at his apartment. He waited for Kelly to unlock the front door, then went inside and ignored Zero's excited greeting, instead going straight into the bedroom. Once there he shut the door behind him and locked it. Then he pulled down the blinds so the room was dark and got on the bed. Curling into a ball and covering his head with a pillow, he squeezed his eyes shut and willed the images to cease.

The restaurant parking lot. Caesar leaning toward Kelly, Bonnie leaning toward Rebecca, Rico honking the horn of a car before running Nathaniel over. He felt insane, rage still coursing through him. As the minutes ticked by, his thoughts started making sense, his anger fading. He soon missed it, since it helped disguise the pain.

He had thought they would be safe. Two damaged soldiers, returning home scarred. He knew Kelly hadn't wanted to hurt him, would never willingly put him through an experience like that. And yet it had happened. In a way it felt inevitable. Nathaniel had been worrying about Kelly since Cancún. His anxiety had begun there, and though he had brief reprieves, the fear remained, bubbling away in the back of his mind. What if Kelly were to fall or be attacked? What if he lost interest? What if Nathaniel failed him in some way, no matter how unintentional, and Kelly was hurt?

Nathaniel had fought against these possibilities. He spent every spare moment trying to shield Kelly. He poured over the details of each new modeling assignment, trying to make sure they were safe and respectable. Even the new prosthetic was born of this anxiety. Kelly was more mobile now, able to run or reach for his phone if—heaven forbid—Nathaniel wasn't there when the worst happened. And in his mind, those nightmares were ongoing, all the worst-case scenarios imaginable. Nathaniel entertained each and kept trying to find ways to prevent them and protect Kelly.

Now he knew that he couldn't. If a kid's birthday party wasn't safe, what was? Nathaniel gripped the pillow even tighter. Some slimy guy had kissed his boyfriend. Kelly could survive that, could survive anything. Look at what he'd been through! What a joke, what arrogance to even think he needed protecting. Kelly, who had been through hell and still had the strength to cock one eyebrow at the world as if to say, "Seriously? You wanna mess with me? Go ahead and try!"

In truth it was Nathaniel who couldn't handle this. He hurt and seethed and ached because of a betrayal from *years* ago. He still hadn't recovered from what Caesar and Rebecca had done, and they were nothing compared to Kelly. Nathaniel had loved them both, but not as much as he loved the guy in the other room. If losing them had hurt that much, was able to send him into a blind rage even now… He was weak. Too weak to protect anyone. He was grateful for Kelly's strength, because it meant he would be okay after today. After what needed to be done. Nathaniel lay there until the slivers of light around the blinds grew dark. He forced himself to revisit the image of Rico kissing Kelly over and over again even though it hurt more each time. Such a thing was inevitable. Someday Kelly would move on and find another guy to kiss him. Nathaniel had only glimpsed the future today.

He steeped in his own misery, tossing aside the pillow, wiping at his tears, punching the mattress in his frustration. Then he forced himself to rise and go to the bedroom door. It was time. Nathaniel was tempted to flip the switch. He hadn't needed to for years. Nathaniel wasn't even sure he *could* shut himself down, turn off his emotions, but he wanted to try. Just not yet. He had to show Kelly his pain, because only then would he understand.

Zero met him in the hallway, tail wagging. He might not be so excited or love Nathaniel quite as much if he knew what was about to happen. Kelly was in the kitchen with a pot of tomato soup simmering on the stove and a grilled cheese sandwich sizzling in a skillet. He looked up, his expression hopeful.

"Hungry?"

Nathaniel shook his head. "We need to talk."

"Okay." Kelly turned off the burners and moved the skillet before joining Nathaniel at the table. "I did *not* kiss him. I was just talking to the guy when he practically jumped me."

"I know," Nathaniel said. "I saw."

Kelly's brow knotted up. "Then why have you been shut in your room this whole time?"

"It hurt," Nathaniel croaked. "Seeing another person kiss you… You have no idea how bad that hurt." He swallowed against the pain. That was enough. Time to flip the switch. He tried but must have been out of practice, because he still ached.

"I'm sorry," Kelly said. "Believe me when I say I didn't like it either."

"It's not your fault. That's what's so fucked up. I knew when I started falling for you that someone might get hurt, but I promised myself I wouldn't be the one to hurt you. And I trusted you would try your hardest not to hurt me. Today didn't break that trust. Neither one of us is at fault, and yet we still got hurt because we love each other."

"That's right," Kelly said. "And it sucks. There's nothing we can do about it, so we should have dinner together while badmouthing the guy. Or are you really going to let something this stupid tear us apart?"

He saw no sense in delaying the inevitable. Doing so would be cruel. Nathaniel looked directly at Kelly, who spoke before he could.

"You better tell me what you're thinking." Kelly's voice was shaking. "Right now!"

"This *will* happen again," Nathaniel explained. "Even if we manage not to hurt each other, eventually one of us will get sick or get bored, or someone else will get in the way. Maybe they won't mean to. Maybe my mom will need me when she's older and I'll have to go to her—"

"I'd go with you," Kelly offered.

"—or maybe one of us will die young or maybe you'll fall out of love with me because emotions can't be controlled. Or maybe we'll get to a point where we want to hurt each other. I know that's hard to imagine now, but relationships only get more complicated as time goes by."

"So we better avoid them?" Kelly snapped. "Why do you even leave the house? Why aren't you constantly scared of getting hit by a car or shot by some random lunatic?"

Nathaniel exhaled. "I never was before. Not until I fell in love with you. Now the idea of you being hurt, even just because I am—I hate it. I don't want to hurt you, but I'm going to now, because if I wait any longer, it'll hurt worse than you could ever imagine. The longer we let this go on, the greater the pain."

"You'll kill me," Kelly said, reaching across the table with trembling hands to touch his. "That isn't a dramatic threat. I won't commit suicide or anything like that, but if you leave me now, it's going to kill me. *That's* how much I love you."

Nathaniel pulled back his hands and looked away. Flip the switch. He clenched his jaw. Flip the goddamn switch! But this pain was too strong to be muted. He exhaled through his nose a few times, his eyes tearing up. "You have to trust me. This is for the best."

"There's something you're not telling me," Kelly said. "What is it? Do you have HIV? Some sort of terminal disease?"

Nathaniel sighed and shook his head. "No."

"Something else. This has to do with your past. If you're going to dump my ass, you can at least tell me. Please!"

"It won't make a difference," Nathaniel said. "People aren't meant to be together like this. I know society pushes the idea, but it's false. We're happier on our own. We're stronger. You especially. Leaving me won't kill you. You never needed me to begin with."

"*I'm* not leaving *you!*" Kelly shouted. "And don't tell me what I need or how I feel. I wasn't happier before I met you. I was okay, but since that first day we spent together, when we ran around Austin trying to figure out how to plan something spontaneous—" His voice cracked. "You don't get to tell me how I feel."

"Fine," Nathaniel said. "Then I'm doing this for me. I can't handle going through this again."

"Through *what*?" Kelly demanded.

"People change," Nathaniel said. "It can't be helped. We love each other now, but you're just starting out and you don't realize how much heartbreak is around the corner. And I admit it. I'm scared of losing you or hurting you or a million other scenarios that keep me up at night. I'm a coward or maybe I'm just crazy. All I know is that I can't handle this anymore."

"You can," Kelly said. "You're so fucking strong. I *know* you can handle this!"

"You can't tell me what I feel, either," Nathaniel said softly. "And you're wrong. I'm not strong. I can't do this anymore. I can't, and I won't."

He breathed in, holding the air in his lungs. Flip the switch. This time he found it. A good thing too. Kelly had determination. He wouldn't cower and slink from the room. Instead he sat and pleaded with Nathaniel to be reasonable. He reminded him of all they had done together, every memory made under a blue sky, and the insanity of throwing that away. He got angry too, told Nathaniel he was being an idiot, weak, naïve. All of it was true, but none of his words changed what needed to be done. Kelly even let down his guard and cried, which only made Nathaniel hate himself more. Kelly kept digging deeper inside himself, finding the strength to keep fighting, until he finally reached his core.

Kelly stood up from the table, eyes hard. "This is going to hurt," he said. "Way more than it does right now, way more than you imagined, because I know how much I love you, and I've felt how much you love me. Your worst nightmare comes true, starting *right now*, unless you risk the future with me."

Nathaniel lowered his eyes, kept his attention on the table as Kelly crouched next to Zero, saying hushed words to him. Nathaniel only heard one. *Goodbye.* Then Kelly gathered his things and went to the apartment door. He didn't open it. Nathaniel waited, fighting the urge to get off his ass and prevent the worst mistake of his life from happening. Doing so would only perpetuate the worst mistake Kelly had ever made. Nathaniel wasn't good enough for him. Kelly deserved better. Maybe he finally realized this, because the door squeaked open. Nathaniel kept his attention on the table, trying to keep his emotions under control. He almost managed, but then Zero whimpered.

Nathaniel took a deep shuddering breath. "I'm sorry," he said, but not to the dog. He looked over to where Kelly had been standing. The hallway was empty. The door already closed. It was too late, but he tried again anyway. "I'm sorry."

Chapter Nineteen

Kelly returned to the apartment the next day, pounding on the door in the early afternoon. Nathaniel did his best to ignore this, having decided that he had done the right thing, if not for himself, then for Kelly. Besides, what more was there to say? Later that night, when Kelly returned again, Nathaniel didn't bother pretending he wasn't home. They had broken up. Kelly needed to accept that. Hiding from him at work wouldn't be easy, so Nathaniel called Marcello and asked a favor.

"You haven't willingly taken time off since your first day," Marcello said. "I had to pretend the office was closed just to be rid of you. Or send you on that assignment to Prague, the one that was mysteriously cancelled when your plane landed."

"Is there any aspect of my life you don't manipulate?"

Marcello chuckled. "Not really, you poor soul. By all means, take a few days off!"

"I was thinking a few weeks," Nathaniel said.

"I see. Planning a romantic get away? Your lovely boyfriend is scheduled to be in the studio next week."

"He'll be there."

The line was silent a moment. "You're not travelling together?"

"My family needs me," Nathaniel said. "I don't want to subject him to two weeks of that."

"Quite so. I don't have much in the way of family myself, but from what I've experienced through others, family gatherings are rather like attending a convention where nobody shares the same interest."

"Exactly," Nathaniel said. "Hold down the fort for me, okay?"

"Naturally."

After hanging up the phone, Nathaniel didn't hesitate. Midnight was steadily approaching, he packed a suitcase anyway, loaded Zero in the backseat, and pointed the car toward Houston. He intended to get a hotel room when he arrived since his parents would be in bed, but he couldn't help himself. He wanted the comfort of familiar surroundings. He was letting himself in the front door when the hall light switched on. His mother appeared wearing her robe, not the slightest bit groggy.

"I couldn't sleep," she said. "Now I know why." She crouched down to pet Zero, who was flipping out with joy, but her attention remained on her son. "Are you okay?"

"Yeah," Nathaniel said. "I just needed to get away."

Ten minutes later they were seated at the kitchen table, sharing a bottle of wine. Nathaniel tried to keep conversation neutral, but Star kept scrutinizing him, her motherly instincts striking close to the truth. "If he left you, then he's a fool. If you're having problems, they can be solved."

"I left him," Nathaniel said, not wanting to play games.

"What happened? What did he do?"

"Nothing." Nathaniel took a swig of wine. "I don't want to get hurt. It's better this way."

"I can see that you're hurting already!"

"And it's enough. I'm done."

His mother sighed. "Honey, if the only reason you broke things off is because you got scared, you need to rethink this."

He stared at his wine instead of replying.

"I like Kelly," his mother pressed.

Nathaniel shrugged. "So do I."

Star remained silent until he looked at her. "You're supposed to learn from the mistakes of your parents," she said.

"Meaning?"

"That if someone is mistreating you, you either do something about it or leave. I'm still ashamed that you had to step in when your father was struggling with his issues. When he was hitting me," she amended. "I'm embarrassed that my own child had to make me see what needed to be done. So if Kelly wasn't good to you, and this is your solution, then fine."

"He wasn't abusive," Nathaniel said. "Kelly is perfect. He's better off without me."

"Then you need to learn a lesson from your father, and for once I mean Victor."

No other name could have captured his attention just then. "How so?"

Star sighed, tapping the base of her wine glass with one manicured nail. "Victor was too self-sacrificing. He loved without discrimination or boundary, which could be frustrating for those of us who loved him back, but I'm not sure he was so generous with himself. Love can be selfish, especially when you do everything in your power to keep the other person with you. That's part of wanting someone else. In such situations, Victor always let go. When I told him I was moving to California with Heath, part of me hoped he would try to stop me, demand that I stay in the Midwest just for him. Or when Jace—Victor's boyfriend—went off to college, Victor never tried to hold him back. That was noble, but I'm not sure nobility and love are compatible. Hearts don't collide without causing collateral damage. If you go through life trying not to hurt anyone, even yourself, you'll probably end up alone. Victor was alone in the end, and I wish more than anything that he hadn't been."

"I'm not alone," Nathaniel said. "I've got Zero. And an awesome mom."

"Neither one of us will be around forever," his mother said gently.

The thought was too depressing to consider. As was the whole conversation. "Can we talk about something else?"

"One more lesson," Star said. "This one from your other father, the one who raised you. When Heath realized he was losing me, he fought hard to change. I swear to you he hasn't come close to making the same mistakes again. That's what love is. It's good that you don't want to hurt Kelly, or be hurt by him, but love means learning from the bruises we give each other so we can avoid them in the future."

"And what did you learn from your bruises?" Nathaniel challenged.

"That I needed to love myself more," his mother replied. "That's what I was trying to say before. Fight for yourself if need be, or fight for the other person if he is slipping away. Just don't give up. Not if you love him and he loves you back. Think about it. Please."

Nathaniel drained his glass and looked away. "I will."

Sitting around the house and feeling miserable slowly became routine. Star forced him to go grocery shopping with her, and Zero insisted on daily walks. Other than those activities, Nathaniel lounged around an entire week, watching old movies on cable. When his cell phone battery died, he didn't bother recharging it. He was dead to the world. He wanted it that way, so when his mother told him that Sheila was coming over, he wasn't happy. He got cleaned up regardless, not wanting to set a bad example for his nephew. He also wanted to be ready to leave the house, just in case his brother started anything.

Dwight was "struggling," as their mother put it, which translated to drinking too much and getting arrested. He'd spent nearly a year in county jail and was only recently out on parole. Sheila was working hard to provide a steady life for Arthur, since Dwight couldn't be relied on. Nathaniel always made sure to ask about them when he called his mom and showered them with presents both practical and extravagant on gift-giving occasions. The rest was up to Sheila. Nathaniel thought she needed to leave Dwight, but he couldn't make that decision for her.

To his great relief, she showed up at the house without her husband. Sheila greeted Nathaniel warmly, but Arthur was much more wary of him, not even wanting a hug.

"Swing set," he demanded, running off through the house toward the backyard.

A few seconds later they heard Star's happy cries, followed by what sounded like an excessive amount of kisses and excited barking.

"Zero is here?" Sheila asked. "That should keep him busy. Arthur loves dogs."

"He's getting big," Nathaniel commented as they settled down on the couch. "How old is he now?"

Sheila's smile was melancholy. "Four."

"Isn't his birthday just around the—"

"He's four years old!" she insisted. "I won't think of him as a minute older until I'm forced to."

Nathaniel laughed. "Time going too fast for you?"

"I'd stop it if I could," Sheila said. "I really would. How are you doing?"

"Ugh," Nathaniel replied. "Let's just say I'm not eager for time to stop. I'd like to speed it up by a decade or two and see how I feel then."

"Kelly?" she asked. When he looked surprised, she added, "Your mom told me."

"Of course she did. You're not here to lecture me about relationships, are you?"

Sheila's tone was ironic. "Sure, I'm practically an expert." Then she sighed. "All I can teach you is what you shouldn't do."

"I've already got that part down," Nathaniel said. "How's my brother?"

Sheila nibbled one of her nails. "Can we go for a walk? Please?"

"Of course. I'll get Arthur and Zero so they can—"

"No, just us. I'll make sure Star is watching them. Okay?"

"Yeah," Nathaniel said, feeling uneasy.

He went to put on his shoes and returned to find Sheila waiting for him at the front door. They strolled in silence for two blocks before she finally spoke.

"I know your brother was rough on you growing up—"

"Abusive," Nathaniel corrected. "Sorry, but I won't pussyfoot around it. He straight up abused me."

Sheila didn't challenge this. She merely nodded. "How did it start?"

"Slowly," he said. "Then it escalated. Why? Has Dwight been hitting you?"

She looked him in the eye. "Never. Not once. I wish that were the issue, because at least I can defend myself."

"Arthur," Nathaniel said, his voice hoarse. "He's hurting Arthur."

Sheila's face crumpled, but she managed to hold back the tears. "Dwight was always the disciplinarian, but lately he's been taking it too far. When he's drunk, I'm scared to leave Arthur alone with him. I won't even use the bathroom without taking him with me."

"Dwight's been hitting him?" Nathaniel demanded. "More than just spanking?"

"I found bruises."

Nathaniel spun around, heading back down the sidewalk.

"Where are you going?"

"To fucking kill him!"

Nathaniel felt hands on his arm, trying to hold him back. Sheila wasn't strong enough to stop him, but her next words halted him in his tracks.

"I don't need another violent hot head! I need your help!"

"What am I supposed to do?" Nathaniel said, turning to face her, his chest heaving. "I couldn't even help myself growing up! What am I supposed to do for your son?"

"I don't know," Sheila said, tears spilling from her eyes. "It's worse than you think. Someone called Child Protective Services. They're going to take Arthur away."

Nathaniel stared at her for a moment, then wrapped his arms around her until she stopped sobbing. "Tell me everything," he said. "We'll get this figured out, I promise. They won't take Arthur away."

Sheila collected herself and spoke. "One of his preschool teachers noticed. Arthur spilled juice all over himself, and they took his shirt off to get him cleaned up. Dwight had grabbed him too hard a couple of days before, so he had bruises. They asked me about it, and I told them the truth, that his father was too rough with him, and that it wouldn't happen again."

"You can't promise that," Nathaniel said. "Not with Dwight."

Sheila continued her story. "CPS showed up at our house later that week. The caseworker wanted to look around, so of course I let her. She seemed satisfied, but while we were talking, your stupid brother came home drunk. I'm not sure if she could tell. He mostly ignored us and went to the bedroom to pass out. Who does that? Who finds Child Protective Services in their home and goes to take a nap?"

"I'm sure she noticed," Nathaniel said. "At the very least she smelled it on him. I'm not trying to upset you more. We need to face the facts so we can plan."

Sheila nodded. "The caseworker asked for character witnesses. I gave her your number. Have you…?"

Nathaniel shook his head. "My phone hasn't been charged. Doesn't matter. I'll call her myself. What else?"

"She asked me to sign a release for Arthur's pediatric records, which I did."

"Will she find anything there?"

Sheila shook her head. "No."

"Good," Nathaniel said, because he hated the idea that Arthur had been hurt enough that he needed to see a doctor. "I won't help you hide what's going on. I hid my own abuse, and that only perpetuated it. You need to leave Dwight. It's the only solution."

"I'm ready," Sheila said. "I don't love him anymore, and I don't want him around Arthur."

"Then tell the caseworker that."

Sheila swallowed. "I'm scared. Of Dwight. Of what he'll do when he finds out. What if he hurts Arthur? I can't watch him all day. What if he takes him out of preschool and runs off somewhere?"

Nathaniel thought about it, neck muscles tensing. She had reason to be frightened because Dwight had always found underhanded ways to retaliate.

"What are we going to do?" Sheila asked.

"I'll talk to him," Nathaniel said. "I'll talk to Dwight. And then I'll talk to this caseworker."

Nathaniel consulted with one of Marcello's lawyers, familiarizing himself with a number of potential outcomes. Then he called the caseworker, Michelle Trout. She was helpful, her tones friendly, but what she said set off warning bells.

"Normally I'd be okay with conducting this interview over the phone, but for this particular case, I think it's best if we talk in person. Let's make an appointment."

Nathaniel agreed, which left him only two days to deal with Dwight. He didn't hesitate. That evening he ate a heavy meal, then went to Sheila's home. They lived in a trailer park, and even though the neighborhood wasn't stellar, she had done her best to provide a good home. Arthur was still feeling wary of men in general. Nathaniel tried to hug him anyway, and did the same to Sheila before entering the living room where his brother was watching a game.

"They're showing this on the big screen down at Shady's Pub," Nathaniel said.

Dwight sat upright, registering surprise. All his drinking was finally catching up with him. Dark bags sagged beneath the once brilliant blue eyes, and his physique, while still hefty enough to be intimidating, wasn't as firm. "What the hell are you doing here?"

"Bored out of my mind," Nathaniel replied. "Did you hear me? The same game is playing at Shady's. Grab a drink with me?"

Dwight narrowed his eyes.

"My treat," Nathaniel prompted.

A hungry grin spread across Dwight's face. "Let's go!"

Arthur was nowhere in sight as they left the mobile home. Sheila didn't ask where they were going or why. She probably assumed Nathaniel planned to talk some sense into his brother, but of course that wasn't possible. Talking *would* solve one problem tonight. Just not in the way she expected.

The drive over to Shady's was tense for Nathaniel, his instincts demanding he keep a constant eye on his brother. He couldn't do so while watching the road. Luckily he'd chosen a bar that was close. "Since when do you care about sports?" Dwight asked.

"I don't," Nathaniel admitted. "I love a good beer though, especially on tap."

"And that made you think of me?"

Nathaniel glanced over at him. "They say drinking alone is a sign that you have a problem. Easy solution, right? I don't know about you, but I plan on getting shitfaced."

Dwight narrowed his eyes. Then he barked laughter. "Let's get our drink on!"

Nathaniel relaxed a little once they were sitting at the bar. Having cold mugs in their hands gave them something to do, and his brother was still into the game, eyes on the screen. Nathaniel matched him drink for drink, glad he had eaten so much at dinner when Dwight suggested they do shots. Nathaniel kept them coming, managing to skip a few without his brother noticing. Not that it helped much. He wasn't used to drinking heavily, and his head was already swimming. He decided to make his move while still capable.

"I hear you've been a little rough on Arthur," he said.

Dwight turned his head, slowly, in Nathaniel's direction. "Is that what you've heard?"

"Yeah."

"Well, we don't want him growing up a pussy, do we?"

"You mean gay?" Nathaniel shrugged. "You beating the crap out of me didn't help much."

"Nope." Dwight knocked back another shot. "I did my best anyway."

"That's not why," Nathaniel said, gesturing to the bartender with an empty beer mug. "You couldn't have known I was gay when we were kids, but you still hurt me every chance you got. That used to puzzle me. For a while I thought there might not be a reason. Then I figured it out. I've known for years."

Dwight's bloodshot eyes bored into him. "Okay, genius. What's your big theory? What did they teach you up in Yale?"

"Actually it's what I learned in Warrensburg. Funny how Gramps is tall, and I'm tall, but you're not."

Dwight scoffed. "And? I'm still big enough to kick your ass!"

"We don't look much alike, do we? Like two sides of a coin. My hair is light, like everyone else in the family. Mom is blonde, dad has brown hair, even our grandparents on either side don't have black hair. Only you. I wonder where that comes from? You've got blue eyes—"

"Like Dad," Dwight said.

"But not like Mom. You look nothing like her at all. That must sting, because I know you love her. She's the only one in this family who hasn't given up on you, right? When's the last time Dad offered to get you a job or spent time alone with you?"

Dwight's lips curled back, revealing his teeth. "You really need to shut your mouth!"

"I figure you'd always known, deep down inside. Or maybe you still have a few fuzzy memories. Remember when Mom's hair used to be black? Except it wasn't her. Not my mom. Yours was a junkie who didn't want you, so she ran off and probably ended up dead in a gutter somewhere. It's true! Mom told me. *My* mom. You just wish she was yours. Hell, you wish you were me!"

The bartender had just set two full beer mugs on the counter when Dwight grabbed one and smacked Nathaniel across the face with it. That hurt. The mug didn't shatter, but it did tumble to the floor. Nathaniel nearly joined it, but he managed to grab the bar to stabilize himself. "When you look at Arthur," he struggled to say, blinking away the beer from his eyes, "when you see his blond hair, does it remind you of me?"

Dwight slugged him, his aim poor, his fist connecting with Nathaniel's forehead, but the force was enough to knock him off the stool. Relying on old habits one last time, Nathaniel balled up on the floor, trying to protect himself as Dwight started kicking. He could get up and fight back, but doing so tonight would ruin everything. Instead he prayed that someone in the bar was feeling heroic. He was in luck. Two guys hauled Dwight away from him, but his brother was twisting and growling, trying to break free. That is, until the bartender leveled a shotgun in his direction. Don't mess with Texas.

Nathaniel stayed where he was, listening to distant police sirens draw near. Even when the officers swarmed into the bar, he remained on the floor, not resisting when they handcuffed him too. "He just attacked me out of the blue," he said as one of the police officers shoved him into the police cruiser. His brother was placed in another. Nathaniel watched as the police spoke to different patrons. Eventually one of the officers returned to the cruiser where he waited and opened the door.

"How are you feeling?" the officer asked.

"Bruised."

"I mean are you sober enough that I can take off those cuffs?"

"Yes, sir."

"You're not going to try anything stupid?"

"No, sir." Nathaniel rubbed his wrists when he was free. "Thanks."

The officer looked him over. "You two are brothers?"

"Unfortunately."

"I'm guessing you don't want to press charges."

"I think it's best if I do," Nathaniel said.

The officer looked surprised. "You know he's out on parole, right? I'm not sure how the parole officer is going to handle this, but you'll only make it worse for him by pressing charges."

"Sounds better than him going home to beat up his kid again."

The officer spit on the ground, then searched his eyes as if assessing how serious Nathaniel was. "I've got two kids of my own."

"Then you understand what's best for them."

The officer nodded. "You'll have to take a ride down to the station with us."

"Whatever I've got to do."

Nathaniel sat in a small office, the walls covered with posters about child welfare or foster care. Most of them were happy and colorful, but he doubted many people who visited this place felt cheered up by them. He wasn't feeling so great himself. He sat across from a woman with long brown hair, high cheekbones, and an open expression. Michelle Trout. She looked him over, no doubt taking in the nasty bruise on one cheek and the red mark on his forehead caused by Dwight's ring.

"Okay," Michelle said, looking down at the papers on her desk. "Nathaniel Courtney." Then she looked up again, stared, and shook her head. "Sorry, but I have to ask. What's with all the..." She gestured at her own face with a pen.

"That's why I'm here," he said. "You want to know the truth about Arthur's situation? His father—my brother—is a violent man. He was abusive to me while we were growing up, and it sickens me to see signs of him treating his own son that way."

Michelle started scribbling notes, her expression somber. "When did you first become aware that Arthur was being abused?"

"Only after the incident you're investigating. The bruises on his arms. Nothing happened before that, because I know Sheila wouldn't have tolerated it."

"You'd be surprised what some mothers tolerate," Michelle said. "Just because she didn't tell you about other incidents, doesn't mean they didn't happen."

"Does she strike you as dishonest? Or as a bad mother?"

Michelle finished writing and glanced up. "No. She was truthful about what happened, or we would have taken Arthur with us that day. I'm more concerned about the father."

"Good, because she needs to stay with her son. She's a perfect mother. The only bad decision I've ever seen her make was marrying my brother."

Michelle nodded sympathetically. "Unfortunately, that can be a pretty big mistake and can have a detrimental effect on the child's environment. Our goal is to help keep children safe, and if one of the parents is a liability—"

"She's leaving him."

"Did she tell you this?"

"Yes."

"But that hasn't happened yet."

"Well, no."

Michelle took a deep breath. "Please don't take this the wrong way, but I hear promises like that all the time. People will say anything to keep from losing their children. Who could blame them? But it makes my job harder because I have to decide who is being truthful and who isn't. You're right that Sheila seems like an honest woman, but that doesn't mean she can't have a weak spot when it comes to her husband."

"Dwight is out of the picture," Nathaniel said. "You probably know he was out on parole. The other day he was arrested for attacking me, and I'm pressing charges. He hasn't gone before a judge yet, but he'll be sent back to prison. There's no chance that he won't."

Michelle held up a hand to stop him so she could keep taking notes. She had a lot to write down, so he turned his attention to the walls again. A framed degree caught his eye. Nathaniel squinted to read the issuing university's name. He chuckled quietly when he saw where it was from. Michelle raised her head.

"Sorry," he said. "Just noticed the degree. My grandparents live in Warrensburg. Small world."

"Small town," Michelle replied. "I grew up there."

"So did my mom."

"Really? What's her name?"

"Star Courtney. Actually back then her last name was Denton. Do you know her?"

Michelle shook her head. "Afraid not." She started writing again and paused. "Actually, that does sound familiar. Did she ever live in Kansas City?"

"Yeah, for a while."

Michelle spluttered laughter. "Yeah! Okay. I didn't know her personally, but I definitely heard *of* her."

Nathaniel scrunched up his face. "I don't like how that sounds."

"Not like that," Michelle said, waving away his concern. "She was sort of dating someone I knew, and that person was also dating... You know what? Ask her. I'm sure she'll get a kick out of it."

"You mean Victor?" Nathaniel asked, his heart thudding. "Victor Hemingway?"

Michelle's jaw dropped. "How in the world did you know that?"

"My mom still talks about him sometimes. You knew him too?"

Michelle regained her composure enough to answer. "Yes."

"What was he like?"

Michelle thought about it. "Cool. He was very cool."

"How so?"

She scrutinized him. "You're awfully interested in who your mom used to date."

"I'm really into our family history," he lied. "Victor was

obviously important to her, but she's biased, so I'm wondering if he really lives up to the legend or not."

"I guess so," Michelle said. "Yeah. People at school talked about him like he was a hero. Once he stood up to one of our worst teachers. More than that, actually. He shoved him up against the blackboard for giving other kids a hard time. He was definitely a legend in that regard. The Victor I knew was different. A little aloof, and very weird, but thoughtful. Always kind. Did things his own way. The sort of person you still think of as the years go by." She hesitated. "I'm afraid he's not with us anymore."

"Suicide," Nathaniel said. He felt the conversation should end there, out of respect. Then again, he wouldn't have another chance like this. "You described him as aloof. My mom said something similar recently, about how he was alone at the end of his life."

Michelle frowned. "We tried being there for him as much as possible, but he didn't make it easy. What happened still haunts me, but we all make our own decisions and have to live with the consequences. I've seen the end of more than one life, and without trying to sound morbid, we either die alone or we—" Her voice cracked a little, so she swallowed and tried again. "Or we die in the arms of the person we love most. I know what I would choose for myself."

"Yeah," Nathaniel said, dropping his gaze to the desk's surface. When he looked up again, Michelle was studying his face curiously. Perhaps she saw some shadow of Victor there.

"Is there something you're not telling me?"

"Probably," he said. "But we're not here to talk about me, are we?"

"No," Michelle said, considering her notes again. "Listen, I appreciate you being here, and for being so honest. I can only do the same. Men don't go to prison forever, not even for breaking their parole. Depending on the judge, Dwight might not even be sent back. If he is, I'd be surprised if he's not out within a year. I know you want to keep Arthur with his mother, but I need to know that he'll be safe. That's my job."

Nathaniel nodded. Getting smacked across the face with a beer mug had bought his nephew a little time, a brief period where he no longer had to fear his father. Nothing more.

* * * * *

We either die alone, or we die in the arms of the person we love most.
These words haunted Nathaniel during the next week. He knew
Michelle wasn't being literal, that most people died with someone
at their bedside or at least waiting outside the hospital room. Still,
the images remained with him. He imagined a future where Zero,
his mother, even Marcello were long since dead. Nathaniel would
be just another face in a nursing home, alone and awaiting the
inevitable. No family, no friends, no lover. Then he imagined the
alternative, him and Kelly growing old together, having to bury
his greatest love and dying of grief soon after. Both scenarios
were bleak, but one less so. With this in mind, when he returned
to Austin, he didn't go first to his apartment. He drove straight
to Kelly's house, put Zero on his leash, and walked with him to
the porch. He rang the bell, awaiting a burst of anger when the
door opened or maybe tears of joy. Instead he got a teenager who
crossed his arms over his chest.

"I told you not to fuck this up," Royal said. Then he dropped
the tough guy act so he could crouch and pet Zero.

"Is your brother here?" Nathaniel asked.

Royal glanced up. "What happened to your face?"

Nathaniel touched his bruised cheek self-consciously. "I got
into a philosophical disagreement."

"Oh."

"Is Kelly home?"

Royal shook his head. "He's gone."

"Where is he?"

Royal stood and looked him in the eyes. "Gone."

"Listen, I messed up, okay? I'm sorry, and I'd like to tell your
brother that."

"You'll have to find him first. He let us take him to the airport,
but he wouldn't tell us which flight he was getting on."

Nathaniel sighed. "If he doesn't want to see me, that's fine. I
don't blame him. You don't have to lie to me."

"He's *gone.*" Royal's expression wavered, anger trying to
banish the hurt. "I'm not happy about it either."

"You're serious?" Nathaniel swore. "Do you know when he'll
be back?"

Royal shook his head. "You can find him, right? You're good
at stuff like that. Kelly always told us that you can do anything."

"Yeah," Nathaniel replied bitterly. "I'm real clever."

He turned and tugged on Zero's leash, walking them back to the car. He drove one block and parked again. He felt like slamming his fist against the steering wheel, but instead leaned his head against it and tried not to cry. Royal was right. He had fucked it all up. Kelly had finally had enough. Maybe once he realized that Nathaniel was gone, he decided to do the same. Except he was stronger and wouldn't come running back after two weeks. He might not ever come back at all.

Nathaniel could find him. Marcello probably had a contact at the airport—a manager or even a flight attendant willing to do a little record searching, but loving Kelly meant respecting his decision, his right to be free. Nathaniel wouldn't force his way back in after forcing Kelly out. That wouldn't be fair. All Nathaniel could do was what he'd done before—look out for Kelly's best interests.

After considering his options, he drove to another house. This time a woman answered the door, but after some prompting, she went to fetch her son.

"Well, well," Layne said, leaning against the doorway seductively. "Does Kelly know you're here?"

"No," Nathaniel grunted.

"Looking for a rebound, are you?" Layne's flirtations ceased suddenly. "You know what? Kelly would kill me. Not worth the risk. Sorry!"

Nathaniel stopped the door from slamming shut. "You know he's gone, right?"

Layne nodded. "He came to one last meeting to say goodbye. It was heartbreaking and deliciously dramatic. He's got amazing style."

"You two are friends?"

"Not real close, but yes."

Not real close was perfect. If Nathaniel tried this with Royal or Bonnie, they would tell Kelly immediately. "Consider yourself his new best friend. You have his email address?"

"I might." Layne peered at him suspiciously. "What happened to your face? Is that from when Rico beat you up?"

"He didn't beat me up! This is from—" Nathaniel shook his head. "It's not important."

"Well it's working for you. Very macho. Maybe I should try

something similar. Of course that would require punching myself in the face. Or maybe a little creative makeup application. I was in drama at school and they have these things called a bruise wheel. This one girl I know tried using it to get her boyfriend in trouble. Lucky for him she totally overdid it and looked more like she'd been working in a coal mine."

Nathaniel took a deep breath, trying to remain patient. "I need a favor. Please."

Layne seemed to struggle internally. Then he nodded. "I'm all ears."

"I need you to stay in touch with Kelly. Frequently. Make sure he's okay. You don't have to tell me where he is or what he's doing unless he's in trouble. Then you let me know immediately."

"Creepy, but also kind of hot." Layne put his hands on his hips. "What's in it for me?"

"Money."

"That'll do!"

"And a paid trip to visit him a least once a year, just to make sure he's really doing okay."

Layne perked up. "Can I get some spy equipment? Like one of those pens with a camera inside? Or maybe a stylish pair of glasses!"

"With a camera inside?"

Layne shrugged. "Whatever."

"I'm serious," Nathaniel said. "I don't want you to spy on him. I just need you to be his guardian angel. Or help me to be. Please."

Layne nodded. "Okay. No problem. Gosh, I wish I had a guy like you in my life!"

Nathaniel grimaced. "Trust me, you really don't."

After making further arrangements with Layne, Nathaniel headed home, but when he got there he found the term no longer applied. The apartment felt empty. Even Zero was silent as they entered, tail not wagging as they walked from room to room, stopping in front of the bed. The side Kelly normally slept on was still unmade. Nathaniel was tempted to leave it that way, just so he would never forget. Then he shook his head, grabbed the sheets and covers, and ripped them off. Even after he had remade the bed with fresh linens, the memories made there remained. By now Zero should be leaping up on the mattress, panting happily as if Nathaniel had changed the sheets just to please him. Instead he lay on the floor with his head on his paws.

"Yeah, me too," Nathaniel said. "Come on. We're sleeping on the couch tonight."

Zero followed him out of the room, Nathaniel pausing in the doorway, hand on the light switch. He looked back at a space that used to be filled with love, laughter, sex, and late night conversations. Now, much like the feeling in his chest, the room was empty.

Interlude

Kelly set the empty wine glass on the table, shaking his head when Nathaniel offered a refill. Just as well. The bottle was nearly empty, the sky growing light outside. Nathaniel watched him carefully, not knowing how Kelly would react now that his story was mostly over.

"Layne," Kelly said, appearing amused. "Do you have any idea how many emails he sends me? Usually it's a funny animal photo with a meme and a little bit of text saying 'Oh, and by the way, how are you doing?'"

"Sorry," Nathaniel said, feeling anything but.

"It's fine. I like him, and he's not a good enough actor to fake liking me. His visits were fun, although now I know why he always clammed up when I mentioned you."

"Was that often?" Nathaniel asked.

"More often than was justified," Kelly murmured in response. "You should be ancient history by now. Forgotten."

Nathaniel swallowed. "Don't say that."

Kelly considered him. Then he sighed. "What happened to Sheila and Arthur? You didn't finish that story."

"I already told you what I did to help."

"Yes, but it sounded like the caseworker felt Arthur still needed to be taken away."

"We're getting off track," Nathaniel said. "I shouldn't have even mentioned that."

"I'd still like to know what happened."

"I'm sure they're fine. Now please, can we focus on us?"

Kelly pursed his lips. "Fine. Is there anything else I need to know?"

Nathaniel looked away. "Caesar."

"What about him?"

"He showed up in my life again a month or two back."

Kelly snorted. "And you told him to fuck off. Right?"

Nathaniel made eye contact. "Not exactly."

"If you think I want to hear about this, you're wrong. I haven't been celibate since we parted ways, but at least I have the decency not to—"

"It's important," Nathaniel interrupted. "It won't take long."

"Okay," Kelly said, leaning back. "Let's hear it."

Part Three
Austin, 2013

Chapter Twenty

Come back to me.

Every sleepless night spent staring at the ceiling, every slow day at work, Nathaniel sent out this silent prayer. His desperate wish. He never truly expected that prayer to be answered, but it was. By the wrong person.

"There's someone here to see you," said Paul, a heavy-set security guard who was forced to play receptionist at times.

"Get rid of them," Nathaniel suggested.

"You sure?" Paul hooked his thumbs in his belt. "He's a good lookin' fella."

"Another wanna-be model," Nathaniel said irritably. "Does he have a name?"

Paul snickered and nodded. "Caesar. Probably thinks he's the next Prince."

"Caesar Hubbard?" Nathaniel asked disbelievingly.

"That's the one."

He stood up, mouth agape, unable to formulate a response.

Paul gave him a knowing expression. "I'll send him up."

Nathaniel nodded, wishing he had a mirror to check himself in. He glanced around his office and started tidying his desk, then had a brief flash of Caesar's always-messy bedroom. Like he would care. Caesar wasn't here to do an inspection. Why was he here at all? Footsteps echoed in the hallway. Nathaniel was still standing. Sitting seemed too casual, so he remained where he was and watched the doorway until it was filled by the past.

Caesar, all grown up. His face was more defined, maturity having chased away any traces of adolescence. The cheekbones stood out more, accentuated by the casual beard, like he only bothered shaving once a week. Waves of dark hair spilled over his ears and halfway down his neck, the natural auburn highlights and brown skin hinting at days spent in the sun. His body was still lanky, arm muscles on display thanks to the loose tank top he wore. Amber eyes met Nathaniel's after looking him over, a white smile flashing a moment later.

"Surprised?"

"Only that it took this long," Nathaniel said, mustering false confidence. "Now I just have to decide what the hell I'm going to do with you."

"I figured you'd either punch me or hug me." Caesar chuckled. "You can guess which I prefer."

Nathaniel did neither. Instead he asked the most pressing question. "What are you doing here?"

"Oh. Your work address was the only one I could find, otherwise I would have showed up at your house unannounced. Nice setup." Caesar strolled closer, looking around. "You've got the coveted corner office. That means you're high on the food chain. What exactly do you do here?"

"Logistics."

"Like shipping?"

"Like everything. What are you doing here? In Austin."

Caesar read his expression. "Still mad at me?"

Nathaniel considered the question. "I don't know."

"Mind if I sit?"

Nathaniel didn't respond.

Caesar remained where he was. "I've been doing a lot of travelling lately, and when I realized I'd be passing through Austin, I thought it would be nice to see each other again. Catch up, compare notes, laugh about the past."

Nathaniel wasn't laughing. "How did you know where to find me?"

Caesar sighed. "I've been following you since the day you left. As much as possible anyway. Who doesn't have a Facebook account?"

"I like my privacy."

"There's no escaping Google Alerts. Your name pops up occasionally. Charity events and stuff like that. I'm proud of you."

"It's my job," Nathaniel said.

Caesar considered him, then shrugged. "I'm proud of you anyway. I might not be a part of your life anymore, but you never stopped being part of mine. I guess that sounds creepy, doesn't it?"

Nathaniel thought of Kelly and averted his eyes. "Not really."

"We were young," Caesar said. "I know it didn't seem like it at the time. I felt so grown up then, but looking back now, I was just a kid. One who made some very stupid mistakes. I'd like to apologize for them, preferably over dinner. Tonight?"

Nathaniel shook his head. "I need to go home and cook. I've got mouths to feed."

Caesar stiffened. "Oh! I didn't know. Uh..."

"Just one mouth, aside from my own."

"A kid?"

"A dog."

Caesar visibly relaxed. "You're messing with me, aren't you?"

"A little." Nathaniel sat, raising an eyebrow to stop Caesar from doing the same. Then he jotted down his address on a scrap of paper and pushed it to the very edge of the desk. "Steak dinner at my house. Tonight. Around seven. Your treat. We can grill in the yard. Bring extra for the dog."

"Sounds good." Caesar stepped forward to take the paper. He was staring at Nathaniel. "You look amazing. Better than ever."

Nathaniel managed to keep his expression neutral. "I've got work to do."

"Okay. See you soon."

Nathaniel remained still until Caesar left the room. Then he turned off the computer monitor, considering himself in the faint reflection. Soon after, he grinned. "Better than ever, huh?" Feeling smug, Nathaniel busied himself with work, already watching the clock.

Nathaniel returned home early to take a shower and put on clothes too dressy for grilling. Then he straightened up the apartment, trying to ignore Zero's questioning expression. "We're having someone over for dinner, that's all." When this didn't satisfy the dog, he realized that Zero probably needed to go for a walk. After taking care of the dog's needs, he gathered some plates, utensils, and condiments, tossed them into a box, and went outside.

Caesar was just getting out of his car as Nathaniel and Zero came down the stairs. He took off his sunglasses, considering the apartment complex. "Almost missed the place," he said with a wry grin. "Figured you'd have a mansion to go along with that corner office."

"It's still being built," Nathaniel said. "Where's the food?"

Caesar went around to the passenger side to fetch loaded plastic bags. This got Zero's attention, who started leaping around his legs. Caesar's expression wasn't amused. He lifted the bags up high, grimacing down at the dog.

"Zero," Nathaniel said. "Come here."

The dog grudgingly obeyed. They walked to the grilling area on one side of the building. Nathaniel had already filled the steel grill box with charcoal before taking his shower. He set about lighting it while Caesar unpacked the grocery bags onto the picnic table. The clinking of bottles attracted his attention.

"Check it out," Caesar said, hand resting on a six-pack. "I actually bought *you* beer for a change. Bet you never thought that would happen!"

"You owe me way more than that," Nathaniel said.

"Then consider this a down payment."

"I'm ready to deposit one now."

"Coming right up!"

Their banter remained light as they drank and grilled the steaks. Only when they were seated did Nathaniel start asking questions.

"Did you graduate from Yale?"

"By the skin of my teeth," Caesar said. "Got a cushy job with my father's company and wasted no time ruining it all."

"What happened?"

Caesar jabbed at his steak. "I'd rather not talk about it."

Nathaniel wasn't okay with that, but he had more pressing questions. "What about you and Rebecca?"

Caesar looked up in surprise. "Ancient history. We weren't a couple or anything. We went our separate ways after you left."

"What a waste."

"Huh?"

Nathaniel frowned. "Considering how much was ruined by what happened, you two should have made something out of the mess. Rebecca could have finally had the boyfriend she always wanted."

Caesar shook his head. "We couldn't look at each other without thinking of you and how guilty we felt. It never would have lasted. So what about you? Anyone special?"

"Yeah," Nathaniel answered. "Someone really special."

"And? Where have you hidden him?"

"He's not here anymore. I let him get away."

"Sorry to hear that. What was his name?"

"None of your fucking business."

Caesar nodded thoughtfully. "Is that a French name? Sounds French to me."

Nathaniel took a swig of his beer. Then he laughed.

Caesar joined him. "Maybe you're right. When everything falls apart, something new should rise from the ashes."

"You're talking about us."

"Why not?"

Nathaniel snorted. "Not a chance in hell. If that's your goal, you should have brought a keg, not a six-pack."

"Duly noted," Caesar said. "You're not far off the mark. I wasn't just passing through Austin. My life fell apart when my parents cut me loose. They're not pleased. Remember when you used to tutor me? How much emphasis they put on my education? They've been grooming me to take over my father's business for as long as I can remember. I feel like I've been studying for the same damn test for most of my life. Now I've finally taken it and failed. No money, no support, no job. They're done with me."

"That's called being an adult," Nathaniel said. "You think my parents still pay my bills? Or that I would expect them to provide me with work if I lost my job?"

"No, of course not. But it's more than that. I made a mistake, and instead of giving me another chance, they replaced me. You remember Peter? My little brother? Now he's—" Caesar sighed. "You know what? None of that matters. I don't want the stupid job because for the first time in my life, I'm finally free to make my own decisions. Yeah, they hurt my feelings, but even I recognize that this is for the best. So that's what I've been doing—exploring what I want to do with my life. Or who I want in it." Caesar leaned forward, his expression earnest. "I drove all the way from Connecticut just to see you."

Nathaniel shoved aside his empty plate, mulling over his feelings. He was tempted. Caesar was handsome, perhaps even more so now. They had a history together, old affections lingering just beneath the surface. And yet, that history also made this an impossible situation. "I'm sorry," he said, shaking his head. "It ended when it ended."

"Why?" Caesar asked, not seeming surprised.

"You know why."

"Seriously, say it out loud. I know where this is going because I've given it a lot of thought." Caesar leaned back. "Fine, I'll say it if you're too polite. You don't want to be with me because I'm a slut."

"That's not what I was thinking."

"Those might not be the exact words, but I bet they were close."

"You're not a slut, because with you it wasn't just about sex." Nathaniel looked him up and down. "You're more like a hustler, but one who's after love instead of money. All the love you can get. You've got a hustler's heart."

Caesar grinned. "I like the sound of that. And you're absolutely right. I'm done denying it. Love is my vice and I'm not very discriminating. Other guys have such a specific type, a whole list of qualifications they go through before letting anyone near. She's gotta be blonde or skinny or fat or rich or dumb or smart. One of my roommates in college broke up with his girlfriend because she didn't like hockey. She was the sweetest thing and willing to put up with his dumb ass, but for him it was a deal-breaker. I'm not saying I don't have standards, but obviously mine are a lot more generous than most."

"That's one way of putting it," Nathaniel muttered.

"I know it's no excuse for what I did. Being able to buy and eat all the candy you want doesn't mean you should. That's something you learn as an adult, and I wish I had understood it back then. I've been around the block. I've fallen in love with all kinds of people and had a lot of bad relationships. A few good ones too. Some play it safe and stick with the first person to love them back, but I was young and dumb enough to risk everything. One benefit of all that experience is clarity. Out of everyone I've been with—all the people I've fallen in love with—none of them compare to you. You're the one."

What a speech. Despite wanting to hate it, Nathaniel felt flattered, longing for carefree days spent in a lover's arms. In an instant he could see the entire story, two people falling in love when they were young, going their separate ways as adults and venturing out into the world, only to come back together when they realized they had it right the first time. How beautiful that would be. A happy ending at last. Caesar's words carried the weight of truth. When the right love was found, when that special person was finally discovered, no one else could compare. That's exactly how Nathaniel felt. Just not about Caesar.

"If you're not going to finish your steak," Nathaniel said, "you should give it to Zero. He didn't eat much this morning."

Caesar looked as though he had been slapped. Then he placed his plate on the ground. They finished their last beers in silence.

"It's chilly," Caesar said, rubbing the bare skin of his arms.

"Yup." His heart maybe, but Nathaniel's body still felt heat. "Wanna go inside? I've got a couple more beers in the fridge."

Caesar chuckled. "I don't know if I can keep up with you. I'm not in college anymore."

That was a yes. Before long they were in the living room. Nathaniel handed Caesar a beer but remained standing as he faced the couch. Caesar sat there, looking around and taking in the details. Zero was on the cushion next to him, appearing slightly puzzled by his presence.

"Nice place," Caesar said, nodding his approval.

"It's enough for a guy and his dog. You still living in Connecticut?"

"Yeah. I have an apartment there a little bigger than this one."

"A little?"

Caesar grinned. "The bedroom closet is bigger than this place. I'm not bragging because it's a burden. I already gave notice. I can't really afford it."

"What's the plan?"

Caesar blinked. "Drive to Texas and win back the love of my life. That's not a plan?"

Nathaniel shook his head, sitting on the edge of the oak coffee table. "Failing that, what are you going to do? I know this will come as a shock, but you'll need a job. Assuming you want to eat."

"Yeah, yeah," Caesar said. "Always gotta remind me of the small details, huh?"

"Yup."

"I'm sure the stamp of approval from Yale will land me something. First I want to figure out where to settle down. I don't even have a hotel."

"Which implies you thought you wouldn't need one."

"I was hoping." Caesar grinned, but when the gesture wasn't returned, his shoulders slumped. "I don't know what I'm going to do with my life. Having ruined everything can be liberating, but also crippling. I'm always tempted to call my dad, beg for another chance. He wouldn't respect that. Hell, I wouldn't respect myself. It's just hard walking the tightrope when you know the net is no longer there. That's another reason I've been thinking of you. Not because I'm looking for someone to take care of me. I'm not. But I always felt safe with you. Excuse me."

Caesar left for the restroom. Nathaniel could hear him blowing his nose, and when he returned, his eyes were watery. Not surprising considering he had exposed his heart at the picnic table, only for Nathaniel to brush it off and into the dirt. That had to hurt. When Caesar sat again, Nathaniel joined him at the other end of the couch. Zero was a chaperone between them, which was good, because as the night wore on and they became increasingly intoxicated, Nathaniel's judgment passed out before he did.

"You can't find a hotel in your condition," he said.

Caesar shrugged. "I'll call a taxi."

"And tell them what? You don't know where to go. Do hotels let drunk people check in?"

Caesar leered. "I'm going to assume they don't because I like where this is going."

Nathaniel pretended not to pick up on this. "You could crash here."

"I saw your big ol' bed," Caesar responded. "It would be a shame if it went to waste."

Those words kicked Nathaniel's judgment in the stomach, causing it to stir. "I tend to sleep on the couch these days."

"Really? Why?"

Because the bed seemed twice as big and empty without Kelly in it. Even after all this time. Squeezing onto the couch with Zero and waking up with a sore neck was easier than facing old memories. "You take the bed," Nathaniel said. "The sheets are clean. I'll sleep out here."

"We can share," Caesar suggested. "It's not like we haven't before."

"It's fine." Nathaniel stood. "I have to go to work tomorrow, so…"

Caesar didn't move. "Are you sure? I feel like I'm imposing. I can take the couch."

"Take the bed. I'll wake you up for breakfast."

"Okay." Caesar finally stood. "Thanks. I really appreciate it."

Nathaniel nodded, made sure he had everything he needed, and felt like he couldn't breathe. Not until the bedroom door was shut with Caesar safely on the other side.

* * * * *

The morning wasn't full of temptation or confused feelings. All the mutual hangover left room for was aspirin, long showers, and a plate of eggs and hash browns. Only afterwards did they feel capable of speech, but Nathaniel had an appointment and Caesar had places to be, so they didn't say much before going their separate ways.

Sweet-talking a client over coffee, visiting a location shoot involving three sisters who all thought they were more famous than Kate Moss, and meeting with one of the company lawyers because a photographer was suing for tripping over his own feet while on the job. Only as the work day came to an end did Nathaniel have time to consider the previous evening, leaving him nostalgic for a time when he would have tumbled into bed with Caesar regardless of the consequences.

As it turned out, he would have another chance. When Nathaniel arrived home after work, Caesar's car was in the parking lot. So was the man himself, hopping out with a smile and opening the trunk to show what he had there. "You bought a keg," Nathaniel said, staring at it.

Caesar grinned shamelessly. "That's what you said it would take."

"After last night, it took me this long to feel human again."

"Hair of the dog," Caesar said. "Best cure there is. Besides, it's Friday night."

Which was usually Foreign Film Friday, as Nathaniel liked to call it, but he wasn't about to admit that. Instead he helped Caesar get the keg upstairs. They spent the evening getting drunk and swapping stories, delving into their past and laughing over the stupidest of details. Caesar made multiple trips to the bathroom, blowing his nose and returning with red eyes each time. They ended up in bed together too, but fully dressed and above the covers, having passed out before anything could happen.

Caesar seemed just as watery-eyed during a late breakfast the next day, so Nathaniel offered to show him around Austin. While this seemed to cheer him up, it turned out to be a bad idea because then Caesar started talking about moving to Austin permanently. On Sunday they even visited a few apartment complexes and some open houses, just to get a feel for the market. That night they worked on the keg again, although with more restraint since Nathaniel needed to work the next day.

The pattern repeated itself. Nathaniel would return home, Caesar would be waiting there, often with a bag of groceries and the promise of a home-cooked meal. Then they would drink and talk, and Nathaniel would struggle with temptation. He tried to combat this by jacking off in the shower each morning, hoping to make himself uninterested in sex, but he discovered how ineffective this was on Thursday morning.

He was straightening up the living room, fluffing the couch cushions and putting them back where they belonged. When he looked up, Caesar was standing there completely naked. Drops of water dripped down his bronze skin, running along the curve of each thin muscle. His body was familiar, although the hair on his chest was denser. His cock was still hanging but at least half-hard, because it looked huge. Or maybe that was caused by the heat from the shower, steam still curling off him. Either way, he was demonstrating more self-control than Nathaniel, who was already so hard that his dick was straining painfully against his jeans.

"I couldn't find a towel," Caesar said.

Nathaniel didn't bother with a witty response. He simply closed the distance between them, letting the wet skin press against his dry clothes as he took Caesar's head in his hands. Then they kissed, the feel of his lips, the smell of his skin—even freshly washed—bringing back a chain of memories: holding each other to stay warm when lost in the woods, staying up all night in Caesar's room just so they could talk, getting drunk in Nathaniel's crappy dorm room while Mr. Jung wasn't there, shouting in a Tex-Mex parking lot where it had all gone terribly wrong. They had a history, both good and bad. And while their time together had a lot of good, the bad had outweighed it enough for Nathaniel to move halfway across the country, give up his college plans, and start from scratch. The bad had even seeped into his next relationship, poisoning it. The bad had cost him much, but he had survived it all. A job, a little apartment, and a furry companion. That felt like a lot. Nathaniel had moved on. But now he was backtracking, making the struggle seem pointless. If he and Caesar were going to end up together again, Nathaniel might as well have stayed at Yale.

He broke the kiss to look down at a mouth-watering cock at full salute. Then he sighed. "Wait here."

"Okay," Caesar said. "Hurry."

"I will." Nathaniel went to the hall closet, grabbed a folded towel, and tossed it to Caesar. Then he went into the kitchen. "Ready for breakfast? I've got some feta and olives. Thought I'd work it into an omelette."

"You're kidding."

"I'm dead serious. I had something similar at a hotel in Athens. You'll love it, trust me."

"That's not what I'm talking about," Caesar said, following him into the kitchen.

Nathaniel turned to look him in the eye, no longer interested in his body. Okay, pretending he was no longer interested. "I know exactly what you're talking about. Get dressed."

Caesar turned without another word and walked away. When he returned fully dressed, he sat in the living room until Nathaniel put two plates on the table and one on the floor. Then Caesar joined him, eyes watery and red. He kept sniffing too.

"Look," Nathaniel said. "I know you're going through a lot, and us being around each other is confusing as hell. It's probably not a good idea—"

"I disagree."

"—*but*, you've got to stop feeling sorry for yourself. No more running off to the bathroom to cry. You got yourself into this mess. You can get yourself out."

"Crying?" Caesar asked.

"Yes. It's pretty obvious. I've heard you in the bathroom blowing your nose."

"Because you don't have any boxes of tissues. It's toilet paper or nothing."

Nathaniel set down his fork and looked at Caesar. The red eyes, the way he was breathing through his open mouth like his nose was stuffed up. Did he have a cold? But he seemed fine normally. Only when they were at home did he seem to—

Zero finished his plate and pressed against Caesar's leg to get his attention, hoping for more.

"You're allergic to dogs," Nathaniel said.

"Most animals," Caesar said with a sniff. "The furry kind, at least. Did you forget?"

"I thought you were upset!"

"I am!" Caesar said. "But I'm not crying. Jesus, is that the only reason you've let me stick around this long?"

No, it wasn't. If Nathaniel was honest, he kept inviting Caesar in because he was increasingly tempted. Even now, despite knowing that he didn't want to date Caesar, he still wanted to have sex with him. Immediately. On the kitchen table. Nathaniel would bend him over it, runny nose and all, and pound the living hell out of him.

"You look angry," Caesar said. "Or horny. I never could tell the difference."

"This isn't working out. You need to leave."

Caesar's jaw went slack. "Then why did you just kiss me?"

"Because I'm an idiot. Eat up. I need to go to work. Find somewhere else to sleep tonight." Nathaniel concentrated on his food. Caesar joined him, halfheartedly consuming a few bites before surrendering the rest to Zero. Nathaniel ignored this, putting on his shoes and collecting what he needed for work. Then he waited by the entrance until Caesar joined him, a hand grabbing his before it could open the door.

"I love you," Caesar said. "I mean it."

Nathaniel nodded. "I love you too. But it doesn't change anything." He shook his hand free and escorted Caesar outside. Then Nathaniel got into his car and drove away.

He knew this wouldn't be the end of it, so he left work early that day and went home to pick up Zero. The dog was thrilled. Less so when he saw their destination. The groomers.

"Do you have an appointment?" the receptionist asked.

"No," Nathaniel replied, "but I'm willing to pay double. Oh, and there's something else I need too."

An hour later he was home again with a trash bag full of fur clippings. He tossed them everywhere—the living room, the kitchen, the bathroom, and especially on the bed. "Hair of the dog. Best cure there is," Nathaniel explained to Zero. "Let's see if it can cure us of an unwanted guest."

When Caesar arrived at his door that evening, as expected, Nathaniel stepped aside to let him in. Ten minutes later, they were outside the door again, Caesar's eyes red and squinty.

"If you start showing up at my work," Nathaniel said, "I'll have a suit made from his fur. Hell, I'll start rolling in his hair every morning while still wet from the shower if that's what it takes."

"The visual is sort of hot," Caesar said, sniffing like mad.

Nathaniel rolled his eyes. He ducked inside for some napkins, handing them to Caesar. "Come on. I'll walk you to your car."

They loitered in the parking lot until Caesar recovered somewhat. He still looked miserable, which made it easier to avoid hugging him or saying something sappy. "I've been where you are before," Nathaniel said. "You feel like the people you love have let you down, and maybe they have, but your happiness was never their responsibility. Figure out what you really want. That doesn't include me. I've moved on. It's time you did too."

"Nathaniel—"

He turned and walked back toward the apartment, unwilling to exchange any more words or make any more memories together. What they had together had died a long time ago. Now it was finally time for it to be buried.

An invitation. A long rectangle of glossy card stock. A sepia image of a broken-down car mere yards from a sign that read *Detroit City Limit*. The photo was exceptional, but the name on the back really caught his eye. Kelly Phillips. Nathaniel turned the card over and over, even carried it with him from room to room. He kept rereading the information on the back, despite having it memorized. A photography exhibition at a local gallery, the date and time, and a brief biography of the artist. That was all. No personal message, no hand-scrawled words. Nathaniel didn't know what this was about, but finding the man who did wasn't difficult.

"What the hell?" he demanded, tossing the invitation on Marcello's desk.

His boss glanced at it before sliding it back toward him. "The Eric Conroy Gallery is run by Tim Wyman. He chooses which artists are exhibited and handles invitations. Perhaps you should speak with him."

Nathaniel plunked down into a chair. "You saw the artist's name?"

"Of course."

"And you expect me to believe you have nothing to do with this?"

Marcello placed a hand over his chest. "I gave you my word! Since that time have I ever tried steering your ship toward more romantic waters? Have I even suggested you take a stroll along the beach?"

"No. You haven't."

"Precisely." Marcello leaned back in his chair and considered him. "Were I in your situation—one of the greatest loves of my life inviting me to see his art—I would leap at the opportunity! A public space isn't ideal for getting—ah—reacquainted, but I never let that stop me before. Will you be attending?"

Nathaniel shook his head, but said, "How could I refuse?"

The week before the gallery opening was pure stress. Nathaniel worked out every other day, feeling presumptuous for doing so, and hours were lost at work imagining scenario after scenario. In many of these daydreams, Kelly ran to him and gave him a hug, refusing to let go again. In others Kelly was cordial, introducing his husband to Nathaniel before moving on to other guests.

No matter what the evening brought, Nathaniel intended to look his best. The day before the exhibition he got a haircut. He also bought a new shirt for the tuxedo he planned to wear. It was too formal for a gallery opening, but Kelly had always liked seeing him wear one, calling him James Bond and making jokes about concealed weapons. Nathaniel made sure his shoes were polished, his teeth flossed and brushed. After showering, he glanced in the mirror and decided to leave the scruff, remembering how he would sometimes use it to tickle different parts of Kelly's body. Then he dressed and, pulse racing, drove across town to the gallery.

He made sure he wasn't the first to arrive, walking slowly along the sidewalk and peering in through the windows. Quite a crowd had gathered already. The main room of the gallery was full, as were the two wings off to each side. He spotted Kelly, who was grinning like an idiot while talking to a handful of young women clearly enamored with him. They weren't alone. Nathaniel stood and stared at his former boyfriend. He looked fantastic, like not a day had gone by. Hell, he positively glowed, which only confirmed that Kelly had been fine during their time apart—had thrived even, judging from his current success. The invitation must have been courtesy and nothing more. Nathaniel had decided to leave when Kelly looked away from his conversation and scanned the room with a flicker of disappointment.

No matter how innocent Kelly's intentions were in inviting him here, Nathaniel supposed it would be rude not to make an appearance. One more insult added to all the injury he'd already caused. With this in mind, he entered the gallery. One of the waiters recognized him—the same staff that was used for Marcello's charity events—and made sure he was offered a glass of champagne. He took one to appear casual. Seeing that Kelly was still occupied, he began browsing the photographs.

Hungrily. Nathaniel had relied solely on Layne's reports to tell him where Kelly had travelled and what he'd been doing, but now he could see it all for himself. Rural farms of the Midwest, animals crowded into their pins. Children playing hopscotch on a city sidewalk, protesters marching in the background. A car show attended by people wearing sweatpants and logo-emblazoned T-shirts, a stark contrast to the polished perfection of the vehicles on display. Nathaniel experienced it all through Kelly's artistic vision. He moved to one of the wings, lost in the imagery. The photos were exceptional. He had known Kelly was talented, but now that skill had refined and matured. The photos echoed passion, an extension of Kelly's personality—emotional and raw.

He was wandering toward the main room when instinct caused him to look to his left. Their eyes met just before he passed through the doorway, Nathaniel pausing there and leaning against it for support, glad he could no longer be seen. The experience had been too intense, a fleeting moment of contact after an eternity of nothing. He waited, expecting Kelly to come after him, to seek confrontation. When this didn't happen, Nathaniel forced himself to start moving again. Kelly was in the main room, cornered by someone with a camera. A fellow enthusiast? No, a reporter, one who would keep him busy.

Nathaniel walked to the opposite wing and browsed more of the photos, his attention torn away occasionally by people he knew. Tim Wyman, who seemed to be negotiating a sale. Marcello, who was encouraging one of the waiters to sneak a glass of champagne. Or two, as it turned out. And William, the guy who had left Kelly broken-hearted. His presence here was unexpected. And unwelcome, considering the implications. Evidently the interview was over because Kelly was at William's side, giving him a tour, confirming what Nathaniel had feared. Kelly had come home and decided to make peace, tie up all his loose ends, including old flames. He wasn't seeking reunion. He was seeking closure. Nathaniel turned away, spotting one of his own loose ends in the crowd.

Jason Grant. Always ushering in the end and proving that nothing lasts forever. Nathaniel's relationship with Caesar. Interrupted by Jason. Twice. Kelly's relationship with William. Ended by Jason. Maybe him being here now was proof that their stories had finally come to an end. One last goodbye before they all went their separate ways.

Or maybe not all of them, because Jason glanced in William's direction, eyes shining. Then he noticed Nathaniel staring and offered a smile. They had never spoken about the past, never admitted their shared history. Pretending seemed pointless now. Why deny the war when standing amidst the ruins? Nathaniel moved through the crowd to reach him.

"I remember you," he said.

Jason nodded. "I've been a waiter for a few of Marcello's parties. We talked once, when, uh—"

"Marcello let you borrow one of his rooms," Nathaniel supplied. "I remembered you back then too."

Jason froze. "What do you mean?"

Nathaniel chuckled. "I knew who you were. And I'm pretty damn sure you remembered me." He offered his hand. "We both survived the Hubbards and their son. That much we have in common."

Jason took his hand gingerly and shook. "Why didn't you say anything back then?"

"And ruin your fairytale night with your lover?" He glanced over to where William was. "It's nice to see you two still together. Gives me renewed faith in love."

"Yeah. Thanks." Jason squirmed a little. "This might be a weird question, but do you hate me?"

Nathaniel put on his best grumpy face. "Why, just because you almost ruined my chances of getting back together with Caesar? Or because you were instrumental in him getting caught by his parents again, making it harder for us to see each other? Or maybe because you slept with him, even when you knew he and I were together?"

Jason was breaking out in a sweat. "That about sums it up."

Nathaniel dropped the act and clapped him on the shoulder. "All water under the bridge. In fact, what you did made it easier to finally leave the guy. I even thought of you when Caesar showed up last month."

"Last month?" Jason said incredulously. "Wait, you've seen him recently?"

Nathaniel nodded. "He rolled into town four or five weeks ago. Had a big sob story about his parents cutting him off and needing a place to stay. I was dumb enough to let him, but after a few weeks of him trying to get back in my pants, I decided I'd had enough. Nothing he could say or do would ever make me take him back. Not after what happened in college."

Jason shook his head. "Wasn't Caesar living on the East Coast?"

"Yeah. He said he came all the way to Austin just to be with me. Said the same thing on my voicemail the other night. I don't think I deleted it." Nathaniel dug out his phone and started pushing buttons. "Want to hear his voice again?"

A few seconds later, Caesar was speaking with a slight slur. *I came all this way just to be with you. I'm still here, and it's not working out, but I can't bring myself to leave. Please. Just call me back. Talk to me. I know we can make this work.*

Nathaniel watched Jason's face as he listened, expecting an eye roll. Instead Jason appeared angry, like he'd heard the exact same story. Recently. "You've seen him too, haven't you?"

Jason frowned. "Where do you think he's been staying?"

"Oh," Nathaniel said. "I didn't realize—"

Jason spun around and stalked toward the exit. Nathaniel stared after him a moment, then looked to William and Kelly, who were deep in conversation. Did that mean Jason and William were no longer together? Or that Kelly and William were an item again? The only certainty was that Caesar was still a hustler looking for his next trick. Thank goodness Nathaniel had kicked him out before making the same mistakes. It wasn't too late to prevent another. He'd been a fool to think Kelly still wanted him. Clearly that wasn't the case.

Nathaniel took a cue from Jason and escaped through the exit, breathing in the fresh air as he headed down the sidewalk. He realized he was still carrying the glass of champagne, but soon found someone to hand it to.

"Are you heading to the office?" Marcello said, puffing from his effort to catch up. "Oh, what an absolute disaster!"

"What are you talking about?"

"The mascara contract!" Marcello brandished his phone. "Didn't you get the message?"

Nathaniel peered at the screen and tried to read, which wasn't easy while Marcello was waving it around. "Just tell me what it says," he snarled in frustration.

"The French are backing out. I think we've been sniped by a different firm."

"That's a seven-figure contract!" Nathaniel shouted, his panic rising along with his voice. "I worked my ass off to secure that deal! What happened?"

"I don't know, but we've got to act now. I'll say my goodbyes and meet you in the office right away."

"It's the middle of the night."

"Not in France, it isn't! Soon it will be morning there, and I suggest we commit ourselves to staying up and getting this fixed. Have you been drinking? Should I send for a car?"

"No," Nathaniel said, handing him the champagne glass and swearing. "And if I was drunk, this news would have sobered me up. What a fucking night."

"I'm afraid it's just beginning. I'll see you soon."

Nathaniel nodded and strode toward his car. At least this crisis would help chase thoughts of Kelly from his mind. During the drive he tried to recall every relevant telephone conversation and email, wondering if something important had been lost in translation. Nathaniel was still shaking his head in disbelief when he stepped into the elevator and punched in the code for Marcello's office. When the doors opened, he strolled in to turn on the computer and stopped short.

Low lighting, candles, and a bottle of wine chilling on the table next to two wrapped presents. A trap. Part of him felt relieved, those seven figures returning to his spreadsheets. Marcello had only lied to get him here. Nathaniel spun around, expecting to find Kelly tied up in one corner. He wasn't there. Not yet. The elevator was no longer responding; Marcello controlling it remotely—a feature of the security system Nathaniel had installed himself. He jabbed at the button anyway before turning to face a camera in one corner of the room.

"It won't work," he said. "If you have any love for me, you'll let me go right now, because this is going to kill me."

The camera stared back stoically. Nathaniel groaned and went to the table, picking up the bottle of wine and immediately recognizing the vintage, the very same he and Kelly had shared when they first met. Then he fingered the two presents, the card of the first addressed to him in Marcello's elegant handwriting.

What is thought lost can still be recovered. The past can be a gateway to the future. I do this for love, with love. Marcello.

He was wrong. Nathaniel wished he wasn't, but the past no longer belonged to this world. He tore at the wrapping paper to find a black-and-white photo, a sliver of time that would remain trapped forever. The two young men running beside each other couldn't be reanimated, color restored to their skin, nor would the dog leap from the frame still wearing that gleeful expression. Zero was at home in an empty apartment. That was the world of today. Nathaniel opened the tag of the other present, his fear confirmed when he saw Kelly's name.

Nathaniel set the framed photo on the table and covered it with the wrapping paper. Then he patrolled the room, blowing out candles, turning off the subtle music, and cranking up the lights. He called a technician to get the elevator operational again. While waiting he took off his tuxedo jacket, undid his bowtie, and rolled up his sleeves. An hour later he finally accepted he was stuck here and sent a text message for someone to take care of Zero because Kelly was probably too smart to fall for one of Marcello's tricks. And if he did? Nathaniel stopped pacing to consider the possibility. If Kelly did show up, if there was hope…

But what could he say to make amends? How could he explain his actions, the lifetime of events that had led to one monumental mistake? He could try. One last time. Tell Kelly the truth. About everything. When he heard the elevator motor whir, bringing someone to the top floor, Nathaniel braced himself to do just that.

Chapter Twenty-one

"That's everything," Nathaniel said. "My whole stupid story." His mouth was dry, so he drained the last of the wine directly from the bottle. He considered the sunlight pouring through the window, then looked at Kelly, who was watching him patiently. "I fucked up three years ago. I made one of the worst decisions of my life, and while I don't think I can ever atone for my sins, please know that I've been suffering. I've been in a hell of my own creation. I probably deserve to spend the rest of my life there. But if there's any chance that you can forgive me…"

Kelly covered his eyes with one hand, rubbing them wearily. Then he took a deep breath and got to his feet. "I'm sorry," he said, shaking his head.

Nathaniel felt dizzy. "What do you mean? What are you sorry for?"

"I don't know," Kelly said. "For wasting your time, even though neither of us chose to be here. I should have stopped you sooner because I knew it wouldn't be enough."

"Not enough?"

"Not enough," Kelly repeated, his cool demeanor breaking. "You were right about Cancún, when you realized we were both damaged. We weren't made for each other, but we were broken in the same way, which is close enough. You were cheated on. You were betrayed. So was I! I'm sorry that your brother is a despicable person, but that abuse made you a survivor. That's something else we have in common. I lost my leg and with it my sense of security and a lot of my self-esteem. Our losses might not be the same, but you know what I would never do? I would never *ever* sit here and tell you that William is the reason we couldn't be together or that losing my leg somehow justified me turning my back on you. I never would have pushed you away, Nathaniel. Never. No matter the reason. But you… You threw me out of your life!"

"I'm sorry."

"So am I, and I wish I'd known your story back then because I've had three years to imagine what could possess you to do such a thing. I kept putting myself in your shoes. What nightmare would I have to go through to make me turn away from the greatest love of my life? I kept trying to find a single reason and kept coming up empty because none of them were good enough. I couldn't find any justification. Now I know that you couldn't either. You didn't want to get hurt, you didn't want to hurt me, but you ended up doing both. Cheating on me would have hurt less because I would have gotten over it. I could have villainized you and made you one more challenge to overcome. Instead I spent the last three years doubting myself and wondering what I did wrong."

"Kelly." Nathaniel stood and took his hands, holding on when he tried to pull away. "You're hurting right now. I know how that feels. I'm hurting too, and I want it to fucking stop. I can't take it any more. So please, how can we fix this?"

"We can't," Kelly said. "Even if I forgave you, the hurt wouldn't disappear. Not completely. Tim was right. That's the shadow cast by every light. You can't love without the hurt, and I don't see the part of your story where you figured that out and learned to accept it."

"What do you think I've been doing these past three years?" Nathaniel demanded. "I've been living with the pain! If I can survive it on my own, I'm pretty damn sure it'll be more bearable with you in my life again."

Kelly looked tempted, but shook his head. "I never would have left you."

"You *did* leave me! Don't pretend your love is perfect, because you could have come back. You could have kept fighting. Instead you gave up on me and left."

"All I was doing is what you asked!" Kelly pulled his hands free. "But maybe you're right. You knew where to find me but never did anything about it. I knew where to find you too, but we both stayed away. Maybe there's a reason for that. Seeing each other here tonight, all these feelings we have, maybe it's just nostalgia."

"It's not," Nathaniel said.

"Then why did we wait so long?" Kelly grabbed the wrapped box from the table, then walked to the elevator. He turned around to address the room, but he was no longer speaking to Nathaniel. "You can either open the doors, or I'm taking the fire escape. One way or another, I'm leaving. Right now."

A moment later, the elevator doors opened. Kelly stepped inside but prevented them from closing again. His lip was trembling as he considered Nathaniel. "I will always love you," he said. "I'm sorry that I failed you too."

Then he let go, the doors sliding shut. Nathaniel moaned, slumped onto the couch, and covered his face with his hands. When he pulled them away again they were wet. He ignored the phone ringing on Marcello's desk, knowing who it would be and not wanting to hear comforting words. Not from him. He only wanted to talk to one person. She would be up by now. Nathaniel stood, leaving the framed photo behind. The elevator came when summoned. He left the building, finding the parking lot empty except for his car.

Nathaniel drove home, but when he got there, he went to the apartment across from his own and knocked on the door. A sleepy-looking kid with brownish-blond hair opened it and hugged Nathaniel's legs automatically before tromping back toward the television, where Zero was helping himself to an unguarded bowl of cereal. Nathaniel shook his head and went to the kitchen. Sheila gasped in surprise. "I didn't hear you come in!"

"Arthur let me in. Might want to talk to him about answering the door without checking to see who's on the other side. Just in case. Oh, and he'll need another bowl of cereal."

"Zero?"

"Yeah. Thanks for taking care of him. I'm glad you got my text."

"No problem. Arthur was thrilled to share his bed with a dog. He pretended to be one too. Coffee?"

"Okay." Nathaniel sat at the kitchen table.

Sheila poured two cups and joined him. "How did it go?" She winced at his expression. "That bad?"

"I deserve worse."

"None of that self-pity crap." Sheila reached across the table to slap his hand. "We've talked about this. Try again. How did it go?"

Nathaniel met her eye. "I opened up to him, told him my life story. I figured the truth was the only way Kelly might forgive me, but it wasn't enough."

"Did you tell him about me and Arthur? What you did for us?"

Nathaniel rolled his eyes. "I didn't want to use that as leverage."

"You relocated us to Austin and supported us until Arthur went to kindergarten, just so I could keep an eye on him. Michelle said she had never seen anything like it. That's not leverage. That's showing him that you're a good man."

"Kelly knows who I am," Nathaniel said. "He's angry that I didn't try to find him sooner and disappointed that he didn't try either. We gave up on each other."

Sheila took a sip of her coffee. "Is that true? Have you given up?"

"What am I going to do?" Nathaniel said. "I offered myself to him. Everything I've got. It wasn't enough."

"You gave him words," Sheila said. "And I have no doubt that they were heartfelt, but sometimes it takes more. You helped me rebuild my life. You rebuilt yours when you left Yale, and Kelly did the same when he decided to leave Austin. Consider that. Then ask yourself if I would ever take Dwight back."

"You're too smart for that."

"And you were too smart to take Caesar back. Why is that?"

"Because there's no way I was going to repeat the same mistakes," Nathaniel said. "Otherwise, everything I've done since then would become meaningless." He blinked a few times. Then he groaned. "That's how Kelly feels, isn't it?"

"Probably."

"Then it's hopeless."

"It's only hopeless if you give up." Sheila sighed. "I'm going to hate myself for saying this, because I really want to be selfish and keep you with me forever, but you can't win Kelly over by staying here. Austin is his past now, and so are you for the time being. That needs to change. If you want to win Kelly again, you need to become a part of his new life."

"He lives in New York," Nathaniel said.

"That's fine. Arthur and I are okay now. We really are."

"Caesar tried to become part of my new life. Look how that turned out."

"He got you drunk every night and strolled into the living room naked one morning. I don't know how you can win back Kelly, but I'm pretty sure you can do better than that. If you don't try, you'll never forgive yourself. Hell, if you don't get your butt up to New York, I'll never forgive you."

"Me neither," Arthur said, padding into the room with a cereal bowl that had been licked clean. He couldn't know what they were talking about, but Nathaniel felt outnumbered anyway.

"New York," he said with an exhausted sigh.

He pictured endless skyscrapers and sidewalks overburdened with anonymous pedestrians. Then he remembered Kelly in the elevator, his lip trembling with emotion, and knew he would travel to the depths of Hell to prevent that from being their last memory of each other.

Layne arrived at Mozart's Coffee wearing huge sunglasses and a shawl concealing most of his head. He glanced around dramatically at the café's raw brick walls and wooden tables, then back at the door he had just walked through, assessing his chances of having been followed. Did he look ridiculous? Yes. And yet, his oddly vintage style made Nathaniel want to rush home and put on a classic spy movie. Something with a glamorous leading lady and a car chase—a convertible racing along the rocky coasts of northern California.

Nathaniel raised a hand to attract attention. Layne approached the table, unwrapping the shawl and removing his shades. He glanced around once more before saying, in hushed conspiring tones, "I need to borrow ten dollars."

Nathaniel sighed and pulled out his wallet.

Layne must have noticed all the bills there because he added, "Better make it twenty. The red velvet cake makes me weak at the knees."

"Here's fifty," Nathaniel said. "Hurry up."

"Can we sit outside? I love the lake view."

Nathaniel gritted his teeth, picked up his coffee, and stood. "I'll find us a seat."

A long wooden deck extended over the edge of Lake Austin, offering an impressive view. Nathaniel secured them a table next to the rail, tense with impatience by the time Layne showed up with a chai latte, a slice of cake, and a smile.

"Don't you just adore this place?"

"It's great," Nathaniel responded. "Care to explain why you dragged me out here instead of sending me what I need via email?"

Layne made a face, sat down, and arranged his items on the table until satisfied. Then he assessed Nathaniel critically and nodded. "It's been a long time," he said. "Years! For all I know, you could have become some crazy junkie with Charles Manson's tattoo on your forehead. You look okay though. I wouldn't kick you out of bed for eating cookies. Hell, I'd leave a trail of Oreos leading right to my pillow, ha ha! Do you like Oreos?"

Nathaniel merely glared.

"I guess not." Layne took a sip of his tea, cutely scrunching up his nose when wiping the foam off his upper lip. Then he pulled a piece of folded paper from his pocket and held it up. "Why do you want Kelly's address? What are you going to do with it?"

"I don't know," Nathaniel said. "I'm moving to New York. It's not like I'm going to run into him by chance, so I thought… I don't know."

"You're just going to sit outside his apartment and hope to be noticed?" Layne sighed wistfully. "I wish I had a stalker. Still, unless you're going to serenade him from the street, you can't just loiter there. It's creepy."

"I'd rather bump into him at his favorite haunts. I don't know where those are, but I'm sure anyone who had visited him recently—and had their ticket paid for by a third party—would have more information than I do."

"We need to talk about those flights," Layne said. "Economy won't do anymore. I need an upgrade."

"You'll need an ambulance if you don't start cooperating."

"Fine." Layne unfolded the paper, which had a printed address on it. He added a few more names and locations, consulting his phone a few times. When he was done, he pushed the paper across the table. "There you go, although you probably won't find him at any of those places. He's been struggling lately."

Nathaniel took the paper, barely glancing at it. "What do you mean?"

"He's broke. Finally blew through all that modeling money. He's been trying to sell his photos but isn't having much luck. Did you see his gallery opening last week? That was his first big break, so maybe he's doing better. All I know is he got totally emo while texting me about how fierce competition is up there." Layne grabbed his phone, thumb swiping the screen over and over again as he scrolled through his history. Then he read aloud. "Everyone's an artist in New York. Everyone except me."

Nathaniel's brow furrowed. "He sold some stuff recently. That should help. Right?"

"If not, are you going to rescue him? Maybe go buy all of his photos without him knowing? God, that would be romantic."

Nathaniel shook his head. "Kelly wouldn't like that." He glanced out over the lake, the water reflecting the orange light of the setting sun. "Then again, I'm not sure what he likes anymore."

The knock at the front door was gentle and unexpected. Nathaniel tore his attention away from the suitcase he was packing, trying to decide who it was and whether to answer it. Arthur tended to kick the door instead of knocking, and Sheila had a key. He didn't expect to see Caesar again, and he knew for a fact that Kelly had flown back to New York. When the gentle rapping repeated, he went to investigate. After peering through the peephole, he felt even more confused as he opened the door.

"Good evening," Marcello said, craning his neck over a huge bouquet of flowers. "May I come in?"

Nathaniel stared, then gestured for him to enter. Zero stirred, spotted Marcello, and began leaping around him, threatening to knock him over. Nathaniel ignored this and proceeded to the living room. When he turned around, a trail of leaves and flower petals marked Marcello's progress, the large man still being harassed by the dog.

"That's enough," Nathaniel said.

Zero changed tactics, hopping up on the couch to secure his favorite spot so he wouldn't have to share it.

Marcello set the bouquet on the coffee table and brushed himself off. "Never have I met such an unruly beast with complete disregard for personal space. Actually, I take that back. In the seventies I had an encounter with a deliciously beefy Turkish man working at a bath house. At least I thought he worked there. Only later did I find out that he had escaped from—"

"What are you doing here?" Nathaniel interrupted.

Marcello hesitated, glancing around the apartment as if to find some pretense. When this failed, his arms flopped to his sides. "The problem with being wrong is that, up until the moment of realization, it feels just like being right. I thought that you and Kelly simply needed to clear the air, but not all bridges are so easily mended. I should have known better. I'm sorry if I put you through any unnecessary pain."

414

"It's fine," Nathaniel said. "Would you like something to drink? I'm pretty sure I have a bottle of champagne in the cupboard. Not chilled, but I can throw it in the freezer for a few minutes."

"No, thank you," Marcello said. "This is no time to celebrate."

He looked... sad? Nathaniel couldn't remember ever seeing him so down. A little pensive at times when talking about friends he had lost or solemn when a business deal didn't go through, but sorrow had never been part of Marcello's repertoire. Not until now. "You read my letter," Nathaniel guessed. "You weren't supposed to. Not yet."

"I tend to overlook the first two words of any sentence beginning with 'do not' so I can act immediately on the remainder."

Nathaniel deciphered this as quickly as he could. "Do not sit with me at the table."

Marcello nodded cordially. "It would be my pleasure." He followed Nathaniel to the corner of the room that functioned as the dining area. He surveyed the apartment again as he moved a chair away from the table and sat. "Considering how much you earn, you can do better than a one-bedroom apartment. That used to puzzle me. At first I thought you were stingy, that you didn't want to invest in a nicer home and instead preferred that the company continued paying your rent."

"I took over the lease after the first three months of living here."

"As I later discovered," Marcello said, nodding in confirmation. "And yet, all these years on, you still live well below your means. You're no penny-pincher. I've seen the amounts you've spent making sure Kelly has what he needs. Prosthetics aren't cheap."

"He has a specialized health insurance plan—"

"Which he doesn't pay a dime for, thanks to a very small foundation that helps people like him. Just one person, in fact. Is he aware of this?"

"Of course not, and don't you dare say a word!"

"My lips—as always—are sealed. Then there is the young woman living across from you, and her child, who you've spared no expense on. I daresay their lives would be quite different if not for the help you provide."

"How do you know about that?" Nathaniel asked.

"You consult with company lawyers. The lawyers consult with me."

Nathaniel sighed. "Look, if this is supposed to be a pep talk about what a good person I am, and how someone will recognize that one day, save your breath. You read my letter. I want Kelly. I'm not giving up on him. Not this time."

Marcello shook his head. "I would never delude myself into thinking I could direct the inclinations of another's heart, especially when I have so little control over my own. I suppose that is why I'm here. I won't stop you from going after Kelly, but why did you feel it necessary to turn in your resignation?"

"To show him I'm willing to make sacrifices. I'm asking permission to be a part of his world, when previously I made him earn the right to be a part of mine. I can't divide my attention anymore or feel like I have obligations that I need to return to eventually. I need to focus on the future because only there can Kelly and I be together."

"I see. And you feel that future doesn't involve Austin?"

"Exactly."

Marcello sniffed and nodded. "You remember Kenneth, your predecessor? When I first met him, I saw someone just as cunning as myself, a person clever enough to keep the business running without me. I'm not getting any younger, and I may have mentioned a severe lack of family in my life. I have none, in fact. At least not of the traditional variety. It's ironic then that Kenneth tried to wrest control of the company from me. Had he simply waited, it all would have been his eventually. I'm glad that didn't come to pass because he lacked one essential trait that you possess in spades. Generosity. That's why I came here singing your praises tonight. Kenneth might have led the company to more profitable horizons, but he would not have bothered with my fundraisers and such. He always treated them as bothersome and unnecessary. I don't have that fear with you. In a way, that's what you're already doing—finding ways to share your success with those who need it most. I'm proud of you, and lately I've become rather fond of the idea of you being there during my final days. Not just as a business partner, or my successor, but rather like a son."

Nathaniel swallowed against the emotions he felt rising. "You're a silly old man. You know that?"

"I take pride in it," Marcello said. "Not so much the old part, but I suppose if I'm willing to trust you with everything else, I can admit it just this once. I'm old and that means I've seen far too many of the best things in my life slip away. Friends and lovers all carried away by the whims of chance. I'm not willing to let you go."

"I need to do this," Nathaniel said. "I'm sorry I'm letting you down, but I do."

Marcello shook his head and smiled. "You're not letting me down. You're living up to my expectations. I'm too selfish to give you my blessing, but please know that I'll be here. No matter what happens in the future, no matter how successful you become in New York, you will always have a home in Austin."

"Thank you," Nathaniel managed to say.

"Now then, let's see about that bottle of champagne. Perhaps I can get you drunk enough to oversleep and miss your flight."

Nathaniel grinned. "It's worth a shot."

The first few days in New York were spent playing tourist and hoping that fate would intervene. While visitors gazed upward in wonder at the advertising blitz in Times Square or walked the Brooklyn Bridge to gawk at the city skyline, Nathaniel scanned the crowds, hoping against the odds that he would find Kelly there. Of course this didn't happen.

On the third night after his arrival, Nathaniel grabbed a few pizza slices on his way back to the hotel, feeling an urge to buy extra for Zero and a pang of sorrow when he remembered the dog was in Austin with Sheila. Nathaniel needed to find an apartment before he brought Zero to New York, so he began his search online while he ate. He kept nudging the search results toward Kelly's neighborhood, managing to find a rental that looked promising. After making an appointment to see the place the next afternoon, he went to his hotel's gym, feeling sluggish from so much eating out.

The next day Nathaniel met with an old man who showed him a small dingy apartment, the walls yellowed with tobacco stains and the carpet so filthy he felt it sticking to his shoes. Nathaniel left the place craving a shower. He hoped Kelly had done better for himself. He lived just a few blocks away. If all the buildings in this neighborhood were that poorly maintained…

Convincing himself he was playing the role of concerned citizen, Nathaniel used the GPS on his phone to map a route to Kelly's address.

Minutes later he was standing outside a brick building, cast-iron fire escapes winding their way down the façade. Nathaniel crossed the street, confirmed that the last name of 'Phillips' was listed among the mailboxes, and was severely tempted to push the buzzer. What would he say? He didn't want to make the same mistake Caesar had, barging in and demanding another chance. Even being caught standing in front of the building would seem creepy rather than charming, so Nathaniel continued on to the nearest subway station.

On his way he spotted an art gallery and stopped to look in the window. The place specialized in photography. Considering the close proximity to Kelly's home, it seemed likely he would be represented there. Nathaniel went inside, eager to find out. He examined each photo carefully, challenging himself to recognize Kelly's work by content alone. He made his way along all the walls in this manner, not finding what he was looking for.

Nathaniel turn to face the room. "Do you have anything by Kelly Phillips?"

The owner walked over to him, repeating the name a few times. "Afraid not, sorry. What's his style? Maybe we have something similar."

"You don't. He's a local artist."

The owner shook his head. "Sorry. I'm not familiar with him."

"He was one of the hottest fashion models a few years back," Nathaniel said, taking out his phone and pulling up a picture to show him.

The owner peered at it. "Are you looking for photos *of* him or—"

"No, he's a professional photographer and artist now. He had a huge exhibition in Austin recently. Just a second." Nathaniel went to the website for the Eric Conroy Gallery, hoping Tim had his shit together when it came to PR. He wasn't disappointed. Not only did the website feature an extensive biography of Kelly and his work, but it also included photos from the gallery opening.

"That's quite the crowd!" the owner said, dollar signs in his eyes.

"Kelly has his fans."

"You say he's local?"

"He lives in this neighborhood, in fact."

The owner narrowed his eyes suspiciously. "Are you his agent?"

Nathaniel laughed. "No. I work for Studio Maltese. Used to, anyway. You've heard of our catalog?"

The owner nodded. "In fact I have!"

"Let's just say that photos of Kelly still rake in money for the studio. I expect the photos he takes will be equally valuable. You should get some in here, see what happens."

"Kelly Phillips," the man repeated. Then he hurried to his desk. "You know, I believe he was in here a few months back. He dropped off his portfolio, but we aren't taking on new artists and… Yes! Here it is!"

"If you don't have room, you don't have room," Nathaniel said casually. "It was nice talking to you. Best of luck with everything."

He left the gallery, keeping a straight face until he was out of sight. Then he turned around and walked backward a few paces, imagining Kelly passing the gallery every day on his way to catch a train, increasingly frustrated that his work wasn't displayed there. *Everyone's an artist in New York. Everyone except me.* Had any of the local galleries given him a chance?

Nathaniel decided to find out. He stopped to get a coffee, searching for galleries that specialized in photography and making a list of the nearest and most prominent. During the next week, while continuing his apartment hunt, he stopped at these galleries, never finding Kelly's work but always casually promoting him before leaving. Some owners were apathetic, but most were salivating with greed by the time Nathaniel left. He always remained anonymous. Kelly preferred to earn his own success, so he probably wouldn't be grateful for Nathaniel's assistance. Regardless, he hoped these efforts helped jump start his reputation.

After a few days, curious if his efforts were having any impact, Nathaniel returned to the original gallery. He decided to go late at night when the gallery was closed so his repeated presence wouldn't cause suspicion. First he strolled by Kelly's building, glancing up at the lit windows and wondering which belonged to him. Then he made his way to the gallery, where he amused himself by pressing his nose against the window. His smile soon faded. The display had changed. Three new photos hung in one corner. One in particular caught his eye, causing goosebumps.

Nathaniel returned the next morning a few minutes after the gallery opened, not caring how this appeared.

"Guess what we got in?" the owner said cheerfully.

"I saw," Nathaniel said, heading for the corner. "Have any of them sold yet?"

"No, but that's not—"

"Good. This one is mine." He stopped in front of an image of a Siberian Husky leaping through the water, front paws in the air, hind legs still partially submersed and surrounded by froth. The animal appeared elemental, a wave in the shape of a dog. *His* dog. Zero. Nathaniel's eyes stung. He rubbed at them, feeling more homesick than he thought possible.

"Animal lover?" the owner asked, clearly puzzled.

"Yeah," Nathaniel managed. He glanced over at the accompanying placard. The title of the piece was *The Best Cure*. The asking price was ridiculous. "I'll take it."

Only when he was back in his hotel room did he wonder if this was a message from Kelly. Had the owner of the gallery said enough to give him away? If so, maybe the image and its title were suggesting that Nathaniel should overcome his heartache as he had before—with the help of his best friend. Maybe Kelly was saying he hoped the hurt would stop for them both some day. Or perhaps it was complete coincidence. Either way, Nathaniel needed to make a decision, to act soon or get over Kelly completely. After thinking about it carefully for many hours, he grabbed his phone and called Marcello.

"How are matters progressing?" his former boss inquired.

"They aren't," Nathaniel said. "Listen, I need a favor."

"Name it and it shall be done."

"I need an escort. The hottest one you've got. Just make sure he's clean. And discreet."

Marcello chuckled. "I thought you'd never ask."

For Nathaniel, morality wasn't a complicated issue. Don't steal, lie, cheat, or kill. Simple as that. Usually. Morality did have some gray areas, such as using someone's phone to track his exact location. He and Kelly had been close enough at one time to share their passwords. If anything is more taxing than breaking up with a lover, it's creating new passwords for multiple accounts, then having to remember them all. Nathaniel hadn't bothered. Kelly hadn't either. That meant the app normally used to track down a lost phone could also be used to follow a lost love. Nathaniel had resisted doing so. Until now.

He stood outside the club, shifting from foot to foot while repeatedly checking his watch. He knew Kelly was inside. So was Harold the escort. His name might be goofy, but the guy was so hot that it was possible to get aroused just by looking at him. Nathaniel knew this for a fact, but he wasn't interested in sampling his wares. Instead, he was more concerned with whether or not he was skilled enough to get the job done.

Nathaniel checked his watch again, still amazed that someone could be confident enough to time such a task. "I'll need twenty minutes," Nathaniel said out loud, mimicking Harold's dry tones. "And that's me taking it slow." Then he rolled his eyes and pushed against the club door, making his way inside.

His arrival went unnoticed, which was good, because at the far end of a u-shaped bar sat Kelly, Harold next to him. They were talking in the dim light, Kelly shaking his head and smiling. What a smoking hot pair they would make! Maybe that's what would happen. Nathaniel's plan wasn't great. He was taking a risk, but that was better than doing nothing. He went to the corner of the bar nearest the door and quietly ordered two glasses of champagne. He checked his watch, wishing the bartender would hurry. Harold had turned sideways to face Kelly, putting a hand over his. Kelly was biting his bottom lip, his eyes sparkling in amusement.

The bartender slid two glasses of champagne across the slick surface. Nathaniel handed him a bill, his attention not leaving the pair as Harold leaned closer. Kelly closed his eyes and did the same. Then they were kissing, which clawed at Nathaniel's heart more than he had expected. He stood, picked up the glasses of champagne, and walked to where they sat. The kiss was still ongoing when he reached them, so he cleared his throat.

Kelly broke it off first, looking up at him and not registering surprise. Not in the slightest. "Fancy seeing you here," he said.

"Yeah." Nathaniel cleared his throat again, nervously this

time. "I don't mean to interrupt. I just wanted to say hello. And that I hope you'll be happy together."

He offered the glasses of champagne, which were accepted. Kelly took a sip, made a sound of appreciation, and then looked him over. "Wow. You saw me kissing another guy, and instead of punching him, you bought him a drink. You've clearly grown as a person."

"Uh…" Nathaniel felt like retreating. Obviously his ruse wasn't working or Kelly would have been more startled. Or more impressed by his maturity, as planned. Instead he was smirking and shaking his head.

"You can leave now," Kelly said.

Nathaniel's stomach sank.

Then Harold stood.

Kelly watched him rise. "It was good seeing you again. Take care."

"You too." Harold chugged his champagne, managed to look hot while burping indiscreetly, and winked at Nathaniel. "Good luck."

After he was gone, Kelly patted the empty stool next to him. "Sit down. You're an idiot."

"Am I?" Nathaniel asked, accepting his invitation.

"Yes. That was an extremely stupid plan."

"It was either that or get extensive plastic surgery so you'd think we'd never met before."

Kelly smiled. "I'm sure I would have recognized a certain part of your body. I can't believe you came all this way! But I'm glad."

Nathaniel swallowed. "I wasn't sure if you'd feel that way."

"I do. I was an emotional mess the last time we met. And tired. I don't want that to be our last memory of each other."

"Me neither," Nathaniel said. "That's why I'm here."

Kelly studied him. "You're here because you wanted to prove that you can handle being hurt. How did it feel seeing me kiss another guy?"

"I wasn't crazy about it," he admitted. "But I'll survive. How did you figure it all out?"

"Harold was in the gay youth group for a time. We don't know each other well, but him being in New York and us running into each other seemed too big a coincidence. So I asked him, and he told the truth. We have history. Not much, but that wasn't the first time we've kissed. How does that make you feel?"

Nathaniel sighed. "Also not thrilled, but these days I'm much more concerned with who you love. And how willing you are to keep on loving him."

"Good. For the record, Harold and I have absolutely nothing in common. His idea of a good time is getting really high and building train models. Except without the trains. He just likes the little people and houses."

"I've been into that myself lately," Nathaniel said with a straight face.

They both laughed.

"I'm also aware of your other activities," Kelly said. "Do you know how many galleries have contacted me recently? They keep talking about a fan of mine, some huge guy who couldn't stop raving about my work."

"He sounds nice," Nathaniel said. "You should hang out with him sometime."

"Okay."

Nathaniel waited for an eye roll or a head shake, but neither came. "Really?"

"Yes," Kelly said. "Since you came all this way, I'll show you around the city. Starting now. Let's get out of here."

Nathaniel stood, happy when Kelly left the still-full glass of champagne where it was. Plying him with alcohol wasn't part of the plan. "Where to first?"

Kelly didn't answer the question. "One more thing," he said. "This isn't a second chance. We aren't testing the waters. I simply want us to end on a high note. Not trapped in an office while unleashing our inner demons. This is the grand finale."

Nathaniel's throat was tight, but he nodded. "Then let's make it a good one."

The subway took them to a Brooklyn soup and sandwich cafe that Kelly promised would be a culinary experience. The soup was fine, but the conversation was better. Kelly was in high spirits, talking about his travels during their time apart and telling little stories, both funny and personal. His voice never carried a trace of accusation or a hint of bitterness. His questions to Nathaniel weren't probing. At least not in the sense that he still sought an explanation. Instead Kelly seemed at peace with everything that had transpired between them and was simply grateful to have these last few hours together.

"I like New York," he said when Nathaniel asked. "I'm just not sure if it's home. I feel like I'm beginning to lose sight of the details. This city is full of so much noise that I can't focus on any one theme. Everything is overlapping, built on the ruins of previous dreams, painted and plastered over and used again. It's beautiful in its own way, but my camera is confused, and I'm still struggling to find an empty space where I fit in. I'm feeling more optimistic since the galleries started calling. You've shown me that I can't wait for an empty space. I need to make one by elbowing my way in and refusing to budge."

Only when they were wandering through Prospect Park, a light breeze swaying the trees around them, did his tone become melancholy. They had left the path and walked across the grass, a wall of bushes halting their progress. They stood in this little remnant of nature, too far from artificial lights to truly see each other. Kelly spoke first.

"I want to apologize for how I acted that night at Marcello's office. I was upset. Not just for the obvious reasons. You kept so much from me when we were together, but I fell in love with you anyway. That made me feel foolish, because how can you love someone without truly knowing who they are? But I did anyway. After we went our separate ways, I wondered if that love could withstand knowing the truth, if anything from your past could prove those feelings false. I shouldn't have worried. The more you talked, the more certain I became. I might not have known all the details, but you're still the man I fell in love with."

"You know what I'm going to ask," Nathaniel said.

"Why," Kelly said. "You want to know why we can't be together now." He fell silent. In the distance came the burble of drunken laughter. The muted beat of hip-hop music. The muffled sound of traffic. Kelly collected his thoughts before he spoke again. "I understand your fear. I didn't at the time. When we were breaking up, you kept telling me how you couldn't handle the pain, couldn't experience that sort of loss again. Afterwards I came really close to losing it. But I didn't. I survived and I healed as much as possible. You have too. I think we've both learned from our time together. There's probably someone out there for each of us who will benefit from that experience."

"I don't want them," Nathaniel said. "I want you. I'm thinking of moving here."

Kelly exhaled. "You need to go home. This isn't where you belong. This isn't even where I belong. It's just an experiment before I move on and keep looking for the right place."

"We had the world," Nathaniel said. "Remember travelling together? All those little expeditions before we returned home again to a worn-out couch and an ornery dog?"

Kelly laughed quietly. "Yes. Those were rich times."

"They aren't lost. We can—" His cell phone vibrated in his pocket, Nathaniel cursing technology. He fiddled in his pocket to reach the right button to make it stop. "Maybe we could travel together, get away from everything and see if we can't find that magic again. No promises or expectations. Just us in a neutral environment. You want a grand finale? Let's make it as grand as possible. Not just carrot soup and a stroll through the park."

"Carrot ginger soup," Kelly corrected. "Come on, it was pretty epic! Did you taste the coriander?"

"If I pretend I did, will you at least think about it? One last adventure together, and maybe the start of a new one. Please." He reached out to take Kelly's hand. His pocket vibrated again, but he refused to acknowledge it.

"Sounds like a swarm of angry bees is living in your pants," Kelly said.

Nathaniel sighed. "Sorry. I'll turn it off." He pulled out the cell phone, barely glancing at the screen as he held down the power button. He released it just in time to stop the phone from shutting down. Ten text messages, three missed calls. That was unusual. The phone vibrated again. Incoming call from Sheila. Nathaniel glanced up, Kelly's face lit by the ambient light.

"It's okay," he said. "Take it if you need to."

Nathaniel tapped the screen and held the phone to his ear. "Hello?"

"Nathaniel?" Sheila sounded panicked. "Oh, thank God! I've been trying to reach you all night."

"What is it? What's wrong?"

There was an ugly sniff on the other end of the phone. "It's Zero. There's been an emergency." Sheila sobbed. "It's pretty bad."

"What do you mean?" Nathaniel said, his voice terse.

"He might need to be put down."

Nathaniel struggled to breathe, listening as Sheila explained. When she was finished, he only managed four words before he hung up. "I'm on my way."

He turned and strode toward the nearest street, surprised when he heard Kelly's voice beside him. "What's going on?"

"You were right," Nathaniel said. "I need to go home. Which way to the closest station? Can you call me a taxi? Fuck!"

Kelly glanced around. Then he pointed. "That way. You'll probably find a taxi already there. What happened?"

"Zero," Nathaniel said, his voice cracking. Then he broke into a run. Kelly kept pace. He must have been in better shape, because when they reached the brightness of a streetlight, Nathaniel was already panting.

"If you want a cab," Kelly said, "you're better off hailing it yourself. They tend to drive right past me, for some reason."

Nathaniel wasn't taking any chances. He walked out in the middle of the street, forcing the next taxi to stop. It honked, but he already had his wallet out. He made sure cash was visible in his hand before he went around to the side of the vehicle.

Kelly approached from the opposite side of the car and said something, but Nathaniel couldn't hear his words over the stopped traffic, more horns blaring.

"I have to go," Nathaniel said, still struggling to catch his breath. "I'm sorry." He got into the car and told the driver the destination. The man didn't hesitate. Nathaniel looked through the back window as Kelly receded into the distance, his expression still bewildered. Then he took out his phone and started making calls, trying to find the quickest way home.

Chapter Twenty-two

Nathaniel caught a last-minute flight, racing through the airport to reach a closing gate. Then he endured a grueling five hours in the air. The plane didn't offer Wi-Fi, so he couldn't use the time to find answers to his questions. Nor could he call Sheila for updates. All he could do was stare out the window and wait. The plane landed at one in the morning. With no luggage to claim, Nathaniel went straight to the airport lobby, the early hour making the space eerily quiet. Sheila was there, face red and swollen from crying. Nathaniel panicked. Was he too late?

"I'm so sorry," she said. "I should have called you right away, but everything happened so quickly and —"

"Is he okay?" Nathaniel croaked. "He's still alive?"

"Of course! I didn't make any decisions. You can see him immediately." She led the way to the parking garage. "Let's go. The emergency clinic is still open."

"Arthur?" Nathaniel asked.

"He's with Marcello. You said I should call him if I ever needed help. I couldn't find a babysitter at the last minute, so…"

Nathaniel tried to imagine Marcello taking care of a child, pictured Arthur wearing a pint-sized version of a suit and waving champagne around while telling droll anecdotes. Then he shook his head to clear the image. None of that mattered right now. Once in the car and on their way, he said, "Tell me everything. Go over it all again."

"I was in the kitchen cleaning up after dinner," Sheila said, eyes fixed on the road ahead. "Arthur came in and said Zero had fallen over. So I wasn't there to see, but I guess they were playing when it happened. When I went to the other room to check —" She needed a moment to get her emotions under control. "He wasn't moving. Don't be shocked when you see him. The vet said that he's stable, but he can only move one of his legs and his head a little. They don't know what happened yet. Something with his spine or a blood clot in the brain. Maybe a stroke. The test results should be there when we get back. The vet wants you to prepare yourself for the worst. Just in case."

"No," Nathaniel said, jaw clenching. "Not a chance in hell."

When they arrived at the veterinary clinic, they had to be buzzed in. This process seemed to take forever. Nathaniel was on the verge of smashing through one of the windows when they were finally granted access.

"He's resting," said Julie, the vet assistant who greeted them, "but he's doing okay."

That was reassuring. "Can I see him?"

"Sure!"

Julie led them down a hallway, past examination rooms, to an area normally reserved for staff. Through the door was a long room, the walls and floor made of concrete. On one side were smaller cages; to the right a row of cells, each with a gate made of chain-link fence. Zero was in one of these, lying on his side on a blanket too thin to provide much comfort.

"I'm here," Nathaniel said, pushing past the vet assistant.

Zero whimpered in response, raising his head, but seemed too weak to keep it upright. The rest of his body remained still except for one of his front legs, which pawed at the air ineffectually. Nathaniel was on his knees, wanting to be brave, but he couldn't help crying. He cradled Zero's head in one arm, kissing his face and looking him over. He didn't smell great, the fur near his hind legs wet with urine.

"Did he have an accident?" Julie asked. "We'll get him cleaned up. The good news is that he ate a little."

Nathaniel glanced to a nearby bowl that still contained a few pieces of kibble. "He has a food allergy."

"I mentioned that when I brought him in," Sheila said. "I thought maybe he had a reaction."

"We only use the best possible food," Julie assured them.

Nathaniel knew from experience that no brand—no matter how pure or expensive—would fail to trigger Zero's allergies. He clamped down on his irritation because what was happening now was more important. Zero was still moving the only leg he could, pawing at him or maybe trying to roll over or sit up. "Calm down," Nathaniel whispered to him. "You're going to be okay. I won't leave you again, I swear."

"Julie?" a new voice said. "What's going on here?"

"Dr. Ward, this is Zero's owner. He just flew in from New York."

Nathaniel turned to see an older man wearing a lab coat, his head topped with a puff of white hair. He didn't offer a hand or any sort of condolences. Instead he seemed agitated.

"Why aren't they in an examination room?"

"He came straight from the airport," Julie said. "He wanted to see his dog."

"That's fine, but we need to do this properly." Dr. Ward addressed him. "Sir, if you could wait in reception, we'll get him moved to a more comfortable environment where we can go over his test results."

Nathaniel looked down at Zero, who still had an eye locked on him. "I can carry him."

"We'll manage, thank you." Dr. Ward gestured to the door. "Please."

Nathaniel rose unwillingly. Julie walked with them to the front room, offering a sympathetic expression. "He's new. Not to the occupation, but to the area." She patted his arm and left them to wait.

Nathaniel took a deep breath, then started pacing, fighting off another wave of emotion.

"I'm sure the test results will tell us something," Sheila said.

She was wrong. When they were finally shown to one of the exam rooms, Zero was on the table. He reacted with as much excitement as he could muster. Nathaniel tried to calm him by holding the paw that kept moving around. His fur was wetter now and smelled better, having been washed.

"Okay," Dr. Ward said, consulting a chart. "We won't have all the lab results until tomorrow. From what I've been able to collect, I feel we can rule out any sort of viral infection as the cause. The X-ray didn't reveal any slipped discs in the spine, and I'm not seeing any tissue masses or inflamed nerves. A stroke is certainly possible, or a tumor in the brain. That would require an MRI to narrow down, but I don't recommend it because of the expense."

"Money is no object," Nathaniel said.

"That's refreshing to hear," Dr. Ward said, "but even if the MRI revealed a tumor, the symptoms I'm seeing suggest it would be near the brainstem. Surgery in that area is invasive and poses many risks. Radiation is a six-week ordeal, and with symptoms this advanced, I can't guarantee results. I know it's difficult, but in situations such as these, I advise owners to start thinking about the dog's quality of life and what would be the most humane decision."

"Meaning?" Nathaniel pressed.

"That if there aren't any improvements in the next few days, putting him to sleep might be the most merciful choice."

Nathaniel's throat felt tight. He started petting Zero, as if this was the last chance he had to do so. Tears were streaking down his cheeks again, but he wasn't sobbing. The pain was too steady for it to shake him.

"Let's see how he does after a full day's rest," Dr. Ward suggested. "We'll get the remaining test results, then we can talk."

Nathaniel nodded. "Can I take him home?"

Dr. Ward took a deep breath. "I'd like to keep him here for observation."

"I won't let him out of my sight," Nathaniel said. "You have my word."

"He needs rest," Dr. Ward said, still not convinced. "The office is closed during the day and will be quiet."

"My place is quiet. I'm taking him home."

Dr. Ward tapped one corner of his clipboard against the table absentmindedly. Then he nodded. "Okay. You'll have to bring him back in tomorrow. I suppose you look strong enough to carry him around."

Nathaniel scooped Zero up. Sheila walked a few paces ahead, opening doors. When they reached her car, Nathaniel placed the dog in the backseat and got in beside him, keeping a hand on his silver fur during the drive, whispering words of comfort and encouragement. When they arrived back at the apartment complex, it was almost four in the morning. Nathaniel had no intention of sleeping, but he encouraged Sheila to do so.

After they said goodbye, Nathaniel put Zero on the couch and went to the kitchen. He had loaded up the freezer before leaving for New York, but now it was getting low. He found a few chicken breasts that he defrosted and baked, keeping tabs on Zero as much as possible. When the food was ready, he cut it into tiny pieces and hand-fed it to the dog. Then he brought in a bowl of water and held Zero's head steady while he lapped at it. That was a good sign. His appetite wasn't as vivacious as usual, but it wasn't gone completely.

Yawning and weary, Nathaniel picked up the dog and carried him into the bedroom. Then he lay beside him, so they were facing each other. He tried to picture a world without this wonderful animal in his life, crying as he did so. Zero stared back, perhaps having similar thoughts. Someday they would have to leave each other. That was a sad fact. At times Nathaniel imagined he would die of grief after Zero passed away. That should be years from now. Not today. Not tomorrow.

Zero closed his eyes, his breathing slowing. Nathaniel watched him carefully, making sure the dog was sleeping and nothing more permanent. Then he found himself drifting toward darkness, his body and mind exhausted.

He awoke to a paw swiping at him repeatedly, a high-pitched whine in his ear. Panic shot through Nathaniel, waking him instantly. Zero was in the same position that he had fallen asleep in, but his eyes were pleading as he whimpered.

"What's wrong?" Nathaniel asked. "Are you in pain?"

Zero yawned, like he sometimes did when Nathaniel was being tiresome. Then he grumbled.

"Potty?" Nathaniel asked.

Another whine.

He rose, slipped on his shoes, and struggled to carry the dog downstairs. When he reached the green lawn behind the apartment complex, he lowered Zero to the ground. His hind legs were useless, but Nathaniel rested him on his haunches, holding up the front of his body. Sure enough, Zero started peeing a few seconds later. What he hadn't been prepared for was him needing to do more. That made a mess, and wasn't very solid, probably thanks to the dog food he'd been fed at the clinic. That meant Nathaniel had to carry him back upstairs to clean him in the bathtub. He noticed it was nearly lunchtime, so after towel-drying the dog and putting him on the couch, Nathaniel scrounged around and came up with a meal.

After they had both eaten, he decided some normalcy would be comforting. He put on a movie, draping Zero over his lap and petting him while it played. He didn't really watch it as his mind entertained endless hopes and fears. Marcello called afterwards, offering his help, but the only thing any of them could do at this point was wait.

He took Zero out for another bathroom break before loading him in the car. They were parked in front of the veterinary clinic an hour before it opened. He waited impatiently, getting out of the car when he saw Julie unlocking the front door.

"How's he doing?" she asked.

"The same," Nathaniel said. "Is that bad?"

Her expression became strained. "It's hard to say. These things take time. Let's get him to one of the rooms so Dr. Ward can check him out."

The veterinarian was silent as he felt different parts of Zero's body, examined his eyes, listened to his heart. Afterwards he shook his head and sighed. "The tests ruled out quite a few things, but unfortunately, they haven't shown us what we're dealing with. I'm still thinking a tumor. Or a stroke. Any increased movement?"

"No," Nathaniel said, grasping desperately for anything. "He was holding his head up pretty well while eating today. And he ate much more."

Dr. Ward didn't seem impressed. "As I said yesterday, there are more tests we could run. Honestly, if this was my own dog, I would start preparing myself."

"You wouldn't do further tests?"

"The extent of his paralysis concerns me. A full recovery is unlikely, no matter the underlying reason. I want my animals to have the best quality of life. The decision is yours, but I would seriously consider euthanasia."

Nathaniel swallowed. Then he asked about the other tests, the procedures and the associated risks, his optimism fading with every detail. Zero would be injected and poked and prodded. He would be exposed to dose after dose of radiation and put on different medications, possibly for nothing, making the last few weeks of his life the most miserable. Nathaniel would rather he slip away peacefully.

"Is it possible to have someone come to my—" He couldn't quite get out the rest of the words, but the doctor understood.

"There is a local service that can administer euthanasia at your home, yes. Would you like their contact information?"

Nathaniel nodded, looking down at Zero and feeling like he had already betrayed his best friend.

When Nathaniel awoke the next day, he prayed for a miracle before opening his eyes. Wet licks on his cheek, or maybe Zero in a different room, chewing up one of his shoes. Instead he found the dog in the same position, whimpering and begging for help. He carried Zero to the yard, cleaned up any carelessness when they were done, and dug through a nearly empty freezer before remembering the lasagna Sheila had brought by yesterday.

Zero ate first, then Nathaniel. Afterwards they sat on the couch, but he didn't turn on the television. Instead he tried to decide how much longer he would let this go on before making an impossible decision. He was staring at the blank television screen when he heard a knock on the door. Sheila with more food, he hoped, because he wasn't looking forward to eating lasagna three times in a row.

Nathaniel rose to answer it. The moment he opened the door, something slammed into him. He knew the feel of that body, recognized the scent of his hair. Nathaniel sobbed and hugged him back. Kelly, in Texas, here in his arms.

"I was on standby all day yesterday," he was saying, "and ended up in Georgia in the middle of the night, but because of some idiot calling in a bomb threat, I missed my connecting flight and had to—"

"Kelly," Nathaniel interrupted. "Shut up."

"Shutting up," Kelly said, still holding him. "How is he?"

Nathaniel squeezed before letting go. "Come see."

He walked down the hall, certain that Zero would be so excited to see Kelly that he'd forget he was sick, hop off the couch, and run right up to him. That didn't happen, but he did bark once before launching into grumbling dog talk. Kelly went to him, kneeling in front of the couch and getting thoroughly licked.

"Marcello filled me in on the details," Kelly said, moving to sit next to the dog. He glanced around the apartment before looking to Nathaniel with concern. "Are you okay?"

"No," he admitted.

"Do they know what's wrong? Is there any sort of treatment?"

Nathaniel couldn't bring himself to say it, so he picked up the business card from the coffee table and gave it to Kelly. The words describing the service were gentle, but their meaning was clear.

"No!" Kelly said.

"I know," Nathaniel responded, "but look at him. He hasn't improved at all."

"Then you've already decided?"

Nathaniel opened his mouth, but was unable to speak.

Kelly appeared angry, but Nathaniel didn't think it was directed at him. He'd felt plenty of anger in the last few days, hating the world for doing this to Zero. Mostly he just felt sad, which is what Kelly's expression shifted to as he leaned over and rested his head against the dog.

"We need to think of what's best for him," Nathaniel said.

Kelly sighed and sat upright again. "What can I do to help?"

"Nothing really. Maybe go to the store. Food is running low."

Kelly continued to stare at him. "You look a little rough."

"Oh." Nathaniel tried smooshing down his hair. "I haven't taken a shower since you last saw me. I didn't want to leave him on his own."

"Go take one now," Kelly said.

Nathaniel hesitated. "He can't potty without help. If he whines, I need to carry him downstairs."

"I can handle it. Or I'll drag you out of the shower. Right now he looks pretty chill, so go get yourself cleaned up. I'll watch him. I promise."

After a little more coaxing, Nathaniel left to take what was supposed to be a very quick shower. Once he was under the hot water, he let himself cry, his thoughts muddled. He felt purged by the time he shut off the water. When dressed again, he returned to the living room. Kelly had a tablet with him and was using it to browse the Internet.

He looked up and nodded his approval. "Much better. Now tell me what you need from the store."

Quite a lot, as it turned out. He was glad to have help. Sheila had offered, but he knew she had her hands full with work and parenting. Marcello was an option, but he'd probably only bring back pâté, truffles, and one of the bag boys. Kelly had practically lived with him, and when he returned from the store—arms full of groceries—it was clear he still remembered which brands Nathaniel preferred.

By evening, Kelly was in the kitchen cooking a beef stew, the aroma mouth-watering. Comfort food. "Dinner time," he said, walking into the living room with one of Zero's bowls. "Better put him on the floor in case it's messy."

Nathaniel hoisted the dog up and placed him on the carpet.

Kelly set the bowl down, but much too far away. "Come get it."

"What are you doing?" Nathaniel asked, taking a step forward.

Kelly held up a hand to stop him. "Let's see what he does."

"That's cruel!"

"Maybe. Look."

Zero raised his head, attention locked on the bowl of stew. He was pawing at the carpet with his good leg, but didn't achieve much.

"Kelly—" Nathaniel said warningly.

Zero pressed his paw harder on the floor, then did the same with his head, trying to drag himself forward. He managed to shift, if only a fraction of an inch.

Kelly moved the bowl close enough that he could eat. "Does it look like he's given up?"

"No," Nathaniel admitted.

"Then don't you give up on him," Kelly said. "Not yet. We're survivors. All three of us."

"Okay," Nathaniel said, his chest tight. "What are we going to do?"

Kelly walked over to the coffee table and picked up his tablet. "Get a second opinion."

Nathaniel stared after him. "I'm glad you're here."

Kelly turned around and smiled. "So am I."

The veterinarian who made a house call two days later was young and pale, curly blond hair reaching his shoulders. He looked more qualified to review video games on YouTube than to treat sick animals, but Kelly assured him that Dr. Colin was not only a fully qualified veterinary neurologist, but that he already had a number of impressive achievements to his name. Nathaniel's hopes plummeted as he watched the vet do the same basic tests that Dr. Ward had done. He knelt next to the couch, felt along Zero's spine, checked his eyes, looked inside his ears, and listened to his heart.

"I'd say it's either a tumor or a stroke," Dr. Colin said, standing up again.

The same diagnosis. Nathaniel was too depressed to roll his eyes. "So what would you do?" he asked. "Pretend this was your dog and you didn't have to worry about the feelings of anyone else."

"Nothing," Dr. Colin said.

"Nothing?"

The veterinarian nodded. "Tests are expensive and in this situation unnecessary because all you need to do is wait and see. If he starts to get worse—stops eating or has any other negative symptoms—then you're dealing with a tumor. We can talk about options then. From what you've told me, he's remained stable."

"His appetite improved after the first day," Nathaniel said.

"Good. If he shows other signs of improvement, I'd say you're dealing with a stroke. Ninety-five percent of dogs recover from strokes. You can't rush Mother Nature though. Some things take a long time to heal. But they do. Eventually."

Nathaniel exchanged a hopeful glance with Kelly. "So you're saying he might get better?"

"I can't promise anything, but yes. You're taking good care of him. He's cleaner than most healthy dogs. Keep it up and see what happens in another week."

They were in high spirits after the veterinarian left. Little had changed, but now they had hope, which was worth the bill they were given. They watched Zero all night, imagining he would hop to his paws at any moment. This didn't happen, but all the chores that needed to be done—carrying him outside to potty and everything else—now seemed a little easier.

Nathaniel slept better too. Kelly took the couch like he'd done the previous nights. He could stay with his parents, but neither of them had suggested the idea. Nathaniel was beneath the sheets, petting Zero in the dim light and about to drift off. Then he heard soft footsteps on the carpet, felt the sheet behind him lift. A moment later, Kelly scooted close, putting an arm around Nathaniel to hold him tight.

"Some things take a long time to heal," Kelly whispered. "But they do."

Nathaniel reached for Kelly's hand, placing his own over it and guiding it to his chest. He pressed it there, not letting go until sleep took them both.

Nathaniel awoke to a whimpering noise like he did every morning. Except this time something was different. Namely the body still pressed against his. From what he could tell, Kelly was wearing nothing but his underwear. Through it he could feel something poking him. Nathaniel allowed himself a chuckle. Then he winced, uncomfortable from sleeping in the same position all night.

Zero whimpered again.

"Okay," he said. "Hold your horses."

He spared the dog a grumpy glare. Zero's head was raised, eyes pleading for a lift outside so he could take care of business. Nathaniel started disentangling himself from Kelly, then did a double take. Zero's head was raised. He was on his belly, both paws neatly in front of him.

"You want to go potty?" Nathaniel asked.

Zero strained, his good arm stretching forward. A second later the other followed. His movements were wobbly and definitely weak, but he managed to scoot himself forward.

"Wake up!" Nathaniel said, elbowing Kelly in the ribs.

"Ow! You're such a monster!"

"Look! He's sitting up!"

He glanced over to confirm that Kelly was looking, surprise spreading across his face. Then glee. "He's getting better!"

"Yeah," Nathaniel said, laughing himself to tears. "He is."

By the end of the day, both of Zero's front legs were doing well. He could now scoot across the carpet, hind legs dragging uselessly behind him. He could also roll over with some effort if feeling uncomfortable. Kelly insisted the dog's tail had wagged briefly when offered a treat. Nathaniel had been in the bathroom at the time, and over the next few hours, repeatedly offered Zero more goodies in the hope that it would happen again. Currently the dog was scooting across the living room to get at a severely mutilated teddy bear he enjoyed chewing.

"He might need crutches," Kelly said musingly, sipping a glass of wine while sitting next to Nathaniel on the couch. "I could give him some pointers."

"I still have your old ones," Nathaniel admitted.

Kelly assessed how serious he was. Then he laughed. "That's so sad!"

"What?" Nathaniel said defensively. "It's not like I cuddle with them at night."

"I'm not sure I believe you," Kelly said with a smirk. "I suppose it *is* kind of sweet."

An awkward moment of tension followed. They hadn't talked

about what had happened last night. Zero had taken all of their energy during the day, and Nathaniel was worried that drawing attention to the progress they had made would somehow ruin it.

"I feel like I've come home again," Kelly said. "Like this is where I belong."

"In Austin?"

"No. Right here. This apartment. This couch."

"Oh." Nathaniel looked around. "I suppose you could take over my lease. I *am* moving to New York, after all." A second later, a pillow smacked him in the face.

"You're lucky I didn't throw the wine instead," Kelly taunted.

"No," Nathaniel countered, his tone serious. "I'm just lucky. If this is what I think it is, then I'm the luckiest man alive."

Kelly set his glass on the table, then stretched out, resting his head in Nathaniel's lap. That felt good, as did reaching down to stroke his hair. A contented silence followed, Nathaniel tempted to press the issue, but he waited until Kelly spoke.

"No promises. That way they can't be broken."

"I'm not scared of any promises. Or commitment."

Kelly rolled over, looking up at him with a disbelieving expression. "*Really?*"

Nathaniel met his gaze. "Want me to propose to you?"

Kelly searched his eyes. "I'm tempted to call your bluff."

"Try me."

Kelly took a deep breath. Then he sat up, seeming a little overwhelmed. "Doesn't seem the most appropriate time. Not with our little patient over there."

They both looked to the dog, who had decided the teddy bear would make a decent pillow. Zero's eyes were closed, his chest rising and falling.

"Looks like you're out of excuses." Nathaniel said, laughing when he saw the panicked response. "Don't worry. I plan to slowly lure you back in. One step at a time."

Kelly batted his eyelashes demurely. "Step one being?"

Nathaniel leaned close for a kiss. Few things could avoid the ravages of time, but their lips touching felt reassuringly familiar. Kelly shifted his body closer, his hands rubbing Nathaniel's chest, his arms, his stomach—touching every part he could reach as if needing reassurance that everything was still there where he'd left it. Then he pulled away.

"One more thing," he said. "I have a boyfriend. In New York."

"Roar," Nathaniel said in deadpan tones, pushing him backward into a laying position. "Growl. I'm so angry and hurt. We can't see each other anymore."

Kelly studied him and laughed. "That was the final test. I promise."

"For me, maybe," Nathaniel said, climbing on top of Kelly. "I plan on testing you in as many ways as you'll let me."

They kissed, Nathaniel grinding against him. Kelly clung to his torso, drawing him near, unable to get enough. Or so it seemed. Just when things were getting really hot, he pushed Nathaniel away.

"Strip for me," he said.

Nathaniel grinned slowly. Then got to his feet. He peeled off his T-shirt, trying to appear confident while wishing he'd hit the gym more often. Kelly seemed impressed enough, giggling when Nathaniel flexed his arms. Then he undid his belt, unbuttoned his jeans, pulled the zipper down slowly and moved the denim flaps aside to reveal his bulge.

"Aren't you going to get undressed too?"

"Not yet," Kelly said. "Keep going."

Nathaniel let his jeans drop, kicking them off. Then he flexed, his cock shifting behind the cotton briefs like a serpent uncoiling.

"Off with them," Kelly commanded.

Nathaniel did as he was told, enjoying how Kelly was on the verge of drooling. Instead he sat up and reached for the tablet.

"Ordering pizza?" Nathaniel joked.

"Nope," Kelly said, holding it up and tapping a button. The device made an artificial shutter noise.

"What are you doing?" Nathaniel said, trying to cover himself.

"Blackmail," Kelly replied. "Hands on your hips."

Nathaniel hesitated. Then he complied. "What's the point of this, exactly?"

"Just a little insurance," Kelly said, taking another photo. "If you ever try to leave me again, I'll send these to Marcello."

Nathaniel shook his head. "Marcello has never shown the slightest bit of interest in me."

"Because he doesn't know what you're packing. If he did, you'd be an underwear model. How's that for role reversal?

I'll be your manager or whatever, making sure none of the photographers get too hands-on."

"We can travel together," Nathaniel said. "Once Zero is better. If that's what you want."

Kelly lowered the tablet and looked at him. "I want to take photos of you. With my real camera."

"That's fine. Anything you want."

Kelly smirked. "Funny. I was just about to make the same offer."

Nathaniel took that as his cue. He undressed Kelly, getting his shirt off first and licking his nipples, nibbling his neck. He wasn't so patient with the pants, except to stop at Kelly's artificial leg.

"You've changed," he teased. "I don't know you anymore."

"That's an X3, baby! It's got all kinds of new features."

"Can it vibrate? I was thinking of humping it."

Kelly slapped his arm playfully. "No, but this version can go in the shower."

"Really?" Nathaniel said, grinning broadly. "So that means it can get wet?"

"Don't hump my leg, and don't come on it!" Kelly rolled his eyes dramatically. "I never should have taken you back."

Nathaniel stopped kidding around. "Say that again."

Kelly eyed him and smiled. "I'm taking you back. You're my man."

"I'm your man," Nathaniel echoed, gently lowering himself on top of Kelly and kissing him. They pressed their naked bodies together, sometimes talking and laughing, other times expressing their emotions physically. They were in no rush, felt no urgency or frustration, even an hour later when Zero stirred and whimpered. They simply got dressed, took him outside, and kept grinning goofily at each other. Like they had all the time in the world. Like their story had only just begun.

440

Epilogue

"To know love is to know loss."

The podium Marcello stood behind did little to conceal his bulk. Like the audience he faced, he was dressed in all black, his expression somber. To his left and right were a number of Kelly's photos, which had been enlarged and placed on easels for the audience to see. In one Zero was running across the yard, his feet barely touching the ground. The next image was of great contrast: Zero in the final days of his illness, his hind legs on a cart with wheels so he wouldn't have to drag them around. Just before the unexpected had happened. A flowered wreath hung off the easel of this photo, causing Nathaniel to swallow painfully.

"Love's greatest challenge is not endurance. Nor is it fidelity or sacrifice. Love's greatest challenge is recovery. A heart that has loved and lost is put through the ultimate trial. Failure means the unthinkable—never loving again. Success brings with it sweet redemption. Not a reprieve from the pain, but compensation in the form of discovery, the knowledge that love comes in infinite forms. All of them unique, all of them of equal importance. And yet, none an adequate substitute for the other. At times such as these, when faced with the end, it can be hard to be so visionary, to see light past the dark. For me especially, because let's face it, I'm the one who has lost the most here." He gestured at the photos on display: Zero, Kelly, and Nathaniel running together at the high school track. One of Kelly at the height of his modeling career, a photoshopped panther striding alongside him. And one of Nathaniel scowling at the camera, arms crossed over his chest. That one was a little surreal, like being not just at a funeral, but his own.

The mood was ruined somewhat when Zero trotted up on stage, still panting from running around the gardens of Marcello's estate. He lifted a leg and urinated on one of the easels, causing a loud snort from next to Nathaniel. He glanced over to see Kelly covering his face in embarrassment. Zero must have spotted a squirrel then, or some other poor creature, because he barked and raced off again. Nathaniel still marveled at how—after nearly three weeks of tediously slow recovery—the dog had awakened one morning his old self. Part of Nathaniel was still waiting for a relapse or another stroke, but he wouldn't let his fear of getting hurt stop him from enjoying every moment they had together. Kelly no longer demanded evidence that Nathaniel had changed, but if he did, there could be no greater proof than the last few months.

Marcello continued his strange farce from on stage. "A wise man once said, 'I may not be able to choose the date of my funeral or avoid showing up for it, but my wake is an event I practice for every single day. Mostly by looking my best while having a drink or two.'"

"Gosh," Nathaniel grumbled. "I wonder who came up with that gem?"

"Why, I did!" Marcello said, appearing flattered. Then he resumed his performance. "Today we say goodbye to three individuals. An ill-behaved beast with an indomitable spirit. A talented and beautiful young man who is much too aggressive in the way he negotiates contracts. And perhaps dearest to me, a brooding man who never lets me do anything fun, and yet for some reason, I can't help but—" Marcello's voice faltered, but he recovered quickly. "Let's just say I'm rather fond of him. So please join me in mourning their passing from our lives to whatever grand adventures await them. While those of us remaining in Austin will be grieving, let us not forget that they will be going to a paradise of their own creation."

The audience clapped, Nathaniel joining them because Marcello always knew how to put on a show, and his offer to throw a going-away party for them had been kind. The funeral theme was a little creepy, but inspired, because it reminded everyone here that some goodbyes were sadder than others.

"I thought he'd never stop talking," Kelly said as he stood. "All I can think of is the buffet. Are you coming?"

Nathaniel shook his head. "I'll catch up with you later."

He met Marcello just as he was stepping off the stage, grabbing him in a hug and—with some effort—lifting him off his feet.

"Oh ho ho!" Marcello said as he was put down again. "You make me feel as dainty as a daisy!"

"Thank you," Nathaniel said. "For everything. Not just this party, but for singling me out in the audience at Yale, taking a chance on me when I decided to drop out, trusting me with your business… just everything. Thank you."

Marcello waved a hand, as if he had done no more than hold open a door for him. "It's been my pleasure. Truly. Just don't thank me for letting you go, because I still haven't given up hope."

Nathaniel sighed. "Don't tempt me. It isn't easy leaving it all behind, but Kelly and I made a promise. If Zero recovered, we would travel together. To see what happens."

"I think we all know what's going to happen," Marcello said. "Surely it has happened many times already! The only difference is this time it will take place in a recreational vehicle, of all things. I would have thought a yacht to be more romantically appropriate."

"You didn't pay me *that* much when I was still working for you," Nathaniel said. "Besides, I know Zero does okay in a car. I'm not sure how he'd handle a boat."

"Just don't forget me," Marcello said. "Oh, and speaking of transportation, when it's time to leave there's a limo out front that will whisk you home. If you must go, you might as well do so in style."

"Thanks," Nathaniel said, putting an arm around his shoulders and walking him toward the party. "And for the record… I'm rather fond of you too."

The rest of the day was spent mingling. Nathaniel didn't have many friends, but Marcello did. Everyone from the company was there, including Tim and his husband, Ben. Sheila was present, of course, along with Arthur, who kept lying in the coffin Marcello had set up for people to have their photos taken in. Morbid, but the kid seemed to get a kick out of it. Kelly's friends were there, people from the youth group who were taking advantage of the open bar. He doubted many of them were old enough, but he tried not to worry about that. Layne had a grip on a guy's arm, and Bonnie was spending every second she could with Kelly. Jason and William were there too, together again, although rumor had it that there was trouble in paradise.

Nathaniel stood at the edge of the party for a while and watched, surprised how many lives had touched his during these years spent in Austin. But now it was time to go.

"Ready?" Kelly asked as the party wore down. The sun

hadn't quite set, but the day had been hot, and most people were eager let their buzzes wear off in the comfort of their own homes.

"Yeah," Nathaniel said.

He sought out Marcello one more time and found speaking too difficult. They both seemed to feel that way, because Marcello didn't offer any words. He simply placed a hand on Nathaniel's cheek and smiled sadly. Then they hugged and parted ways.

As promised, a limo was waiting out front. Zero hopped in first. Nathaniel and Kelly climbed in after him. The driver seemed to know where he was going because the car was in motion before they gave any signal, the doors locking. That struck Nathaniel as odd, but he didn't have much time to reflect on it because Kelly was holding up two envelopes he'd found, each labeled with one of their names.

"What are these?"

"I don't know," Nathaniel said, but he recognized the handwriting. He looked toward the front of the vehicle.

The driver's window was down, and he seemed to be keeping tabs on them. Or maybe he was just nosey.

"Would you mind pulling over?" Nathaniel said. "We've decided to walk."

The driver's eyes met his in the rearview mirror. "Sorry, sir, but I can't do that."

"Didn't think so," Nathaniel said. Then he looked to Kelly, who sat across from him. "Trapped again. Let's see what the old man has in store for us."

They opened their envelopes and found that both contained contracts. Nathaniel's was familiar because it was the same one he'd worked under for all these years. The only difference was a few new paragraphs added to the end. He read them carefully, shaking his head in disbelief. Then he started laughing. "What's yours say?"

"It's a job offer," Kelly replied. "Working for Marcello. I'd be senior art director, which according to this means my 'sole responsibility' would be to 'increase the catalog of available material to a higher standard than typical of stock photography, offering clientele access to imagery of an artistic caliber.'"

"So basically you keep taking your photos, but now you're guaranteed to get paid for it."

Kelly nodded. "I've had worse offers, and I'm not exactly

fond of pimping myself to galleries. What's yours say?"

"He's just offering me my old job back," Nathaniel said. He didn't mention that it now included the promise that he would one day inherit the studio when Marcello stepped down. They had time to discuss that later, and Nathaniel didn't want Kelly to feel too tempted if this wasn't what he truly wanted.

"There is a certain joy in being young," Marcello's voice said over the limousine sound system, "and in reveling in spontaneity, but I promise you that many who are no longer young wish they had planned for the future. This practiced traveler intends to provide you with the benefit of his experience while still allowing for your inevitable follies."

"Is this a recording?" Nathaniel asked.

"Yes, sir," the driver confirmed.

"By now I hope you've reviewed your contracts. No doubt you feel they contradict your plans. Please note, however, that the start date for each position has been left empty. My proposition is that you have your adventures, experience all that life has to offer, and if ever you find yourselves longing for stability once again, that you consider filling in those blank spots with a date of your choosing. Every adventurer should have a home to return to. And a family. I hope you both realize that your home—and much of your family—is here in Austin. I wish you both well."

The recording ended. Kelly was still grinning. "What do you think? Half a year? Three months?"

"Before we come back?" Nathaniel shook his head. "I think we should decide when we're ready. There's no rush."

Kelly exhaled and nodded. "Okay."

The limousine slowed, then pulled into a driveway. At first Nathaniel thought they were at Kelly's house, but the yard was much bigger and the trees taller, meaning the neighborhood was older. He didn't know where they were, but he did recognize the used RV in the driveway, because he and Kelly had bought it last week.

"Now what?" Nathaniel asked.

"Sir," the driver said, arm outstretched to offer another pair of envelopes.

They were small, and as Nathaniel took them, he felt hard, flat shapes inside. He already knew what they were when giving one to Kelly.

"The man is insane," Nathaniel muttered.

Kelly laughed, dumping the contents into his hand. A key. "He just wants to make sure we come home again."

"So he made sure we have a home to come back to."

"Do you think he's renting it or…"

Nathaniel shook his head helplessly. "Who knows? Let's go find out."

The keys worked on the front door. The lights were already on inside, illuminating all of Nathaniel's belongings, which had been relocated without his knowledge. They weren't enough to fill a house, but that was probably part of the plan. They found paperwork on the kitchen table. Nathaniel sat down and flipped through it. The house was theirs, if they wanted it. All they had to do was sign. Kelly and Zero ran from room to room, while Nathaniel stayed in the kitchen, reading the papers and trying to come to terms with everything. He ignored the two additional envelopes that awaited them, and instead joined Kelly in the fenced backyard. Perfect for Zero.

When they returned inside, Kelly repeated the same question he'd been asking over and over: "This is ours? Seriously?"

"If we want," Nathaniel said. "It's up to us."

"Gosh, let me think about it," Kelly said, chuckling madly.

Nathaniel joined him.

"What are these?" Kelly said, grabbing the final two envelopes. They were small and square, and as he felt one, he made a funny face. "I think he planned out our entire future. And I mean *all* of it."

Nathaniel took the envelope with his name written on it. Soon he understood Kelly's reaction. They shook out the contents at the same time, a ring landing in each of their palms.

"Weird," Kelly said. He tried putting his on and shook his head. "Mine's too big."

"Mine's too small," Nathaniel said. "It barely fits my pinky. He must have gotten them mixed up. Here."

"Trade you!"

They held out the rings to each other, and at the same time, realized the significance. Then they froze.

"Are these engagement rings?" Kelly asked nervously. "Or more?"

Nathaniel locked eyes with him. "Does it matter?"

"You tell me."

"I'm ready for anything," Nathaniel said, taking his hand. "That's what these rings will be. A promise. As long as it involves you, I'm game."

He slid the ring on one of Kelly's fingers, and allowed the same to be done to him. Zero's claws clicked across the floor, then he plonked down on his haunches, staring up at them happily. Sort of like he was presiding over a wedding. Kelly and Nathaniel laughed, then looked at each other, lost for words, but certain that the best was yet to come.

———————

Hear the story in their own words...

Many of the *Something Like...* books are available on audio too. Listen to Tim's tale while you jog with him, or ignore your fellow airline passengers while experiencing Jace's story again. Find out which books are available and listen to free chapters at the link below:

http://www.jaybellbooks.com/audiobooks/

Something Like Characters: Series One

Now you can own art worthy of hanging in the Eric Conroy gallery! This first series of cards features five original illustrations created by Andreas Bell, the same hunky guy who does the cover illustrations for the *Something Like…* books. Each card depicts one of your favorite characters (we hope!) with a selected quote by them on the opposite side. The sixth card features unobscured cover art from the first four books in the series, and will be personalized to you and autographed by Jay Bell. (That's me!) Find out more details at our store. We've got T-shirts and all kinds of stuff too!

http://www.jaybellbooks.com/merchandise/

Also by Jay Bell
Kamikaze Boys

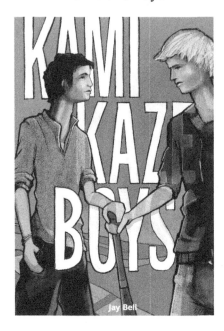

True love is worth fighting for.

My name is Connor Williams and people say I'm crazy. But that's not who I am. They also think I'm straight, and mean, and dangerous. But that's not who I am. The stories people tell, all those legends which made me an outsider—they don't mean a thing. Only my mother and my younger brother matter to me. Funny then that I find myself wanting to stand up for someone else. David Henry, that kind-of-cute guy who keeps to himself, he's about to get his ass beat by a bunch of dudes bigger than him. I could look away, let him be one more causality of this cruel world… But that's not who I am.

Kamikaze Boys, a Lambda Literary award winning novel, is a story of love triumphant as two young men walk a perilous path in the hopes of saving each other.

For more information, please see:
www.jaybellbooks.com

Made in the USA
Las Vegas, NV
02 December 2024

13162697R00267